Praise for
THE ENDLESS FRONTIER
Books:

" . . . those interested in space flight in general will find
THE ENDLESS FRONTIER exceptionally worthwhile.''
—The American Library Association *Booklist*

"Pournelle is infectiously optimistic about solutions to the
Earth's problems. Entertaining and exhilarating. Highly
recommended.''

—*Science Fiction and Fantasy Book Review*

"If more people would only listen to Pournelle (and the rest
of us), we could mobilize the national/international will and
put an end to worries about energy crises, resource
shortages, pollution, crowding, and all the rest of the
doomster fears.''

—Tom Easton, *Analog*

CITIES IN SPACE

Edited by JERRY POURNELLE with John F. Carr

ACE BOOKS, NEW YORK

CITIES IN SPACE

An Ace Book / published by arrangement with
the editors

PRINTING HISTORY
Ace edition / September 1991

ISBN: 0-441-10591-2

Ace Books are published by The Berkley Publishing Group,
200 Madison Avenue, New York, New York 10016.
The name ''ACE'' and the ''A'' logo
are trademarks belonging to Charter Communications, Inc.

PRINTED IN THE UNITED STATES OF AMERICA

10 9 8 7 6 5 4 3 2 1

ACKNOWLEDGMENTS

The editors gratefully acknowledge that research for some of the nonfiction essays in this book, including the introductory essay, "The Endless Frontier," was supported in part by grants from the Vaughn Foundation. Responsibility for opinions expressed in this work remains solely with the authors.

This book is dedicated to the work and memory of Robert A. Heinlein.

CONTENTS

The Endless Frontier

⌐⌐

JERRY POURNELLE

EVER SINCE the L-5 Society was absorbed into the National Space Society and became part of yet another cheering section for NASA, the real space enthusiasts have had no public voice. Fortunately, we have had a champion in Vice President Dan Quayle, who, as head of the National Space Council, quietly kept LAND-SAT going, disputed NASA's bureaucracy in a number of key matters, and sponsored the SSX proposal.

Then there's High Frontier. General Dan Graham, former head of the DIA, started High Frontier to promote the Strategic Defense Initiative (SDI); but it has become a general purpose space advocacy organization, and publishes the *Journal of Practical Applications in Space. (JPAS*, 2800 Shirlington Road, Suite 405A, Arlington, VA 22206, $30/year.) It's no coincidence that the editor is Aleta Jackson, the former chapters chairman for L-5.

The Space Community has a number of diverse views, and it's impossible to characterize them all. However, there are two major "factions" in the community: those who believe we must go to space because of military necessity, and those who believe that we must go to space because of economic, scientific, and social imperatives.

The military realists are afraid that if we closely couple space defenses and economic investment in space we will get neither; and the United States will not survive.

The space cadets note the historic tendency of all societies to devote more and more of their product to bureaucratic structure, and are afraid that if we do not invest heavily for the economic exploitation of space, the economy will stagnate as the government

1

share of GNP grows more rapidly than the GNP itself. Soon there will be nothing to invest.

My own view is that if we as a free society—I will not here debate the proposition that, on balance, we still live in a free society—are to survive, we must have:

- Strategic defenses.
- Private enterprise in space.
- Government investment in space technology development.

Without strategic defenses the nation will not survive the next shift in the arms race. As I write this, some form of nuclear disarmament looks more likely than at any time since the end of World War II. However, we can not, nor can anyone in the Soviet Union—including Gorbachev himself—guarantee that *glasnost* will continue.

THE U.S.S.R. TODAY

In early 1990 I went to the Soviet Union for the first time. Obviously, one can hardly become an expert by spending a week in a foreign capital. Of course I had some familiarity with the U.S.S.R. before I went; but despite all my reading, there were a number of surprises, as well as changes.

First, the good news: *glasnost*, "openness," is in full force, and that *is* working, at a pace that surprises everyone.

On the other hand, *perestroika*, economic reorganization, is not working. Everyone we met says things are getting worse, not better. The major effect of *perestroika* is to allow a free market in a limited number of goods. For example, farmers, after meeting their quota for goods to be delivered to the state wholesale grocery distributors, are now allowed to set up shop in public markets and sell whatever else they've grown. That's quite a change: a few years ago it would be considered an "economic crime" with severe penalties.

Moscow is at the latitude of Juneau, Alaska: the growing season is short. The city is thus chronically in need of fresh vegetables during the winter. The major vegetable seems to be cucumbers. At the International Hotel, one of Moscow's top hotels, we had cucumbers at three meals a day. Only once did we get carrots, and then only one carrot each. They were quite proud of those carrots. The only time we had sliced tomatoes was at a very high-level luncheon in the private dining room of the *Praga*, said to be the best restaurant in Moscow. In a word, fresh vegetables in winter and spring are rare in Moscow.

In the state stores, cucumbers are sold for one rouble per kilo. Alas, there were none for sale. The state grocery stores had kasha, rice, wheat flour, butter, milk, and what looked like beef chuck, all for sale at *very* reasonable prices—you could buy enough oatmeal to live on for a month for about six roubles—but little else, and no vegetables at all. However, in the farmers markets, cucumbers are readily available for twenty to thirty roubles per kilo.

Now, what's a rouble worth? That's not a simple question. At the state currency exchange booths, it was six roubles to a dollar. The street price was between fourteen and eighteen roubles per dollar, depending on how hard you negotiate. (I didn't, but a former U.S. ambassador down the hall from us did, and got eighteen.) Looked at that way, twenty roubles doesn't sound like much for two pounds of cucumbers; a bit less than you'd pay at a U.S. supermarket. However: the average Russian salary is three hundred roubles a month. Some make less. Most retirees, including retired engineers as well as bus drivers, get one hundred roubles a month. Five to twenty percent of your monthly income is a *lot* to pay for a kilo of cucumbers.

In other words, the first stages of *perestroika* have produced more goods, but now they're no longer for sale at prices most can afford. Before *perestroika* you had to stand in line for cucumbers, but you could afford them. Now you don't stand in lines, but the prices are very high.

ECONOMIC DISINCENTIVES

Cooperatives make too much money, so now the Soviet government—while claiming to be in favor of *perestroika*—hampers them in every possible way. Joint ventures, in which Soviet institutions (and thus, indirectly, the government) own half, have an easier time of it.

The Tekhnika operation thought it had a way around the problem. Tekhnika was a cooperative, which is something like a western private corporation, but as they found out, with fewer rights.

Tekhnika salvaged waste logs and branches from Soviet rivers; the Soviet lumber operations operate with the usual Soviet efficiency, which is to say they're very wasteful. Tekhnika was able to pay good prices for river gleanings, which were exported to

Japan. Japan is desperate for lumber of any kind to use for everything from paper pulp to toothpicks, so there was no trouble selling there. In Japan, Tekhnika bought PC clones; they could get a complete machine for about five hundred U.S. dollars, roughly equivalent to three thousand roubles. Such machines sell in the U.S.S.R. for thirty thousand to fifty thousand roubles and more. Business was good.

Too good. Many Russians resent profits. They don't believe anyone can do anything worth, say, twenty-five thousand roubles a year when the annual base salary of a Soviet engineer is under four thousand roubles. Tekhnika came to the attention of the authorities. Regulations were devised. Special taxes amounting to more than 50 percent were imposed, and applied retroactively. Barter was forbidden. Pretty soon Tekhnika shut down. Incidentally, their high profits were disclosed when one of the partners loyally paid his Party dues from his earnings, writing a check for ninety-two thousand roubles to an institution that paid him one hundred thirty roubles a month.

For many Russians, who have nothing to sell or barter, their only solace is the traditional remedy—vodka. Once again there are long lines in front of state liquor stores. Gorbachev's anti-alcohol campaign, a multi-billion-rouble failure like our own Prohibition, has cost the government billions in lost sales. Moonshine is no longer a boom business and construction workers are no longer drinking cheap perfume. But vodka caps can be seen popping out of passing car windows, not exactly a reassuring vision.

To many Soviets, the man responsible for all this confusion and sorry state of affairs is Gorbachev, who is ripping the country apart with his crazy ideas, bringing it to the edge of civil and internal war. One hears terms such as the "disintegration of the state" and the "paralysis of power" used by Soviet politicians and intellectuals to describe the present regime. The election of new local councils, many of which are run by deputies with strong democratic views, is seen by much of the public to be responsible for the catastrophic decline of public order and economic disintegration.

According to *The Christian Science Monitor:* "The most serious breakdown in status occurred in 1989, when the Soviet state and its political infra-structure—the party apparatus—lost any remaining measure of prestige in society. Surveys conducted in 1989 indicated that less than 5 percent of the population respected the party, and less than 20 percent respected the central and local governments."

The forces arrayed against Gorbachev's "reforms" are legion. Gorbachev himself talks grimly about an army of eighteen billion bureaucrats. Apparatchiks in fancy apartments along *Kutuzovsky Prospekt*, each willing to fight for his privileges, and longing for a return to the old order. Moscow itself contains thousands, possibly millions, of these gray bureaucrats, each guarding his own special interest and privilege.

Many reformers fear an alliance between the apparatchiks and the hard-liners, who still dream of the none too distant days of Soviet Empire and monolithic military machine. Most hard-line communists, militarists, and nationalists have one thing in common—they loathe Gorbachev and his reforms. They yearn for strong central leadership and share a hatred of the West and its many corrupting influences. So far they have been hibernating, but everywhere in Moscow reformers and intellectuals worry about the sleeping bear suddenly awakening.

The "Soviet Kipling," hard-line Stalinist writer Alexander Prokhanov, decries the policies of Gorbachev and his foreign minister, Eduard A. Shevardnadze, for smashing the Soviet Empire and destroying its favored geo-political position. He especially holds Gorbachev responsible for giving away Eastern Europe and the prize of World War II, East Germany. "Sometimes the policies of Foreign Minister Shevardnadze seem to be the policies of a madman," he tells people. "If the head of Soviet foreign policy was Henry Kissinger and not Shevardnadze, he would act this way."

Prokhanov sees the Soviet Union as a precious gem, the jewel of three thousand years of historical synthesis, put in place by Lenin and Stalin, and now threatened by the insane policies of Gorbachev and his "reformers." The Soviet Union today "is like a big body without a skeleton and with reckless brains."

The great nationalist Piotr Proskurin worries about the destiny of Russia. "Russia is giving far more than it is taking out," he complains. "Seventy to eighty billion roubles is earned by Russia but is dispersed throughout the republics. It is a kind of colonialism in reverse which must be stopped immediately." Proskurin's great worry is the Muslim republics where the birthrate is better than four times that of Russians, who now make up barely 50.8 percent of the population.

Mate all this to the troubled Baltic republics and the future of the Soviet Union is murky indeed. The economic contribution of the Baltics is not critical to the Soviet Union, but their example could be fatal. If the Ukraine, the second largest Soviet republic with a population of some fifty-two million, secedes from the U.S.S.R., the Soviet Union house of state will rock to its very foundations.

The Ukraine is the largest *European* producer of grains, sugar, beef, and dairy products. It leads Europe in natural resources, such as coal, natural gas, manganese, and iron ore. Its industries drive the Soviet Union; over two thirds of its national product are taken out of the Ukraine without recompense. During the last election, some two hundred thousand Soviet troops were brought from various republics to conduct maneuvers.

Henrich Altuyanin, a Ukranian pro-independence candidate, declares: "Today it is Lithuania—tomorrow the Caucasian republics—and the day after tomorrow it will be the Ukraine."

U.S. STRATEGY IN THE AGE OF PERESTROIKA

Indeed: the surest way to insure the survival of both *glasnost* and *perestroika* is for the United States to maintain the capability of waging high-tech war, and in particular, to have an economically *deployable* strategic defense system. So long as we have that, any possible successor to Gorbachev will understand that there is no way out. A return to the Cold War will be a return to the massive costs of that war to the Soviet Union, with no prospect of winning anything worthwhile. Reagan told Gorbachev in Iceland that the U.S. intended to maintain technological superiority, and that SDI was a major key to that. It was the beginning of the end for the Cold War.

Note that it is not necessary for the U.S. to deploy SDI to deal with the U.S.S.R. What is necessary is a credible capability for doing so—which means access to space at reasonable costs. At the moment we don't have such access. Later in this book we will describe one system, SSX, that can supply that need.

The growing Soviet instability is not the only incentive for the U.S. to take and keep a strategic presence in space. There are literally dozens of potential conflicts which could conceivably explode into wars affecting the interests of both the U.S. and U.S.S.R. It is very much in our national interest, for example, that we be able to prevent anyone in the Middle East from launching IRBM's at anyone else. It is not difficult to supply other examples.

Thus even a deployed SDI need not be an "astrodome over the U.S.A."; which is as well, because that's impossible. No one, including President Reagan, ever imagined a strategic defense system that would be 100 percent effective against a massive all-out city-buster attack by the U.S.S.R. On the other hand, it is extremely difficult to think of any reason the U.S.S.R. would launch such an attack. The gripping hand is that a system need not be 100 percent effective against the U.S.S.R. to be 100 percent effective against *everyone else*; while a 50 percent effective system so complicates the Soviet war plan that there is no reason for the U.S.S.R. ever to attack us even if the leadership is replaced with an expansionist and aggressive faction.

And, of course, a large space effort like SDI can, if conducted intelligently, stimulate private enterprise as well as protect the nation.

SPACE AS INVESTMENT

We do have the capability to do both. To be specific: the construction of a Lunar Base and SDI will together cost less than the sum of the individual efforts. The best consensus we can get says that the two will cost about one and a half times as much as either. Once free enterprise has low-cost access to space, the needed quantum jump in U.S. economy will be inevitable. Space resources are *new* wealth.

It is also possible to do SDI in ways that do little to benefit the economy. That must not happen.

The major challenge to American is productivity. The space program can make dramatic changes in U.S. industrial productivity. In colonial times the founding fathers were keen on canals; they knew that providing access to the new frontier would more than pay for itself. Toll roads and toll canals were often built under government sponsorship and support.

The best investment we could make today would be to lower the cost of access to the space environment.

There are a number of ways to get into space. One, SSX, is described later in this book. Another is ORION, which uses nuclear fission/fusion bombs to launch and propel a *large* spaceship. We could, with a single ORION, put a four-million-pound base on the Moon. This would be more than enough for a self-sustaining colony. It is, of course, unlikely that we'd use a launch system that required exploding a couple of dozen nuclear weapons in the atmosphere (and in fact there's a treaty that prevents that) even though the atmospheric contamination could be kept to very small levels.

However, we really could develop a ground-based laser launching system, like the one used in my story "Consort." Electric power for those lasers could originally come from nuclear power plants, were it not for our national nuclear phobia. A more expensive—but certainly feasible—alternative is space-based solar power satellites. These satellites can be placed in orbit, *or* at the Lunar poles.

Once electric power flows from space, laser launching systems will drastically lower the cost of space access; an economic spiral whose maximum output cannot at present be calculated would begin.

Economics and investment are boring subjects. We need to talk about it, but economics has little power to stir the blood. Large goals and large dreams electrify the people. Where there is no vision, the people perish.

The return to the Moon is such a dream. Unlike the space station—which remains necessary—the establishment of a Lunar settlement, permanently inhabited, has the power to draw the people toward it.

It is also an investment. Large returns on that investment are as certain as returns on any investment have ever been.

It is nearly certain that we must do *something*, and fairly soon. Through history, civilizations have inexorably converted larger and larger portions of their output into structure: into regulation and bureaucracy, rules and laws and state employees. The end result of that looks like India.

Europe was headed that way when the discovery of the Americas changed all the rules. China, interestingly, very nearly discovered Europe: the Chinese navy had more and better ships than Vasco da Gama, and a Chinese treasure fleet actually reached India before the Mandarin bureaucracy, rightly fearing the effects of opening up new frontiers, dismantled the fleet. China turned inward as Europe turned outward.

We once again have an opportunity to look outward; we once again have a chance to escape the inevitable trend toward bureaucracy and regulation and the stifling of initiative; to escape the fate that so concerned Alexis de Tocqueville over a hundred years ago.

Tocqueville wrote of democracy with approval; but he also examined how democracies perish; and he said:

"I think, then, that the species of oppression by which democratic nations are menaced is unlike anything that ever before existed in the world; our contemporaries will find no prototype of it in their memories. I seek in vain for an expression that will accurately convey the whole of the idea I have formed of it; the old words *despotism* and *tyranny* are inappropriate; the thing itself is new, and since I cannot name it, I must seek to define it.

"I seek to trace the novel features under which despotism may appear in the world. The first thing that strikes the observation is an innumerable multitude of men, all equal and alike, incessantly endeavoring to procure the petty and paltry pleasures with which they glut their lives. Each of them, living apart, is as a stranger to the fate of all the rest; his children and his private friends constitute to him the whole of mankind. As for the rest of his fellow citizens, he is close to them but he does not see them; he touches them, but he does not feel them; he exists only in himself and for himself alone; and if his kindred still remain to him, he may be said at any rate to have lost his country.

"Above this race of men stands an immense and tutelary power, which takes upon itself to secure their gratifications and to watch over their fate. That power is absolute, minute, regular, provident, and mild. It would be like the authority of a parent if, like that authority, its object was to prepare men for manhood; but it seeks, on the contrary, to keep them in perpetual childhood; it is well content that the people should rejoice, provided they think of nothing but rejoicing. For their happiness such a government willingly labors, but it chooses to be the sole agent and the only arbiter of that happiness; it provides for their security, foresees and supplies their necessities, facilitates their pleasures, manages their principal concerns, directs their industry, regulates the descent of property, and subdivides their inheritances: what remains, but to spare them all the care of thinking and all the trouble of living?

"Thus every day it renders the exercise of the free agency of man less useful and less frequent; it circumscribes the will within a narrower and narrower range and gradually robs a man of all uses of himself. The principle of equality has prepared men for these things; it has predisposed men to endure them, and often to look on them as benefits.

"After having successively taken each member of the

community in its powerful grasp and fashioned him at will, the supreme power then extends its arm over the whole community. It covers the surface of society with a network of small complicated rules, minute and uniform, through which the most original minds and the most energetic characters cannot penetrate to rise above the crowd. The will of man is not shattered, but softened, bent, and guided; men are seldom forced by it to act but they are constantly restrained from acting. Such a power does not destroy, but it prevents existence; it does not tyrannize, but it compresses, enervates, extinguishes, and stupefies a people, till each nation is rescued to nothing better than a flock of timid and industrious animals, of which the government is the shepherd.

"I have often thought that servitude of the regular, quiet, and gentle kind which I have just described might be combined more easily than is commonly believed with some of the outward forms of freedom. . . ."

So spoke Tocqueville; and if those words were disturbing twenty years ago, they are frightening now. Every day we see more trends toward this nameless despotism, this new thing which "might even establish itself under the wing of the sovereignty of the people."

Yet we have the means to escape that fate. We have the means to give mankind a new direction: to leap into the endless frontier.

Consort

卍

JERRY POURNELLE

THE SENATOR LOOKED from the bureau with its chipped paint and cracked mirror to the expensive woman seated on the sagging bed. My God, he thought. What if one of my constituents could see me now? Or the press people got wind of this?

He opened the leather attaché case and turned knobs on the console inside. Green lights winked reassuringly. He took a deep breath and turned to the girl.

"Laurie Jo, would it surprise you to know I don't give a damn whether the President is a crook or not?" the senator asked.

"Then why are you here?" Her voice was soft, with a note of confidence, almost triumphant.

Senator Hayden shook his head. This is a hell of a thing. The Senate Majority Leader meets with the richest woman in the whole goddamn world, and the only way we can trust each other is to come to a place like this. She picks the highway and I pick the motel. Both of us have scramblers goin', and we're still not sure nobody's makin' a tape. Hell of a thing.

"Because you might be able to *prove* President Tolland's a crook. Maybe make a lot of people believe it," Hayden said.

"I can."

"Yeah." She sounds so damned confident, and if what she sent me's a good sample of what she's got, she can do it, all right. "That's what scares me, Laurie Jo. The country can't take it again."

He drew in a lungful of air. It smelled faintly of gin. Hayden exhaled heavily and sank into the room's only chair. One of the springs was loose, and it jabbed him. "Christ Almighty!" he exploded.

11

"First Watergate. No sooner'n we get over that, and we're in a depression. Inflation. Oil crisis. The Equity Trust business. One damn thing after another. And when the Party gets together a real reform wing and wins the election, Tolland's own Solicitor General finds the Equity people right next to the President!

"So half the White House staff goes, and we get past that somehow and people still got something to believe in, and you're tellin' me you can prove the President was in on all of it. Laurie Jo, you just can't do that to the country!"

She spread her skirts across her knees and wished she'd taken the chair. She never liked sitting without a backrest. The interview was distasteful, and she wished there were another way, but she didn't know one. We're so nearly out of all this, she thought. So very near.

"DING."

It was a sound in her mind, but not one the senator could hear. He was saying something about public confidence. She half listened to him, while she thought, "I WAS NOT TO BE DISTURBED."

"MISTER MC CARTNEY SAYS IT IS VERY IMPORTANT. SIGNOR ANTONELLI IS CONCERNED ABOUT HIS NEXT SHIPMENT."

"WILL IT BE ON TIME?" she thought.

"ONLY HALF. HIS BIOLOGICALS WILL BE TWO DAYS LATE," the computer link told her. The system was a luxury she sometimes regretted: not the cost, because a million dollars was very little to her; but although the implanted transceiver link gave her access to all of her holdings and allowed her to control the empire she owned, it gave her no peace.

"TELL MC CARTNEY TO STALL. I WILL CALL ANTONELLI IN TWO HOURS," she thought.

"MISTER MC CARTNEY SAYS ANTONELLI WILL NOT WAIT."

"TELL MC CARTNEY TO DORK HIMSELF."

"ACKNOWLEDGED."

"AND LEAVE ME ALONE."

"OUT."

And that takes care of that, she thought. The computer was programmed to take her insulting commands and translate them into something more polite; it wouldn't do to annoy one of her most important executives. If he needed to be disciplined, she'd do it face to face.

The senator had stopped talking and was looking at her. "I can prove it, Barry. All of it. But I don't want to."

Senator Hayden felt very old. "We're almost out of the slump," he said. He wasn't speaking directly to Laurie Jo any longer, and he didn't look at her. "Got the biggest R&D budget in twenty years. Unemployment's down a point. People are beginning to have some confidence again." There was peeling wallpaper in one corner of the room. Senator Hayden balled his hands into fists and the nails dug into his palms.

When he had control of himself, he met her eyes and was startled again at how blue they were. Dark red hair, oval face, blue eyes, expensive clothes; she's damn near every man's dream of a woman, and she's got me. I never made a dishonest deal in my life, but God help me, she's got me.

I have to deal, but— "Has MacKenzie seen your stuff? Does he know?"

Laurie Jo nodded. "Aeneas didn't want to believe it. Your media friends aren't the only ones who want to think Greg Tolland's an honest man. But he's got no choice now. He has to believe it."

"Then we can't deal," Hayden said. "What the hell are you wasting my time for? MacKenzie won't deal. He'll kamikaze." And do I admire him or hate him for that?

There's something inhuman about a man who thinks he's justice personified. The last guy who got tagged as "The Incorruptible" was that Robespierre character, and his own cronies cut his head off when they couldn't take him any longer.

"I'll take care of Aeneas," Laurie Jo said.

"How?"

"You'll have to trust me."

"I've already trusted you. I'm here, aren't I?" But he shook his head sadly. "Maybe I know more'n you think. I know MacKenzie connected up with you after he left the White House. God knows you're enough woman to turn any man around, but you don't know him, Laurie Jo, you don't know him at all if you think—"

"I have known Aeneas MacKenzie for almost twenty years," she said. "And I've been in love with him since the first day I met him. The two years we lived together were the happiest either of us ever had."

"Sure," Barry Hayden said. "Sure. You knew him back in the old days before Greg Tolland was anything much. So did I. I told you, maybe I know more'n you think. But goddam it, you didn't see him for ten, twelve years—''

"Sixteen years," she said. "And we had only a few weeks after that." Glorious weeks, but Greg Tolland couldn't leave us alone. He had to spoil even that. Damn him! I have more than one reason to hate Greg Tolland— ''Why don't you listen instead of talking all the time? I can handle Aeneas. You want political peace and quiet for a few years, and I can give them to you.''

I don't listen because I'm afraid of what I'll hear, the senator thought. Because I never wanted this day to come, and I knew it would when I went into politics, but I managed for this long, and it got to lookin' like it never would come and now I'm in a cheap motel room about to be told the price of whatever honor I've got left.

God help us, she's got all the cards. If anybody can shut MacKenzie up—

The room still smelled of cheap gin, and the senator tasted bile at the back of his throat. "OK, Laurie Jo, what do I have to do?''

Aeneas MacKenzie switched off the newscast and stared vacantly at the blank screen. There had been nothing about President Greg Tolland, and it disturbed him.

His office was a small cubicle of the main corridor. It was large enough for a desk as well as the viewscreen and console that not only gave him instant access to every file and data bank on *Heimdall* Station, but also a link with the master Hansen data banks on Earth below. He disliked microfilm and readout screens and would greatly have preferred to work with printed reports and documents, but that wasn't possible. Every kilogram of mass was important when it had to go into orbit.

There was never enough mass at *Heimdall*. Energy was no problem; through the viewport he could see solar cells plastered over every surface, and further away was the power station, a large mirror reflecting onto a boiler and turbine. Everything could be recycled except reaction mass: but whenever the scooters went out to collect supply pods boosted up from Earth, that mass was lost forever. The recent survey team sent to the Moon had cost hideously, leaving the station short of fuel for its own operations.

He worked steadily on the production schedules, balancing the station's inadequate manpower reserves to fill the most critical orders without taking anyone off the *Valkyrie* project. It was an impossible task, and he felt a sense of pride in his partial success. It was a strange job for the former Solicitor General of the United

States, but he believed his legal training helped; and he was able to get the crew to work harder than they had thought they could.

Get *Valkyrie* finished, Laurie Jo had said. It must be done as quickly as possible, no matter what it does to the production schedules. She'd said that, but she couldn't have meant it; Aeneas knew what would happen if *Heimdall* didn't continue sending down space-manufactured products. *Heimdall* was a valuable installation, now that there were no risks left in building it, and Laurie Jo's partners were ruthless; if she defaulted on deliveries, they'd take it away from her.

Eventually the assignments were done. By taking a construction shift himself (he estimated his value at 65% as productive as a trained rigger, double what it had been when he first tried the work) he could put another man on completing the new biological production compartment. The schedule would work, but there was no slack in it.

When he was done, he left the small compartment and strode through the corridor outside. He was careful to close and dog the airtight entryway into his office, as he was careful about everything he did. As he walked, his eyes automatically scanned the shining metallic cloth of *Heimdall*'s inner walls, but he was no more aware of that than he was of the low spin gravity and Coriolis effect.

The corridor curved upwards in front of and behind him. When he reached the doorway to the Chief Engineer's office, it stood open in defiance of regulations. Aeneas nodded wryly and ignored it. Kittridge Penrose made the regulations in the first place, and Aeneas only enforced them. Presumably Penrose knew what he was doing. If he doesn't, Aeneas thought, we're all in trouble.

Penrose was in the office, as Aeneas knew he would be; one of his prerogatives was to know where everyone was. The engineer was at his desk. A complex diagram filled the screen to his left, and Penrose was carefully drawing lines with a light pen. He looked up as Aeneas came into the office. "What's up, boss?"

"I don't know." Aeneas peered at the screen. Penrose noticed the puzzled look and touched buttons on the console below the picture. The diagram changed, not blinking out to be replaced, but rearranging itself until it showed an isometric view which Aeneas recognized instantly.

"Right on schedule," Penrose said. "Just playing about with some possible improvements. There she is, *Valkyrie*, all ready to go."

"Except for the engines."

Penrose shrugged. "You can't have everything. Nothing new

from Miss Hansen about getting that little item taken care of?''

''Not yet.''

''Heh. She'll manage it.'' Penrose went back to his game with the light pen. ''I used to think my part of this was the real work,'' the engineer said. He sketched in another line. ''But it isn't. I just design the stuff. It's you people who get it built.''

''Thanks.'' And it's true enough: Laurie Jo put together the syndicate to finance this whole station.

''Sure. Meant that, you know,'' Penrose said. ''You've done about as well as Captain Shorey. Didn't think you'd be much as commander here, but I was wrong.''

Now that, Aeneas thought, is high praise indeed. And I suppose it's even true. I do fill a needed function here. Something I didn't do when I was down there with Laurie Jo. Down there I was a Prince Consort, and nothing else.

True enough I came here because I was the only one she could trust to take control, but I've been more than just her agent.

''Sit down, boss,'' Penrose said. ''Have a drink. You look like you're in need of one.''

''Thanks, I'll pass the drink.'' He took the other chair and watched as Penrose worked. I could never do that, he thought, but there aren't a lot of jobs up here that I can't do now. . . .

The newscast haunted him. Laurie Jo had the whole story, all the evidence needed to bring Greg Tolland down. We can prove the President of the United States is a criminal. Why hasn't she done it? Why?

I don't even dare call and ask her. We can't know someone isn't listening in. We can't trust codes, we can't even trust our own computer banks, and how have things come to this for the United States?

''Got a couple of new reports from the Lunatics,'' Penrose said. ''Had a chance to go over them?''

''No. That's what I came to talk to you about.'' The console would have given him instant communications with Penrose or anyone else aboard *Heimdall*, but Aeneas always preferred to go to his people rather than speak to them as an impersonal voice.

''Pretty good strike,'' Penrose said. ''Another deposit of hydrides and quite a lot of mica. No question about it, we've got everything we need.''

Aeneas nodded. It was curious: hydrogen is by orders of magnitude the most common element in the universe, but it had been hard to find on the Moon. There were oxides, and given the plentiful energy available in space that meant plenty of oxygen to breathe, but hydrogen was rare.

Now the Lunar Survey Team sent up from *Heimdall* had found hydrogen locked into various minerals. It was available, and the colony was possible—if they could get there. The survey team's fuel requirements had eaten up a lot of the mass boosted up to *Heimdall*, and without more efficient Earth orbit to lunar orbit transport it would take a long time to make a colony self-sustaining.

"We've either got to bring the survey party home or send another supply capsule," Penrose was saying. "Which is it?"

"Like to hold off that decision as long as we can." And please don't ask why. I don't know why. Just that Laurie Jo says do it this way.

Penrose frowned. "If you'll authorize some monkey motion, we can do the preliminaries for going either way. That'll hold off the decision another couple of weeks. No more than that, though."

"All right. Do it that way."

"What's eating you, Aeneas?"

"Nothing. I've been up here too long."

"Sure." Kit Penrose didn't say that he'd been aboard *Heimdall* nearly two years longer than MacKenzie's eighteen months, but he didn't have to.

Of course, Penrose thought, I've had my girl here with me; and MacKenzie's seen his precisely twice since he's been here, a couple of weekends and back she went to look after the money. Wonder what it's like to sleep with the big boss? What a silly thing to wonder about.

The diagram faded and another view came on the screen. "There she is," Penrose said. "Lovely, isn't she?"

Valkyrie may have been lovely to an engineer, but she was hardly a work of art. There was no symmetry to the ship. Since she would never land, she had neither top nor bottom, only fore and aft. "All we need is the NERVA, and we're all set," Penrose said. "No reason why the whole Moon colony staff can't go out a week after we have the engines."

"Yes."

"Christ, how can you be so cold about it? Moon base. Plenty of mass. Metals to work with. Who knows, maybe even radio-actives. We can cut loose from those bastards down there!" He waved at the viewport where Earth filled the sky before the station slowly turned again to show the sequined black velvet of space. "And we've very nearly done it."

"Very nearly." But we haven't done it, and I don't see how we can.

"What we need are those military aerospace-planes," Penrose said. His voice became more serious. "I expect they'll be coming round for visits whether we invite them or not, you know."

"Yes. Well, we got on with their chaps all right—"

"Sure," Penrose said. "Sure. Visiting astronauts and all that lot. Proud to show them around. Even so, I can't say I'm happy they can get up here whenever they like. . . ."

"Nor I." Aeneas opened a hinged panel beside the desk and took out a coffee cup. He filled it from a spigot near Penrose's hand. "Cannonshot," he said.

"I beg your pardon?"

"In the old days, national law reached out to sea as far as cannonballs could be fired from shore. Three miles, more or less. It became the legal boundary of a nation's sovereignty. There used to be a lot of talk about international law in space, and the rest of it, but it will probably be settled by something like cannonshot again. When the national governments can get up here easily, they'll assert control."

"Like to be gone when that happens," Penrose said. "Can't say I want more regulations and red tape and committees. Had enough of that lot."

"So have we all." Aeneas drank the coffee. "So have we all."

Penrose laughed. "That's a strange thing to say, considering that you were one of the prime movers of the People's Alliance."

"Maybe I've learned something from the experience." Aeneas stared moodily into his coffee cup. I wasn't wrong, he thought. But I wasn't right either. There's got to be more than comfort and security, and we didn't think of that, because the Cause was all the adventure *we* needed.

I wonder how long it will take them to make space tame? Forms to fill out, regulations always enforced, not because of safety but because they're regulations . . .

Penrose looked at the digital readouts above his drafting console: Greenwich time, and Mountain Daylight time. "Big shipment coming up next pass over Baja. I'd best be getting ready for it."

"Yes." Aeneas listened without paying much attention as Penrose told him what the big lasers in southern Baja would send up this time. It didn't really concern him yet, and when he needed to know more, the information would be available through his desk console.

As the engineer talked, Aeneas remembered what it had been

like to watch the launches: the field covered with lasers, their mirrors all focusing onto the one large mirror beneath the tramway. The squat shapes of the capsules on the tramway, each waiting to be brought over the launching mirror and thrust upward by the stabbing light, looking as if they were lifted by a fantastically swift-growing tree rising out of the desert; the thrumming note of the pulsed beam singing in hot desert air.

It had been the most magnificent sight he had ever seen, and Laurie Jo had built it all. Now she was ready to move onward, but her partners were not. They were content to own *Heimdall* and sell its products, raking in billions from the miracles that could be wrought in space.

Biologicals of every conceivable kind. Crystals of an ultimate purity grown in mass production and infected with precisely the right contaminants, all grown in mass production.

Heimdall had revolutionized more than one industry. Already there were hand calculators with thousands of words of memory space, all made from the chips grown in orbit. Deserts bloomed as the production crews sent down membranes that would pass fresh water and keep salt back; they too could be made cheaply only in zero gravity conditions.

Why take high risks on a Moon base when there was so much more potential to exploit in orbital production? The investors could prove that more money was to be made through expanding *Heimdall* than through sending *Valkyrie* exploring. They remembered that they would never have invested in space production at all if Laurie Jo hadn't bullied them into it, and that had been enough to give her some freedom of action; but they could not see profits in the Moon for many years to come.

And they're right, Aeneas thought. Laurie Jo doesn't plan for the next phase to make profits, not for a long time.

She wants the stars for herself. And what do I want? Lord God, I miss her. But I'm *needed* here. I have work to do, and I'd better get at it.

The airline reception lounge was no longer crowded. A few minutes before, it had been filled with Secret Service men and Hansen Security agents. Now there was only one of each in the room with Laurie Jo. They stayed at opposite ends of the big room, and they eyed each other like hostile dogs.

"Relax, Miguel," Laurie Jo said. "Between us there are enough security people to protect an army. The President will be safe enough—"

"*Sí, Doña* Laura." The elderly man's eyes never left the long-haired younger man at the other end of the room. "I am willing to believe *he* is safe enough."

"For heaven's sake, I'm meeting the President of the United States!"

"*Sí, Doña* Laura. *Don* Aeneas has told me of this man who has become President here. I do not care for this."

"Jesus." The Secret Service man curled his lip in contempt. "How did you do it?" he demanded.

"How did I do what, Mr. Coleman?" she asked.

"Turn MacKenzie against the President! Fifteen years he was with the Chief. Fifteen years with the People's Alliance. Now you've got him telling tales about the Chief to your peasant friend there—"

"Miguel is not a peasant."

"Ah, *Doña* Laura, but I am. Go on, *señor*. Tell us of this strange thing you do not understand." There was amusement in the old *vaquero's* eyes.

"Skip it. It just doesn't make sense, that's all."

"Perhaps my *patrona* bribed *Don* Aeneas," Miguel said.

"That will do," Laurie Jo said. Miguel nodded and was silent.

"Bullshit," Coleman said. "Nobody ever got to MacKenzie. Nobody has *his* price. Not in money, anyway." He looked at Laurie Jo in disbelief. He didn't think her unattractive, but he couldn't believe she was enough woman to drive a man insane.

"You're rather young to know Aeneas that well," Laurie Jo said.

"I joined the People's Alliance before the campaign." There was pride in the agent's voice. "Stood guard watches over the Chief. Helped in the office. MacKenzie was with us every day. He's not hard to know, not like some party types."

"INFORMATION," Laurie Jo thought. "COLEMAN FIRST NAME UNKNOWN, SECRET SERVICE AGENT. RECENTLY APPOINTED. SUMMARY."

"COLEMAN, THEODORE RAYMOND. AGE 25. PAID STAFF, PEOPLE'S ALLIANCE UNTIL INAUGURATION OF PRESIDENT GREGORY TOLLAND. APPOINTED TO SECRET SERVICE BY ORDERS OF PRESIDENT TO TAKE EFFECT INAUGURAL DAY. EDUCATION—"

"SUFFICIENT." Laurie Jo nodded to herself. Coleman hadn't been like the career Secret Service men. There were a lot of young people like Coleman in the undercover services lately, party loyalists who had known Greg before the election.

Personally loyal bodyguards have been the mark of tyrants for three thousand years, she thought. But some of the really great leaders have had them as well. Can any President do without them? Can I?

Not here. But I won't need guards on the Moon. I won't—

"DING."

"WHAT NOW?"

"THERE IS A GENERAL STRIKE PLANNED IN BOLIVIA. TWO HANSEN AGENTS HAVE INFILTRATED THE UNION. THEY HAVE FOUND OUT THE DATE OF THE STRIKE, AND WERE DISCOVERED WHEN TRANSMITTING THEIR IN-FORMATION. SUPERINTENDENT HARLOW WISHES TO TAKE IMMEDIATE ACTION TO RESCUE THEM. WILL YOU APPROVE?"

"GIVE HARLOW FULL AUTHORIZATION TO TAKE WHATEVER ACTION HE THINKS REQUIRED. REPORT WHEN HIS PLANS ARE COMPLETE BUT BEFORE EXE-CUTION."

"ACKNOWLEDGED."

Another damned problem, she thought. Harlow was a good man, but he thought in pretty drastic terms. What will that do to our other holdings in Bolivia? One thing, it will hurt my partner worse than it will hurt me. I'll have to think about this. Later, now I've got something more important.

The door opened to admit another Secret Service man. "Chief's on the way," he said.

"DO NOT CALL ME FOR ANY PURPOSE," she thought.

"ACKNOWLEDGED."

It was almost comical. The Secret Service men wouldn't leave until Miguel had gone, and Miguel wouldn't leave his *patrona* alone with the Secret Service men. Finally they all backed out together, and Laurie Jo was alone for a moment. Then President Greg Tolland came in.

He's still President, she thought. No matter that I've known him twenty years and fought him for half that time. There's an aura that goes with the office, and Greg wears it well. "Good afternoon, Mr. President."

"Senator Hayden says I should talk to you," Tolland said.

"Aren't you even going to say hello?" She thought he looked very old; yet she knew he was only a few years older than herself, one of the youngest men ever to be elected to the office.

"What should I say, Laurie Jo? That I wish you well? I do, but you wouldn't believe that. That I'd like to be friends? Would you believe me if I said that? I do wish we could be friends, but I hate everything you stand for.''

"Well said, sir!" She applauded. "But there's no audience here." And you only hate that the fortune I inherited wasn't used to help your political ambitions, not that I have it. You always were more comfortable with wealthy people than Aeneas was.

He grinned wryly. It was a famous grin, and Laurie Jo could remember when Congressman Tolland had practiced it with Aeneas and herself as his only audience. It seemed so very long ago, back in the days when her life was simple and she hadn't known who her father was, or that one day she would inherit his wealth.

"Mind if I sit down?"

She shrugged. "Why ask? But please do."

He took one of the expensively covered lounge chairs and waited until she'd done the same. "I ask because this is your place."

True enough. I own the airline. But it's hardly my home and this is hardly a social visit. "Can I get you anything? Your agents have sampled everything at the bar—"

"I'll have a bourbon, then. They shouldn't have done that. Here, I'll get—"

"It's all right. I know where everything is." She poured drinks for both of them. "Your young men don't trust me. One of them even accused me of seducing Aeneas away from you."

"Didn't you."

She handed him the drink. "Oh good God, Greg. You don't have to be careful what you say to me. Nothing I could tape could make things worse than I can make them right now. And I give you my word, nobody's listening."

His eyes narrowed. For a moment he resembled a trapped animal.

"Believe that, Greg. There's no way out," she said. "With what I already had and what Aeneas knows—"

"I'll never know how I put up with that fanatic S.O.B. for so long."

"That's beneath you, Greg. You wouldn't be President if Aeneas hadn't helped you."

"Not true."

It is true, but why go on? And yet— "Why have you turned so hard against him? Because he wouldn't sell out and you did?"

"Maybe I had no choice, Laurie Jo. Maybe I'd got so far out on so many limbs that I couldn't retreat, and when I came crashing down the Alliance would come down with me. Maybe I thought it was better that we win how ever we had to than go on leading a noble lost cause. This isn't what we came here to talk about. Senator Hayden says you've got a proposition for me.''

"Yes." And how Barry Hayden hates all of this. Another victim of patriotism. Another? Am I including Greg Tolland in that category? And what difference does it make? "It's simple enough, Greg. I can see that you'll be allowed to finish your term without any problems from me. Or from Aeneas. I can have the Hansen papers and network stop their campaigns against you. I won't switch to your support.''

"Wouldn't want it. That would look too fishy. What's your price for all this?''

"You weren't always this direct.''

"What the hell do you want, Laurie Jo? You've got the President of the United States asking your favor. You want me to crawl too?''

"No. All right, the first price is your total retirement from politics when your term is over. You don't make that promise to me. You'll give it to Barry Hayden.''

"Maybe. I'll think about it. What do you want for yourself?''

"I want a big payload delivered to *Heimdall*.''

"What the hell?''

"You've got those big military aerospace planes. I want something carried to orbit.''

"I'll think about it.''

"You'll do it.''

"I don't know." He stared into his glass. "If it means this much to you, it's important. I'd guess it's tied in with that lunar survey party, right? Your Moon colony plans?''

She didn't answer.

"That's got to be it." He drained the cocktail and began laughing. "You can't throw me out because you'd never get anyone else to agree to this! It's pretty funny, Laurie Jo. You and Mr. Clean. You *need* me! More than just this once, too, I expect— What is it you want delivered?''

"Just a big payload.''

Tolland laughed again. "I can find out, you know. I've still got a few people inside your operation.''

"I suppose you do. All right, I've got a working NERVA engine for *Valkyrie*. It's too big for the laser launching system. We could send it up in pieces, but it would take a long time to get it assembled and checked out." And I don't have a long time. I'm running out of time. . . .

"So you want me to hand over the Moon to a private company. That's what it amounts to, isn't it? The People's Alliance was formed to break up irresponsible power like yours, and you want me to hand you the Moon."

"That's my price, Greg. You won't like the alternative."

"Yeah. It's still pretty funny. A couple more years and you won't have a goddam monopoly on manned space stations. So you want me to help you get away."

"Something like that. We see things differently."

"You know you're doomed, don't you? Laurie Jo, it's over. You sit there in your big office and decide things for the whole world. Who asked you to? It's time the people had a say over their lives. You think I'm ambitious. Maybe. But for all of it, everything I've done has been in the right direction. At least I'm not building up a personal empire that's as anachronistic as a dinosaur!"

"Spare me the political speeches, Greg." God, he means it. Or he thinks he does. He can justify anything he does because he's the agent for the people, but what does it mean in the real world? Just how much comfort is it to know it's all for the good of the people when you're caught in the machinery? "I won't argue with you. I've got something you need, and I'm willing to sell."

"And you get the Moon as a private fief."

"If you want to think of it that way, go ahead. But if you want to be President three months from now, you'll do as I ask."

"And why should I think you'll keep your bargain?"

"When have I ever broken my promises?" Laurie Jo asked.

"Don't know. Tell you what, get MacKenzie to promise. That way I'll be sure you mean it."

"I'll do better than that. Aeneas and I are both going to the Moon. We can hardly interfere with you from there."

"You are crazy, aren't you?" Tolland's face showed wonder but not doubt. "You know you're going to lose a lot. You can't manage your empire from the Moon."

"I know." And how long could I hold out to begin with? And for what? "Greg, you just don't understand that power's no use, money's no use, unless it's for something that counts."

"And getting to the Moon is that big?" He shook his head in disbelief. "You're crazy."

"So are a lot of us, then. I've got ten volunteers for every opening. Pretty good people, too—as you should know."

"Yeah. I know." Tolland got up and wandered around the big

room until he came to the bar. He filled his glass with ice cubes and water, then added a tiny splash of whiskey. "You've got some of my best people away from me. You can pay them more—"

"I can, but I don't have to. You still don't understand, do you? It's not my money, and it's not my control over the Moon colony that counts. What's important is this will be one place that you don't control."

"Hah. I hadn't thought I was that unpopular with the engineers."

"I don't mean you personally," Laurie Jo said. "Your image control people have done well. But, Greg, can't you understand that some of us want out of your system?"

"Aeneas too?"

"Yes." More than any of us, because he knows better than any of us what it's going to be like—

"I should have known he'd go to you after I threw him out."

"There wasn't anywhere else he could go. Mr. President, this isn't getting us anywhere. You'll never understand us, so why try? Just send up that payload and you'll be rid of us. You may even be lucky. We'll lose people in the lunar colony. Maybe we'll all be killed."

"And you're willing to chance that—"

"I told you, you won't understand us. Don't try. Just send up my payload."

"I'll think about it," Tolland said. "But your other conditions are off. No promises. No political deals." The President stood and went to the door. He turned defiantly. "You get the Moon. That ought to be enough."

He felt dizzy and it was hard to breathe in the high gravity of Earth. When he poured a drink, he almost spilled it, because he was unconsciously allowing for the displacement usual in *Heimdall*'s centrifugal gravity. Now he sat weakly in the large chair.

The Atlantic Ocean lay outside his window, and he watched the moving lights of ships. The room lights came on suddenly, startling him.

"What—*Miguel!*" Laurie Jo shouted. Then she laughed foolishly. "*No está nada. Deseo solamente estar, por favor.*" She came into the room as Miguel closed the door behind her. "Hello, Aeneas. I might have known. No one else could get in here without someone telling me—"

He stood with an effort. "Didn't mean to startle you." He stood uncomfortably, wishing for her, cursing himself for not telling her he was coming. But I wanted to shock you, he thought.

"You didn't really. I think .Greg has called off his dogs. I'm safe enough. But—you're not!"

"I'll take my chances."

"Why are we standing here like this?" she asked. She moved toward him. He stood rigidly for a moment, but then stepped across the tiny space that separated them, and they were together again.

For how long? he thought. How long do we have this time? But then it didn't matter any more.

"Laurie Jo—"

"Not yet." She poured coffee for both of them and yawned. Her outstretched arms waved toward the blue waters far below their terrace. "Let's have a few minutes more."

They sat in silence. She tried to watch the Atlantic, but the silence stretched on. "All right, darling. What is it?"

"There's been nothing on the newscasts about Greg. And then I got a signal. Prepare *Valkyrie* at once. The engines will be up, intact."

"And you wondered if there was a connection?" she asked.

"I knew there was a connection." There was no emotion in his voice, and that frightened her.

"I've bought us the stars, Aeneas. The engines will go up in a week. Tested, ready for installation. And you've done the rest, you and Kit. We can go to the Moon, with all the equipment for the colony—"

"Yes. And Greg Tolland stays on."

She wanted to shout. What is that to you? she wanted to say. But she couldn't. "It was his price. The only one he'd take."

"It's too high."

She drew the thin silk robe around herself. Despite the bright sun she felt suddenly cold. "I've already agreed. I've given Greg my word."

"But I haven't. And you didn't tell me you were doing this."

"How could I? You wouldn't have agreed!"

"Precisely—"

"I can't lie to you, Aeneas." And now what do I lose? You? Everything I've worked for? Both? "The deal hasn't been made. Greg wants your word too."

"And if I don't give it?"

"Then he won't send up the engines. You're close enough to know what happens then. I'm at the edge of losing control of

Heimdall to my partners. This is my only chance.''

But it didn't have to be, he thought. You're in trouble because you insisted on speeding up the schedule, no matter what the cost, and it cost a lot. Technicians pulled off production work for *Valkyrie*. The Lunatic expedition. ''You've put me in a hell of a fix, Laurie Jo.''

''Damn you! Aeneas MacKenzie, damn you anyway!'' He tried to speak, but the rush of words stopped him as she shouted in anger. ''Who appointed you guardian of the people? You and your damned honor! You're ready to throw away everything, and for what? For revenge on Greg Tolland!''

''But that's not true! I don't want revenge.''

''Then what do you want, Aeneas?''

''I wanted out, Laurie Jo. It was you who insisted that I direct your agents in the investigation. I was finished with all that. I was willing to leave well enough alone, until we found—'' Until it was clear that Greg Tolland had known everything. Until it was clear that he wasn't an honest man betrayed, that he was corrupt to the core, and had been for years. Until I couldn't help knowing that I'd spent most of my life electing— ''You intended this all along, didn't you?'' His voice was gentle and very sad.

Her anger was gone. It was impossible to keep it when he failed to respond. ''Yes,'' she said. ''It was the only way.''

''The only way—''

''For us.'' She wouldn't meet his eyes. ''What was I supposed to do, Aeneas? What kind of life do we have here? It takes every minute I have to keep Hansen Enterprises. Greg Tolland has already tried to have you killed. You were safe enough in *Heimdall*, but what good was that? With you there and me here? And I couldn't keep the station if I lived there.'' And we've got so little time. We lost so many years, and there are so few left.

They were silent for a moment. Gulls cried in the wind, and overhead a jet thundered.

''And now I've done it,'' she said. ''We can go to the Moon. I can arrange more supplies. *Valkyrie* doesn't cost so much to operate, and we'll have nearly everything we need to build the colony anyway. We can do it, Aeneas. We can found the first lunar colony, and be free of all this.''

''But only if I agree—''

''Yes.''

''Laurie Jo, would you give up the Moon venture for me?''

''Don't ask me to. Would you give up your vendetta against Greg for the Moon?''

He stood and came around the table. She seemed helpless and vulnerable, and he put his hands on her shoulders. She looked up in surprise: his face was quite calm now.

"No," he said. "But I'll do as you ask. Not for the Moon, Laurie Jo. For you."

She stood and embraced him, but as they clung to each other she couldn't help thinking, thank God, he's not incorruptible after all. He's not more than human.

She felt almost sad.

Two delta shapes, one above the other; below both was the enormous bulk of the expendable fuel tank which powered the ramjet of the atmospheric booster. The big ships sat atop a thick, solid rocket that would boost them to ram speed.

All that, Laurie Jo thought. All that, merely to get into orbit. And before the spaceplanes and shuttles, there were the disintegrating totem poles. No wonder space was an unattractive gamble until I built my lasers.

The lasers had not been a gamble for her. A great part of the investment was in the power plants, and they made huge profits. The price she paid for *Heimdall* and *Valkyrie* hadn't been in money.

There were other costs, though, she thought. Officials bribed to expedite construction permits. Endless meetings to hold together a syndicate of international bankers. Deals with people who needed their money laundered. It would have been so easy to be part of the idle rich. Instead of parties I went to meetings, and I've yet to live with a man I love except for those few weeks we had.

And now I'm almost forty years old, and I have no children. But we will have! The doctors tell me I have a few years left, and we'll make the most of them.

They were taken up the elevator into the upper ship. It was huge, a squat triangle that could carry forty thousand kilos in one payload, and do it without the 30-g stresses of the laser system. They entered by the crew access door, but she could see her technicians making a final examination of the nuclear engine in the cargo compartment.

She was placed in the acceleration couch by an Air Force officer. Aeneas was across a narrow passageway, and there were no other passengers. The young A.F. captain had a worried frown, as if he couldn't understand why this mission had suddenly been ordered, and why two strange civilians were going with a cargo for *Heimdall*.

You wouldn't want to know, my young friend, Laurie Jo thought. You wouldn't want to know at all.

Motors whined as the big clamshell doors of the cargo compartment were closed down. The A.F. officer went forward into the crew compartment. Lights flashed on the instrument board mounted in the forward part of the passenger bay, but Laurie Jo didn't understand what they meant.

"DING."

"MY GOD, WHAT NOW?"

"SIGNOR ANTONELLI HAS JUST NOW HEARD THAT YOU ARE GOING UP TO HEIMDALL. HE IS VERY DISTURBED."

I'll just bet he is, Laurie Jo thought. She glanced across the aisle at Aeneas. He was watching the display.

"TELL SIGNOR ANTONELLI TO GO PLAY WITH HIMSELF."

"I HAVE NO TRANSLATION ROUTINE FOR THAT EXPRESSION."

"I DON'T WANT IT TRANSLATED. TELL HIM TO GO PLAY WITH HIMSELF."

There was a long pause. Something rumbled in the ship, then there were clanking noises as the gantries were drawn away.

"MISTER MC CARTNEY IS VERY DISTRUBED ABOUT YOUR LAST MESSAGE AND ASKS THAT YOU RECONSIDER."

"TELL MC CARTNEY TO GO PLAY WITH HIMSELF TOO. CANCEL THAT. ASK MISTER MC CARTNEY TO SPEAK WITH SIGNOR ANTONELLI. I AM TAKING A VACATION. MC CARTNEY IS IN CHARGE. HE WILL HAVE TO MANAGE AS BEST HE CAN."

"ACKNOWLEDGED."

"Hear this. Liftoff in thirty seconds. Twenty-nine. Twenty-eight. Twenty-seven . . ."

The count reached zero, and there was nothing for an eternity. Then the ship lifted, pushing her into the couch. After a few moments there was nothing, another agonizing moment before the ramjets caught. Even inside the compartment they could hear the roaring thunder before that, too, began to fade. The ship lifted, leveled, and banked to go on course for the trajectory that would take it into an orbit matching *Heimdall*'s.

"GET MC CARTNEY ON THE LINE."

There was silence.

Out of range, she thought. She smiled and turned to Aeneas. "We did it," she said.

"Yes."

"You don't sound very excited."

He turned and smiled, and his hand reached out for hers, but they were too far apart. The ship angled steeply upward, and the roar of the ramjets grew louder again, then there was more weight as the rockets cut in. Seconds later the orbital vehicle separated from the carrier.

Laurie Jo looked through the thick viewport. The islands below were laid out like a map, their outlines obscured by cotton clouds far below them. The carrier ship banked off steeply and began its descent as the orbiter continued to climb.

Done, she thought. But she looked again at Aeneas, and he was staring back toward the United States and the world they had left behind.

"They don't need us, Aeneas," she said carefully.

"No. They don't need me at all."

She smiled softly. "But I need you. I always will."

The Free Agent

rl

MICHAEL CASSUTT

With the reluctance of the U.S. government to move quickly into space, companies are being formed to respond to NASA's lethargy and business's growing need for communications and other types of satellites. Thus far, most of these new companies have been small private firms with limited capital. Without the resources of an international corporation or the deep pockets of a national government, they've been forced to re-engineer and retool older launch and rocket technology.

So far most of their launches have resulted in resounding failures, like the October 5, 1989, suborbital rocket launched by the American Rocket Company, which failed to leave the launching pad. Instead of rising majestically, it fell over and burst into flames. The good news was that the vehicle did not explode; the bad news is that the American Rocket Company was forced by this failure and other financial problems to lay off about sixty employees. Then it lost its president in an accident. The future is uncertain.

Other small firms have suffered crippling losses. Space Services, Inc. took a hard blow when the *Consort 2* suborbital vehicle exploded thirty-seven seconds into its maiden flight over White Sands Missile Range in New Mexico. Despite heavy investor reluctance, companies continue to try to develop and build their own launch systems.

One day soon, one of these privately owned companies is going to do it right. The Davis Aerospace Company has been working for five years on a promising design for an unmanned heavy-lift launch system again called the *Consort*. The boost engines are each fabricated into the individual recovery capsules so they can be refurbished and used again after their recovery on Earth. Through the use of the *Consort* or similar vehicles it is hoped that cost per pound to low Earth orbit can be reduced as low as three hundred dollars per pound. We have our money on the SSX, but more on that later.

Right now it is still a big crap shoot; no one knows what design will be most successful, or shot down by NASA as it protects its turf as the sole proprietor of space launches and satellite delivery. While it's frustrating now, in the long run it matters little. Destiny will have its day; the human race will push off this tiny orb as our ancestors pushed themselves out of the primordial oceans.

For now, the future is murky. But out there some nation or strong-minded group of individuals will ride the torch into space, whether for mankind, or for their own private demons, as in this story by Michael Cassutt.

HE'S BEEN WAITING a long time for this launch.

In his ears a familiar voice ran calmly through the old chant: "Six . . . five . . . ignition sequence start . . . booster commit . . ." He heard rumbling in his headset. ". . . Two . . . one . . . liftoff . . ." And the screen in front of him blossomed with numbers cycling every third of a second.

"Tower cleared," the capcom said.

"Roger, Davey." Mendoza didn't get too excited. After all, there was nothing that could happen that he hadn't rehearsed a hundred times.

"Pitch ten degrees." "Roger." Thirty seconds into the flight and mark. He wasn't much for chit-chat and neither was the capcom. Mendoza wasn't loafing, though. He had something like forty-seven different functions to monitor on the main display.

Any significant deviation from the optimax curves, and he would have to switch to PILOT mode—which would make the launch that much more interesting. "All systems are go," he said.

"No fooling," the capcom replied, laughing.

He thought about what was waiting, up there in the wild black yonder. The Space Operations Center, of course, that misshapen heap that would eventually be a real space station, if they ever got their act together, if they ever got the money. And "Kosmograd," the first space city, with its four, or was it five, dozen Russians and Cubans and Germans. "SRB sep in ten." "Roger."

Suddenly his screens went blank. *Total* power failure? Hydraulics? It was impossible— "What the hell's going on?"

"Time's up for today," the capcom said.

Damn. "I thought I had a whole hour." He popped the release on the couch and tilted it back twenty degrees to a relatively comfortable recline. The shuttle's cabin windows no longer showed a receding Florida coastline and blue sky—just gray phosphor nothingness.

"Sorry, but the One-Fifteen crew came in early. Bambi says they caught some heavy timeline changes yesterday and he wants a chance to run through them before the meeting in Hugh's office." Hugh was Hugh Dickinson, the Director of Flight Crew Operations, Mendoza's boss. Bambi was Wally Baumberger, prime crew commander for STS-115, the next shuttle flight.

Prime crew. Jerry Mendoza was about as far from that high status as you could get, and still be an astronaut. Prime crew members didn't have to crawl out of bed at six in the morning to steal some time on the center's only single-system simulator. He was lucky to get time at all.

"What the hell are you doing in here, Mendoza, working up a strafing run on Washington?" Bambi squeezed into the cabin. He was bald and ugly and had been in the program since '81.

"That's an idea," Mendoza said, getting out of the commander's couch. "With Senator Stooker's house as ground zero. Of course, you guys could save his life by taking me along. Just give me an air mattress and deck space, and you won't hear a word."

"Not even an occasional cry of pain?" That was McIntyre, the pilot.

He got out of her way, too, feeling somewhat like a best man on the honeymoon. "Not a peep. What are you real astronauts running today, anyway?"

Bambi looked unhappier than usual. "You won't want to hear what I have to tell you—"

"Oh, heck, I can take it, Bambi. I'm a war veteran. . . ."

They laughed. "It's a sardine flight, Jerry. One dozen goddamn *passengers*, if you can believe that. Four Congresspeople and the rest writers and VIPs. Six hours, three orbits."

"Just like John Glenn," Mendoza said.

"Who's that?" McIntyre asked, and everybody laughed again.

He left the simulator cabin, taking the steps carefully. The war had given him a souvenir, a plastic fragment in his left knee, nothing that would seriously hamper his mobility—wouldn't the NASA doctors love to get hold of that—but every once in a while he felt some stiffness in it, especially on a damp spring morning like this. He picked up a cup of coffee and, sipping at it, trudged down the dark hall to his office. He switched on the light and, reflexively glancing at the outdated nameplate (CAPT. MENDOZA), saw a note taped to the door. He grabbed the slip and read: 4:55, REGGIE GILLIAM CALLED. WCL TOMORROW A.M.

Reggie Gilliam—now who the hell was that? The press had started to leave him alone in the past couple of months. He couldn't place the name in Washington, either. So he crumpled the note and tossed it in the wastebasket, then sat down at his all-too-neat desk.

He picked up the phone and called home. His son answered sleepily. "Hey," he said, "aren't you supposed to be getting ready for school?"

"It's *Friday*, Dad."

"Oh. Let me talk to your mother."

Jeannie got on the phone. "Is something wrong, Jerry?"

He winced. Has it gotten that bad? "No, nothing's wrong. They just bumped me out of the simulator for Bambi's crew."

"Damn them, haven't they done enough to you already?"

"It's okay, hon. It was just your typical routine last-minute emergency. You know how it goes. At least Bambi said hello to me this time."

"How thoughtful of him."

"Don't be nasty," he said. "What are you doing today?"

"Oh, I promised Mr. Shivello that I'd come in for a few hours this morning." Jeannie worked as a researcher for a lawyer, a good job because it gave her relative freedom during the day.

"What about Erik?" He kept telling himself he was too old-fashioned, wanting his wife home during the day with the boy.

"I'm dropping him off at Little League on the way. What about you?"

"Well, I *was* gonna sit in the simulator until . . . oh, about an hour from now, then I was gonna drop the tapes off at Dickinson's office, you know, just to remind him that I'm still alive. Then I thought I would go to the debriefing for the One-Fourteen crew and find some ass to kiss. Since step A didn't happen, I may just sit here and *siesta* all day."

"Jerry."

"Ah . . . I know. I'll do something. I did get a message here, from some guy named Gilliam. Reggie Gilliam. Is that someone I should know?"

"Isn't he on TV—?"

"Christ, that's *all* I need today."

"—No, that's another—"

"He's a baseball player, Dad."

"What are you doing on the line?"

"You can tap into it from the console upstairs."

The kid had no shame. "I never knew that. What kind of baseball player?"

"Pretty good. He's an All-Star, plays centerfield for the Washington Americans." Erik yawned. "But he's pretty old now. I think he's almost forty."

Mendoza was forty-two. "He's supposed to call me today."

"Great! Can you get an autograph for me?"

"*Eric*—" Jeannie said.

"I'll see," Mendoza said. "I'll see what I can do."

He was on his way to lunch when the call came. "Mr. Gilliam is on the phone," the secretary said, pronouncing the name as Gill-em.

"Okay." He picked up the receiver.

The first words Gilliam said were, "Tell your secretary I may be in love with her."

Jesus, one of those. "Sure, but she's about sixty." That wasn't true, but he was in no mood to play good old boy games.

"The charm works on all ages," Gilliam said. "This is Reggie Gilliam, Mr. Mendoza."

"Pleased to meet you."

"I called to see if you would be interested in flying down here to talk about a business proposition."

"Down where, Mr. Gilliam?"

"Reggie—St. Pete. At my expense, of course."

"I'm not making any endorsements or investments at the moment . . . Reggie."

"This is more of—what would you call it?—a professional engagement."

Mendoza wanted to laugh. "Just for the sake of speculation, Reggie, what does a baseball player want with an astronaut?"

"Well, for starters, Gerardo, I've got a space vehicle, and you're just the man to fly it."

II

He had hoped the change in locale might bring a change in the weather, but if anything, Mendoza felt even hotter and sweatier when he got off the plane at Tampa-St. Pete. Well, it was only fair: he hadn't been able to quit replaying last night's argument with Jeannie, either. At least Erik had wanted him to go.

On the drive to the airport he had picked up a flimsy paperback called *Who's Who in Baseball 1996* and a *Sporting News*. The paper contained a jargon-loaded survey of "Spring Training—The Grapefruit League," embedded in which was a whole paragraph about Reggie Gilliam:

. . . Gilliam has been the bomber of yesteryear this spring. His shoulder seems completely recovered from rotator cuff surgery in fall 1994 that limited him to pinch-hitting roles for most of 1995. At 38 he still runs well (asked about his "wheels" he says "They're like full-warranty, steel-belted radials.") and is looking forward to the two years remaining on his lucrative contract.

That helped a bit, and the *Who's Who* book filled in the gaps. Born in '57 in Chicago, Gilliam was a two-year College All-Star at Arizona State; drafted by the Mets, he jumped straight to the big leagues at age 21. NL Rookie of the Year for 1979 . . . a couple of early batting titles, lots of big, booming home runs . . . the dive into the free-agent market at age 25, which got him a five-year, four-million-dollar contract. Thirteen years later he was still going strong and making more money than ever.

That Gilliam: commercials, candy bars, T-shirts.

"Captain Mendoza?"

He had taken one step into the sweltering terminal building when a pretty black woman called his name.

"I'm Eunice Christian, Mr. Gilliam's secretary. We have a car waiting for you, if you'll come with me."

"Glad to."

"Did you check any luggage?"

"I just have the overnight bag." He let her take it and followed her to the VIP lounge. He enjoyed the walk through; the lounge was mercifully air-conditioned, and Ms. Christian was wearing one of the new miniskirts, which Jeannie swore she would never wear.

The car was a Mercedes limo with opaque windows. Mendoza got in the back, and the door, as if by magic, closed behind him.

"Captain Mendoza, I'm George Dungee." A neatly bearded black man in a dashiki and sunglasses extended his hand. "Reggie's adviser."

"Where is Reggie?"

"At the ballpark." He glanced at a Piaget wrist unit. "The workout should be over shortly after we arrive."

The limo had started without Mendoza's knowing. So much for the astronaut's keen sense of equilibrium.

"How was your flight?"

He had been sandwiched between a shaven-skulled college boy who smelled of cigarette smoke and ether (he always felt vaguely ill on commercial liners) and a business woman who kept mumbling into a pocket recorder as she flipped noisily through a mess of hard copy paper. "Fine," he said.

"How long will you be able to stay with us?"

"I have to be back in Houston tomorrow night."

"Are you in a position, Captain, to take leave from your program—or would you have to resign in order to do some work for Reggie?"

Mendoza couldn't help smiling. "Don't you think that's a bit premature, Mr. Dungee?" The lawyer was busy extracting a dark Thai stick from a silver case. He lit it and offered Mendoza the first hit. "No, thanks."

Dungee wasn't so refined as to dislike doping alone. He inhaled, held it without visible effect, then exhaled gently. "Please don't be offended, Captain. Working with a man like Reggie requires a certain amount of pre-preparation."

"I assume you know my situation, or you wouldn't have invited me down here in the first place."

Dungee coughed slightly. "It was impossible to . . . ignore the reports of your . . . how shall we say? . . . differences of opinion with the NASA hierarchy. No, I was simply anxious to save time later, should you decide to accept Reggie's offer."

"That's understandable. But what, exactly, is this wonderful offer?"

"I *am* sorry. I was under the impression that Reggie had told you all about it."

"He just told me that he was looking for a rocket jockey."

Dungee snuffed his cigarette. "That *is* typical." He didn't look happy. "And slightly inaccurate as well. Briefly, Captain, Reggie's management and investment firm has acquired a Pirri-Weiss capsule and plans to place it in orbit within the next few weeks."

"Those pods don't require crew, Mr. Dungee."

"For retrieval by the Space Operations Center, that is true. But for rendezvous with Kosmograd, our studies show that a trained pilot must be on board."

"I didn't know Kosmograd was taking P-W shipments."

"Let's just say that the system is still in its infancy."

"I'll be damned." The Pirri-Weiss pods were bullet-shaped capsules that were fired into orbit at the tip of high-energy carbon dioxide lasers, which super-heated the air at the base of each capsule, expelling it. It was like having a jet engine without having to carry the fuel. Exxon's pod launcher had been in operation since '93. The Arizona facilities were leased to any party with half a million dollars, usually European or small American firms who wanted payloads delivered to space but couldn't afford room on the Shuttle or on Arianne. NASA, of course, didn't use the pod system: its total mass-to-orbit capability was only 1500 kilograms a launch, less than a fiftieth what a Shuttle could deliver. The fact that a great majority of NASA's payloads massed 1500 kg or less hadn't changed the policy, nor was it likely to change any time soon. Mendoza had learned that the hard way.

"Is there a problem, Captain?"

"Well—the kind of maneuver you've described, Mr. Dungee, is tricky enough with a Shuttle. The minimum requirements are an on-board guidance system, which means a trio of reliable processors, delta-vee capability, which would mean adding at least a pair of engines, not to mention maneuvering fuel. I can't say that I care for the splashdown method of recovery, either. It's perfectly okay to dump cargo in the ocean and pick it up at leisure, but I think I might get seasick. I don't even want to *think* about the political problems."

"The political problems will be taken care of, I assure you," Dungee said. "But—your honest opinion, now. Is a P-W capsule even capable of such a flight? I'm just parroting a feasibility study, you understand. Would *you* fly one?"

"Without getting into the problem of payload, of which you could have damn little, and using off-the-shelf hardware, yes, it *can* be done and I *could* do it. Hell, they were doing plane changes and first-orbit rendezvous with Gemini capsules thirty years ago."

"I see." Dungee rubbed his upper lip. "Frankly, Captain, I was hoping you would say that it was impossible."

The limo pulled into the parking lot of Landreaux Field and Mendoza got out alone, Dungee having assured him that his bag would be taken on to the hotel, and that he would be riding over with Gilliam.

The cool ride had relaxed him and actually chilled him, and the hot Florida sun felt comforting as he walked up the concrete ramp to the battered old grandstand. He could hear distant shouts, occasional laughs, and bats cracking into balls. Houston, Dickinson and Jeannie might have ceased to exist.

The Americans' workout was still in progress. Players threw back and forth along the foul lines while others sprinted in the outfield. Inside the batting cage at home plate one skinny kid, wearing number 88 on his uniform, took cuts at a series of looping curves lobbed by a burly, bearded pitcher. The screen protecting the mound was unnecessary, because young 88's hits either dribbled foul or blooped lazily to the infielders. Mendoza figured there were almost a hundred players out there. Where was Gilliam?

The stands, however, were all but empty. Four or five elderly men sat in the shade beneath the press box, high above home plate. Mendoza preferred to wait in the sun. He could see one spectator sitting a few rows back of the first base dugout.

"Excuse me," he said, "do you know how much longer they're going to be practicing?"

"About another fifteen minutes or so." It was a kid. "Two more guys have to take their turns in the cage."

"Thanks. Mind if I sit here?"

"No, no, go right ahead, man."

Mendoza took the nearest seat and glanced at the kid. He was black, something that hadn't been completely obvious at first because his skin was so light. Beneath an official Americans baseball cap the kid's hair was cropped right down to the scalp, and he wore a T-shirt with the "A" logo. There was an expensive-looking cane laid across the seat next to him. Mendoza couldn't help looking at his legs, which were bone-thin and braced. Poor little bastard. He was probably some local kid who just lived for spring training and the chance to watch the major leaguers up close.

"How do they look?" he asked.

The kid squinted. "Oh, they'll be lucky to finish third this year. They've got some pretty good pitchers, but they're awful fragile. I don't know how their arms'll hold up when it gets to be August.

The fielding is very shaky and they've only got a couple of consistent hitters. Now, if they were in the Central Division they might have a chance—but the National East is real tough this year, especially New York and Atlanta.''

Mendoza could feel his local-cripple theory drying up and blowing away. "Ah, which one of these guys is Gilliam?"

"Number four," the kid said.

"I don't see him anywhere—"

"You need to talk to him?" Mendoza nodded. The kid moved the cane and lifted a Sony processor pack out of the seat. He set it on his lap and touched a key. "He's off doing windsprints in right field now. He'll have a couple of hours off before the afternoon workout, which will be light,'cause they're playing a couple of intrasquad games against St. Louis tomorrow."

"Does that processor tell you all that?"

"Oh, keeping track of training is just something I'm doing for fun," the kid said cheerfully. "Later on Roger Wolfe, the manager, is going to come over here and give me half a dozen potential lineups for the game tomorrow as well as the reports on injuries and player development, you know? I'll feed it into the machine, which is already programmed with a routine of my own design, including the most recent information on the Cardinals, and it'll give me a lineup that should be ideal for the game."

"Jesus, *I* never played baseball like that."

"You still gotta play the game, man. It just gives you better information, that's all. See, since it's spring training and the games don't count, the program aims for maximum player development. There are some guys who always seem to have trouble getting it together and this helps. *During* the season, what you'd want to do is model as many different games with as many different lineups as possible each day, then pick your starters based on the results. But it's still baseball. You still got three strikes."

Mendoza got up, shaking his head. "You work for the team, I guess."

"I help out."

The grandstand ended just past first base, and Mendoza found himself walking at field level along a chain fence toward the outfield. There was a group of players on the other side resting from windsprints. A couple of them were real giants; some, to Mendoza's surprise, weren't any bigger than he was. Number four was definitely one of the big guys—probably six-five, huge shoulders, black as midnight, and going bald. He didn't look too tired, either.

He pointed at Mendoza. "All right, *Gerardo!* Be with you in a minute." He picked up his cap and called to a nearby coach. "Hey, Ellie, tell Roger I'm gonna take off for a while. I'll be back in plenty of time for the PM workout, okay?"

The coach frowned, but Gilliam didn't seem to care. He exited through a gate and, with Mendoza tagging along behind, headed toward the parking lots. "Damn," he said, "you'd think I asked the guy to go tell Shamu there ain't no fish for lunch."

"I didn't mean to interrupt your workout."

"It's no problem. We've got a new manager this year who does everything by the numbers. He likes the idea that I'm what he calls 'ten percent ahead of projection,' but I've got one other number that he pays more attention to, and that's a million-four every year. Thanks, by the way, for coming down here. I hate doing business on the telephone." He dug car keys out of his uniform pocket and opened the doors of a yellow Bricklin Steamer that looked two sizes too small for him. Mendoza was slightly disappointed. After Dungee's limo, he'd expected Gilliam himself to have a private chopper at the very least. They pulled out.

"Did Dungee fill you in on the job at all?"

"Sort of. He says you're buying a pod and firing it up to Kosmograd."

"Doesn't sound too complicated when you put it like that. Yeah, we've got a pod and a cargo and a launch date six weeks from now, and we need a hotshot pilot to see that it all gets done."

Mendoza wished he could take off his jacket. "Boeing has a bunch of people who've driven the pods, and there are a lot of ex-NASA or European guys available."

"True, but . . . well, let's just say I hate to see anyone getting blacklisted."

"Who might that be?"

"Come on, Gerardo, don't try to shit a bullshitter. You're in it up to your neck with NASA 'cause of that testimony last year, that senator you got ticked off at you—"

"—And it's only because I'm a beaner that they haven't bounced my ass out of there yet, huh?"

Gilliam shrugged. "It's still a white man's world, lots of ways. Besides, you've got other things goin' for you. You know how it is, too, when you're looking for a ballplayer that's gonna win ball games, you don't always automatically grab the biggest or the fastest—"

"—Or the blackest."

Gilliam looked sideways at him and laughed. "You got it. It's attitude that makes the difference. I figure that *you've* got a winning attitude. You'd *have* to have it, otherwise you'd give up.''

Mendoza concentrated on the worn-out fast-food joints along the road. This was all he needed: a fading, millionaire jock full of locker room smarts and cosmic visions. He was beginning to wish he had stayed in Houston, fight or no fight.

"There's one thing that always bugged me about NASA and all these space people," Gilliam went on, "and that's because they always seemed to think that the only people who might ever want to get out there where the wind don't blow is white guys with white shirts and glasses. Captain Kirk, boring mothers like that.''

"That isn't quite true.''

"True *enough*, man. Most of them are all the same, the ones making the decisions, that is. They're all these bookworm types who spent all their time playing with computers when they were kids, you remember? Well, hell, I don't want to run down somebody just 'cause they like machines . . . that's just one kind of dedication, I suppose. But now and then you've got to get out in the sunshine . . . chase a little pussy, put the pedal to the floor. You can't just sit there and look at the numbers and say, 'Shit, they don't add up.' ''

"Some of the early guys were pretty rowdy.''

"I've heard that—most of them didn't stick around too long, either. They found out that it wasn't any fun doing things the way NASA made you do them. No magic at all, goddamn reporters running after you all the time, all this boring junk on the TV. Why didn't they just leave everybody the hell alone, don't mention everything that's going on. Just come on the TV some day and say, 'In ten minutes we're going to fire some guy into space. Take a look.' *That* would have been exciting. Like those Mars pictures, with the pink sky?''

"I've seen them.''

"*That* was interesting. It's like new turf. Everybody likes to see something new like that.''

They were in the parking lot of the Hilton by now. Gilliam stopped the car. "So what would you say to fifty thousand?''

"Fifty thousand what?''

"Fifty thousand bucks, you start in a week or whenever you can get loose, arrange the training and all that jazz, and do that launch. Half to start, half when it's over.''

Fifty thousand dollars was more than NASA paid him in a whole year. It was more than the Air Force used to pay him in two.

"I'll think about it and call you on Monday, how's that?"

"Good enough."

"It *is* a lot of money," Jeannie said.

"It could also be a lot of trouble," Mendoza answered. They were just finishing dinner. Erik had already bolted out to the back yard. "I mean, Christ, I might be signing up to be some sort of interstellar smuggler or something. *God* doesn't know what goes up in those pods sometimes, and I hate getting messed up with anything the Russians are involved in." He picked up the dishes and carried them into the kitchen.

Jeannie followed. "I don't think that's worth worrying about, Jerry. They're just businessmen, after all. You were the one who told me that eventually all these private investors were going to start putting things into space. Now that someone's actually starting to do that, you think they're smugglers."

"I guess I just don't know if it would do *me* any good—"

"Honestly, Jerry—is NASA doing you any good right now? You've done nothing but blabber on about this project since you came back. You *want* to do it, I can tell. At least it would get you back into space. Hugh Dickinson isn't going to send you up again, that's for sure."

"Well, that *isn't* for sure. I mean, Dickinson could fall over dead tomorrow, Stooker might get beat in his primary, you know. Besides, the agency has been awfully touchy about granting leave—"

"*Jerry!*" She put her hands on her ample hips and looked at him angrily. "Right now Alan Weisman and Peggy Holt are on leave to do *research*, and they won't be back for a *year*. You're only going to need *one* month—without pay!—and it could easily be justified as a fact-finding mission." She turned back to the sink. "If nothing else, do it for me. This is the first thing you've shown any interest in since that stupid meeting last *year*—"

He hated to be told what he already knew, but she was right: since his fall from grace, he had been sinking further and further into a terminal crouch, crawling far under a rock, just as NASA hoped he would. Of course he had gone through the right-stuff motions—it was expected that an astro jock would get up at 5 A.M. to show that he couldn't be beaten down—but he still came home wanting only to sleep or watch TV. And that was a good way to get fat, old, and useless.

He closed the cupboard door and eased up behind Jeannie,

slipping his hands around her waist, rocking against her. "I feel a certain interest returning," he murmured.

She took her soapy hands out of the water and turned toward him.

The phone rang.

"God damn it."

She smiled. "Go ahead."

He went to the desk and noticed that the calling number displayed on the auto-sec was familiar. "That's Dickinson."

"Good. He can be the first to know you're taking a leave."

He touched the receiver. "Hey," he said. "What was that you called this—a fact-finding mission?"

III

"Please give your status report," the "capcom" said.

"Guidance, go," Mendoza replied. "Life support, go . . . Thrusters armed." He wanted to laugh. There was the sum total of the data he had to relay. Now he knew what it had been like for Yuri Gagarin or any of the early astronauts. Spam in a can.

"Go for burn in one minute. Please check your RCS auto."

"Right on." He adjusted the headset, which kept slipping down, and squirmed in his seat. It was a little too hot for comfort inside the Yuma simulators of Exxon's Space Delivery Division. For five hundred bucks an hour you'd think the air-conditioning would work. Mendoza hoped the sloppiness didn't extend to the pod's life-support systems. "RCS to auto." He made a red mark on his homemade checklist. Exxon would have provided one, but he preferred his own.

"Twenty seconds to burn."

The "command console" of a Pirri-Weiss pod bore about as much resemblance to that of a Shuttle as the dashboard of a golf cart did to a Mercedes. There was just one display screen—no backup dials and gauges, either—a stick, a firing panel for the three tiny maneuvering thrusters, and a guidance system that was literally nothing more than a box bolted to the table top. The life support was good for twenty-four hours "if you breathed slow," and the sanitary facilities might as well have been dispensed with altogether.

"Five seconds."

He let the automatic guidance tweak him into the proper orientation for the burn. Plane changes were necessary because Exxon's launcher could only put pods into orbit for the Space Ops Center—this year, anyway. It took burns on two successive orbits to move a pod to Kosmograd's inclination. With its big blasters, of course, a Shuttle could make such a change with one small burn. But going by pod was going no-frills.

"Firing," Mendoza said. The numbers on the screen ran in their various appointed directions for thirty seconds—a long time for a burn—then stopped abruptly.

"This must be shutdown."

"That's correct, Captain."

"What's the new orbit look like?"

"One forty by one ninety, inclination—"

"Jesus! That's too damn elliptical." He started to rub his forehead. This is what happened when you used third-hand rockets. If any of the little engines fired two seconds too long or too short, the pod could very well be dumped into an orbit it could never get out of. Mendoza certainly wouldn't have fuel to maneuver to safety, and just how likely were the Russians—or NASA—to send somebody after him?

"Let's go through this again. I'd like to do it right, just once."

Someone was knocking on the door. Dungee. "May I talk with you for a moment, Captain?"

Mendoza got up. "Yeah. I've been meaning to ask you a couple of things." He followed the lawyer into the corridor. "Besides, you're paying for it."

"How are things going, by the way?"

"Well, let's just say it's a good thing my insurance agent isn't here to see me. I've got no real backup systems, fail-safes that keep failing, no pressure suits on board . . ."

"You did get the initial fee."

"Yeah, that I got. But, tell me something, Mr. Dungee. With me and the engines and the extra fuel, I figure there's maybe room for less than a hundred kilograms of paying cargo. Call it two hundred pounds, if I skip lunch. Now, the only thing I can think of, off hand, that's worth that kind of money, is heroin."

Dungee laughed and, by way of evading the question, opened the door into the launch center's tiny lobby. Through the glass, which looked in on the "control room," Mendoza could see half a dozen teams of operators clustered around their screens. And there was another set of observers inside the glass in the rear of the room. Something about them bothered Mendoza. "Are those people Russians?"

"Some of them," Dungee said. "You may even know that one—Colonel Vovkin?"

He sure did. Yuri Vovkin was the shortest of the four Russians (there were also a couple of Americans, blacks), a trim, sharp-featured man with a styled beard and designer casual clothes. "Yeah, I met Vovkin about three years ago, down in Houston. Smart man, but he's a shark. I wonder what he's doing here?"

"I believe he's touring the States with a trade delegation." Dungee smiled. "At least that's what he said when we were introduced a while ago."

One of the Americans was directing Vovkin's attention toward a station where a pair of unseen operators worked. The cosmonaut slipped his hands into his expensive pockets and stepped away from the group, which continued its slow procession around the room.

Apparently he wanted a better look—at what? The facilities at Baikonur were twice as good as these.

"Let's go inside," Dungee said.

"Let's finish our discussion first," Mendoza said. "It's not such a big deal. I only want to know what it is that I'm supposed to deliver to Kosmograd."

"That's what I propose to clear up," the lawyer said. "Inside."

Mendoza hesitated, then gave in, expecting Dungee to call the Russians over for one of their famous "spontaneous" meetings. But the Russians were halfway to the other exit. Vovkin did catch Mendoza's eye, giving a little wave.

"There," Dungee was saying.

The lawyer nodded toward the console that had seemed so fascinating to the Russians. Toward one of the operators, a black teenager with heavy braces on his legs, wearing a T-shirt that said Washington Americans on it.

"What the hell is this?" Mendoza demanded.

"Captain Mendoza, meet Buddy Gilliam—"

"We've met," the kid said, getting painfully to his feet.

"Reggie Gilliam's son," Dungee went on. "Your passenger."

"I didn't sign up to be a baby-sitter," Mendoza said.

Reggie Gilliam leaned against the wall beneath a No Smoking sign and lit a cigarette, "No one's asking you to be a baby-sitter. All you've got to do is drive the car—baby'll take care of his own ass. Hey, want some help with that?"

"No," Mendoza snapped, reaching around his back to zip up the two halves of the pressure suit. "And it isn't that simple. We'll forget the business of misrepresentation, for the moment. What you don't seem to understand is that this cockamamie flight is dangerous for me, and I know what to expect. It's ten times more dangerous for a healthy person who isn't trained. God knows what could happen to somebody who's . . . ah. . . ."

"Lordie, somebody who is crippled." Gilliam sounded like an Amen-shouting Baptist.

"Yeah, somebody who is crippled. It could kill him." He wriggled inside the suit. Not a great fit, but it would do: they would only be underwater in the neutral buoyancy tank for two hours. This sort of work, here at NASA/Marshall, was something Mendoza always looked forward to. Floating free all afternoon. "I mean, this isn't Space Mountain. Look, I think it's great for a guy to want to buy his kid a ride in space. I've got a kid myself. But goddamnit, if you waited about three years you could probably get him a ride on the Shuttle, if that's all you want."

Gilliam sneered. "Now who's doing the misrepresentation? NASA's got a list a mile long of fat cats and VIPs they want to give rides to. A nigger kid who can't walk is going to be down about number four million." He put out his cigarette after two puffs and tossed it toward a wastebasket. It missed. "No, I'm gonna keep on with this thing my way. That's usually how you get it done, man. Now, you took the job, and you've got to make a choice: do it, or go back to sitting on NASA's bench."

Mendoza had his helmet over his head. He held it there.

"Look," Gilliam said. "I'm sorry about the snake dance, okay? But if I'd called you up one day and said, 'Hey, Astronaut Mendoza, could I borrow you for a month so's you can take my po' crippled kid for a ride in space?' you'd have called de po-lice. At least this way you had the chance to check out all the equipment with nothing else hanging over you. If it'll work for you, it'll work for the two of you."

He clicked the helmet down, leaving the faceplate open. "We'll see, then. Today he gets Space Cadet Lesson Number One—how to move in zero-G without puking all over yourself. And he's going to have to go through a lot more lessons before he gets into that pod."

"That's cool. I can stand it."

Mendoza plugged the suit into the testing kit. "I hope *he* can stand it."

Gilliam was taking swings with an imaginary baseball bat. "Buddy was telling me you two met down in Florida."

"Yeah. I thought he was a fan or something."

"Well, hell, he is. He's into lots of stuff—most of it I can't figure out, I tell you. He was running around with all this *Star*

Wars and *Star Trek* jazz when he was little, even before he got crippled.''

"How'd that happen, anyway?" He was curious about it: how would a pro jock like Reggie Gilliam take to a crippled son? How would he?

"Accident." Gilliam took another swing. "Him and a friend whose daddy worked at Rockwell—this was when I was with the Angels—were screwing around with some model rocket one day, and the son of a bitch blew up on them. Buddy got some metal in his spine."

"What happened to the other kid?"

"Killed him dead."

The suit checked out. Mendoza phoned the technicians who were prepping Buddy and told them he'd be down in a minute. "That's really too bad."

"Maybe it's the Lord's way," Gilliam said quietly. "I don't know. I think he would have wanted to try to play ball, but that's a hell of a risky thing to be planning on—that I know for sure. And he was always better with these electronic things, anyway. After the accident he started paying more attention to school, too, which was good, because his momma and I were broke up by then and I was on the road a lot. Damn, but he's a sharp little bastard, the stuff he comes up with. He was the one turned me on to this space business, did you know that?"

Mendoza thought of Erik, another sharp little bastard, always tampering with the household computer system—a system which still managed to confuse Mendoza from time to time. "They're all like that these days," he said.

"I suppose they've gotta be." Gilliam slammed one big fist into an equally big palm. "So what is this here? You going swimming on my time?"

"You could call it that. It's more like deep-sea diving, only you don't get wet."

Gilliam laughed. "Well, watch out for Shamu. I've got to get back to Atlanta. Too many white guys in white shirts running around here. You want anything else, just turn on that Mexican temper and let me know."

"One thing," he said.

"Shoot."

"No more goddamn surprises, okay?"

Gilliam made a little pistol with his hand and fired it at Mendoza. "You got it. See you in Yuma next week."

Halfway through the test with Buddy, Mendoza looked over at

the tank's observation window, and there was Reggie Gilliam, big as life, with his face pressed up to the glass.

Mendoza knew that face. You could see it on any ten-year-old boy at any big league ballgame.

"Okay, this orbit would probably work, and we've got fuel left over," Mendoza said. They had been in the simulator since nine, and it was almost one now. In two days rehearsals would be over, and it would be Real Life. None too soon for Mendoza.

"Let's get right to the fun part," he told the capcom. "Put us about a thousand meters short of Kosmograd, and let's do the rendezvous one more time. For luck."

"Okay," the operator said. "Give me a minute to re-cycle."

"Take it." He stood up and glanced at Buddy, in the next seat. "I'm going to get some air. Do you want to go out?"

"I'll be okay right here."

"Okay." There wasn't a hell of a lot for the kid to do. In fact, Mendoza had considered doing the simulator work without him altogether, but Air Force and NASA habits were too strong. And it was best for the kid to know what was going on. It might save time later on.

The two of them didn't talk much, alone. TV reporters had cornered them several times, during which interviews Buddy tended to sound like a press agent's dream—a real junior cadet of the Rocket Patrol—with stories of his accident, his interest in microprocessors, his work at Yuma during summer vacation, his father. Mendoza, on the other hand, tried to smile and be as boring as possible, expounding endlessly on the advantages of cheap surface-to-orbit transport systems that did not require massive tax-payer subsidies, the endless frontier, space colonies. The TV people learned to leave him out of things. The viewers, however, must have thought he and Buddy were old pals . . . the skilled if somewhat disgraced astronaut trying to win back his wings, and the plucky kid. But the only private conversation they had had remained the baseball chat in Florida that first day. It wasn't dislike; Mendoza thought the teenager was bright, polite, and probably pushed into this whole project by his hotdog father, who was currently struggling at bat for the Americans, now five games out of first. Circumstances also kept them apart. Mendoza flew back to Houston for weekends, and Buddy spent most of his free time in physical therapy and survival training. Even when they were both at Yuma, Mendoza did a lot of worrying about fuel, delta-vee, re-entry angles, and his Russian.

"Ready," the operator said. "One thousand and closing at one-fifty."

"Roger," Mendoza said. He tweaked the thrusters twice, more to get the feel of them than anything else, which cut the closing velocity to one-twenty. The guidance computer fired the tiny RCS thrusters to compensate for any wobbles in the main engines. The docking would be tricky. A pod was a lot like an egg—strong in its own way, but if you rapped the edge just right. . . .

"Five hundred, closing at ninety."

"Rog." With his eyes on the radar display, he punched in a good four-second burn that brought them to a dead stop relative to the ghost space station one hundred meters away. From this point it would be like putting a car in a garage.

Except that the goddamn display was flashing red. "I've got a program alert," Mendoza said. "The board's dumping all the data—"

"Hold on," the operator said. "Ah . . . hell."

"Christ."

"Check the DOS terminal switches," Buddy said.

Mendoza couldn't help looking. Sure enough, two of the switches were set to AUTO, which meant that every time Mendoza manually fired the thrusters, the guidance computer went a little nuts.

"What about that, capcom?" Mendoza said.

"Checks out."

He flipped the switches into the right position. The board cleared. Mendoza looked at his checklist and saw DOS MODE TO MANUAL checked in red. So how had the switches gotten in the wrong mode?

He shut off the intercom. "Buddy, look, I know this is only a simulation and you can't get hurt, but don't ever screw around with these switches—"

"I didn't."

"Well, somebody did. Just remember that I'm the pilot—you're cargo, even if you do have your own pocket computer."

Buddy looped the carry strap of his processor around his neck. "Whatever you say, Commodore."

Mendoza stared at the kid long enough for his temper to flare up and cool down. Well, who knew what had happened? People made mistakes in simulators all the time, since you were always aware that it wasn't real. People made fatal mistakes in orbit, leaving switches in the wrong position, anything. Buddy wasn't dumb enough to try to help . . . but Mendoza suspected that the kid played astronaut when he was out of the cabin. *He* would have. "I think we ought to take a break for lunch."

"Fine." Buddy reached down and locked his braces into their walking position, grabbed his cane, and stood up. As he squeezed past Mendoza, however, he moved a little too fast, and his stiff right leg caught on the chair—

"Damn!"

He started to topple in slow motion. Mendoza twisted around and stuck out an arm, which didn't do much good. They hit the floor together, Mendoza on the bottom.

After a moment Mendoza said, "Are you all right?"

"Yeah." Buddy struggled upright and even gave Mendoza a hand. "Sorry," he said grimly.

"Hey, Buddy, tell me something. Are you sure you want to go through with this? I tell you, I'm not that crazy about this Mickey Mouse set-up—"

"No way, man," he said. "It's gonna work, and we're gonna go. Both of us." He turned to leave the simulator.

"Hey, Buddy," Mendoza said. He handed him the processor. "Here."

He watched him go, clumping loudly through the door, wondering, what have I gotten into?

IV

"Your new boss seems a little more . . . understanding . . . of human needs . . . than NASA . . ." Jeannie said, whispering between nibbles at his chest. They lay together in the cool morning darkness of Mendoza's hotel room. "And they even paid for my ticket."

"Yeah, and Howard Johnson's has bigger beds than the Cape." He laughed and rolled onto his side, cradling her. "But some things, they do not change. I really have to start getting ready."

"How long?"

He looked at his new Piaget watch. "They start firing the unmanned pods in three hours. I go about forty minutes later. End of the bus again."

As if to urge him out of bed, the clock radio came to life with an old country and western song. " 'Mama, don't let your babies grow up to be spacemen,' " Jeannie said, laughing. "Well, at least this morning you're finally getting a chance to make history."

"What history? Seven or eight people have ridden pods before me. One of them even docked at Kosmograd. This is no big deal."

"No," she said firmly, "this is history. The first . . . totally frivolous space flight."

His turn to laugh. "That's a great thing to be famous for." He went into the bathroom and turned on the shower. "I guess I'll have to take it, though, won't I?"

"Hugh Dickinson will take it."

"What's that supposed to mean?"

"He called just before I left Houston. He wanted to know when you were launching."

"Did you tell him," he said from the bathroom, "that they've got this new thing nowadays called television, you can have one right in your own house, it's got all the latest news—"

"*Jerry*. He was just looking for an excuse to wish you good luck."

"And probably to let me know he'd be watching if I screwed up."

"He told me to ask you to come see him as soon as you get back. Something about a tour aboard the Space Operations Center—"

Well, by God . . . "Aw, you're making that up. You just want me out of town for six months. I bet you've got a boyfriend—"

She threw a towel at him. "I've got a *vato* for a husband. He wants to go to Mars."

"Doesn't everybody?"

"Not me," she said, slipping into his arms for a last kiss. "At least, not till I get you some breakfast."

He closed the shower door and let the water run completely over his head, drumming on his skull and filling his ears. Poor man's sensory-deprivation tank. He tended to do it on mornings when it was still dark, when he felt unusually close to El Muerto. He was all too aware of what could happen to him before the sun set . . . decapitation in a crash . . . suffocation because of a guidance error . . . immolation . . . decompression, explosive or otherwise . . . drowning, even.

Jesu, Mendoza, enough of that. Think of the Endless Frontier . . . monster cylinder-cities turning in an eternal march . . . the mountains of the moon . . . the plains below Olympica, where surely the angels waited. Do this right today, and all of this shall I give you.

And take it, I will, *gracias*.

"Home Run, this is Yuma. We show you go for your burn. Good luck."

"Roger, Yuma," Mendoza said. "In . . . two minutes."

Below, beyond the tiny port, the barren land of Grandfather Raul slipped by . . . Sonora. It had taken two hundred years, but eventually the dirt and the heat had driven the Mendozas across the border to Tucson, and Raul to a lifetime of bussing tables and fixing cars. Now, just three hours past, on this day, Raul's seed had risen from that same brown earth high into the sky at the tip of a finger of light. Imagine! Grandpa had died before Jerry ever got into NASA, but he would have liked the idea: he was always on the lookout for a "new deal." Get there first, Gerardo! And shoot the first Anglo who come along!

"What's so funny?" Buddy said.

"Was I laughing?"

"Yeah. You aren't going space-happy on me, are you?"

"Hell, not an old rocket jockey like me. No way." He pushed himself back to the seat and belted down. He looked at the screen. "One minute."

Now he could think of nothing but the approach to Kosmograd . . . a dolphin trying to mate with a whale. "If God had meant Man to perform rendezvous and docking in free-fall," he said, "He would have given us processors in our heads."

"Did you ever hit a baseball?" Buddy asked.

Mendoza laughed. "Maybe that's my problem. Your old man should be flying this thing. Twenty seconds."

He looked at the switches and his checklist for the tenth time. "Five . . . four . . . three . . . two . . . initiate—"

Burn!

And then thoughts of Buddy, grandpa, and whales went away.

There was, of all things, a cool cloth on his forehead, and it felt good, but the mere thought of moving or opening his eyes brought on an Olympica-sized headache.

"Hold still, man," Buddy ordered.

"I can't tell if I'm moving or not."

"You're moving all right—about eight clicks a second, okay? Just don't turn your head. You've got a bump the size of a baseball on it."

For some reason he thought that was pretty goddamn funny.

"The burn?" What had happened? It had to be over by *now*—

"It went okay," Buddy said. "Shut down right on time. Give me your arm."

He did. "What's okay mean? How long have I been out?"

"Fifteen minutes or so."

"God *damn*—" A spray touched his arm. Presently his head felt better, and, slowly, he opened his eyes. The display showed them close enough to projection to be safe. "Wow."

"The strap busted when the engines kicked in," Buddy said, floating freely in the tiny cabin. "Cheap mother. I heard a thump, and you were out cold."

Radar showed them just two thousand meters from Kosmograd, and closing nicely. He rolled the pod with the RCS—and there was the big beacon itself, right out there in the port. "How did we get from the burn to station-keep?" he asked.

The kid pushed himself back toward his own couch. "I, uh, fired the engines the second time."

"Oh." His head started to hurt again. He closed his eyes and began to rub them. "Good job."

"You aren't mad?"

"I'm mad at the goddamn strap. Other than that—you've got to do what you've got to do." He looked at Buddy, noticing that the kid's T-shirt was torn in the front. That's where he'd gotten the "cloth." "Good improvisation there." He thumbed the mike to hail Kosmograd and tried to recall the last time in his life he had been knocked unconscious. He couldn't remember a time.

"Kosmograd, Home Run. *Zstrasvitye*. Hi."

"Welcome to Space City, Home Run," a Scots-accented voice replied. "Are ye ready for approach figures?"

"*Da*, Space City." Docking would take twenty minutes, getting out of the pod another fifteen. Allow a couple of hours for the Russians to service the pod and load the return cargo, time for Jerry and Buddy to sightsee. Another three hours for re-entry and return.

With luck, he would be back on Earth for late dinner—certainly drinks. "Let's see if the Mexican kid can park this 'rider."

"Okay, Commodore," Buddy said.

Just call me Walt—Walt Disney, Mendoza thought.

"What do you mean, you're not going back?"

Mendoza's head started to hurt again. In front of him Buddy floated back and forth between the narrow walls of the Kosmograd People's Infirmary, not daring to look him in the eyes. A Russian doctor hovered nearby. "That's what I said. I'm not going back."

"Could you excuse us for a moment?" Mendoza asked the doctor. He felt stupid about it, but he needed a diversion.

"Of course," the woman replied, smiling. "We understand completely the need for Party discipline."

"*Spaseebah*. Thank you." When she was gone he turned to Buddy again. "You can't just decide to *stay* here, kid. This isn't the goddamn Moscow Hilton or something—"

"I know that, man. I'm immigrating."

"Oh, really?" He couldn't help being sarcastic. "Permanent, or are you just looking for a green card?"

"I'm staying for good."

"Grow *up*, Buddy. This is like . . . the pioneers up here. They don't have room for hardship cases."

"I've got some skills!" he said. "I know processors."

Yuri Vovkin appeared in the hatchway. "Captain Mendoza, Comrade Gilliam, very nice to be seeing both of you again. There is a problem?"

"Colonel," Buddy said.

"Buddy, wait a minute!"

"I want to apply for political asylum here, under the UN Charter."

"Asylum *granted!*" Vovkin crowed. "We are always happy to assist those feeling the tyranny of capitalist system."

Mendoza suddenly felt very tired. Trade delegation. No more goddamn surprises . . . huh. "You bastards had this all worked out."

"A good socialist is always prepared," Vovkin said.

Mendoza grabbed Buddy's shoulder. "What about your father?"

The kid spun away. "He'll dig it. He knows better than anyone, that down there I'll never be anything but a cripple." With very little clumsiness Buddy tucked himself into a full somersault right in front of Mendoza's face. Then the kid started to laugh. "Up *here*, man, *I've* got the chance to be a superstar."

V

After a month it was finally possible for Mendoza to step outside without facing at least one reporter. Tonight he sat in a first-base seat at the Dome, watching the Americans beat the hell out of the Astros. Reggie Gilliam doubled twice and played well, though he seemed slow on the bases. It didn't make much difference to the huge crowd, which cheered madly any time Gilliam and the ball got within ten feet of each other.

Were they cheering a ballplayer? Or were they just here to get a look at the man who sent his son into space?

"Hey, Gerardo!"

He had waited for the crowd to thin out before trying to battle

up the aisles. Gilliam was hollering at him from the playing field.
"Go down to the clubhouse door!"

Should he? Aside from the day right after the mission they had
not talked. "Okay." He waved.

"Give me ten minutes!"

It was fifteen minutes, but the door eventually opened. "Let's
go up to the lounge for a while," Gilliam said. Mendoza followed
him to an elevator, which shot to the top floor of the Dome. "I
talked to Buddy yesterday," the big man said.

"How's he doing?"

"He's learning Russian, by God. I can't understand him when
he starts up with it."

"That's good. He'll need it."

"I hear you're going up again." They found seats in the lounge,
which was deserted except for the bartender, who was closing
down.

"In a couple of months, on the Shuttle this time." He paused
as Gilliam strolled to the bar, grabbed a bottle from behind it, and
returned. "Space Ops Center, Systems Engineer, that's me."

"Then what?"

"I don't know. I'm staying in touch with Exxon—"

Gilliam poured two glasses of clear liquid. "Let's drink to that,
then."

"What is this, white lightning?"

"No, but that might be a good name for it. It's vodka."

Mendoza tasted it. "What kind?"

Gilliam held up the bottle and swiveled in his chair so that he
faced the night sky. "I was thinking of calling it Old Space Ranger,
or something like that, once it gets out in the open." He looked
back and winked. "Right now, you understand, this is *very* expensive hooch."

"You son of a bitch," Mendoza said. "I thought that shipment
was photovoltaics or something like that. Wonder drugs."

"Some folks consider this stuff a wonder drug, Gerardo. No,
this is genuine, space-distilled booze, selling right now at fifteen
thousand bucks a bottle, mostly to collectors, of course, and we
have to pay a hell of a licensing fee to Vovkin's Iranian account.
But you did bring back thirty bottles, and, you know, a little
thinning doesn't seem to hurt it. . . ."

"I'll bet you didn't even lose money on this thing."

"Oh, some, on paper. But it was worth it, and it'll get cheaper
from now on." The big man got up and went to the window,

pointing up to the sky with his drink. "Can you see that goddamn thing from here?"

"Later tonight, I think," Mendoza said. "It should rise in the southeast . . . if you stay up to watch."

Gilliam set the drink down and made some little mock swings with his imaginary bat. "Those people up there, Gerardo, they gonna play sports, do you think?"

"Sure. Someday."

"Damn! I wonder what kind?" He grinned. "You think they might want a good outfielder?"

What *Are* These Lagrange Points, Anyway?

⊞

DOUG BEASON

Despite its use as the title of the L-5 Society, a lot of people misuse and don't completely understand what Lagrange Points are and where they're located. First of all, they are not *points*—but orbits that have radii of several *hundred* kilometers. I could tell you more, but instead, I'll let Doug Beason, who is both a particle physicist and serving officer in the U.S. Air Force, tell you everything you ever wanted to know about the Earth–Moon Trojan Points.

L-5: LAGRANGE COLONIES.

The name conjures up images of vast, slowly rotating cylinders, filled with thousands of people . . . or giant wheels, silently revolving in space to provide the gravity needed to survive. They hold the future of humanity: mankind, swept off the Earth and flung into an artificial habitat, living in an island-space paradise.

Masters from Heinlein to Varley have written tales about Lagrange colonies. It's a heroic vision—a dream of optimism, piercing the veil of budget cuts and shortsighted bureaucrats: if the human race is going to survive it *must* advance into space.

And L-5 is the stepping-stone.

But before we go charging off into the endless frontier, just what *are* these Lagrange points, anyway? And why are they supposed to be so good for space colonies?

Joseph Louis Lagrange (1736–1813) was a French mathematician, perhaps most famous for developing "Lagrangian Mechanics," a worldview of physics that uses energy principles instead of forces to describe the way the universe evolves. It's a revolutionary, and as it turns out, powerfully elegant way of describing physical interactions. Without "Lagrangians," the evolution of modern physics would not have been possible.

But it wasn't this esoteric branch of physics that vaulted Joe's name into the science fiction hall of fame. As a hobby, he was attracted to the so-called "N-body" problem. And from this grew the roots of Lagrange points.

Newton's laws define the motion of two bodies due to their mutual interaction. People can accurately calculate how two objects move relative to each other. For example, when two objects rotate around each other, it's easy to calculate what the system will look like at some point in the future. All you have to do is to set up the differential equations of motion and solve them using high school calculus. That's all there is to the "two-body" problem.

The N-body problem is just as straightforward. In theory, one can calculate the interaction of "N" number of bodies, N being 3, 4, 5, 6 . . . and so on. And like the two-body problem, all one has to do is to apply the Newtonian equations of motion to the system.

Doing so, one finds that ten integrals of the equations of motion exist for an arbitrary system of N objects (six equations describe the motion of the center-of-mass, three more describe the angular momentum and the last conserves total energy). This still doesn't present a problem, because in the world of physics, simplifying assumptions *always* enable one to find the answer.

Or nearly always.

(Ever hear the one about a farmer taking a sick cow to a Physics Department for a checkup, and the physicist's diagnosis based on his assumption: "Consider a spherical cow. . . .")

Scientists quickly found out that when simplifying mathematical tools were applied to analyzing the interaction of three or more bodies, the problem quickly became intractable; meaning their calculations proved many-bodied systems should fly apart, crash into each other, or just plain blow up.

Now this was serious problem—systems having more than two

bodies could obviously interact without becoming unstable; look at the solar system, for example. The planets orbit the sun in a well-ordered manner, and they certainly don't fly apart. So one of the big problems of the day was how to solve the N-body problem, and come up with answers that made sense. And believe it or not, it is *still* a hot topic of research.

In 1772, Lagrange discovered an elegant approximation to the three-body problem. By assuming that one of the three masses was negligible when compared to the other two masses, he established there were certain equilibrium solutions. For example, an artificial satellite has negligible mass when compared to the Earth and moon. Lagrange made some other assumptions—like the bodies must move in perfectly circular orbits—but they're really beyond the scope of this article.

Without getting into the gory mathematics (perturbation analysis, for those interested), for two massive bodies rotating around each other, one of Lagrange's solutions showed that the third, smaller body could sit at one of five equilibrium points. Naturally, these points came to be known as *Lagrange points*. The diagram below shows their location:

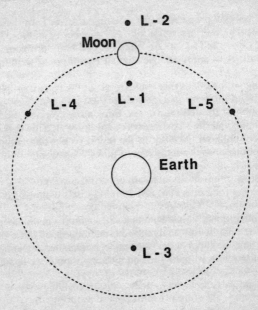

This isn't the end of the story: as it turns out, only *two* of the five equilibrium points are stable.

For a quick explanation of stability, here are two more diagrams:

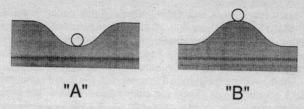

"A"   **"B"**

Figure "A" shows a ball trapped in a hole. This is an example of a locally stable equilibrium. When you push on the ball, the ball oscillates about the bottom of the hole—a "libration" point. (That is unless you give the ball too much of a push; then it will pop up out of the hole and move away—hence the adjective "local.") The point is that for small displacements, the ball will always return to its original starting place (or point of equilibrium).

Figure "B" shows an example of an unstable equilibrium. The ball sits balanced on the top of the hill—a point of local equilibrium. Now if you push the ball, it falls from its equilibrium position, accelerates away and *will not return*.

You can quickly imagine a third type of equilibrium: neutral equilibrium. This occurs when the ball in Figures A and B lies on a *flat* surface. If given a push, the ball neither oscillates about its equilibrium point or accelerates away. It just continues to move until slowed by friction.

The three types of equilibrium are not constrained to gravitational forces. All "central body" or "inverse square" forces can have these equilibrium points—the electromagnetic force is one example.

But for our N-body problem, we'll just consider the force due to gravity. And obviously, it is more desirable to have an object at a stable equilibrium point than at an unstable one if you want the object to stay in place.

In the same manner, the points L-4 and L-5 are the only stable equilibrium points for the Earth–moon system. If a space colony were placed at L-5 (or L-4 for that matter), the colony would remain there, oscillating (or maybe even orbiting) about the center. Placed at L-1, L-2, or L-3 the colony would move into some erratic orbit, shooting off into space if barely nudged.

So why is L-5 used for space colonies and not L-4? One site isn't any better or worse than the other—it's probably just that L-5 sounds sexier than L-4.

And do the points really exist? After all, up to now what we've discussed is just theory.

As it turns out, Kordelewski suggested that meteoric particles would occupy L-4 and L-5 if the Lagrange points were really stationary. Furthermore, these particles should be barely visible as faint nebulosities, which indeed, is the case. So we know Lagrange points exist for the Earth–moon system.

Up to now, we've assumed that only the Earth and moon affect the Lagrange points. There are other factors, such as the moon's eccentricity (how circular its orbit is). Another element is the influence of the sun, Jupiter, and the other planets. As it turns out, they all affect the precise location of L-4 and L-5, as well as how an object at those points will oscillate. Thus, the very idea of having a dimensionless dot describe the Lagrange point begins to grow suspect.

One way to think of the Lagrange points is not as points at all, but instead as a *volume* in three-dimensional space. The region has fuzzy boundaries which constantly change, depending on the location of the sun and other planets. Objects inside the "Lagrange region" oscillate as expected; only when the objects oscillate too much (remember "locally stable equilibrium") are they in danger of leaving the region of stability.

One solution for the Lagrange regions shows that it is possible for masses to *orbit* about the Lagrange point. These orbits may be hundreds of kilometers in radius, allowing *several* colonies to exist at the Lagrange "point."

So there you have it. The Lagrange points L-4 and L-5 are simply "volumes of stability," ready to hold space colonies. They reside in the same orbit as the moon, on the vertices of an equilateral triangle with the Earth and moon.

This means the colonists must use the same astrodynamic parameters to get to the stable Lagrange points as to get to the moon. In other words, to get to L-4 or L-5, you'd need to use the same type of orbit as you would in getting to the moon. This is one reason the Lagrange points are so attractive as locations for space colonies. They're far enough away from the Earth so as not to be bothered by man-made space debris, but yet they're close enough to reach within a few days time, traveling in a minimum-energy trajectory such as a Hohmann orbit (also called a "doubly tangent" orbit).

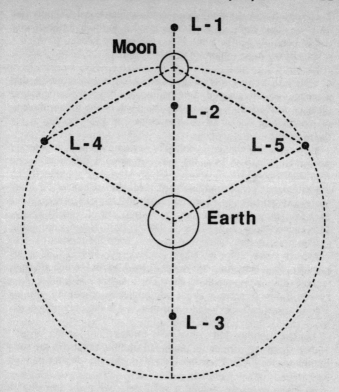

But why go to all the trouble of putting colonies at L-4 or L-5? What about orbits closer to the Earth? If habitats were placed in lunar or Earth orbit, they would experience frequent solar eclipses. This would deprive the space colonies of the energy and sunlight they need for survival.

Then what about placing the colonies in orbits large enough around the Earth so the eclipses are kept at a minimum? This would make it difficult to ship the enormous amount of material to where the colony was being constructed. That brings us to another, equally compelling reason for locating the colonies at the stable Lagrange points.

Three criteria must be minimized to establish a colony: the travel time to the colony, the amount of station-keeping to keep a colony active, and the amount of propulsion needed to reach the colony.

These criteria cannot all be minimized simultaneously. If only one criterion could be relaxed, the time it takes to travel to the colony would certainly be the best. Thus, the energy needed to reach a space colony is an important consideration.

Before we go charging off to minimize energy, we first have to realize that two kinds of separation exist in space: metric distance and velocity change. Spaceships must travel the same metric distance to reach L-5 from either the Earth or the moon; there is no compelling reason to put the colony at L-5 because of the difference in metric distance.

However, the change in velocity (or equivalently, in *energy*) needed to reach L-5 from the Earth or moon *is* different. To go from the moon to L-5, a spaceship must change its velocity by 2.9 kilometers per second (km/sec); a velocity change of 12.7 km/sec is needed to travel from the Earth to L-5, *450 percent more than from the moon to L-5*. In fact, the majority of velocity change (8.6 km/sec) is needed to rocket from the Earth to low Earth orbit.

The point is this: launching material from the moon to L-5 to construct space colonies takes less energy, and is thus much cheaper, than launching the material from Earth—much cheaper, in fact, than even launching from Earth to low Earth orbit. As a result, if you're serious about building a space colony, placing the colony at L-5 and using lunar material is the only way to go.

Lagrange points don't only exist for the Earth–moon system. In fact, Lagrange originally predicted stability points for the sun–Jupiter system. The Lagrange points for the sun–Jupiter pair are known as "Trojan" points.

In 1906, Wolf discovered a small asteroid at the sun–Jupiter Lagrange point. He named the asteroid after the Greek hero Achilles, giving rise to the "Trojan" designation. As with L-4 and L-5, the Trojan points lie in the plane of Jupiter's orbit, sixty degrees preceding and following Jupiter. There are more than a dozen known members of the two stable Trojan points, equally distributed between them.

Some theories speculate that these Trojan planets were once satellites of Jupiter. It can be shown mathematically that the conservative equations of mass, momentum, and energy are satisfied for such a captive system.

(For the interested reader, *Astrodynamics* by Baker and *The Foundations of Astrodynamics* by Roy are two excellent texts that jump right into the mathematics. *Space Settlements*: *A Design Study*, a NASA publication, is probably the best overall source.)

■ ■ ■

So what good are Lagrange points? Aside from being a mathematical curiosity, they exist in nature and are as real as anything on Earth. Lagrange points provide a means for humanity to expand into space, and not be enslaved as groundhogs.

Man's jaunts into space skim the upper atmosphere; and the few lunar expeditions were too short to even pretend to exist autonomously from the Earth. Even a geosynchronous satellite is bound to its blue-green master, constantly being reminded of where it came from and who controls its destiny.

But a *Lagrange* colony—!

It's far enough from Earth to obtain an identity of its own; far enough away to evolve from mankind's pettiness. But yet, still close enough to have that secure feeling . . . just in case.

Lagrange points: what's the bottom line? As Niven and Pournelle so succinctly wrote, "Think of it as evolution in action."

Preparing mankind for that next giant leap . . . *to the stars*!

The Christmas Count

⌐⌐

HENRY MELTON

Living in a space colony is going to be far different from the life we know here on Earth. Studies are underway now at the Antarctic on the effects of isolation on human interactions and health. All this, of course, will help prepare us for life in a space colony, but there will be differences too. Space colonies are not static environments but have their own ecologies, which polar bases and submarines do not have.

On Earth, ecological concerns are important; this is true. Yet, rarely can an individual see the effects of his actions on the world around him. This will not be true aboard a space habitat; the old maxim, "for every action, there is a reaction," will become a part of the fabric of everyday life—as we see in Henry Melton's "The Christmas Count."

FRED JERRET SQUINTED his eyes against the light. The sun was a white band of light stretching high across the sky. The checkerboard fields of the farms he knew to be on the other side of the sky were washed out in the glare. There was no change. Winter should have come by now—it was past four P.M.

"Fred," his wife, Dot, called across the field to him, as she stood at the back porch of their gray stone farm house. "Fred, I need the list."

"Okay! I'm coming." Reluctantly, he stepped from furrow to furrow in the caked black earth until he reached the wide patch of grass he kept as a backyard for the kids to play in.

Waiting out in the field wouldn't make winter happen any faster. He had been a farmer for too many years to try to second-guess the climate control computer. The *Piedmont Herald* would publish the day, but no one knew the exact moment. The weather in their farming world was at the mercy of a real-time computer system far too concerned with solar flares and the heat balance of their self-contained space colony to give out predictions.

Fred had a couple of bucks down in the 4:15–4:20 spot in the betting pool that the boys at the general store were keeping. He had wanted four P.M., but that spot had been taken. *Just as well*, he thought. *Maybe I'll win anyway*.

Dot had vanished back into the house, and he slowed his pace a trifle. He was born a farmer, and today he needed to be outside, soaking up the peace he knew was always there in his fields.

Joey had been gone all day, vanished at first sunlight. He had not asked to leave. It was a deliberate escape from the chores he knew he was responsible for. Fred thought of the scolding he would give the boy. There was a sick anger in his stomach. He had said those words before, when Tim, his oldest, was sixteen.

A distant metallic rumble, like the legendary pre-space locomotives on rails, stopped Fred in his tracks. It was difficult to see through the hazy sky that clouded the center of this cylindrical world, but he knew it was the sun shutters. Three great metal gates had moved on their courses, restricting and channeling the sunlight that entered the world of Piedmont, shifting the energy balance. For the next few weeks, more heat would be radiated from the back side of this enclosed world than would be let through the great mirrors. It would get colder. Winter had begun.

Fred looked at his watch and shook his head. Missed it by three minutes.

Inside, Dot looked up as he entered. "Winter's come," he informed her. "Here's the list." He handed the clipboard to her. "I thought we had finished with the kitchen."

Dot gave him a twisted little grin. "Well . . . I have to reduce the roach count." She pushed the selector button on the clipboard a few times until the roach count appeared on the display plate. She subtracted two from the count and then gave it back to Fred.

He shook his head. "Dot, this is not the day to kill roaches. This is Christmas Eve. Today we count the beasties, not try to wipe them out."

She curled her lower lip. "But they asked for it. I had my pumpkin pies cooling on the cabinet and those two came after them. I wasn't about to let them get on my pies!"

Fred tried to hide a smile. "Pumpkin, hmmm. Well, if it was pumpkin, I won't turn you in. But don't tell David about it. He will take it as approval to go hunting the rats in the woodpile again."

Dot nodded, then looked out the kitchen window to the fields and the woods beyond. "Where are Kim and David? Haven't they finished yet? With winter here, dark will come sooner."

"Maybe I had better go looking for them. I've got all the livestock counted and I keyed in the changes in the acreages for the insect estimates." He sniffed the kitchen air. "How soon is food?"

"Maybe another hour. By the way, are you sure we won't have any guests for Christmas dinner tomorrow?"

He shrugged. "I guess not. I made the invitations, but everyone was taken." He was not terribly surprised. After all there were three farming families for every one of the city folk. Dot had come from Galvin, a manufacturing world that circled the Point in the same lazy orbit as Piedmont. The world she had grown up in was nothing but one big city. Even after all these years as his wife, living on the soil, she still tended to think of that city as a big place, rather than the handful of support and maintenance people it actually was.

He continued. "I thought Charlie from river maintenance might come, but his wife had already made other arrangements." Maybe it would be better with just family this year. If there was company coming, Dot would work herself to exhaustion to get the house spotlessly clean.

Outside, the air was already getting cooler. Fred looked over his fields, freshly planted and waiting for the winter to make its appearance, and then leave for the long growing season.

Fred expected the winter to be colder than usual this year. The ant infestation down by Southport had hurt a dozen farmers. A good solid freeze or two would wipe out the nests.

Spot came bounding across the fields to meet him. Fred clapped his hands together and the dog jumped high to snap the imaginary treat out of the air. Spot knew there was nothing there, but he liked to play the game. Sometimes Fred would fool him with the real thing.

Off to the east, a neighbor's dog barked. Spot lost interest in Fred and raced off, voicing his challenge. Fred could just spot the tiny figures in the next farm over. The curve of the ground rose enough to show a man building his Christmas fire. Fred glanced at his watch and hurried on.

The strip of woods that bordered the Jerret farm was partly on his property, so he was responsible for it in the count. It was the kids' job to help him with that.

The high-pitched shout of five-year-old David helped him locate them quickly. Kim and David were having a leaf fight. Fred adjusted his path slightly so he kept out of sight behind a stand of oak as he approached. Just yesterday, ten-year-old Kim had gotten a scolding from her mother about getting leaves in her hair. Fred waited until the last moment, then stepped out from behind a tree just as David was dumping a double handful of leaves onto his older sister's head.

"David!" Fred used his stern-father voice. Both kids jumped. David spilled most of the leaves off to the side of his target. He guiltily brushed his hands against his trousers.

"Yes, Daddy?" he asked timidly.

Fred let a moment of silence grow. But he had no intention of doing anything about the leaves. The kids would get the necessary dusting from their mother. It was her restriction, she would enforce it. Personally, Fred had nice memories of playing in the leaves when he was younger.

"David, you are going to have to help me with the fire. Have you two finished your counts?"

David pouted. "Why do I have to help with the fire? That is Joey's job."

"Joey is not back yet." His voice showed a little impatience. "Now did you finish your counts?"

Kim gave a warning glance at her brother. Now was not the time to complain about chores, not with Joey being out late again. Daddy was likely going to be in a bad mood until he came home.

She spoke up, "Yes. We counted twenty-two squirrels, and nine rabbits. The mice don't seem to be as bad this year, there were only ten in the sample square. I didn't spot the badger, but there were fresh signs."

Fred tapped in the numbers on the clipboard. "Are you sure all of these were on our side of the boundary line? We are not supposed to count the animals on any other property."

She nodded. "I'm sure. I think the rabbits moved their hole down by the gully since the last count."

"How about the birds?"

"I didn't see any crows, but I saw five orioles. David claims to have seen a cowbird, but I didn't."

Fred nodded. "If David saw it, we count it. The climate computer needs to know everything we see, so it can plan the right amount of rain to make and plan how many days of winter we need."

"And summer?" asked David.

Fred smiled. "Yes, and summer. That's why we have four counts: the Christmas Count, the Easter Count, the Earthday Count, and the Harvest Count. We have a small, special world here in Piedmont and the counts are one of the ways we take care of our home."

David's attention had already wandered off to something in the sky by the time Fred had finished saying that. But Kim was older, and this time the words seemed to make some kind of impression on her.

David pointed. "Daddy, look."

Up high, halfway to the patchwork of fields on the other side of the sky, was a tiny speck moving south. A man-shape and a set of wings. It was too high for them to hear the sputtering of the tiny engine.

"A flier," Fred said, "trying to make the run to Southport. He'd better hurry." He looked at his watch. "And we had better run. Dark will come in five minutes."

Darkness, when it came, closed down over Piedmont like the lid on a large cedar chest. The distant rumble of the shutters followed as the sound hurried to catch up with the shadow, like black thunder chasing the stroke of darkness. With only the light leak around the sun shutters to provide a pale imitation of moonlight, they had to step carefully as they made their way back to the house.

David shouted, "Hey look! Lights in the sky!"

And there were. First a dozen yellow lights scattered across the far side of the sky, then more, as farmers all through Piedmont lit the traditional Christmas Eve fire. Dot came out of the house, rubbing her hands on the towel at her waist. She, too, started up at the sight.

"Hurry and help me, David," Fred said to his youngest. "We have to get our fire going."

"Aww. Why do I have to . . ."

"None of that!" Fred spoke sharply. "Santa is coming in just a few hours. This is not the time to act up."

"Yes, Davie," taunted his sister. "If you're naughty, Santa won't give you anything."

"Kim," commanded Dot, "come on and help me set the fireside table." Kim's face twisted as she realized she had trapped herself into helping her mother.

As the door closed, David heard his mother's voice rise sharply. "Kim Jerret, what is that in your hair?"

David giggled.

David was not really strong enough to help much with the firebuilding, but his father believed in chores for the children, even if it meant more work for him. They had the stack of wood placed in the firepit, ready for lighting by the time the dinner was served.

"Can I light it now, Daddy?" David asked. Fred shook his head.

Dot looked up at her husband with a question in her eyes. He turned away, looking briefly at the road that led past the front of their property. Joey had been late getting home several times before. But it was Christmas Eve! He shook off a rising flood of anger and frustration. He couldn't let Christmas be spoiled for the other kids.

He said, "Let's just sit here for a little bit and enjoy the lights."

Dot insisted they eat while the food was still hot. Helplessly, Fred felt the liquid trickle of an old hurt as they watched the lights flickering above. Empty places at the family table again.

Joey was at a difficult age. His older brother had been the same—staying out later and later with his friends. The role and restrictions of being a child were too much for him to bear. The harder his father fought to keep control, the more Joey managed to slip away.

His brother Tim had vanished one day, leaving a note saying that he had left to apprentice as a shuttle pilot. That had been two years ago. Christmas that first year had been hard, with that vacant chair as a constant reminder of a part of them that was gone.

The second year Tim sent Christmas presents for the kids, and a letter for his parents. They wrote back, but it was clear that their son had left for good. He was a regular pilot, with a regular run among the different orbital worlds. He had a life of his own, and it did not include Piedmont. Fred's boy would never be a farmer like his father.

"Why do we light a fire on Christmas Eve, Daddy?" Kim asked.

His little girl was growing up, too. He smiled at her as she stared up at the display above.

"There are a couple of reasons. When I was a boy, my father told me that Piedmont had started the Christmas fires to remind us of the stars in the night sky of Earth."

"What is the other reason?"

Fred went over to the storage shed and picked up a bag of powder from the shelf. He set it down on the bench before the kids. "This is seeding powder. We put it on the fire and it helps the formation of raindrops. Piedmont is a special world and we have to take care of it in a lot of little ways."

David asked, as he stuck his finger in the grayish powder, "Does it make snow, too?"

Fred laughed. "Yes, it helps make snow, too."

"Good, let's light it!" David grabbed the bag and headed over to the fire.

Fred was quick on his feet and grabbed the bag before the boy had dumped it. "Okay. But we have to sprinkle the powder over the fire carefully."

Kim wanted to help, but Fred ruled that since David had helped build the fire, he ought to be the one to start it. They soon had a blazing fire and he showed David the proper way to toss the little scoops of powder over the fire.

In the yellow light, Fred noticed tears in Dot's eyes. He moved to her side. Christmas was a time for extremes. If you didn't feel wonderful, you felt horrible. He held her hand as they watched the flames.

He tried to smile, to feel as happy as his two little ones. But it was so hard. He squeezed Dot's hand. She squeezed back.

"Hey!" Kim pointed. "Here comes Joey!"

And sure enough, the bouncy white light of a bicycle on a dirt road was visible in the night. They all watched it as it pulled up and Joey walked up to the fireside.

He came right up to the flames and rubbed his hands. "This feels good. It's getting cold."

"Where have you been?" Fred tried to keep his voice level. There would be nothing good in having another shouting match like last time he returned home late.

Joey looked at his father's face and then looked back to the fire. "Mr. Grey, the scout troop leader, he asked me to help. Troop Two was supposed to handle the count on the Common." He shrugged, carefully watching the flames. "It took longer than we thought."

Fred nodded. He had heard it before. He sighed. "Dot, could you heat up something for Joey?" To Joey, he said, "David had to do your chores today. He gets your allowance, too."

David squealed in delight. Joey started to protest, then thought better of it.

It took an hour or more for the fire to die down to a red piping bed of coals. With Dot leading, they sang Christmas carols.

David asked, "How can Santa get to every house in one night?"

Kim eagerly explained, "He has a magic flier so he can land and take off real quick. He comes in a red shuttle and visits all the worlds in the circuit all in one night."

Fred always held his breath when the little ones asked about Santa. He dreaded the moment when they would ask if Santa was real. For David, at least, the moment had not yet come. He was just a little too young to guess at such a great conspiracy. At least his older ones were firmly coached not to give away the secret to the younger ones, at least not on purpose.

Across the landscape, like a metallic rolling thunder, the clank of the great doors of the Northport docking hangar clanked shut.

Kim and David started shouting, "Santa's here! Santa's ship is here!"

Distant voices, far too distant to resolve into anything more than the sound of humanity, told of all the world's children cheering the coming of Santa.

Dot said, "Okay. Bedtime, kids." She hustled them off to bed, giving David his medicine and getting Kim to wash her hair. Bedtime was never quick and easy with kids, not even on Christmas Eve.

It was much later that Dot came back to join Fred as he tended the bed of coals. "*Woooo!* It's cold." She rubbed her hands together before the warmth of the coals, then sat down on the bench next to him. He put his arm around her.

Quiet moments, and a spot of warmth on a cold night—that and love can drain the stress of the day. They sat and breathed the frosty air, and enjoyed the moment.

"Oh," Fred asked, "did you upload the clipboard file?"

"Mmm. I plugged it into house storage. The midnight poll will upload it to central." She leaned her head against his shoulder and laughed. "Did you see Kim's hair? She must have rolled in the leaves!"

"No," he contradicted. "David dumped those on her. I caught them at it in the woods."

"Why didn't you tell me? I gave her quite a scold."

"If she didn't snitch on him, why should I? Besides, I would have liked to play in the leaves, too, if they would have let me."

She poked him in the ribs. "Impossible. Farm kids! And you're the worst of the lot."

Fred nodded. "Good kids," he said quietly.

"All of them," she agreed.

Then, a touch of wetness on her cheek turned Dot's eyes to the sky above them. "Snow! It's starting to snow."

Drifting down in lazy swirls, large snowflakes were suddenly filling the air. Minute by minute, the white stuff increased, until it became clear that they had to get up and go inside or get wet from all the snow melting on them.

"It will be a good snow this year," Fred said, getting to his feet and helping his wife up. "Good for snowmen."

"And don't forget Santa."

Almost on cue, they heard a strange sound faintly through the snow-muffled air. The sound of a flier. But no one would be flying on a night like this! And the sound was becoming louder, as if the flyer was coming down.

Neither of them spoke. Her hand gripped his tighter when the flier flickered into view at the edge of the field. The wings tilted up, the sputtering died. A man in a heavy suit, carrying a large bag over his shoulder, set the flier back on its struts. He walked toward them.

"Tim?" Dot spoke.

"Son?" Fred asked.

The young man's face, dimly lit by the rosy glow of the coals, was one big smile. "Mom, Dad. Sorry I'm late." Then words were lost in a joyous round of bear hugs and happy tears.

"I couldn't get here any sooner," he explained. "Northport control had me delay docking so that I could be Santa's ship this year. I'm sorry I didn't warn you I was coming. It took some fancy last-minute schedule swapping with the regular pilot to get me here. And then I almost got lost in the snow." He shook his head in embarrassment. "I had forgotten about the snow."

"Just so you are here." His mother gave him another hug. "All my children are here."

"Dot!" said Fred, as the thought struck him. "Go correct the count, quickly before the midnight upload. Our family is six—in our Christmas Count tonight."

Three Poems

WILLIAM JOHN WATKINS, BRUCE BOSTON, and
JOHN GILLESPIE MAGEE, JR.

Imagery in fiction is always limited in scope, a
slave to storyline and characterization. It is only
in verse that a poet can open the lens and attempt
to shine the light of imagination on those things of
which the rest of us but dream. Here we see life
in space through the vision of three talented drea-
mers.

THE LAGRANGE LEAGUE STATIONARY HABITATS

We are a legend—cities in the sky,
six scattered seeds and, on the moon, one more.
We are the high frontier, but not so high
death cannot reach and take us as we soar
above the sordid earth. Make no mistake,
this paradise was built from blood and loss.

The welder tumbles outward with a snake
of tether trailing out and back across
the structure he won't live to occupy;
the sun behind him dwindling, the roar
of last blood pumping in his ears,
the ache of so much left undone.

            There is a gloss
to everything up here, a ghostly shine
that glows where death and beauty intertwine.

                —WILLIAM JOHN WATKINS

WHEN SILVER PLUMS FALL
JumpShift/AgriStat IV/2048 Sidereal

In the chambered nautilus
of a decaying orbit,
with the liquid acceleration
of tiny butterflies
along my stranded veins
orchestras of artillery
unmoor our homescape
from its slackened tether.

Ah the lean telemetry
and calculated yearning
of the adamantine impulse
as it primes and propels
our tumbling hemisphere
in waves which splay
the sky grasses flat.

When silver plums fall
past lives unsettled
in the sudden violence
of seasons borne awry,
I am quartered to earth
in mock crucifixion
by the whine dark rush
of velocity's climb.

When silver plums fall
in anachronous time
and noon is noon again
in the nocturnal remission
of an eastering sun,

our envelope of air
stutters with leaves.

O how the plates
and stanchions vibrate
to the quickening strain,
how the rivulets flood
our concave terrain
as we are flung to apogee
by the coda's roar.

In a chambered nautilus
taut upon its line,
the finely drifted snow
of an artificial winter
blankets the fires,
obscures the dislocations
of unnatural disaster.

In night beyond our night
the silver plums fall,
and rise against the
vacuum.

—BRUCE BOSTON

HIGH FLIGHT

Oh, I have slipped the surly bonds of earth
        and danced the skies on laughter-silvered wings.
Sunward I've climbed, and joined the tumbling mirth
        Of sun-split clouds—and done a hundred things
You have not dreamed of—wheeled and
        soared and swung.
Chased the shouting wing along, and flung
        my eager craft through footless halls of air.
Up the long, delirious, burning blue
        I've topped the windswept heights with easy grace
Where never lark, or even eagle flew.
        And, while with silent, lifting mind I've trod

The high untrespassed sanctity of space
        Put out my hand, and touched the face of God.

—JOHN GILLESPIE MAGEE, JR.

Lifeguard

⌐⌐

DOUG BEASON

I first met Dr. Beason when he was doing a tour of duty as a professor of physics at the United States Air Force Academy in Colorado Springs. He has since gone to an Air Force weapons lab.

I think Robert would have liked this story. It certainly was intended to please him.

Heinlein, Robert A. (hīn līn), n. 1. 1907–1988, American writer and space enthusiast. 2. Water depository for the stable (L-4, L-5) Lagrange colonies. Two water tanks, each 1 kilometer thick and 2 kilometers in diameter, counterrotate (10 rev/hr) at opposite ends of a 2-kilometer-long cylinder. A byproduct of the revolving water tanks is a vacillating, water-free tunnel extending along the zero-gee core of each water tank; low air pressure and high water temperature in the water tank result in a boiling point near 52 degrees Centigrade for the water . . .

Second Triumvirate Dictionary

NO MATTER WHAT you've heard, being a sixteen-year-old female in the *Heinlein* is not exciting. And no, we don't swim with our clothes off. The water is much too hot for that—you'd boil after two minutes, no matter what the holos show you. Besides, it's all trick holography, and the touri *really* get upset when they find out we wear wetsuits. But we keep the air pressure low enough that the water boils to make up for it.

Anyway, I was guarding when the *Forward* docked, so I missed the first gaggle of touri this month. They're probably out gawking at the Swimmers now, so I have to make doubly sure no one gets hurt on my shift. This was my last run anyway, and things are pretty quiet.

I peered through the tunnel of water that surrounded me and made out the shimmering electrostatic curtain that protected the restcove. The water tank's wall was coming up fast—too fast for a safe landing. It was still over four hundred meters away, but I had to start thinking about slowing down; I was moving at least twice as fast as I should have. The body has these certain warning signals that kick in when you're doing something stupid: my heart started palpitating and I grew suddenly chilled—which was ridiculous, because the tank was up to at least fifty-five Cee today, lots warmer than usual.

The restcove grew larger through the tunnel; it couldn't have been more than two hundred meters away by now. Oh well, this was the end of my shift, and I hadn't spotted any Jumpers—might as well make the most of it and Jump myself.

I threw my buoy up at the water above me. The motion sent me moving slowly in the opposite direction—down, toward the bottom of the tunnel. This is the hard part—I didn't leave much room to spare . . .

The buoy skipped across the water, grabbed at the surface, then dove outcore, toward deep water. I was jerked up when the buoy hit and smacked against the water. It hurt—stopping forward momentum in zero-gee makes you a believer!—but I had other things to worry about. I was trolled in the water as the buoy picked up speed on its way down.

When I passed the twentieth glowglobe, I drew my legs up under me. I should hit bottom . . . any . . . second . . . *now*! I jumped for the tunnel, clawing my way up through the kilometer of water above me. As the gravity decreased, I pulled myself up faster, pointing slightly inward to adjust for coriolis.

The pseudosurface was a warbling ripple above me. I felt cocky, so I angled toward the restcove. If I planned it right, I'd pop out just at the viewports, break the pseudosurface, and manage to get eight flips in before I hit the water at the top of the tunnel. That oughta pop a few eyeballs out . . .

I misjudged the surface. I must have caught a bubble as it burst, because I only had time to get five flips off before I realized that

I was going to hit the top of the tunnel sooner than I thought. Instead of twenty meters of open air, I flew through fifteen. That's not much when you're trying to get in those extra turns.

I hit the water on my back with a *pop*. The spray was something else. It must have taken five minutes for all the water to diffuse from the zero-gee core back down to where the pseudosurface boiled.

Feeling foolish, I half-dog paddled, half-skipped across the pseudosurface to the restcove, then trudged up the stickum and entered through the electrostatic curtain. Soloette was there with three touri, all male.

She looked like she was in heaven. I was about to sail past her to post my report when she said to the men, "Oh, and this is my best friend I've been telling you about. Astar, meet Randall, Justin, and Phillip. They're laying over for a few days until the lunar shuttle gets back; they're with the Computer Upgrade Project at Tycho Station."

One of the men grinned stupidly—from the size of his arms he had to be a weight lifter. Or walk on his hands. Another was a runt, and the last—the cute one, of course—couldn't keep his eyes off Soloette.

I said, "Hi, glad to meet you," and turned away, but a male voice stopped me. The weight lifter.

"Hey, wait." He looked me up and down; I wasn't used to being stared at. My face grew warm as he said, "I'm Justin Kenlai. Do you swim here a lot?"

I managed to make one of my typical brillant statements. "Uh?" Then, "Sure, what do you think I am—a touri?"

Soloette interrupted and motioned with her eyes to the chronometer embedded over the entrance to the water tank. "Astar, aren't you about done with your shift?"

"Uh, yeah. That was my last run before my lunch break."

Soloette looked smug. "I tell you what—why don't you join us for lunch at the Bifrost? It won't take more than an hour. How does that sound?"

I smiled sweetly. "Soloette, don't you think the men would like to try somewhere a little less formal?" Translated: *The Bifrost will blow my food allowance for the month!*

She batted her eyes. "Now, Astar, they're only going to be here a few days. We might as well show them the high spots." In other words: *Don't blow it for me!*

She's flipped over every new guy for the past two months; might as well let her have her fun. "All right," I grudgingly agreed. "If they want to."

"Well?" asked Soloette, looking to the men.

"Sounds good to me, if you're both coming with us," said Justin, smiling at me.

I shrugged. "Sure, why not."

"Great." Soloette was practically drooling. She said, "Astar, I'll take them there while you change out of your 'suit. Ten minutes?"

"If you want." I turned to go. "Uh, nice meeting all of you. See you there."

"Sure."

They managed to make it out of the restcove without hurting themselves. I quickchanged, then bounced to my apartment to get something a little more appropriate for the Bifrost Lounge. After all, if I'm going to use up Daddy's rations, might as well go in style.

The apartment was empty. Daddy's the *Heinlein*'s chief hydrologist and was still at the L-4 colonies for the week, so I was able to grab the ration cube without him protesting.

They were already seated by the time I got there. Aalicen was doing the ballet today, so Soloette had managed to wrangle an area nearby the dance space. Justin attempted to get up when I approached, but was jerked back into his seat by the webbed belting. His arms bulged as he strained against the straps; I thought he was going to break the belt. He looked sheepish. "Sorry."

"S'all right." I grinned. "Sometimes that's the only way to tell the touri in here. Don't want you floating into the middle of Aalicen's dance." I looked around. "We're missing someone." *The runt*.

"Phillip's stomach didn't feel too well," said Randall. "He wanted us to go on without him."

"Whatever." It was fine with me; the fewer people here meant the faster I could get back to 'guarding.

We punched in our orders and sat in silence until the weight lifter—sorry, until Justin—spoke up. "You said something about a dance?"

I nodded toward the dance space, demarcated by bundles of fine-mesh netting. "Aalicen is doing the floorshow today: classic punk ballet. The netting ensures she doesn't stray too far from the dance space. Sometimes she can get pretty worked up if the crowd interacts well with her."

"Umm, I've never seen zero-gee ballet."

"It's great. In fact, next to swimming, it's the most popular attraction here."

We were interrupted by Aalicen's entrance. She spun around the volume encompassing her dance space, then bounced through a train of holographs projected around the chamber. The music seemed to change with every swirl. It still strikes me every time I watch her—which isn't often, because of the prices in here.

We were finally served; Aalicen's dance set a pleasant mood for lunch. Justin turned to me and said, "I've seen holos on swimming in your water tanks. It looks exciting."

"It is," I agreed. "I really enjoy it. In fact, I could probably do it forever. If it wasn't for school, I'd probably be lifeguarding most of the time."

"Is it hard swimming here?"

"Are you kidding? Three- and four-year-old kids do it all the time. They even make Jumping look easy."

Justin was quiet for a moment. "Do you think I could try it?"

"Swimming? Why not? If you want, I'll take both of you after lunch."

Justin looked pleased. "That would be fun."

I toyed with my food. "What about you—did you ever 'guard back on Earth?"

Randall looked abruptly up, then back down at his plate. Justin poked at his food and said, "To tell you the truth, I never had the chance. You see, when I was younger, I—"

He was drowned out by applause as Aalicen completed her set. Randall leaned over the table and said, "She's great. If she wanted, I bet she could make a million on Earth." He looked to Soloette. "Do you think she'll ever try?"

The table grew quiet. Soloette managed to answer quickly, "No, I don't think so; she likes it too much here. Besides, she wouldn't be able to do half of what she does here down there." She turned her attention to me and said urgently, "Astar, isn't it time for your shift?"

The atmosphere seemed tense. "Er, yes . . . I guess it is." I unstrapped and floated up. I wasn't quite finished, but Randall had touched a nerve best left alone for now. "Randall, Justin—sorry to cut this short. I've got to get back to the tank."

"No problem. We understand."

"Fine, then I'll see you all later?"

Soloette answered, "We'll be right behind you." She held my eye. "Go on. I'll get these guys fitted out in wetsuits. We'll meet you in the restcove."

I overrode their objections to my paying for my own meal, and left. Reaching the water tank, I changed and made it into the restcove just as my shift started.

I scanned the sonarholo for traffic in the water; it was virtually deserted. Then I kicked into the water tank. The tunnel was boiling in a Dantean frenzy, water popping as bubbles fought their way up from the bottom of the tank. Sailing through the tunnel, I thought about lunch: Soloette would do *anything* to get a man to come back here. Lucky I was more particular than she is; besides, I wasn't ready to get involved. I'm having too much fun just 'guarding.

Oh, *bother*. The restcove on the outer wall was coming up fast. I'd have to let the buoy slow me down. That's what I get for thinking about men.

I spotted them on my approach to the main restcove. Soloette had done a pretty good job of fitting them with wetsuits; they resembled neon signs in their hot-pink novice suits.

The colonists spruced their suits up a little more to style: Soloette's radiated an ever-changing hue of colors, rippling through the rainbow from blood maroon to deep indigo and back again. If there had been gravity in the restcove, the guys' eyes would be rolling on the floor.

My own suit was the straight dayglow orange Lifeguards wear on duty. My last "civilian" wetsuit was more of a mockup of a wraparound toga—but I'd outgrown that years ago, and since taking my Lifeguard duties seriously, had saved Daddy money by not investing in a mantrap like Soloette's.

Soloette hadn't worn this one lately—there hadn't been any men as eligible as these around for a while—but I had to admit that she filled the suit rather nicely. She had bulges and curves in just the right places, and the suit seemed to play on that, making her more attractive than usual. In fact, you couldn't tell the signs of near zero-gee living—which infested everyone who lived here for more than six months.

I closed in on the restcove at a safe speed. It was about twenty meters away. I flipped and hit feet first, trudged up the stickum, through the electrostatic curtain, and into the restcove. I tried to sound cheery. "How do the suits feel?"

Justin answered my call, "Confining." He grunted and leaned over to tighten a strap, and began to float up from the effort. I grabbed a handhold, reached out and hauled him back. He looked bewildered, but managed to get out, "Thanks."

"Sure. Just be careful; it takes a while to get acclimated to zero-gee."

"I guess. But what do we need this gear for?"

"You'd boil if you didn't wear the wetsuit; the water tanks are a heat sink. The *Heinlein* doesn't have heatvanes or IR transmitters like the other colonies to get rid of waste heat, so we dump it in the water."

Justin twisted his forehead. "If you say so, but what about the mask?"

It dawned on me that Soloette was being awfully quiet. I glanced over at her, but she ignored me. I said, "It's for the low air pressure. The combination of the low pressure and high temperature puts the vapor pressure at just the right point for the water to boil."

"Why do you want to do that?"

Soloette dimpled and looked at Randall. She said, "So touri like you will come here. Since we're the water depository for the consortium, it's the only drawing point we have over the other, newer colonies. It's just another way to get more touri to visit."

I said under my breath, "And it still doesn't pack them in."

Randall tried to join in. "I don't understand why you can't just dump the heat into space. Isn't space supposed to be cold—three degrees, or something like that?" He looked quizzically at Soloette, who just smiled.

I rolled my eyes and started to explain—was it because they were *men*, or because they were groundhogs, that they didn't know better? As I opened my mouth, Soloette's face went vacant and she said: "I don't know much about the mechanics of it, but I do know it's fun to swim in boiling water."

Soloette was hanging all over Randall. If there had been any obscenity laws here, she'd be in the pokey for life. I asked, "How's his suit?"

"Couldn't be better." She almost purred. If she was bad at lunch, this was worse. It could get sickening.

"All right, then," I said. "Check your masks and we're ready to go."

I showed Justin how to make sure his mask was snug—something they should have checked at the equipment rental—then turned to exit the restcove. "When you leave, you'll feel a slight tingling. Don't worry, that's just the electrostatic curtain that keeps most of the water out, and the restcove dry. If you're scared, use the handholds. If you want to walk, there's stickum all around the port; just be sure to keep one foot on the stickum until you're ready to go into the tunnel. Otherwise, you'll float out and it could take a while to get you back.''

Soloette spoke up, sounding intelligent for the first time all day. ''Are you going to tell them about the buoys?''

''I was getting to that.'' I pulled a buoy from my waist belt. ''There are two restcoves. One here,'' I pointed behind me with the buoy, ''and another at the end of the tunnel, one kilometer away. If you're moving too slowly, or find yourself moving too fast toward either restcove, just toss your buoy toward the water. The little bugger is a waterjet with a homing device that makes a geodesic for the bottom of the tank. You don't have to go all the way to the bottom, of course, when the buoy pulls you down. But if you do go to the bottom, you can kick back up to the tunnel. I recommend that as soon as you hit the water, you let go of the buoy. I guarantee you'll slow down once you hit the pseudosurface.''

Randall spoke nervously. ''How far is the bottom?''

''A kilometer from the axis—about nine hundred ninety meters below the water's surface. That's approximate; the tunnel is about twenty meters in radius, plus or minus several meters, taking into account the pseudosurface.''

It didn't help any; Randall seemed more upset. ''Uh, nine hundred and ninety meters seems awfully deep to go swimming. I know I can't go any deeper than a few meters or so back—''

''—on Earth.'' I finished for him. ''Don't worry. The pressure at the bottom of the water tank corresponds to about three meters of water on Earth. The difference is that our gravity is variable. It increases from zero at the center of the tunnel, to a max of about two percent of a gee at the rim. It's very comfortable, and you don't even have to worry about the bends: you can't get them at these pressures. Also, there are glowglobes floating every fifty meters apart, radially and axially, so you won't have to worry about having enough light to see.

''One more thing. If you get disoriented in the water, shoot out your buoy. It'll take you to the bottom, and from there you can get back to the surface by crawling to a wall. But don't try blowing bubbles to find out which way is up,'cause it won't work. The bubbles move too slowly, and with the coriolis force acting on them, it will only make things worse.''

Randall had a blank stare. I started to explain, but noticed that Justin nodded, so I closed my mouth. Soloette still hadn't pitched in to help me. She was playing the dumb-wahoo role to attract Randall, and it looked like it was working.

I needed to get back on my patrol through the tunnel. I briskly went through the remainder of the ingress procedures, and when there were no questions, led them out through the electrostatic curtain. Justin stayed at the edge of the restcove, still hanging on to the handhold. I had to speak louder than normal to get over the roar of the boiling water and the muffling of the mask. "Any questions?" They shook their heads.

Soloette called out, "I'll take them on out, Astar. Go ahead with your patrol."

"Thanks." I ducked back in to check the sonarholo. There were one or two Drifters in the tunnel and maybe half a dozen Jumpers actually in the water. No problem. I got back into the tank, crouched, then leapt out toward the far end of the tunnel and flipped over to watch Soloette and the guys as they receded. They left the restcove holding hands as a group and moved slowly into the tunnel. They weren't traveling anywhere near as fast as I, but at least they made the incursion into the water tank.

I flipped back over to see where I was heading as I approached the halfway mark. I was traveling a little too fast, so I released a buoy. As it hit I was jerked backwards, and headed for the water. I skipped on the surface and managed to flail my arms to get back on track in the center of the tunnel. It looks hard, but all it takes is practice.

I landed on the outer restcove and checked the sonarholo again. All Swimmers—Drifters and Jumpers—were still active. There was nothing out of the ordinary, so I jumped back toward the main restcove to take a blow for a while.

Soloette, Randall, and Justin were about a third of the way through the tunnel. I timed the buoy just right so I stopped about ten meters ahead of them. Soloette caught me by the arm to join them, slowing their progress even more.

As I started to speak, a Jumper broke water ahead of us, coming up from the surface, through the tunnel, and up into the water. She had done a good job of keeping control as she broke surface; Randall and Justin's mouths sagged in their masks.

The guys looked a little wary. "How do you like it so far?" I yelled.

"S'all right." Justin was craning his neck all around. "I feel as though the water will collapse all around me."

I laughed. "Don't worry—it can't. The worst that could happen would be for the colony to stop rotating—then the water would just float up into the tunnel. With your mask and wetsuit on, you're safe."

Justin flashed me a smile through the mask. "I'd like to try the water."

"Sure. Randall, how about you?"

Randall clung to Soloette's arm. He refused to answer, but Soloette didn't seem to mind. I turned back to Justin. "Want to Jump through the tunnel?"

"Huh?"

"All we do is get to the bottom of the water tank, kick off, and head for the surface. It's not as easy as it looks, though. You'll not only have to judge the pseudosurface when you pop through the tunnel, but you'll have to fight the coriolis on the way up. It will push you sideways, and the faster you go, the more you'll have to fight it."

"How do you get around it?"

"By stroking and leaning into the force. If you try to glide, you'll get all screwed up."

"Sure, when do we go?"

I glanced over to Soloette and Randall. She shook her head slightly. Randall didn't speak; he was trembling slightly. Soloette motioned with her head for me to go on without them. She shouldn't have any trouble if he didn't lose his head.

When we were about three hundred meters from the far restcove, I shouted to Justin, "Ready?" All he could do was grin and give a thumbs up. I motioned for him to grab his buoy. "After you toss it, just hold on tight and let it take you to the bottom."

"Right."

I counted to three out loud, then in tandem we threw the buoy down. It hit water and immediately started down. We had drifted up from the momentum of tossing the device, but as soon as the line grew taut, we were jerked down with it.

Justin hit water first—with an audible "ooof" as he was pulled under. (Once in the water I kicked to catch up, then grabbed on to his hand.) He nodded; he was all right. I motioned for him to turn off the buoy, and he complied, so we sank downward at a slower pace than usual. We passed several glowglobes on the way; Justin motioned excitedly at the first one, but quickly became accustomed to them.

I caught myself grinning. I don't know why—it sure wasn't because of Justin. He was okay for a guy: cute, I guess fairly bright if he was a programmer, and he *did* have muscles.

Then it hit me what I was really grinning about: I was getting caught up in Soloette's incessant drive to *find a man*. That's the last thing I needed. I shoved the thought firmly out of my mind and let go of his hand.

As we approached bottom, I tapped Justin on the shoulder and rotated till I was feet down, ready to absorb the landing with my legs. Justin should have been following my lead, but he remained head down, flexing his arms as though he was going to land with his hands rather than his feet. I frantically pulled at him, but he waved me off. The idiot wants to kill himself!

I tried to reach over to him, but he batted me away. I got ready to grab him and make a geodesic for the restcove after he cracked his skull. We passed the final glowglobe before the bottom. Two meters . . . one meter . . .

I hit bottom and collapsed to the deck, not bouncing. As I turned to grab Justin, he sprang from the bottom using his arms, and shot up, into the water. *Zen!* I followed, not holding back. He flipped over and started stroking against the coriolis. As we moved faster, we were pushed even harder in a direction perpendicular to our motion. Justin did a pretty good job of compensating for it.

The surface was coming up. I was wary about trying anything fancy when we popped up, so I decided just to follow Justin and shoot through the tunnel.

There was a Drifter right in our path as we broke air. I screamed for Justin as I tossed a buoy behind me. Justin did the same, and we both were jerked backwards to where we had popped out of the water. I let go of the buoy and hit the water.

Justin let out a whoop. He's hurt! I *knew* something would happen. I stroked over to him, grabbed his elbow, and hauled him up to the surface. We bounced around in the breaking bubbles as I yelled into his mask, "Are you all right?"

He was grinning. "Yeah, that was great! It was like having the universe revolve around you when we hit the tunnel. I've never had so much fun—"

"You mean you're okay?" I demanded.

"Sure. Let's go again. I could do this forever." He must have noticed my look through my mask. "Hey, Astar, what's the matter? We missed the person floating in the tunnel, didn't we?"

I pulled away, angry. "Yeah, we did. Now what were you trying to pull by landing on the bottom with your hands? You could have broken your neck." He shrugged and avoided answering. I pointed toward the restcove. "Come on, we can talk in there." I started the half-dog paddle, half-skimming it took to get up to the tunnel. Justin followed—slowly, because he was only using his arms—but he was still pretty proficient for a beginner.

When we reached the restcove, Justin stopped me. "Hey, why the sudden turnaround? What's going on?"

I recited the first nine 6-j symbols under my breath and tried to cool down. "Look, Justin. That was a stupid thing to do out there."

"So?"

Oh, bother! "So, look: I shouldn't have taken you down to the bottom on your first time out. And if I had known what kind of hare-brained stunt you'd pull—" I sputtered, trying to bawl him out, but I wasn't too good at it.

Justin shrugged. "I did all right."

"Sure, but you could have cracked your skull and killed yourself—and on my shift. Even if you hadn't been killed, it could have meant I'd never pull Lifeguard duty again."

"So what's the big deal? It's not that important, is it?"

"Justin Kenlai, you just don't understand. I'm sorry. Perhaps you'd better get hooked back up with that friend Randall of yours. If you'll excuse me, I've got to make another pass through the tunnel. Just go into the restcove and stay out of the water, would you?" I turned to go, and just as I kicked, Justin grabbed on to a handhold and pulled me in.

"Now wait one damn minute. Just what the hell is going on? One minute we're having a great time swimming, and the next you're bawling me out for landing on the bottom with my hands. If you really want to know why I did it, I'll tell you. But I want to know what's wrong with you, first."

Daddy told me that I could freeze a Tokamak with my stare if I wanted to. He said I inherited that—and my looks—from Mom.

So I stared at Justin, and to leave no mistake about the matter, I froze the air in the restcove with my reply: "I *said* I have a job to do, Mr. Kenlai. Now, if you please." I kicked through the electrostatic curtain and into the tunnel.

I wiped away water from my eyes that just happened to splash in, making them all red and teary. As I shot to the other side, I nearly missed colliding with a Drifter. Funny . . . that's *never* happened twice in one day before.

Daddy was still gone, but I didn't mind. I liked being alone in the apartment sometimes so I could just think. The week had been going fine until those guys had shown up.

The door beeped angrily. I ignored it until I realized it wasn't going to stop, then flung it open. Soloette slowly drifted in.

"What's the matter?" she asked. I lowered my eyes and muttered something about being asleep.

Soloette nodded, obviously unimpressed. "Justin wanted to know where you were. Said he hadn't seen you since swimming yesterday."

"What did he say?"

Soloette frowned. "Say? He just wanted to know where you were, that's all."

"He didn't say anything about the swim?"

Soloette answered slowly. "No, should he?"

It didn't make sense—but then again, men never do. I tried to sluff it off. "No, I guess not." I pushed over to the kitchen and scanned the menu for something sweet.

Soloette floated beside me. "What's wrong?"

"Nothing!" I punched up a glucose-covered tofu bar.

Soloette raise an eyebrow. "Oh? Miss Calorie-Conscious getting surly again?" She twirled me by the elbow, sending us both spinning. "Astar, something happened in that water tank. This is your best buddy talking. Now what's up?"

After I got through explaining Justin's near miss with the Drifters in the tunnel, and how he was *a lot* better swimmer than I thought he should be, Soloette tried to chase down my tears as they started floating around the kitchen. We laughed, and she held my hands. "Astar, I'm asking Randall to visit me after he's through at Tycho Station."

"For how long?"

"As long as he wants."

I stopped sniffing and managed to raise a brow. "After two days? You're starting to sound like the holos. Besides, you're only seventeen."

Soloette ignored it. "He's not as intelligent as Justin is, but he's cute and he's well off. I think I can talk him into staying; I've almost convinced him to move here after he's done."

I bit my lip. "Soloette, if he comes back, are you going to propose to him?"

"You bet!"

"Before or after you tell him about the *Heinlein*?"

Silence. Then Soloette spoke with a trace of anger. "That's between Randall and me, Astar. Don't you *dare* tell him—or Justin, for that matter."

"Just be fair to him, Soloette."

After a few more minutes of forced conversation, Soloette

found an excuse to leave. I never did eat that tofu bar. Darn those tears!

I saw Justin three more times after that. He took me back to the Bifrost the night after my talk with Soloette. I don't think he cared much for our home-grown version of tequila, but we had fun anyway. He wouldn't let me take him to any of the gravity decks, so we stayed in zero-gee the whole time, which was fine with me. And I didn't take him swimming.

I even let him kiss me twice too, but each time I put off the other advances. I mean, it just wasn't *fair* to him. It would never work with us. And besides, I couldn't tie him down here. I'd seen what happened to Daddy, and I've heard Daddy talk after he'd had too much to snort. He really misses Earth, and for all it's worth, I couldn't tie Justin down like that.

I was pulling Lifeguard duty on the day Justin's shuttle was supposed to leave. I couldn't believe it had been only three days.

I sailed through the tunnel, and as I approached the restcove, I caught sight of him. No way to get around it. I passed through the electrostatic curtain and removed my mask. I said, "Sorry I couldn't see you off; we're kinda busy with the new touri who just came in."

"I understand."

Did he really? I doubted it. "Well, thanks for everything—it's been nice knowing you." I stuck out my hand.

He stared at it. "Is that all? Astar, I thought we had something more than that going between us."

Oh, *bother*! I shook my head. "It was fun, Justin, but . . ." I tried to change the subject. "We can always keep in touch through Randall."

"Randall isn't coming back through here."

My jaw dropped. "What?"

"Randall changed his ticket two hours ago. He won't talk about it, but he's going back by way of the L-4 group. He doesn't want to lay over here again."

"Oh." I repositioned myself. "Did he say why?" Justin shook his head. I scanned the sonarholo. There was a large group— probably that new gaggle of touri—drifting in the tunnel. They were safe for now; I had time to talk. I drew in a breath. "Justin, I like you *a lot*, but I can't ask you to come back. And I think that's the reason Randall decided not to either."

"Huh?"

"Look. Soloette and I were born here on the *Heinlein*. We've never been off of it." I tried to make a point by switching gears. "What's the max gravity here?"

Justin looked startled. "Why, two one-hundredths that of Earth. At least, that's what you told me. Why?"

I sighed. "That's why. I've *never* experienced more gravity than that, and for most of my life, I've lived in zero-gee. You wanted to know why being a Lifeguard is so important to me? It's because it's the only thing I can do to keep in shape. Some people dance, some are tour guides: I lifeguard. If I didn't, my joints would meld from calcification and I'd turn into an oversized balloon. I can never leave the *Heinlein*, can't you see? I can't even go to other colonies. They have too much gravity at their outer core, and they're not built in decks like the *Heinlein*, so they don't have a zero-gee living space. I'm stuck here forever, Justin. *I can't leave*.

"That's why I can't ask you to come back. If something did happen between us, you'd be stuck here forever. And I bet that's why Randall didn't want to get involved with Soloette; he could never take her off the *Heinlein*." I wonder how he found out. I'll bet Soloette sure didn't tell him.

My voice trembled. "I can't do that to you, Justin. I've already got one man to worry about: my father. Since Mother died, he's trapped here because of me. The only time he gets away is on business trips, but he still has to come back to me. I can't let that happen to you."

Justin opened his mouth to say something when the alarm went off. *Collision!* The sonarholo showed a large group near the rest-cove, skimming the pseudosurface.

I shot out the restcove, adjusting my mask while in flight. There was a gaggle of people—at least seven touri, judging from their hot-pink wetsuits—clawing at the air in the tunnel. Bodies were separating and I could hear screams over the roar of the boiling water. I couldn't tell what happened, but it's even money some hotdog Jumper probably thought she could impress them by Jumping through their group.

As I closed in, I spotted several objects tumbling away from the gaggle. Some of their masks were ripped off! There must have been four or five masks drifting in the tunnel, whirling aimlessly away from the crowd.

I picked out those who needed help the most and flailed myself toward them. I shot off a buoy, which skipped against the water when I stopped it, and bounced, putting me right in front of one group. I gathered up three kids and an adult and started kicking for the restcove.

Two more groups were splashing around. *Unspeakable!* We should never have let that many in here at once. And if anyone drowns, they'll close the water tanks forever.

I pushed the first group toward the restcove, kicking in the water to give me support. Although they were weightless, their mass gave them a hefty amount of inertia I had to overcome.

I got them on the stickum, pushed them through the electrostatic curtain, and bounced back for the other two groups. Two people were splashing around at the surface of the water, and a third twirled wildly in the tunnel. I made a split-second decision and went for the two. The lone one would have to wait. I let off my last buoy, managed to grab the two, and started hauling them back to the restcove. One of them was going nutso on me. I tried to slug him.

The groundhog ripped my mask off! I drew in several breaths of near-nothing. I tried to concentrate: just make for the restcove, and forget about the other one still out here. The silvery stickum delineating the restcove seemed light-years away. I stroked, kicked, and pushed the squirming groundhogs ahead of me. It looked as though we were going to make it.

A dark object shot out from the restcove over me; another Lifeguard must have been nearby. At least I wouldn't have to rescue the last one myself. We reached the restcove and I pushed them onto the stickum, then inside the electrostatic curtain, where I gasped pressurized air for the first time in a minute.

I ran my hands over the touri I had hauled in. Everything seemed to be all right. At least they were still breathing. I looked up at one in the first group I rescued. "How's the Lifeguard doing that went after your buddy?"

The touri coughed. "It wasn't a Lifeguard—or at least not one in a wetsuit—just somebody who was in the restcove."

Turning my attention back to the tunnel, my body yammered with adrenaline: *Where's Justin!* The idiot had shot into the water, *sans* wetsuit, mask, or anything. The sonarholo showed them about five meters below the surface, fifty meters out. I grabbed a mask and shot out of the restcove, into the tunnel. I couldn't see anything below me—maybe they were farther from the side than I thought.

That's when it hit me that I didn't have a buoy to slow me down.

I started rotating, gyrating, and everything else I could think of, trying to hit water, but nothing helped. I was helpless—so I fumed all the way over to the other side. Finally reaching the farside restcove, I grabbed three buoys and shot back to the main restcove, craning my neck, scanning the water for any sight of them.

I thought I saw something, so I let off a buoy, dropped, and looked around—just a couple of kids from the *Heinlein*. I dog-paddled and skipped across the surface until I was up in the tunnel again.

The inner restcove was about fifty meters away when I spotted them. They had reached the stickum, and Justin was using his hands, trying to pull the touri past the electrostatic curtain. An arm reached through from the restcove and hauled them both inside.

I hit the stickum too fast, bounced, and headed back in the opposite direction. Cursing, I let go with another buoy, which grabbed the water, and I made it on my own to the restcove.

Breaking through the electrostatic curtain, I just made it as they were fitting Justin with an oxygen bottle. I reached over and touched his face. It was Mars red—at least second-degree burns. I started crying and they pushed me away. He felt so *hot!*

After what seemed to be forever, they finally started to move him out. I collared one of the medics and demanded, ''Is he all right?''

Justin coughed. I pushed my way to him. He was barely audible as he bleared at me and grinned. ''It takes a lot more than a little swimming pool to kill this ole boy.''

I held his head in my hands. ''You stupid . . .'' I was at a loss for words; if Daddy could see me now, he'd faint. ''Why did you do it?''

The medics tried to move him, but Justin stopped them. He coughed again and said, ''You were in trouble, and the kid might have died.''

''Still—!''

He made an effort to pat my arm. ''And I didn't get a chance to finish what we were talking about.''

And *I* thought I switched gears fast! Oh, no. Tears started to well in my eyes. ''I already told you, Justin. I *can't*—''

''Let me finish,'' he interrupted. ''You made a comment about my arms. Why do you think I never use my feet to push off . . . or to swim with . . . or why I never go down to your gravity decks? Because I *can't*, that's why. Look, Astar, I've been paralyzed from the waist down since I was a child. I was in a diving accident and the doctors couldn't grow the nerve endings back. Back on

Earth, the only thing I can do is work with my arms.

"But here I'm a whole person . . . and if I come back, I won't be trapped. It's the only place I can be like everyone else. Now will you at least give me a chance when I come back?"

Funny. To this day, I can't ever recall saying yes to him. As they moved him to emergency, I think I was crying too hard to remember.

But I do remember everyone in the restcove clapping.

New Worlds in Space

NORMAN SPINRAD

While I don't always agree with Norman Spinrad's conclusions, I know of few people who can spin an old idea more provocatively. In "New Worlds in Space," especially commissioned for this volume, Norman gives us a *new* look at space habitats and the people who will live in them. I'm not sure I agree with all of his conclusions—in fact, I hope a few of them are dead wrong—but it's not a vision of the future you're likely to forget.

THE FRENCH CRITIC Michel Butor once suggested quite seriously (or at least in perfect deadpan) that science fiction writers get together, agree on a desirable consensus future, and then, by setting all their stories and novels in this collective dreamworld, imprint it upon the public consciousness and thereby call it into being.

It seemed rather silly at the time.

True, one collective dream had always been thematically central to science fiction, and more, dear to the hearts of most of the people who wrote and read it as a vision of the future much to be desired in the real world. Science fiction, in point of fact, if not by theoretical definition, could hardly be science fiction without it.

If there is one collective value held by the "science fiction community'' as a whole, it is a belief in our destiny as a space-faring species.

But far from agreeing on a future in space and setting all their stories and novels in it, science fiction writers followed their own individual stars and created not a collective dream but a rich profusion of alternate futures and multiplex realities.

This view of the future as a multiplexity of possibilities, rather than a collective dreamcastle awaiting construction, is, of course, science fiction's greatest strength as a visionary literature.

Nor did science fiction's refusal to champion a collective prescription for a space program vitiate its successful social role as a major spiritual, and even mystical, inspiration of Project Apollo.

While science fiction never did predict the details of Project Apollo (let alone champion anything so apparently ludicrous as going to the moon via brute force rocketry directly from the surface of the Earth without building an orbital space station first), many were the astronauts and space scientists whose careers were set in motion by its multiple visions of space-faring futures.

Then came Gerard O'Neil and the L-5 Movement.

O'Neil, a Princeton professor, set his students the task of designing a space colony and ended up so convinced of the result's practical viability that he became dedicated to getting the "L-5 Colony" built.

What his class came up with was a cylindrical canister, perhaps ten miles long and able to support a population of 10,000, stabilized at Lagrange Point 5, one of the gravitationally stable libration points equidistant from the Earth and the moon. It would rotate about its long axis to supply artificial gravity. Large movable solar mirrors would supply the power to run it and artificial daylight for the self-contained ecology which would provide the food and oxygen for its inhabitants.

The proposal was worked out in considerable detail, and designed so that the project could be begun with modified existing technology. And it was even provided with an economic justification, rather optimistically designed to persuade Congress to cough up the funding.

First, a fleet of Shuttles and Heavy Lift Vehicles, big unmanned freight boosters derived from Shuttle technology, would be used to boost enough personnel and material into Earth Orbit to build the so-called "Construction Shack," a rather large space station, which would then be ferried to the L-5 point.

Meanwhile, or perhaps afterward, using the Construction Shack as logistical support, a base would be established on the moon.

The lunar surface would then be mined for the raw materials with which to build the actual L-5 Colony. Taking advantage of the low lunar gravity, a monster railgun, an electromagnetic mass-driver powered by a nuclear reactor, could be used to boost raw materials from the lunar surface to the L-5 point construction site.

With a lunar gravity one-sixth that of Earth, the energy required to boost a given mass out of the lunar gravity well would be one-sixth of that required to boost the same mass into Earth orbit; indeed, given the lack of a lunar atmosphere and, therefore, no energy loss due to atmospheric heating, even less. And by using an electromagnetic railgun powered by a reactor on the lunar surface to catapult the payload to lunar escape velocity, no fuel mass would have to be boosted along with it, meaning a further reduction in energy costs F.O.B. Lagrange point 5.

What this would mean, at least in theory, is that lunar raw materials could be delivered to the L-5 construction site at a fraction of the cost of boosting the necessary material out of the terrestrial gravity well by rocket, making the whole, enormous project economically feasible.

But not, of course, exactly inexpensive. Even the most optimistic projections put a price tag north of one hundred billion dollars on the project, and even if the cost would be spread out over a decade or more, it would still take some tall talking to convince Congress to fund it.

Even if the Congress was convinced that a city in space with a population of ten thousand could really be built within a decade at an annual cost that would not bankrupt the nation, they would have to be shown an economic payback to justify the expense.

O'Neil's proposal took that into account, too. Once completed, the L-5 Colony, using cheap raw materials boosted out of the light lunar gravity well, and working under optimized conditions of gravity and temperature, would be able to build large numbers of enormous solar mirrors. The mirrors would be placed in Earth orbit and, equipped with microwave transmitters, would beam abundant and cheap solar energy to ground stations; enough renewable, clean, safe, ecologically sound energy from space to free the planet forever from the need to use fossil fuels or nuclear power sources.

Needless to say, most of the L-5 colony concept had been anticipated in science fiction. Space stations had long been a staple of the genre. The huge self-contained artificial world, at least in terms of the powered "generation ship," is a concept at least as old as Robert A. Heinlein's "Universe." Putting the thing at an

Earth-Moon libration point instead of in a conventional orbit about an astronomical body was foreshadowed by George O. Smith's *Venus Equilateral* series, in which a space station is placed in stable position at a Venusian Trojan point, and what it is doing is indeed beaming solar power to the Earth. Even the lunar mass-driver and its economic consequences were described in great detail in Heinlein's *The Moon Is a Harsh Mistress*.

In a sense, then, O'Neil's L-5 concept was cobbled together out of decades worth of science-fictional space colonies, or, to put it another way, decades worth of science fiction had explored so many possible variations on this piece of macrotechnology, that just about anything O'Neil could have come up with would have been anticipated somewhere in the literature.

But O'Neil's design was quite specific and unique, just like Project Apollo. It was long anticipated by science fiction in its generality and scattered detail, but never quite appeared in the literature in its actual nuts and bolts and systems form.

And when the L-5 Society was founded as a lobbying group whose political goal was actually to get a space colony built, a strange new thing began to happen.

It was only natural for many science fiction writers to support the goal of the L-5 Society; some were active in the organization itself, and science fiction fandom, of course, was the most fertile ground for space lobby recruitment.

Space lobbyists became part of the science fiction convention scene, the L-5 proposal became a popular panel item and topic of barroom conversation, and while M. Butor's proposal was never to my knowledge seriously advanced, he would no doubt have smiled contentedly at what evolved out of this general process.

The L-5 Colony became a collective consensus image.

The science fiction genre had evolved plenty of consensus images before. The interplanetary rocket. The robot. The wheel-shaped space station. Hyperdrive. The raygun. Hive mind. The list, though not endless, is quite extensive.

But never before had a specific engineering proposal injected itself like a virus into the species DNA of the genre, replicating itself in stories by many writers. Instead of frontier technology mirroring science fiction, science fiction was emulating and promoting the program of the L-5 Society.

L-5 Colonies abounded in stories and novels, and they were called just that, when they were not called "O'Neil Colonies." The place of Gerard O'Neil in future history became a given. Generally speaking, these fictional L-5 Colonies were all very much like each other, and were all pretty much as described by O'Neil.

Was this merely a matter of science fiction writers staying au courant with space science and adopting the L-5 design as the obvious form of the large space colony?

Perhaps a certain intellectual laziness was indeed involved; easier to do a quick rewrite of O'Neil's detailed description of your setting than to reinvent the wheel from scratch. But on careful retrospective consideration, the L-5 concept was far from the optimum inevitable in space colony design.

For one thing, living around the interior circumference of a huge spinning cylinder in order to enjoy Earth-normal gravity means that most of the enclosed volume of your colony is useless, empty space. The most efficient shape, in terms of surface to volume ratio, and therefore of cost, would be spherical.

The only justification for a cylinder is so that it can be spun on its long axis to provide uniform "artificial gravity" on its interior surface.

And that might not work either.

I took considerable ribbing as a science fiction writer on the subject of artificial gravity from astronaut Wally Schirra at the Global Vision seminar in Tokyo.

Centrifugal force, he insisted, is *not* the same thing as artificial gravity because your head is rotating somewhat slower than your feet and subject therefore to Coriolis forces. The price of maintaining spin gravity on the interior surface of anything other than a cylinder of truly enormous proportions would be a permanent case of vertigo for all of its inhabitants.

The shorter the axis of rotation, the greater the gut-wrenching effect, the greater the length of the moment arm, the closer centrifugal "gravity" approaches the real thing. Meaning that, in terms of both geometrically efficient enclosure of *usable* space and achieving maximum rotation diameter with minimal mass, the good old wheel-shaped space station makes more sense than the cylindrical L-5 Colony.

But it's hard to imagine a rotating torus big enough to overcome the Coriolis effect, either. Two discs tethered together by a kilometers-long cable and rotating about a common center is probably going to be the best way to make bearable spin gravity remotely affordable.

Furthermore, while boost costs of delivering lunar raw materials to the L-5 point with which to build both the L-5 Colony and solar power satellites might be much lower than boosting the same mass from the Earth, the costs of prospecting and mining the lunar surface would be a different story. Figuring in the enormous cost of building the L-5 Colony itself, it's hard to see how a world network of solar satellites could be built more cheaply using O'Neil's grandiose scheme than by building them on the Earth's surface, as fit-together modules, if necessary, and using Shuttles and Heavy Lifters to deploy them.

As with Project Apollo, all those old SF stories were right, and the real-world engineering concepts were wrong.

Why then did the L-5 Colony achieve at least for a time the status of a consensus image à la Butor?

Precisely, I believe, for Butor's reason.

A future for the human race in space had long been the central collective dream of science fiction. Project Apollo had validated the vision and given science fiction writers an exaggerated sense of their ability to direct the national psyche toward its destiny in space. But Project Apollo had been a false first step—not our vision at all—and it had turned out to be a dead end in terms of our expansion into space.

The L-5 proposal, however, whatever its possible design flaws, had real-world plausibility. Here was a detailed developer's blue-print for a city in space that could be built without real techno-logical breakthroughs; a dreamcastle that those already born might expect to be able to move into. Timothy Leary even concocted a sardonic scheme to finance the building of the space development by pre-selling lots inside it.

Then too, this was the first time that the science fiction com-munity had been subject to real lobbying—and lobbying for a cause to which, in general, it had already long since been con-verted.

The Butorism seemed relatively benign, subtle, and apolitical. Readers were mercifully spared a flood of science fictional So-cialist Realism depicting the heroic struggle of the scientists, work-ers, and SF fans to build utopia in space. Comparatively few of the stories and novels were directly *about* the construction of an L-5 Colony. Writers simply tended to write in O'Neil's projected artifact whenever the tale called for a colony in space. It was as innocent as the time-honored employment of "Tuckerisms," the injection of names or personas of real SF figures into fictional futures.

Or was it?

In retrospect, as we shall soon see, maybe not.

For one thing, taking O'Neil's design as a given tended to freeze further fictional speculation on space habitat design, while encouraging a design with serious conceptual flaws, and the construction of an artifact so expensive that it had no hope of being taken seriously by Congress, even before the Pentagon gobbled up the lion's share of the space budget.

Second, as science fiction writers began to use the L-5 Colony as a consensus setting, a kind of thematic consensus began to accrete around the artifact, a collective vision of the future of the solar system at least halfway to becoming ideology.

Indeed, in certain quarters, that ideology was preexistent. The American myth of the frontier is older than American science fiction, and long before the L-5 concept was even a gleam in O'Neil's eye, it had been moved to the Asteroid Belt by science fiction writers of a laissez-faire libertarian bent.

The asteroids (colonial America or the Old West) were seen as the free frontier, the future of economic (and sometimes political) freedom, colonized by rugged individualists who were fighting for economic and/or political independence from wicked, degenerate, collectivist, played-out Earth (Old Europe or the effete East). Out there in the Belt, with its limitless mineral resources, its low-g environment, and its wide open spaces, was the future of the species, and as for poor old polluted, over-populated, screwed-up Earth: tough shit.

In part, this myth of the "Free Asteroids" served as a venue for laissez-faire libertarian political fables, but it was also a reflection of a certain viewpoint within the SF community, the one that divides the species into free-thinking, future-oriented SF fans (the Belters of the free frontier) and "mundanes," which is to say the rest of humanity (poor played-out old Earth).

Not all of this stuff had a libertarian political message, and not all of it limited the frontier to the Asteroid Belt, but all of it displayed much the same attitude toward Earth and what it stood for. Poor old Earth was unsalvageable and, at best, must be left to stew in its own juices while the boldest and the brightest headed in the direction of Pluto.

The advent of the L-5 proposal and the lobbying efforts of the L-5 Society within the SF community pushed these tendencies to their logical extremes.

The L-5 Colony would be built with material from beyond Earth's gravity well. It would have its own self-contained ecology and draw its energy from the sun. Thus it would be a brand new world entire, a new start, fashioned entirely by the hand of man, completely self-sufficient, a society independent not only from

Earth but from reliance upon the resources of any planetary surface, from geology, weather, the natural realm itself.

"Planetary chauvinism" became a buzzword, meaning that the future of the species lay in self-created artificial worlds, that while the mundanes were left to wallow in their own self-created mess on Earth, star-faring man would conquer not other planets as much as the tabula rasa of space itself.

What was more, what was *much* more, was that SF writers and readers felt that this was a dreamworld they could actually build for themselves precisely as Michel Butor suggested. Detailed engineering plans for the L-5 Colony existed; given the money and political commitment, it could be built well within the lifetimes of those now living. A lobbying effort to build a constituency for the funding was already under way, and science fiction had helped to successfully inspire Project Apollo. So, if the SF community, if SF *writers*, did their bit, why we might actually get to *live* in our collective vision, we might actually be able to leave the mundacity of Earth and move into our dreamcastle in space, become the heroes and heroines of our own science fiction stories.

Fiction, however, even science fiction, is not written in a political and social vacuum, and in the 1970s and early 1980s, when the bulk of this stuff was being written, America was sliding into economic decline. The prosperous middle class was under financial and social pressure, most of the science fiction and space advocacy community came from that background, and so the collective utopian dream of the L-5 Colony also reflected the social and political longings of the beleaguered middle class.

So there was a sameness to most of these fictional L-5 Colonies, a sameness of more than technological framework, a sameness mirrored nicely in the title of Somtow Sucharitkul's "Mallworld" series, a uniformity of social vision epitomized, with weird appropriateness, by the closed society of "Todos Santos," the huge self-contained habitat in *Oath of Fealty* by Larry Niven and Jerry Pournelle.

Weird because Todos Santos is not an L-5 Colony but a kind of "Festung Los Angeles," a giant self-contained suburb-cum-fortress plunked down in the festering midst of a socially, politically, and economically degenerate future L.A.: "Mallworld" with a vengeance.

Appropriate because *Oath of Fealty* quite openly, and with sophisticated political consciousness, depicts the middle-class vision of a beleaguered technocratic utopia surrounded by lumpenproletarian social degeneracy that other writers placed in outer space.

It's all there in words of one syllable. Todos Santos is bright and clean and shiny and technologically up-to-date. It is a corporate utopia run with tight but unobtrusive security by dedicated technocrats. It is entirely self-contained, a pocket universe that, if fitted with artificial gravity and a life-support system and boosted out of the gravity well, would be rather indistinguishable from a space colony. No slums. No sleazy red-light districts. Openly designed as a safe, secure, rather antiseptic middle-class fortress. Even the name means "All Saints" in Spanish, as if to declare that lesser social beings need not apply.

Thus the outcome of this stage of science fiction's love affair with Butorism—a collective vision of bright, clean, ecologically, economically, and socially self-contained technocratic, middle-class suburbs in space, with no poor people, no streets gangs, no cockroaches, and no dogshit on the streets. Vast, spanking shopping malls and neat housing developments and no freeway gridlock between. All floating airily unconcerned above a Third World faevella called Earth.

Then came the cyberpunks.

While much as been written about Cyberpunk as a literary movement, the point here is that so-called cyberpunks like William Gibson, Bruce Sterling, and John Shirley share with their supposed opponents, so-called "humanists" like Kim Stanley Robinson, Michael Swanwick, and Walter Jon Williams, a new collective vision of space colonization that's quite different from that of the L-5 enthusiasts.

Take *eight* novels written in a mere four-year span by six writers with no other collective identity—*The Memory of Whiteness* and *Icehenge* by Kim Stanley Robinson, *Eclipse* by John Shirley, *Voice of the Whirlwind* by Walter Jon Williams, *Neuromancer* and *Count Zero* by William Gibson, *Schismatrix* by Bruce Sterling, and *Vacuum Flowers* by Michael Swanwick—all of which, viewed together, converge on quite a new collective conception of space colonization.

All of these works are set a century or three in the future. In most of them, the action wanders about a thoroughly colonized solar system. Gibson, Williams, and Swanwick emphasize artificial habitats while Robinson places a bit more emphasis on asteroids and satellites, and Shirley's extraterrestrial setting is confined to an Earth-orbiting city, but in all of these books, the terraformed surfaces of major planets do not hold the bulk of humanity's extraterrestrial population.

In some of these novels, the solar system is a patchwork of independent states, in some a patchwork of corporate fiefdoms, in others a complex political mélange of both, but in *none* of them does a system-wide government of any coherent sort prevail, nor does Earth dominate its far-flung sons and daughters.

Indeed, in most of these novels, Earth is either a backwater, a degenerate mess, a corporate battleground, or, in the case of *Vacuum Flowers*, even the homeland of a hive mind hostile to space-going man.

Aside from the shared vision of space, these are very different books by very different writers. In terms of style, theme, focus, politics, and aesthetics, these novels are about as similar as say, *Dr. Strangelove*, *Bug Jack Barron*, *The Handmaid's Tale*, *Failsafe*, and *On Wings of Song*, all of which are set in the United States in the relatively near future.

But since *their* similar future venues are all entirely imaginary, they reflect not extrapolation from a shared real political geography but the outline of a new emerging collective vision of the human future in space.

So far, that vision seems not unlike most of the futures depicted in the previous generation of novels in which space colonization was under the influence of the L-5 proposal.

But in most of these newer novels, Earth's gravity well, far from being something to simulate artificially, is something to escape from, and most of the characters would much prefer to live in a very low- or zero-g environment, which is seen as the next stage in human evolution, the equivalent of lungfish leaving the sea for the land, or our primate forebears descending from the ancestral trees.

And *these* space colonies are emphatically *not* spanking clean mallworlds; well-run, technocratic, middle-class suburban bastions reproduced in space, à la the collective vision inspired by Gerard O'Neil and the L-5 movement.

John Shirley's space city has a rigid class structure, a pre-revolutionary atmosphere, and all the neat, clean, well-maintained, middle-class stability of Jersey City or Beirut. Gibson extends a corporately balkanized Earthside culture seamlessly into space, along with its streetwise outlaw underbelly, and Williams does something similar.

Robinson's solar system is a thoroughly colonized and politically balkanized one, too, albeit a more positive and prosperous one, economically and especially aesthetically. It is a richly complex and baroque version of evolved solar man, rather than the decaying space city of Shirley or Gibson's corporate social darwinism.

Swanwick's solar system in *Vacuum Flowers* lies somewhere in between. Once again we have political balkanization and a profusion of space habitats—moons, asteroids, artificial worlds in clusters and clouds, even "dyson worlds" in the Oort Cloud. But while a good many of them are fetid slums and the majority of them are literally barnacled with the irksome vacuum flowers of the title, and none of them run with the antiseptic perfection of the ideal L-5 Colony, there is room inside for Robinson's high cultural style, too.

And Swanwick's space habitats have a decidedly organic flavor. The vacuum flowers were originally designed to soak up the inevitable leakage of air and garbage for efficient recycling and grew so out of control that hulls need continual scraping. Giant mutated trees fill the interior spaces of many of them by design, forming complex three-dimensional mazes, forests with winding trails and unplanned peripatetic villages. These habitats really *are* little worlds in space, with all the chaotic unplanned complexity of living ecologies.

Bruce Sterling also gives us a profusion of diverse artificial worlds and balkanized political complexity, through the ebb and flow of the fortunes of the two main human factions, the Mechs (cyborgers) and the Shapers (genetic engineers), until the crosscurrents finally create a mélange not merely of cultures but of "daughter species" so complex that almost any somatic variation is possible.

And that is Sterling's thematic point, the central point of the new collective image of the future of humanity's destiny as a space-going species, and what contrasts it so starkly to the technocratic middle-class utopias inspired by the L-5 movement. That given time, technology, genetic engineering, and the evolutionary impulse toward adaptation through diversity, the habitats we construct for ourselves in space—be they terraformed comets, asteroids, and moons or new man-made worlds—will sooner or later evolve into environments as ecologically complex, politically fragmented, and recomplicated as the so-called "natural realm," the mosaic of ecospheres, cultures, social classes, and ways of life we presently see on Earth.

If this new collective vision is a form of "Butorism," too, it is Butorism of a peculiarly paradoxical sort, different in kind, not merely in specific content, from the earlier version with its cookie cutter O'Neil Colonies, a vision that serves to renovate science fiction's hoary romantic promise of our solar system as the playpen of the infinite possible.

Way back when the Soviet and American space programs were only gleams in SF's collective eye, in the days of Edgar Rice Burroughs, Leigh Brackett, Jack Vance, Ray Bradbury, C. L. Moore, and company, the solar system was an Arabian Nights fantasy, replete with dying Martian civilizations, Venusian jungles, space pirates, Elder Races, an open-ended sense of wonder, and the promise of the infinitely possible in our own stellar backyard.

The pictures and data from real planetary probes banished all these baroque possibilities from our solar system in terms of science fictional plausibility and relegated the wonderful worlds just beyond our gravity well to the far stars, to a literary dreamworld not even our children were likely to reach.

Gerard O'Neil and his L-5 proposal gave us a new vision of our future within the solar system: a reachable, attainable vision of bright, clean, well-ordered artificial worlds in space, an escape from the ecological pollution, resource depletion, poverty, collectivism, and unseemly, unplanned, natural chaos of poor old Earth.

But in the light of the new emerging collective vision, we can see clearly enough that it was a pale shadow of what we seem to have lost.

In place of Barsoom and Venusburg and scantily clad catwomen on the moon, we were offered a middle-class, controlled, relentlessly suburban collective vision of our space-faring future—technocratic, enclosed, antiseptic, socially mean-spirited, reminiscent somehow of the bleak unadorned architectural futurism of the Bauhaus school, from which the romantic impulse and the organic sense of cultural ornamentation and social richness had been banished, along with ghettos, underclasses, countercultures, and interesting nightlife—a future in which pallid order reigned triumphant over tasty chaos, Velveeta on Wonder bread, rather than a ripe, runny brie messily smeared on crusty pumpernickel.

Cyberpunk was, among other things, a reaction against this well-ordered, denatured, inorganic, white middle class, essentially socially fascist vision of the future, of high technology as inherently the property of the ruling power structure, as an instrumentality of social and political control, as the servant of order.

No way, José, says Gibson in *Neuromancer* and *Count Zero*.

"The street finds its own uses for technology." Technology will not eliminate the sensibility of the street, of underclasses, ghettos, countercultures, and class struggle, say Shirley in *Eclipse* and Williams in *Hardwired* and *Voice of the Whirlwind*.

And it's not just a matter of street culture, Robinson demonstrates in *Icehenge* and *The Memory of Whiteness*. As technology advances, as we not only move out into the solar system but attain the ability to mold worlds entirely according to our own desire, our cultures—even on the highest levels—will become *more* baroque, not more simplified; more chaotic in a positive, aesthetic sense, not more predictably ordered and boring.

Nor must we necessarily lose our oldest source of environmental surprise, recomplication, and unpredictability, even in artificial space colonies, as Swanwick demonstrates in *Vacuum Flowers*: ongoing organic evolution itself.

We may genetically engineer the elements of closed artificial ecosystems, but precisely to the extent that they are successful—that they *do* cohere as self-contained ecosystems—will they develop the ability to mutate and adapt to the conditions of space habitations in ways we never predicted or intended. Even our designer organisms will find their own uses for technology, as Swanwick's "vacuum flowers" so powerfully demonstrate.

Indeed, as we see in *Schismatrix*, the advance of technology, the colonization of the solar system, the ability to construct worlds of any idiosyncratic design out of the void itself, and ultimately the power of human consciousness to redesign its own biological matrixes to whim and fashion, will in the end make us both the masters and creations of a new kind of evolution: human-created, faster, more diverse, and infinitely more complex and baroque than anything that has presently come into being on the surface of the Earth.

"The universe is not only stranger than we think, it is stranger than we *can* think," J. B. Priestly once declared.

How wrong he was! The endless diversity of environments we can create in space and the endlessly diverse self-created mutations of humanity we will turn ourselves into when we inhabit them will be stranger and more varied by far than anything in the so-called "natural realm."

Thus do the thesis of "cyberpunk" and the antithesis of "humanism" unite in the synthesis of science fiction's new collective vision of our multiplex, organic, futures in space, futures in which humanity evolves into a space-faring species in a far deeper sense, in which we not only create new living worlds, but evolve along with them.

Thus, too, its happy paradox. In a sense, many science fiction writers do seem to be taking Michel Butor's advice. They have come together to create a new collective dream of space. But this collective dream is not a vision of uniformity but of infinitely multiplexed diversity, not of order and control but of chaos and romanticism reborn.

A vision that gives us back the dream of the solar system as an Arabian Nights fantasy of the infinitely possible, of marvelous and terrifying lands just beyond Earth's gravity well, ours not merely to conquer but to create. A literary creation achievable not by the willful disregard of the scientific realities but through their imaginative utilization.

The street finds its own uses for technology.

So does science fiction.

And so does the process of evolution itself.

There will always be more things in the heavens above the Earth, Horatio, than are dreamt of by your philosophers.

Think of it as evolution in action.

The Software Plague

⊓⌐

JOHN PARK

Recently, I was a speaker at Loscon, the science fiction convention of the Los Angeles Science Fiction and Fantasy Society. One standard feature of SF conventions is the panel discussion, in which a couple of science fiction writers get together with a couple of experts and amuse an audience of readers and fans. Often writers aren't told what panels the convention authorities are putting them on: by assumption we're experts on everything, and if we're not, we ought to be.

Anyway, that's how I found myself sitting at a table with Dr. Judd Lundt of the UCLA prosthetics department, and Phyllis, a woman who has one of the latest model artificial arms, discussing the state of the art in modern prosthetics.

As to why they'd chosen me for this panel: Some years ago I wrote an article about efforts at Rockefeller University to decode the human brain's communication systems. The notion was, if they could figure out how your brain processes information coming in through your ears, it should be possible to connect up a gizmo that would squirt the knowledge in directly. I even made use of that concept in a novel (*Oath of Fealty* by Larry Niven and Jerry Pournelle). In my story, a city manager has a radio link computer interface implanted in his head and can thus directly communicate with the city's data banks.

There is *The Moon Is a Harsh Mistress* by Robert Heinlein; in that story the main character is actually better off by not having one of his biological arms. He keeps a crop of prostheses, each with specialized tools, such as finger/screwdriver in one, and a laser welding outfit in "the number 3 arm."

None of this has a bit to do with present day reality. The sad truth is that modern prosthetics look pretty good—Phyllis was happy with the appearance of hers, and indeed her employer didn't know for weeks that one of her arms wasn't natural—but there's not a lot of functionality there. Phyllis can raise and lower it, and the hand operates well enough that she can put a can of soda in it and close the fingers *en bloc*, after which she can manage to drink from the can pretty naturally, but anything much more complex than that just isn't in the cards. There's really nothing about Phyllis' arm that couldn't have been done ten years ago, and it's surely nothing like what the Six Million Dollar Man had.

Why isn't prosthetic technology better? "The Six Million Dollar Man" came on the air long enough ago that we were supposed to be impressed by what is now a pretty small amount of money, so we've had the idea for a long time. We've certainly had a number of developments in control equipment in the past few years. It would be no great trick to put a microchip and several servo motors on that arm, so that it could complete quite complex actions; but we haven't done any of that.

The problem is hardware and lack of research funds. For a while the Veterans Administration was deeply involved in prosthetics research, but for some reason has dropped out. Dr. Lund didn't want to say why. My speculation is that VA doesn't want to do research because if they develop better prosthetics they'll be expected to provide them to all the veteran amputees, and they don't have the budget to do that; but that's just a guess. What isn't a guess is that almost nobody is funding high-tech prosthetic research and development, and prosthetic devices are built one at a time, handmade, so there's no economy of scale in their construction.

That is a pity, because the potential payoff could be high, not just in increased comfort and functionality for amputees, but in technology for industrial use. After all, what a prosthetic device attached to a human can do, it can do at a remote distance as well—as for instance in an orbiting satellite, or deep in a mine, or in a hazardous waste dump. The fact is that the development of better prosthetics would lead directly to better . . . what? We really don't have a word for what I have in mind.

Imagine a mechanical man that looks much like a human being. It might have some specialized limbs; no need to limit it to the human shape which evolutionists tell us was derived from the starfish. It will probably have an on-board computer. What it won't have is a brain. Instead, the brain will be in a human being in a remote location.

What do we call that device? By convention, it's not a "robot," since that word implies something self-controlled. I've got Word Finder installed in my word processor, so let's see what synonyms it offers for robot.

There are two: "automation" and "android." My remote-controlled man is surely not an android, since that's generally understood to be a biological robot. Automaton doesn't quite fit either; and at 3:30 in the morning I don't seem to be up to coining a new word, which is a pity. Maybe I'll think of something later. Meanwhile, I think we ought to be inventing it.

The benefits could be considerable. In the first place, giving amputees replacement limbs isn't just an act of charity—or in the case of veterans: justice—it's also a good investment in increased productivity. As a simple business proposition, I suspect that the return in increased taxes and decreased welfare payments would more than match the R&D required.

A further return would be increased capability for telecommuting. We're already seeing small computers revolutionize office work; there's no reason

my idea can't have a similar effect on light industry.
It wouldn't even cost much.

In "The Software Plague," John Park takes us
even farther into the future of the human/machine
interface, to a time where computer evolution
forces us to compete with our own creations . . .

THE CLANG OF drowned bells and the prickle of cinnamon
gravel: I was hooked into the ship's sensors, listening to magnetic
fields and tasting cosmic rays, when Sheena's call came on line.
The implant in my cortex sounded a faint chime and switched me
to the navigation sensors. Over there, once more, was the glittering
tangle of the starship complex, there the pale fat pillow of Jupiter;
there lay Europa like a great fractured crystal ball, and somewhere
over my imaginary shoulder was the cruel stabbing point of the
sun. The implant hung a red circle around Dawson Base on Europa
to show me where the call was coming from, and then Sheena
appeared.

Just head and shoulders, her hair tied back, so that the streak
of grey above her left temple was hidden among the black. The
LED interface socket at her right temple was empty; for a moment
I wished she'd used wide-band transmission. With the implants
knitting into the synapses, wide-banding can be almost as good
as real sex—some people claim it's better. In any case, it's the
best you can do across twenty kiloklicks. But this wasn't the time.

She said, "You nearly through out there, Martin?"

"Just finishing Harley's data; it peaked four hours ago. Practically down to background again now. What's up?"

"I just got in from orbit. The backup for the communications
net is down—software problems. Dave called to tell you: he thinks
it's sabotage."

"Dave thinks metal fatigue and sunset and toothaches are sabotage. Why does he have to call me every time?"

"Be nice," she said. "And—we've got visitors."

"Oh yes? Who?"

"Surprise. And besides . . ."

"Yeah?"

"Miss you." She grinned. "Been dreaming of vampires
again."

So I cut short the rest of Harley's data, and went into my

nightflier mode. I spread my wings and planed through the eternal dark, watching the worlds turn about me and the stars hanging poised, and feeling just a little eternal myself.

With the ship parked at the orbital relay, I had to disconnect myself for the shuttle down to Europa. It's always disorienting, being penned in your own body again after your senses have been opened to the whole electromagnetic spectrum and more. The drop in free fall gave me time to adjust; and anyway, I didn't want to find myself addicted to using the implants.

The carways were less bright than usual when I made my way from the terminal; it took me a moment to realize that all the advertising holos were dark. Evidently the communications breakdown was more serious than I'd expected. And when I got into Number 2782 the IndiVid, which should have been ready to feed holos into our implants, was dead. Instead, the holo-vid was on, with a newscast from Earth showing riots and anti-tech demonstrations under smog-yellow skies. Sheena was curled up on the air-mat in front of it, but the wall screen was lit beside her. It was ablaze with enhanced stars and the immense glittering latticework of the starship construction bay, and I could tell from her posture and the look on her face that she wouldn't be awake to anything else. I watched her, then went over and took her hands. I whispered, "No, Sheena. It's not for us." We've got too many recessive genes; Sol is the only star we get to visit.

I studied her face as she turned to me. A broken dream transforming to quiet joy in the curve of a cheek, the smoothing of a brow. Her face was thin, with a straight nose and high cheekbones. That evening she was wearing the brown jump suit that matched her eyes, and some of our magic jewelry: antique carbon resistors and metal oxide capacitors strung together as bracelet and necklace. Her hair was loose and it billowed behind her in the flow from the air mat, silvered by the unreachable stars. I wasn't using the RAM option on the implant, but some things stay in the memory. Whenever I think of Sheena now, that's how I see her.

We had an hour to ourselves, to play; we used our new invention which produced modulated radio-frequency radiation to stimulate certain neuron-implant interfaces. The generators were hidden in the antique jewelry; feedback and modulation were provided through our implants. The effect was like a direct line to the pleasure center. Away from the two foci, though, the interference patterns played absolute hell with any unshielded electronics—including other implants—which is one reason why emitters at those frequencies are illegal on Europa. But we'd shielded our bedroom meticulously, and no one ever found out.

Afterwards I left to see Dave and his theories about the communications breakdown and to deliver Harley's data, while Sheena went to meet our still-secret guests.

I found Dave Stromberg hooked up to an interface bank in the back of the auxiliary communications room. While I waited for him to disconnect, I stood by the window and watched a group of steelworkers from the starship marching under the fluorescents on their way to the red light district. I decided I could cope with Dave's paranoia today, as long as he didn't start whining or insisting on calling me Mr. Juarez.

He unhooked and came over, smoothing his white smock, his red hair flopping over his eyes. "God, it's a mess in there. Bastards are starting to play rough. I couldn't even get in far enough to do a proper diagnosis. I'm glad you came, Mr. Juarez; you don't know—"

"Call me Martin, Dave. Now, just who d'you think is starting to play rough?"

"I don't know, do I? You're in the reserve Militia, not me. I can't do it all, Mr. Juarez. But if we don't stop them soon, the whole city's going to be one big software crash."

I sighed. It seemed everyone in Dawson was in the reserve Militia, with nothing to do because it all came to me. "What makes you so sure this isn't just another power bump or something?"

"Look at this." He showed me a holo of the circuit bank, filled with a tracery of red lines. "Look, the thing's tied itself in a knot. That doesn't just happen; someone fed a virus program into it. Only thing it could have been."

"You sure about that?"

"Of course," he said, tugging his sleeves straight, and I knew the whine was coming. "If only someone would listen to me, and tighten the defenses on the software. I've worked up codes that'll keep out anything on the market. Guaranteed. But they won't listen. They keep piling the whole system onto the same software base. They think I'm crazy. Just you, Mr. Juarez, you listen to me."

I swallowed a couple of things and said, "Dave, if this is sabotage, do you have anything that could give us a lead, any evidence at all?"

He frowned, gnawing his forefinger. "But it's so *obvious* someone's doing it . . . Yeah, I've got it: the way those latchings are used—it's like Amato-Singh's work."

"You mean the Mars traffic control program?" I said, managing to keep a straight face.

"They're like that, but the sequencing's different; someone who knows how to modify—"

The whine had gone again; he was starting to invoke the arcana of his art. I cut him off. "Okay, Dave, thanks. I'll see if I can get this checked out."

"Talk to them about my defenses, too, Mr. Juarez."

"Right, Dave."

I was sorry my patience with Dave had worn thin, but he had been finding sabotage and designing software defenses against it for so long that keeping him at arm's length was a reflex now. His holo of the circuit bank did not look peculiar, though.

After that I decided I didn't want to experience Harley as well just then, so I left a message with his cyber and went to find Sheena and our visitors.

The Arcade is the high-gravity quarter of Dawson; it's brought up to Earth normal by two old Blinc-Rigamonti generators, prototypes that hadn't tested out well enough in vacuum to meet the starship specs. The management charges three times a reasonable price for anything you do there, plus seventy-five a minute for using their gravity; but it's worth the cost just to keep in shape, for those of us who still think of going back.

Though Sheena had abandoned that dream for a less realizable one, she still wouldn't admit it to herself, and it was her idea to meet in Plato's Cave on the far side of the Arcade.

The cyber at the lock took my identifiche in its claw and passed it under its scanner. Its metal arm was still bright, and something in the way it moved suggested the whole cyber was new. I wondered briefly who it had been, and what he or she had been convicted of, or had died of. The cyber checked my prints, skin and breath analyses, and my implant code, then handed my fiche back. The lock rotated half a revolution and swung open.

I moved carefully through the gravity gradient at the entrance until my body had adjusted to full weight. Past the memorial fir trees in their hydroponics I came to the Square, where half a dozen steelyarders on two-year hitches at the starship were clustered around a news holo. They were identifiable by the lack of LED couplers in their temples, and by the way they watched the holo. It was showing the last stages in the trial of a hydroponics tech-

nician for embezzling air rations. Third offense. If—when—the
cybers computed him guilty, he would be carted off to the meat
shop, and the salvageable part of his brain turned into a useful
cyber. The steelyarders obviously knew about our justice, and
didn't like it; I could feel their eyes on my own LED coupler as
I walked past.

A grizzled man in plumber's green in need of a wash stumbled
across my path, his hands groping in front of him. He stopped
with a sudden grin, and his head swung from side to side as though
he were listening for something, while his eyes snapped back and
forth in some kind of scanning raster. Then he went on again. I
knew the symptoms. Going silicon, they called it, though the
implants were all bio-organic semiconductors and had been for
twenty years—which was why they could infiltrate the neural
circuitry and start to take over.

Past the Square was an old-fashioned Earth-type dark alley,
complete with garbage in the gutter and—this time—two fuel-tug
jockeys, both male, linked temple to temple by an optic cable,
and squirming together in electro-neuronic ecstasy.

One thing about the Arcade: you can be sure it's not going to
change much from month to month.

I reached the Cave, and found Sheena as I'd expected, sitting
by the starwindow, watching a fuel-scoop labor up from Jupiter,
loaded with light isotopes for the starship. Two people were sitting
opposite her: a blond young woman in a green jump suit—and
Victor Sixl. I had known him for seven years, but I hardly recognized him. He was thinner than I remembered, his hair was
tawny rather than red, and streaked with grey, and there were
more lines on his face than I had ever expected to see. His eyes
were sunken, and they held an expression I could not fathom.
Wanting to ask, "My God, what's been happening to you?" I
said, "Well, hi, Victor; it's been a hell of a long time."

He smiled broadly, transforming his face; then he jumped up
and shook hands with a sudden nervous intensity. Under his heavy
brows his eyes seemed to glitter.

"Three years, Martin," he said with a grin. "It's aged you.
Made you look mature."

"Thanks."

We sat down; he introduced Greensleeves as Frederika, and
explained that they had arrived on Europa three weeks earlier from
the Ultra Long-wave Telescope complex on Ceres, and had just
found out that we were here. "Thought you two were still ice-
fishing on Ganymede. Come on, the first bottle's on us. None of

that wine you kept trying to poison me with; this is a celebration."
So we punched for hard liquor at high-g prices. As we drank, I
noticed his eyes again: intense and constantly searching, while
Frederika's seemed to watch everything with ironic patience. He
turned to Sheena. "You still piloting that overgrown firecracker?"

"Arturo?" Sheena said with a grin. "Did Newton like apples?
Art's the last one around now, so I've no competition for spares
and I've taken options on all the solid booster production of the
four satellites. As long as there's someone to sell me fuel, and
Arturo holds together, I'll keep him running, you bet."

"It's good to know some things don't change. I bet you're still
a walking arsenal, too."

She took off her necklace. "This is the latest." I had thought
for a moment she was going to show him her half of our rf
generator, but instead she twisted open one of the fat megohm
resistors. It came apart and she put half on the table. After four
seconds it gave off a flash like a welding arc. When our eyes
adjusted again, there was just a blackened shell on the star-flecked
glass top. "Useful distraction in emergencies," said Sheena. "Or
for signaling—though I don't know where I'd be if I had to use
that to call for help. Actually it's just an ordinary photo-detonator
for blasting sticks, dolled up in that casing. It's perfectly safe."

Frederika nodded and smiled lazily, drawing the tip of one slim
finger down the condensation on her glass.

Victor was examining the necklace. "You always were a witch
with those things," he said, handing it back. "A real witch."

Sheena laughed. "No one's called me that for three years.
Martin says I'm a lost sea nymph; but then he's just a vampire in
disguise."

"Well," said Frederika, leaning towards me and toying with a
copper ankh at her throat, "he does look the part."

Victor turned from Sheena to me and then back. "You both
seem happy here," he said. "That's good, but have you ever
thought of leaving, moving outward?"

Sheena looked at him. "That might be interesting . . ."

"You mean to Titan?" I said. "From what I've heard they
don't have B-R generators there at any price. We'd never get
back."

"You're right about the generators," said Victor. "But they
also don't have trouble—yet."

Frederika nodded and leaned forward to fix me with ultramarine
eyes under long blond lashes. "We left ULT because the complex
was getting just too dangerous to live in. They had power failures

all the time. The computer would crash and cripple the whole station. We'd have to live without the air recyclers for ten hours. And one time all the thermostatting failed for a day.''

Victor leaned forward as well. "I tell you, Sheena, it's bad trouble back there, and it's coming from further in.''

"Sabotage?" I said for the second time in two hours. "Do you know who's doing it?''

"No, we don't." He turned his eyes on me. "Ah, you have suspicions too. Has it got this far already?''

"Just a few glitches, and some pretty vandalism," I said, not too convincingly.

"Perhaps you're still safe then," Victor said. "Let's drink to that.''

As we lowered our glasses, Sheena said, to break the mood, "Hey d'you remember that time on Ganymede when all the lights went out on number Eleven—?''

They both started laughing before she had finished the sentence, and then Victor started telling her about that time on Dione when . . . I stopped listening, and had another drink, remembering Dave and his fantasies, and wondering how safe we would all be in another three years.

We ordered more drinks. Frederika started telling me about Ceres, and how they'd spent the long voyage up to Jupiter. On the screen, the fuel-tug rendezvoused with its shuttle. By the time it had exchanged full tanks for empty, and dived back toward Jupiter for another load, Frederika was starting to describe some of the more interesting things she'd found to do in zero-g.

But by then Victor and Sheena were sitting at the same side of the table, and he was handing her a cassette cube, which she placed against the coupler in her temple and replayed. I saw her face change then; I saw the same expression I'd seen when I came in and found her by the wall screen. I wanted to say something, ask what was going on, but she'd turned to Victor with that look still on her face, and he was talking quietly and intensely to her, and she was all attention, and the glass in my hand came up to my mouth without my thinking about it.

Later I noticed they were whispering together the way spacemen did in the pulps when their radios had failed—helmets together to conduct the sound—except that I could see they weren't wearing helmets.

Soon after that I noticed how far Frederika's green jump suit had opened down the front.

We must all have kept drinking for a while, because the next thing I remember, it was dark, and I was upside down, but it didn't matter, because gravity was Europa normal again and I was half floating. Someone giggled, and I found I was struggling with the fastenings of the green jump suit. I realized the reason I was having difficulty was that she kept trying to string an optic cable between our temples, while I kept trying to stop her. She seemed to have her end of it secured, but it came free as she brought the other end towards my head, and then I got the last of the fastenings undone, and the cable went drifting away to a far corner of the room.

Much, much later, I was sprawled across my hammock, with my stomach contents indistinguishable from my brains, and alone. I spent some time trying to understand exactly what had happened, and then some more time wondering if I could move. Finally I pushed myself out of the hammock and found my way to the bathroom. When I came back, slightly more human, I noticed the length of optic cable coiled behind our herbarium. I picked it up. It wasn't a local product. Wincing, I made the implant adjust my eyes to read the maker's name etched onto its coupling boss. Van Strien. The name was vaguely familiar, but there was no reference to it in my hardware. I wrapped the cable around my hand, and closed my fist so that it made a knuckleduster, but I was just procrastinating; I didn't even know what I wanted to hit. So I threw the cable back into the corner and went next door to look for Sheena.

She was there, strapped at her work bench so that she could use both hands without floating away. She didn't speak or look up when I came in. I stood behind her, waiting, and finally muttered, "You've taken up sculpture again." She was bent over a block of brownish plastic, working on it with fast, nervous movements of a scalpel, and she went on as though she hadn't heard me. I was still feeling too sick to get mad, so I swallowed and put my hands on her shoulders. "Sheena. What is it?"

She stopped working abruptly, turned her head, and blinked. "It's going to be a pair of bookends," she said. "A souvenir for Victor. He's leaving, you know."

She turned and bent over the plastic again. "I've got to finish them."

She seemed to have forgotten I was there. I walked out, and heard the door click behind me.

I decided to take Harley his cosmic ray data. He had started going silicon months before; now he was almost incapable of getting outside, and he relied on people like me to supply data for his research projects. I found him curled up in his hammock, sucking synthavite from one of half a dozen squirt bulbs, while an optic cable snaked out of a mass of wiring and microprocessor cubes to his temple. After thirty seconds or so he noticed me.

"Harley," I said, "you look like hell."

His eyes flickered; he lifted one hand, and let it float down. "Yeah, suppose I do. Don't feel like hell, though. *You* look like hell; what's up? Hey—you got the numbers? That why you're here?"

"Right, Harley. But give me a diskpak. No way I'm messing with your synapses, man."

"Do you good," he said, "widen your outlook beyond the sins of the flesh." But he handed over the diskpak.

It's a peculiar, clinical sensation, interfacing with a machine; I still don't understand the attraction. I handed him the loaded cube and watched him devour the data. The change in his expression while he was hooked up made me uncomfortable. There was a kind of hunger in it that looked unpleasantly familiar. I didn't want that sort of need working on me or on anyone I cared about.

He took more than two minutes, and by the end I was looking for something to keep my mind occupied. He came out of it looking drained, and I handed him a coil of optic cable that had been lying beside me.

"Harley, is all this stuff made locally?"

He nodded, his mouth twitching, his eyes blinking independently. I glanced away from his face, and said, "A firm named Van Strien makes some; know anything about them?"

"Van Strien," he muttered, and from the way his eyes steadied, I could tell he was running a memory search. His hands jerked. "Yeah. Van Strien of Olympia—that's Mars, not the Big Tube— they make optical hardware. Stuff's pretty good for the price. Seventy klicks per dB at five hundred nanometers. But it's not worth the import cost if you're thinking of buying, Martin. I'm not paying you that much for mass spec data."

I shrugged. "Just curious. Saw the name on a piece of cable someone was showing me." One or two things were beginning to slot together in my mind, but they weren't making much sense yet.

I left Harley muttering and twitching in his own digitally enhanced universe again, and decided I'd better get hold of Victor and Frederika. I didn't know their address, but Sheena would have to. I found a call box with its *Operational* light still glowing, but when my call had wormed its way through a tangle of static, all I reached was our cyber telling me that Sheena was busy and could not be disturbed. Before I could set about overriding that, the static got worse, and the line died on me.

I thought about it, and decided I wasn't ready to go back and start a fight with Sheena, and that Dave was my next best bet.

I caught the shuttle car to the communications center, and found Dave at his desk, trying to cope with half a dozen crises at once.

"It's spreading," he muttered. "They're really flaying us now."

This time I didn't feel like smiling. "What's happening exactly?"

"Virus programs in half the network. I'm shutting down the sections one by one and sending a team in to clean them out. But it's spreading faster than we can keep up." He pointed to the holo array showing traffic in the parking orbit. "That's the only thing that's a hundred percent right now. If we can't stop the spread before I go off shift, I'm going to quarantine every piece of software in the Base, if it means shutting down the city for a week."

"Do you know where it's coming from?"

"Everywhere, nowhere, I don't know. Haven't you found anything, Mr. Juarez?"

"That's what I've come to see you about. Can you dig into arrival records and tell me where I can find one Victor Sixl, and a woman named Frederika something. Arrived three weeks ago."

He wiped his hair back from his eyes. "Christ, I don't even know if that much is still up." He plugged a cable into his temple, frowned, then shook his head and began keying commands into his desk console. After a few seconds he nodded. "Okay, here we are. Victor Sixl, Frederika von Mannheim"—he paused, staring at the screen—"arrived twenty-seventh from Phobos, with a stopover at Ceres ULT. Moved twice since they got here. Now at three-zero-one theta, sector four. You think they're the ones behind this, Mr. Juarez?"

He sounded anxious. I shook my head. "No, just some people who might give me some more clues. Thanks, Dave."

I caught the next car to sector four. Three-zero-one was closed and, when I used my Militia pass key, empty. They had moved again; I was less surprised than I might have been. I tried calling Sheena twice, got through for half a minute the second time, and met the same response from our cyber as before.

I had been on the return car for two minutes when it came to a dead stop, with all its cybers inactive, evidently as the result of a crash at the transit control. It took me five hours to work my way out of the transit tunnel, and then through corridors packed with angry steelyarders and closed by emergency doors for half an hour at a time, and get back to the communications center.

Dave had gone off shift two hours earlier, Marcie at the next desk told me. He'd been working for nineteen hours straight, and he'd just quarantined the system when his girlfriend came for him. When I raised my eyebrows, Marcie started to explain about the blond woman in green with the old-fashioned name. I'd hurriedly thanked her, and was turning to go looking for them, when I noticed what was on Dave's desk. Yes, Marcie said, they had been a present from that lady: she'd said he needed something to make the place look more friendly.

The present was a pair of brown plastic bookends, each carved in the shape of an amiable witch with two fat resistors under her arm.

It took me twenty minutes to get to Dave's apartment, and another two to convince myself he wasn't answering, and to use the Militia pass. For a moment I was certain I'd made a fool of myself; then my eyes adjusted to the dark, and I saw the two of them clearly. Dave was sprawled across a couch, bleeding from his face and neck, and he clutched one end of an optic cable in his left hand. Frederika was lying about two meters away from him. The cable was still at her temple, and she twitched when I closed the door.

I slapped skin-seal from the apartment's emergency kit over Dave's wounds, and gave him a transfusion.

As I pulled the needle out, his eyes flickered, then opened. "Worked, Mr. Juarez," he whispered; "my software defenses, they worked." He opened his right hand to show me a diskpak cube, and fainted again.

I hesitated, then took the cube and put it in my pocket and went to look at Frederika. One of her eyes jerked, tracking me; the other hunted at random. Her jaw quivered as I approached. Then her hand twitched, and I saw scalpel tips flicker from under her fingernails. From her lips came a sound like the buzz of an idling machine. I swallowed and backed away.

After I had got medical attention for Dave, I went back to see Harley. He was still curled up in his hammock, wired into his hardware.

"Harley," I said, "I want you to tell me about virus programs. What happened to Amato-Singh's work on Mars? What makes people go silicon?"

"Say, Martin, it's you again, is it?" He returned to my reality slowly. "Ask me one at a time, okay? I can't do more than one at a time, Martin."

"Okay, let's start with virus programs. You feed them into a computer, and they take it over, control its software. They're weapons, right?"

"Now they are; but when they started out, they were just a way of making best use of whatever hardware was free at the moment."

"Okay, but now they're weapons. Who makes them?"

"You want a list? It'll be out of date by the time I give it to you."

"Who makes them on Mars?"

"Lots of people." His eyes flickered, steadied. "You know what happened to Syrtis?"

"No."

"That's right. Nobody does. No one's supposed to know anything happened, but it just vanished off the map for six days as far as communications were concerned. But the word is that someone was developing Amato-Singh's codes into weapons software there."

"Okay. That fits. Now, the other end of the thing. Could there be a program that alters the behavior of our implants, that makes them start to take over the user?"

"Now there's a funny thing. No one here knows what factors make someone like me amenable and you not. Plenty of ideas, but no real data. But I know three groups were doing research on that five years ago; two of them on Mars. So either they've all failed to make one iota of progress since then, or they're not being allowed to publish. I know which one I'd believe."

"Right," I said. "Okay, now put it all together. Could we have a virus program that takes over the implant, and makes that take over the carrier, turns him into an agent—a vector that passes the virus to others and infects any software around? Because if there could be such a thing, Harley, we may have a plague on our hands."

He considered, and was starting to speak when we heard the explosion.

I shoved him back into his hammock and dashed to the communications center; I got there in time to get several lungfuls of smoke helping to get the fire under control and the wounded out. The last part of the center which had been working fully, the orbital traffic monitor, was going to be down for two or three days. It took me a minute to realize what that meant, and then I took the first working car home.

Sheena had gone, of course.

I walked around the apartment cursing my stupidity. I was only reserve Militia, and no one on Europa had any real experience of major crime. But that didn't help.

I looked at her workroom. It was the same room it had always been, and yet it would never be the same again. Tools and ICs were scattered across the workbench. Holos of Vesuvius, Fuji, Olympus on the side wall. Half a dozen music cubes among the tree-fern pots. I picked up one of the cubes. *Four-D Damnation* by Möhwald and the Wolf Pack. It had come out when we were both in the tunneling teams on Ganymede—when we'd met. We still kept playing it, though neither of us liked the piece very much. I opened my fingers and wished there was enough gravity to smash the cube on the edge of the bench; it merely glanced off with a faint click and floated to the floor, and left me still wondering what else I could have done, what I was going to do for the rest of my time in Dawson, and why I had to stand there in that unbearable room.

The cube had landed among some curls of brown plastic from Sheena's carving. I bent and picked one up, touched it to my tongue.

In some sense I'd known what it was ever since I'd smelt the smoke in the communications center, but I'd been ignoring the knowledge, because I hadn't wanted to think about what must have happened to Sheena's mind to make her carve solid booster fuel into a bomb.

Now I realized that was how I'd find her again. I recorded a report for Henriksen of Security, started to feed it to his cyber, then realized what I was doing and made my way to his office. There I eventually found a pen and some paper, and left a longhand summary on his desk. Then I climbed to the departure lock and waited for an orbital shuttle.

Drowned bells and cinnamon gravel. I was looking for something other than cosmic rays this time, and I adjusted the settings of the mass spectrometer. I found the salty drizzle of caesium ions from the thrusters of transfer ships, and then I found what I wanted. Carbon dioxide, metal particles, ice, and soot with absorbed organics: I could track the exhaust from Sheena's boosters, and even estimate the thrust vector from the intensity distribution. I spread my wings and set out after them. For two hours I followed the trail; they seemed to be in a transfer orbit for Ganymede, but were still burning fuel. The radar was a clutter of space junk without an identifiable echo. Finally I detected a burst of power, a course change. I lost the trail for half an hour, burned docking fuel to backtrack, found it again, and twenty minutes later I was sure where they were heading.

I examined Dave's defense cube and made what preparations I could, and five hours later was putting out grapples to dock at the starship bay.

The kliegs and welding arcs were dead; the scaffolding seemed deserted, and most of the personnel craft had gone. I could see Sheena's ship pulled in against the cylindrical service dock. Otherwise there was just the dark lattice of the scaffolding and the cetacean bulk of the starship itself. I guessed that they'd had computer trouble too, and had cleared the site until it was sorted out.

In response to my Militia call sign, a passenger tube was extruded and mated to my air-lock. I checked that I was as ready as I could be and climbed into it.

The official who met me seemed genuine enough. He pointed out that the site was undergoing a Class Three emergency, and while I could not be required to leave since I had Militia authority, I would be there at my own risk. He checked my fiche with a cyber, and then said that as there were not likely to be any more visitors, he would be glad to accompany me in my investigations.

His eyes were moving independently.

"No," I said; "I don't want to put you to any trouble."

He followed me to the exit. "I must insist." When I turned, there was a pistol in his hand.

"Thought you people were strictly software," I said. "You sure you know how to handle that?"

He ignored that and waved me into a storage hold. Victor was there with four others, and a mass of electronics. The five were all enmeshed in wiring. Their eyes were open, but they did not appear to see me. Then Victor stirred; his eyes focused; he stripped the cable from his temple, freed himself of a tangle of wires, and came toward me. "Martin," he said, "I'm glad it was you who came."

I said half-truthfully: "You realize of course that the head of Security knows I'm searching for you. If I don't report back in thirty minutes, the alarm will go out and they'll come looking. They'll have a platoon of riot troops here within twenty-four hours."

"I'm sure you're right," Victor said. "But we won't be here by then. Nor will most of this."

I didn't say anything. I knew what a kilo of rocket fuel could do as an explosive; they had a ton of it in Sheena's ship.

He saw my expression. "You don't understand, Martin. Yes, we destroy, but we are fighting for our existence. We are the hunted; your kind is the hunter. I'm not being figurative: there are men from the inner worlds seeking us now. If we didn't take this course, it would be only a matter of time before we were identified and destroyed. As it is, we have saved ourselves as individuals, and helped preserve our race. If Europa and the other worlds we have seeded do survive, it will be as our colonies. Then, perhaps, we may return."

I said, "You've just explained why we hunt you."

"You find me callous? I find you ridiculous. You and your kind hold the greatest evolutionary advance since the flint hand-axe, literally in your heads, and you treat it as a toy—those of you who aren't too afraid to use it at all. You're still the same death-haunted creatures that daubed the Lascaux caves. Why should I care for such a race, even if it did not hate me? Our survival now depends on abandoning the past. It is regrettable, but you have forced us to it. Instead, we have embraced the future, let it change us. And it has made us immortal."

He gestured to the banks of electronics. "We can inhabit a matrix of semi-conductors as comfortably as that complex of fats and proteins we were born into. In a few hours we shall do so. Yet our perceptions will be wider than any possible for either flesh or machine alone. We are what you have turned back from, Martin, and you are paying a greater price in knowledge and intelligence— in wisdom—than you can hope to comprehend. That shell of a starship is not ready for human occupants, but it is already sufficient for our needs. We will destroy here what we cannot use, but with that ship and its tanks of helium as refrigerant, we will be free to explore our own natures until the solar system is fit to receive us."

"They'll come after you; they'll want that ship."

"They have enough chaos of their own to deal with at the moment," he said. "And besides, you will be here to misdirect and delay them. I assure you, you will be eager to do so."

Now we were getting to the point. "You'll have to damage me beyond repair if you want to get that program into me," I said. "I'll fight anyone who comes near."

Victor nodded, and one of the others freed himself and went

behind the array of electronics. He came back leading Sheena.

"You've gone pale, Martin," Victor said. "Are you afraid?"

"No," I said thickly, "not afraid."

"I assure you, she's unharmed. Once she is through the incubation period, she will be fully one of us, and we have enough facilities on the starship to help her through the hardest phase. You yourself will be helping her now. In its early stages, the program demands to be transmitted. Failure to do so becomes quite distressing to the carrier. Or do you intend to fight her too?"

Before I could move, the man who had brought me seized my arms from behind. Victor produced a length of optic cable, and Sheena came toward me. I could still have twisted, bitten and kicked—but not without hurting her.

The connections were made to our temples, and the circuit opened between us. I was aware of darkness, and a threat.

"Sheena," I whispered.

The darkness eddied, thickened. Something was creeping toward me.

"Sheena, it's me."

"Martin." Her voice was thin and remote, like a worn-out recording. "I tried to stop it."

"I know," I said. "It's all right."

The thing in the dark reached out.

"I can't hold it back, Martin. I'm sorry. I'm so sorry."

"It's all right. Just follow me."

As Dave's defense programs met the intruder in a burst of crimson, I twisted the control on my half of our rf generator. Sheena swayed as the counterattack shocked her through the implant, but her fingers went to the silvery capacitor at the center of her necklace. She twisted it and fell forward, and I ripped the cable from her temple and caught her in my arms as the world blew up in rainbow fire.

I held her and shivered and wept, and felt her shivering against me as the modulations passed between us. For a moment I could believe that nothing had changed since the previous evening when I had found her watching the wall screen. Then I became aware of the others, thrown into convulsions by the induction field. I lowered Sheena to the ground and turned to see the official with the gun trying to rise to his knees and make his fingers close on the butt of the weapon. I kicked him under the jaw and took the gun away.

Victor got to his feet, took two steps toward me, and fell again. I went and grabbed him by the hair.

"Victor! Can you hear me?"

"Turn it off."

"Not yet."

"I can't tell you where we came from. None of us can. It's blocked. Turn it off."

"That's not what I want," I said. "How can I stop what's happening to her? How do I get her back?"

"You can't. She's one of us. The program will destroy her if you try to cancel it. Turn it off. You're too late."

"Am I?" I carried Sheena to the door, made sure the rf generators had enough power to run for several hours, and threw them back into the storage bay. Then I ran with her to the airlock.

I got Sheena back to Europa, and Henriksen finally sent over a ship to collect what was left of the saboteurs. But Victor was right. It was too late for her. In the next weeks I watched the program take over the rest of her mind. Dave's software enabled us to clean up the mess in Dawson before it got much worse. Most of the carriers wound up as cybers, but all Security ever extracted from any of them about where the program had come from, or why, was the name Helsing. Henriksen swears he'll track down this Helsing, whoever he is, and make him pay, and I'm sure he will. Unless I find him first.

It needed some wire-pulling, but I got Sheena's brain out of Dawson. I had her cleared for the starship and wired into the sensor bank. Since then the ship had been completed, named the *Gilgamesh*, and fueled for its voyage. Tomorrow its trials will be complete and it goes into transfer orbit, and after that, I'll have no more reason to stay here. I'll terminate my contract and take the next light-clipper to Phobos. But I'll watch until the starship is out of sight, and pray that somewhere behind the crystal eyes and metal nerves, among the semiconductors and the cyberprotein, there is still the ghost of an awareness that once ached for such a journey through night to the infinite stars.

Blindsight

ROBERT SILVERBERG

Robert Silverberg is one of the finest prose styl-
ists writing science fiction today. However, Bob can
do more than write elegant prose: he can shock,
delight, surprise and—most importantly—enter-
tain.

THAT'S MY MARK, Juanito told himself. That one, there. That
one for sure.

He stared at the new dinkos coming off the midday shuttle from
Earth. The one he meant to go for was the one with no eyes at
all, blank from brow to bridge of nose, just the merest suggestions
of shadowy pits below the smooth skin of the forehead. As if the
eyes had been erased, Juanito thought. But in fact they had probably never been there in the first place. It didn't look like a retrofit
gene job, more like a prenatal splice.

He knew he had to move fast. There was plenty of competition.
Fifteen, twenty couriers here in the waiting room, gathering like
vultures, and they were some of the best: Ricky, Lola, Kluge.
Nattathaniel. Delilah. Everybody looked hungry today. Juanito
couldn't afford to get shut out. He hadn't worked in six weeks,
and it was time. His last job had been a fast-talking, fancy-dancing
Hungarian, wanted on Commonplace and maybe two or three other
satellite worlds for dealing in plutonium. Juanito had milked that
one for all it was worth, but you can milk only so long. The
newcomers learn the system, they melt in and become invisible,

131

and there's no reason for them to go on paying. So then you have to find a new client.

"Okay," Juanito said, looking around challengingly. "There's mine. The weird one. The one with half a face. Anybody else want him?"

Kluge laughed and said, "He's all yours, man."

"Yeah," Delilah said, with a little shudder. "All yours." That saddened him, her chiming in like that. It had always disappointed Juanito that Delilah didn't have his kind of imagination. "Christ," she said. "I bet he'll be plenty trouble."

"Trouble's what pays best," Juanito said. "You want to go for the easy ones, that's fine with me." He grinned at her and waved at the others. "If we're all agreed, I think I'll head downstairs now. See you later, people."

He started to move inward and downward along the shuttle-hub wall. Dazzling sunlight glinted off the docking module's silvery rim, and off the Earth shuttle's thick columnar docking shaft, wedged into the center of the module like a spear through a doughnut. On the far side of the wall the new dinkos were making their wobbly way past the glowing ten-meter-high portrait of El Supremo and on into the red fiberglass tent that was the fumigation chamber. As usual, they were having a hard time with the low gravity. Here at the hub it was one-sixteenth-g, max.

Juanito always wondered about the newcomers, why they were here, what they were fleeing. Only two kinds of people ever came to Valparaiso, those who wanted to hide and those who wanted to seek. The place was nothing but an enormous spacegoing safe house. You wanted to be left alone, you came to Valparaiso and bought yourself some privacy. But that implied that you had done something that made other people not want to let you alone. There was always some of both going on here, some hiding, some seeking, El Supremo looking down benignly on it all, raking in his cut. And not just El Supremo.

Down below, the new dinkos were trying to walk jaunty, to walk mean. But that was hard to do when you were keeping your body all clenched up as if you were afraid of drifting into mid-air if you put your foot down too hard. Juanito loved it, the way they were crunching along, that constipated shuffle of theirs.

Gravity stuff didn't ever bother Juanito. He had spent all his life out here in the satellite worlds and he took it for granted that the pull was going to fluctuate according to your distance from the hub. You automatically made compensating adjustments, that was all. Juanito found it hard to understand a place where the gravity would be the same everywhere all the time. He had never set foot on Earth or any of the other natural planets, didn't care to, didn't expect to.

The guard on duty at the quarantine gate was an android. His name, his label, whatever it was, was something like Velcro Exxon. Juanito had seen him at this gate before. As he came up close the android glanced at him and said, "Working again so soon, Juanito?"

"Man has to eat, no?"

The android shrugged. Eating wasn't all that important to him, most likely. "Weren't you working that plutonium peddler out of Commonplace?"

Juanito said, smiling, "What plutonium peddler?"

"Sure," said the android. "I hear you."

He held out his waxy-skinned hand and Juanito put a fifty-callaghano currency plaque in it. The usual fee for illicit entry to the customs tank was only thirty-five callies, but Juanito believed in spreading the wealth, especially where the authorities were concerned. They didn't *have* to let you in here, after all. Some days more couriers showed up than there were dinkos, and then the gate guards had to allocate. Overpaying the guards was simply a smart investment.

"Thank you kindly," the android said. "Thank you very much." He hit the scanner override. Juanito stepped through the security shield into the customs tank and looked around for his mark.

The new dinkos were being herded into the fumigation chamber now. They were annoyed about that—they always were—but the guards kept them moving right along through the puffy bursts of pink and green and yellow sprays that came from the ceiling nozzles. Nobody got out of customs quarantine without passing through that chamber. El Supremo was paranoid about the entry of exotic microorganisms into Valparaiso's closed-cycle ecology. El Supremo was paranoid about a lot of things. You didn't get to be sole and absolute ruler of your own little satellite world, and stay that way for thirty-seven years, without a heavy component of paranoia in your makeup.

Juanito leaned up against the great curving glass wall of the customs tank and peered through the mists of sterilizer fog. The rest of the couriers were starting to come in now. Juanito watched them singling out potential clients. Most of the dinkos were signing up as soon as the deal was explained, but as always a few were shaking off help and setting out by themselves. Cheapskates, Juanito thought. Assholes and wimps, Juanito thought. But they'd find out. It wasn't possible to get started on Valparaiso without a courier, no matter how sharp you thought you were. Valparaiso was a free enterprise zone, after all. If you knew the rules, you were pretty much safe from all harm here forever. If not, not.

Time to make the approach, Juanito figured.

It was easy enough finding the blind man. He was much taller than the other dinkos, a big burly man some thirty-odd years old, heavy bones, powerful muscles. In the bright glaring light his blank forehead gleamed like a reflecting beacon. The low gravity didn't seem to trouble him much, nor his blindness. His movements along the customs track were easy, confident, almost graceful.

Juanito sauntered over and said, "I'll be your courier, sir. Juanito Holt." He barely came up to the blind man's elbow.

"Courier?"

"New arrival assistance service. Facilitate your entry arrangements. Customs clearance, currency exchange, hotel accommodations, permanent settlement papers if that's what you intend. Also special services by arrangement."

Juanito stared up expectantly at the blank face. The eyeless man looked back at him in a blunt straight-on way, what would have been strong eye contact if the dinko had had eyes. That was eerie. What was even eerier was the sense Juanito had that the eyeless man was seeing him clearly. For just a moment he wondered who was going to be controlling whom in this deal.

"What kind of special services?"

"Anything else you need," Juanito said.

"Anything?"

"Anything. This is Valparaiso, sir."

"Mmm. What's your fee?"

"Two thousand callaghanos a week for the basic. Specials are extra, according."

"How much is that in Capbloc dollars, your basic?"

Juanito told him.

"That's not so bad," the blind man said.

"Two weeks minimum, payable in advance."

"Mmm," said the blind man again. Again that intense eyeless gaze, seeing right through him. "How old are you?" he asked suddenly.

"Seventeen," Juanito blurted, caught off guard.

"And you're good, are you?"

"I'm the best. I was born here. I know everybody."

"I'm going to be needing the best. You take electronic hand-shake?"

"Sure," Juanito said. This was too easy. He wondered if he should have asked three kilocallies a week, but it was too late now. He pulled his flex terminal from his tunic pocket and slipped his fingers into it. "Unity Callaghan Bank of Valparaiso. That's code 22–44–66, and you might as well give it a default key, because it's the only bank here. Account 1133, that's mine."

The blind man donned his own terminal and deftly tapped the number pad on his wrist. Then he grasped Juanito's hand firmly in his until the sensors overlapped, and made the transfer of funds. Juanito touched for confirm and a bright green $+cl.\ 4000$ lit up on the screen in his palm. The payee's name was Victor Farkas, out of an account in the Royal Amalgamated Bank of Liechtenstein.

"Liechtenstein," Juanito said. "That's an Earth country?"

"Very small one. Between Austria and Switzerland."

"I've heard of Switzerland. You live on Liechtenstein?"

"No," Farkas said. "I bank there. *In* Liechtenstein, is what Earth people say. Except for islands. Liechtenstein isn't an island. Can we get out of this place now?"

"One more transfer," Juanito said. "Pump your entry software across to me. Baggage claim, passport, visa. Make things much easier for us both, getting out of here."

"Make it easier for you to disappear with my suitcase, yes. And I'd never find you again, would I?"

"Do you think I'd do that?"

"I'm more profitable to you if you don't."

"You've got to trust your courier, Mr. Farkas. If you can't trust your courier, you can't trust anybody at all on Valparaiso."

"I know that," Farkas said.

Collecting Farkas' baggage and getting him clear of the customs tank took another half an hour and cost about 200 callies in mis-cellaneous bribes, which was about standard. Everyone from the baggage-handling androids to the cute, snotty teller at the currency-exchange booth had to be bought. Juanito understood that things didn't work that way on most worlds; but Valparaiso, he knew, was different from most worlds. In a place where the chief industry was the protection of fugitives, it made sense that the basis of the economy would be the recycling of bribes.

Farkas didn't seem to be any sort of fugitive, though. While he was waiting for the baggage Juanito pulled a readout on the software that the blind man had pumped over to him and saw that Farkas was here on a visitor's visa, six week limit. So he was a seeker, not a hider. Well, that was okay. It was possible to turn a profit working either side of the deal. Running traces wasn't Juanito's usual number, but he figured he could adapt.

The other thing that Farkas didn't seem to be was blind. As they emerged from the customs tank he turned and pointed back at the huge portrait of El Supremo and said, "Who's that? Your President?"

"The Defender, that's his title. The Generalissimo. El Supremo, Don Eduardo Callaghan." Then it sank in and Juanito said, blinking, "Pardon me. You can *see* that picture, Mr. Farkas?"

"In a manner of speaking."

"I don't follow. Can you see or can't you?"

"Yes and no."

"Thanks a lot, Mr. Farkas."

"We can talk more about it later," Farkas said.

Juanito always put new dinkos in the same hotel, the San Bernardito, four kilometers out from the hub in the rim community of Cajamarca. "This way," he told Farkas. "We have to take the elevator at C Spoke."

Farkas didn't seem to have any trouble following him. Every now and then Juanito glanced back, and there was the big man three or four paces behind him, marching along steadily down the corridor. No eyes, Juanito thought, but somehow he can see. He definitely can see.

The four-kilometer elevator ride down C Spoke to the rim was spectacular all the way. The elevator was a glass-walled chamber inside a glass-walled tube that ran along the outside of the spoke, and it let you see everything: the whole great complex of wheels within wheels that was the Earth-orbit artificial world of Valparaiso, the seven great structural spokes radiating from the hub to the distant wheel of the rim, each spoke bearing its seven glass-and-aluminum globes that contained the residential zones and business sectors and farmlands and recreational zones and forest reserves. As the elevator descended—the gravity rising as you went down, climbing toward an Earth-one pull in the rim towns—you had a view of the sun's dazzling glint on the adjacent spokes, and an occasional glimpse of the great blue belly of Earth filling up the sky a hundred fifty thousand kilometers away, and the twinkling hordes of other satellite worlds in their nearby orbits, like a swarm of jellyfish dancing in a vast black ocean. That was what everybody who came up from Earth said: "Like jellyfish in the ocean." Juanito didn't understand how a fish could be made out of jelly, or how a satellite world with seven spokes looked anything like a fish of any kind, but that was what they all said.

Farkas didn't say anything about jellyfish. But in some fashion or other he did indeed seem to be taking in the view. He stood close to the elevator's glass wall in deep concentration, gripping the rail, not saying a thing. Now and then he made a little hissing sound as something particularly awesome went by outside. Juanito studied him with sidelong glances. What could he possibly see? Nothing seemed to be moving beneath those shadowy places where his eyes should have been. Yet somehow he was seeing out of that broad blank stretch of gleaming skin above his nose. It was damned disconcerting. It was downright weird.

The San Bernardito gave Farkas a rim-side room, facing the stars. Juanito paid the hotel clerks to treat his clients right. That was something his father had taught him when he was just a kid who wasn't old enough to know a Schwarzchild singularity from an ace in the hole. "Pay for what you're going to need," his father kept saying. "Buy it and at least there's a chance it'll be there when you have to have it." His father had been a revolutionary in Central America during the time of the Empire. He would have been Prime Minister if the revolution had come out the right way. But it hadn't.

"You want me to help you unpack?" Juanito said.

"I can manage."

"Sure," Juanito said.

He stood by the window, looking at the sky. Like all the other satellite worlds, Valparaiso was shielded from cosmic ray damage and stray meteoroids by a double shell filled with a three-meter-thick layer of lunar slag. Rows of V-shaped apertures ran down the outer skin of the shield, mirror-faced to admit sunlight but not hard radiation; and the hotel had lined its rooms up so each one on this side had a view of space through the V's. The whole town of Cajamarca was facing darkwise now, and the stars were glittering fiercely.

When Juanito turned from the window he saw that Farkas had hung his clothes neatly in the closet and was shaving—methodically, precisely—with a little hand-held laser.

"Can I ask you something personal?" Juanito said.

"You want to know how I see."

"It's pretty amazing, I have to say."

"I don't see. Not really. I'm just as blind as you think I am."

"Then how—"

"It's called blindsight," Farkas said. "Proprioceptive vision."

"What?"

Farkas chuckled. "There's all sorts of data bouncing around that doesn't have the form of reflected light, which is what your eyes see. A million vibrations besides those that happen to be in the visual part of the electromagnetic spectrum are shimmering in this room. Air currents pass around things and are deformed by what they encounter. And it isn't only the air currents. Objects have mass, they have heat, they have—the term won't make any sense to you—*shapeweight*. A quality having to do with the interaction of mass and form. Does that mean anything to you? No, I guess not. Look, there's a lot of information available beyond what you can see with eyes, if you want it. I want it."

"You use some kind of machine to pick it up?" Juanito asked.

Farkas tapped his forehead. "It's in here. I was born with it."

"Some kind of sensing organ instead of eyes?"

"That's pretty close."

"What do you see, then? What do things look like to you?"

"What do they look like to you?" Farkas said. "What does a chair look like to you?"

"Well, it's got four legs, and a back—"

"What does a leg look like?"

"It's longer than it is wide."

"Right." Farkas knelt and ran his hands along the black tubular legs of the ugly little chair beside the bed. "I touch the chair, I feel the shape of the legs. But I don't see leg-shaped shapes."

"What then?"

"Silver globes that roll away into fat curves. The back part of the chair bends double and folds into itself. The bed's a bright pool of mercury with long green spikes coming up. You're six blue spheres stacked one on top of another, with a thick orange cable running through them. And so on."

"Blue?" Juanito said. "Orange? How do you know anything about colors?"

"The same way you do. I call one color blue, another one orange. I don't know if they're anything like your blue or orange, but so what? My blue is always blue for me. It's different from the color I see as red and the one I see as green. Orange is always orange. It's a matter of relationships. You follow?"

"No," Juanito said. "How can you possibly make sense out

of anything? What you see doesn't have anything to do with the
real color or shape or position of anything.''

Farkas shook his head. ''Wrong, Juanito. For me, what I see
is the real shape and color and position. It's all I've ever known.
If they were able to retrofit me with normal eyes now, which I'm
told would be less than fifty-fifty likely to succeed and tremen-
dously risky besides, I'd be lost trying to find my way around in
your world. It would take me years to learn how. Or maybe
forever. But I do all right, in mine. I understand, by touching
things, that what I see by blindsight isn't the 'actual' shape. But
I see in consistent equivalents. Do you follow? A chair always
looks like what I think of as a chair, even though I know that
chairs aren't really shaped anything like that. If you could see
things the way I do it would all look like something out of another
dimension. It *is* something out of another dimension, really. The
information I operate by is different from what you use, that's all.
And the world I move through looks completely different from
the world that normal people see. But I do see, in my own way.
I perceive objects and establish relationships between them, I make
spatial perceptions, just as you do. Do you follow, Juanito? Do
you follow?''

Juanito considered that. How very weird it sounded. To see the
world in funhouse distortions, blobs and spheres and orange cables
and glimmering pools of mercury. Weird, very weird. After a
moment he said, ''And you were born like this?''

''That's right.''

''Some kind of genetic accident?''

''Not an accident,'' Farkas said quietly. ''I was an experiment.
A master gene-splicer worked me over in my mother's womb.''

''Right,'' Juanito said. ''You know, that's actually the first
thing I guessed when I saw you come off the shuttle. This has to
be some kind of splice effect, I said. But why . . . why . . .'' He
faltered. ''Does it bother you to talk about this stuff?''

''Not really.''

''Why would your parents have allowed—''

''They didn't have any choice, Juanito.''

''Isn't that illegal? Involuntary splicing?''

''Of course,'' Farkas said. ''So what?''

''But who would do that to—''

''This was in the Free State of Kazakhstan, which you've never
heard of. It was one of the new countries formed out of the Soviet
Union, which you've also probably never heard of, after the
Breakup. My father was Hungarian consul at Tashkent. He was

killed in the Breakup and my mother, who was pregnant, was volunteered for the experiments in prenatal genetic surgery then being carried out in that city under Chinese auspices. A lot of remarkable work was done there in those years. They were trying to breed new and useful kinds of human beings to serve the new republic. I was one of the experiments in extending the human perceptual range. I was supposed to have normal sight plus blind-sight, but I didn't quite work out that way.''

"You sound very calm about it," Juanito said.

"What good is getting angry?"

"My father used to say that too," Juanito said. "Don't get angry, get even. He was in politics, the Central American Empire. When the revolution failed he took sanctuary here."

"So did the surgeon who did my prenatal splice," Farkas said. "Fifteen years ago. He's still living here."

"Of course," Juanito said, as everything fell into place.

"The man's name is Wu Fang-shui," Juanito said. "He'd be about seventy-five years old, Chinese, and that's all I know, except there'll be a lot of money in finding him. There can't be that many Chinese on Valparaiso, right?"

"He won't still be Chinese," Kluge said.

Delilah said, "He might not even still be a he."

"I've thought of that," said Juanito. "All the same, it ought to be possible to trace him."

"Who you going to use for the trace?" Kluge asked.

Juanito gave him a steady stare. "Going to do it myself."

"You?"

"Me, myself. Why the hell not?"

"You never did a trace, did you?"

"There's always a first," Juanito said, still staring.

He thought he knew why Kluge was poking at him. A certain quantity of the business done on Valparaiso involved finding people who had hidden themselves here and selling them to their pursuers, but up till now Juanito had stayed away from that side of the profession. He earned his money by helping dinkos go underground on Valparaiso, not by selling people out. One reason for that was that nobody yet had happened to offer him a really profitable trace deal; but another was that he was the son of a former fugitive himself. Someone had been hired to do a trace on his own father seven years back, which was how his father had come to be assassinated. Juanito preferred to work the sanctuary side of things.

He was also a professional, though. He was in the business of providing service, period. If he didn't find the runaway gene surgeon for Farkas, somebody else would. And Farkas was his client. Juanito felt it was important to do things in a professional way.

"If I run into problems," he said, "I might subcontract. In the meanwhile I just thought I'd let you know, in case you happened to stumble on a lead. I'll pay finders' fees. And you know it'll be good money."

"Wu Fang-shui," Kluge said. "I'll see what I can do."

"Me too," said Delilah.

"Hell," Juanito said. "How many people are there on Valparaiso all together? Maybe nine hundred thousand? I can think of fifty right away who can't possibly be the guy I'm looking for. That narrows the odds some. What I have to do is just go on narrowing, right? Right?"

In fact he didn't feel very optimistic. He was going to do his best; but the whole system on Valparaiso was heavily weighted in favor of helping those who wanted to hide stay hidden.

Even Farkas realized that. "The privacy laws here are very strict, aren't they?"

With a smile Juanito said, "They're just about the only laws we have, you know? The sacredness of sanctuary. It is the compassion of El Supremo that has turned Valparaiso into a place of refuge for fugitives of all sorts, and we are not supposed to interfere with the compassion of El Supremo."

"Which is very expensive compassion, I understand."

"Very. Sanctuary fees are renewable annually. Anyone who harms a permanent resident who is living here under the compassion of El Supremo is bringing about a reduction in El Supremo's annual income, you see? Which doesn't sit well with the Generalissimo."

They were in the Villanueva Cafe, E Spoke. They had been touring Valparaiso all day long, back and forth from rim to hub, going up one spoke and down the other. Farkas said he wanted to experience as much of Valparaiso as he could. Not to see; to *experience*. He was insatiable, prowling around everywhere, gobbling it all up, soaking it in. Farkas had never been to one of the satellite worlds before. It amazed him, he said, that there were forests and lakes here, broad fields of wheat and rice, fruit orchards, herds of goats and cattle. Apparently he had expected the place to be nothing more than a bunch of aluminum struts and grim concrete boxes with everybody living on food pills, or something. People from Earth never seemed to comprehend that the larger satellite worlds were comfortable places with blue skies, fleecy clouds, lovely gardens, handsome buildings of steel and brick and glass.

Farkas said, "How do you go about tracing a fugitive, then?"

"There are always ways. Everybody knows somebody who knows something about someone. Information is bought here the same way compassion is."

"From the Generalissimo?" Farkas said, startled.

"From his officials, sometimes. If done with great care. Care is important, because lives are at risk. There are also couriers who have information to sell. We all know a great deal that we are not supposed to know."

"I suppose you know a great many fugitives by sight, your-self?"

"Some," Juanito said. "You see that man, sitting by the win-dow?" He frowned. "I don't know, can you see him? To me he looks around sixty, bald head, thick lips, no chin?"

"I see him, yes. He looks a little different to me."

"I bet he does. He ran a swindle at one of the Luna domes, sold phony stock in an offshore monopoly fund that didn't exist, fifty million Capbloc dollars. He pays plenty to live here. This one here—You see? With the blonde woman?—an embezzler, that one, very good with computers, reamed a bank in Singapore for almost its entire capital. Him over there, he pretended to be Pope. Can you believe that? Everybody in Rio de Janeiro did."

"Wait a minute," Farkas said. "How do I know you're not making all this up?"

"You don't," Juanito said amiably. "But I'm not."

"So we just sit here like this and you expose the identities of three fugitives to me free of charge?"

"It wouldn't be free," Juanito said, "if they were people you were looking for."

"What if they were? And my claiming to be looking for a Wu Fang-shui just a cover?"

"You aren't looking for any of them," Juanito said.

"No," said Farkas. "I'm not." He sipped his drink, something green and cloudy. "How come these men haven't done a better job of concealing their identities?" he asked.

"They think they have," said Juanito.

Getting leads was a slow business, and expensive. Juanito left Farkas to wander the spokes of Valparaiso on his own, and headed off to the usual sources of information: his father's friends, other couriers, and even the headquarters of the Unity Party, El Supremo's grass-roots organization, where it wasn't hard to find someone who knew something and had a price for it. Juanito was cautious. Middle-aged Chinese gentleman I'm trying to locate, he said. Why? Nobody asked. Could be any reason, anything from wanting to blow him away on contract to handing him a million-Capbloc-dollar lottery prize that he had won last year on New Yucatan. Nobody asked for reasons on Valparaiso.

There was a man named Federigo who had been with Juanito's father in the Costa Rica days who knew a woman who knew a man who had a freemartin neuter companion who had formerly belonged to someone high up in the Census Department. There were fees to pay at every step of the way, but it was Farkas' money, what the hell, and by the end of the week Juanito had access to the immigration data stored on golden megachips somewhere in the depths of the hub. The data down there wasn't going to provide anybody with Wu Fang-shui's phone number. But what it could tell Juanito, and did, eight hundred callaghanos later, was how many ethnic Chinese were living on Valparaiso and how long ago they had arrived.

"There are nineteen of them altogether," he reported to Farkas. "Eleven of them are women."

"So? Changing sex is no big deal," Farkas said.

"Agreed. The women are all under fifty, though. The oldest of the men is sixty-two. The longest that any of them has been on Valparaiso is nine years."

"Would you say that rules them all out? Age can be altered just as easily as sex."

"But date of arrival can't be, so far as I know. And you say that your Wu Fang-shui came here fifteen years back. Unless you're wrong about that, he can't be any of those Chinese. Your Wu Fang-shui, if he isn't dead by now, has signed up for some other racial mix, I'd say."

"He isn't dead," Farkas said.

"You sure of that?"

"He was still alive three months ago, and in touch with his family on Earth. He's got a brother in Tashkent."

"Shit," Juanito said. "Ask the brother what name he's going under up here, then."

"We did. We couldn't get it."

"Ask him harder."

"We asked him too hard," said Farkas. "Now the information isn't available anymore. Not from him, anyway."

Juanito checked out the nineteen Chinese, just to be certain. It didn't cost much and it didn't take much time, and there was always the chance that Dr. Wu had cooked his immigration data somehow. But the quest led nowhere. Juanito found six of them all in one shot, playing some Chinese game in a social club in the town of Havana de Cuba on Spoke B, and they went right on laughing and pushing the little porcelain counters around while he stood there kibitzing. They didn't *act* like sanctuarios. They were all shorter than Juanito, too, which meant either that they weren't Dr. Wu, who was tall for a Chinese, or that Dr. Wu had been willing to have his legs chopped down by fifteen centimeters for the sake of a more efficient disguise. It was possible, but it wasn't too likely.

The other thirteen were all much too young or too convincingly female or too this or too that. Juanito crossed them all off his list. From the outset he hadn't thought Wu would still be Chinese, anyway.

He kept on looking. One trail went cold, and then another, and then another. By now he was starting to think Dr. Wu must have heard that a man with no eyes was looking for him, and had gone even deeper underground, or off Valparaiso entirely. Juanito paid a friend at the hub spaceport to keep watch on departure manifests for him. Nothing came of that. Then someone reminded him that there was a colony of old-time, hard-core sanctuary types living in and around the town of El Mirador on Spoke D, people who had a genuine aversion to being bothered. He went there. Because he was known to be the son of a murdered fugitive himself, nobody hassled him: he of all people wouldn't be likely to be running a trace, would he?

The visit yielded no directly useful result. He couldn't risk asking questions and nothing was showing on the surface. But he came away with the strong feeling that El Mirador was the answer.

"Take me there," Farkas said.

"I can't do that. It's a low-profile town. Strangers aren't welcome. You'll stick out like a dinosaur."

"Take me," Farkas repeated.

"If Wu's there and he gets even a glimpse of you, he'll know right away that there's a contract out for him and he'll vanish so fast you won't believe it."

"Take me to El Mirador," said Farkas. "It's my money, isn't it?"

"Right," Juanito said. "Let's go to El Mirador."

El Mirador was midway between hub and rim on its spoke. There were great glass windows punched in its shield that provided a colossal view of all the rest of Valparaiso and the stars and the sun and the moon and the Earth and everything. A solar eclipse was going on when Juanito and Farkas arrived: the Earth was plastered right over the sun with nothing but one squidge of hot light showing down below like a diamond blazing on a golden ring. Purple shadows engulfed the town, deep and thick, a heavy velvet curtain falling over everything.

Juanito tried to describe what he saw. Farkas made an impatient brushing gesture.

"I know, I know. I feel it in my teeth." They stood on a big peoplemover escalator leading down into the town plaza. "The sun is long and thin right now, like the blade of an axe. The Earth has six sides, each one glowing a different color."

Juanito gaped at the eyeless man in amazement.

"Wu is here," Farkas said. "Down there, in the plaza. I feel his presence."

"From five hundred meters away?"

"Come with me."

"What do we do if he really is?"

"Are you armed?"

"I have a spike, yes."

"Good. Tune it to shock, and don't use it at all if you can help it. I don't want you to hurt him in any way."

"I understand. You want to kill him yourself, in your own sweet time."

"Just be careful not to hurt him," Farkas said. "Come on."

It was an old-fashioned-looking town, cobblestone plaza, little cafés around its perimeter and a fountain in the middle. About ten thousand people lived there and it seemed as if they were all out in the plaza sipping drinks and watching the eclipse. Juanito was grateful for the eclipse. No one paid any attention to them as they came floating down the peoplemover and strode into the plaza. Hell of a thing, he thought. You walk into town with a man with no eyes walking right behind you and nobody even notices. But when the sunshine comes back on it may be different.

"There he is," Farkas whispered. "To the left, maybe fifty meters, sixty."

Juanito peered through the purple gloom at the plazafront café beyond the next one. A dozen or so people were sitting in small groups at curbside tables under iridescent fiberglass awnings, drinking, chatting, taking it easy. Just another casual afternoon in good old cozy El Mirador on sleepy old Valparaiso.

Farkas stood sideways to keep his strange face partly concealed. Out of the corner of his mouth he said, "Wu is the one sitting by himself at the front table."

"The only one sitting alone is a woman, maybe fifty, fifty-five years old, long reddish hair, big nose, dowdy clothes ten years out of fashion."

"That's Wu."

"How can you be so sure?"

"It's possible to retrofit your body to make it look entirely different on the outside. You can't change the non-visual information, the stuff I pick up by blindsight. What Dr. Wu looked like to me, the last time I saw him, was a cubical block of black metal polished bright as a mirror, sitting on top of a pyramid-shaped copper-colored pedestal. I was nine years old then, but I promised myself I wouldn't ever forget what he looked like, and I haven't. That's what the person sitting over there by herself looks like."

Juanito stared. He still saw a plain-looking woman in a rumpled old-fashioned suit. They did wonders with retrofitting these days, he knew: they could make almost any sort of body grow on you, like clothing on a clothesrack, by fiddling with your DNA. But still Juanito had trouble thinking of that woman over there as a sinister Chinese gene-splicer in disguise, and he had even more trouble seeing her as a polished cube sitting on top of a coppery pyramid.

"What do you want to do now?" he asked.

"Let's go over and sit down alongside her. Keep that spike of yours ready. But I hope you don't use it."

"If we put the arm on her and she's not Wu," Juanito said, "it's going to get me in a hell of a lot of trouble, particularly if she's paying El Supremo for sanctuary. Sanctuary people get very stuffy when their privacy is violated. You'll be expelled and I'll be fined a fortune and a half and I might wind up getting expelled too, and then what?"

"That's Dr. Wu," Farkas said. "Watch him react when he sees me, and then you'll believe it."

"We'll still be violating sanctuary. All he has to do is yell for the police."

"We need to make it clear to him right away," said Farkas, "that that would be a foolish move. You follow?"

"But I don't hurt him," Juanito said.

"No. Not in any fashion. You simply demonstrate a willingness to hurt him if it should become necessary. Let's go, now. You sit down first, ask politely if it's okay for you to share the table, make some comment about the eclipse. I'll come over maybe thirty seconds after you. All clear? Good. Go ahead, now."

"You have to be insane," the red-haired woman said. But she was sweating in an astonishing way and her fingers were knotting together like anguished snakes. "I'm not any kind of doctor and my name isn't Wu or Fu or whatever you said, and you have exactly two seconds to get away from me." She seemed unable to take her eyes from Farkas' smooth blank forehead. Farkas didn't move. After a moment she said in a different tone of voice, "What kind of thing are you, anyway?"

She isn't Wu, Juanito decided.

The real Wu wouldn't have asked a question like that. Besides, this was definitely a woman. She was absolutely convincing around the jaws, along the hairline, the soft flesh behind her chin. Women were different from men in all those places. Something about her wrists. The way she sat. A lot of other things. There weren't any genetic surgeons good enough to do a retrofit this convincing. Juanito peered at her eyes, trying to see the place where the Chinese fold had been, but there wasn't a trace of it. Her eyes were blue-gray. All Chinese had brown eyes, didn't they?

Farkas said, leaning in close and hard, "My name is Victor Farkas, Doctor. I was born in Tashkent during the Breakup. My mother was the wife of the Hungarian consul, and you did a gene-splice job on the fetus she was carrying. That was your specialty, tectogenetic reconstruction. You don't remember that? You deleted my eyes and gave me blindsight instead, Doctor."

The woman looked down and away. Color came to her cheeks. Something heavy seemed to be stirring within her. Juanito began to change his mind. Maybe there really were some gene surgeons who could do a retrofit this good, he thought.

"None of this is true," she said. "You're simply a lunatic. I can show you who I am. I have papers. You have no right to harass me like this."

"I don't want to hurt you in any way, Doctor."

"I am not a doctor."

"Could you be a doctor again? For a price?"

Juanito swung around, astounded, to look at Farkas.

"I will not listen to this," the woman said. "You will go away from me this instant or I summon the patrol."

Farkas said, "We have a project, Dr. Wu. My engineering group, a division of a corporation whose name I'm sure you know. An experimental spacedrive, the first interstellar voyage, faster-than-light travel. We're three years away from a launch."

The woman rose. "This madness does not interest me."

"The faster-than-light field distorts vision," Farkas went on. He didn't appear to notice that she was standing and looked about ready to bolt. "It disrupts vision entirely, in fact. Perception becomes totally abnormal. A crew with normal vision wouldn't be able to function in any way. But it turns out that someone with blindsight can adapt fairly easily to the peculiar changes that the field induces."

"I have no interest in hearing about—"

"It's been tested, actually. With me as the subject. But I can't make the voyage alone. We have a crew of five and they've volunteered for tectogenetic retrofits to give them what I have. We don't know anyone else who has your experience in that area. We'd like you to come out of retirement, Dr. Wu. We'll set up a complete lab for you on a nearby satellite world, whatever equipment you need. And pay you very well. And insure your safety all the time you're gone from Valparaiso. What do you say?"

The red-haired woman was trembling and slowly backing away.

"No," she said. "It was such a long time ago. Whatever skills I had, I have forgotten, I have buried."

So Farkas was right all along, Juanito thought.

"You can give yourself a refresher course. I don't think it's possible really to forget a gift like yours, do you?" Farkas said.

"No. Please. Let me be."

Juanito was amazed at how cockeyed his whole handle on the situation had been from the start.

Farkas didn't seem at all angry with the gene surgeon. He hadn't come here for vengeance, Juanito realized. Just to cut a deal.

"Where's he going?" Farkas said suddenly. "Don't let him get away, Juanito."

The woman—Wu—was moving faster now, not quite running but sidling away at a steady pace, back into the enclosed part of the café. Farkas gestured sharply and Juanito began to follow. The spike he was carrying could deliver a stun-level jolt at fifteen paces. But he couldn't just spike her down in this crowd, not if

she had sanctuary protection, not in El Mirador of all places.
There'd be fifty sanctuarios on top of him in a minute. They'd
grab him and club him and sell his foreskin to the Generalissimo's
men for two and a half callies.

The café was crowded and dark. Juanito caught sight of her
somewhere near the back, near the restrooms. Go on, he thought.
Go into the ladies' room. I'll follow you right in there. I don't
give a damn about that.

But she went past the restrooms and ducked into an alcove near
the kitchen instead. Two waiters laden with trays came by, scowling at Juanito to get out of the way. It took him a moment to pass
around them, and by then he could no longer see the red-haired
woman. He knew he was going to have big trouble with Farkas
if he lost her in here. Farkas was going to have a fit. Farkas would
try to stiff him on this week's pay, most likely. Two thousand
callies down the drain, not even counting the extra charges.

Then a hand reached out of the shadows and seized his wrist
with surprising ferocity. He was dragged a little way into a claus-
trophobic games room dense with crackling green haze coming
from some bizarre machine on the far wall. The red-haired
woman glared at him, wild-eyed. "He wants to kill me, doesn't he? That's
all bullshit about having me do retrofit operations, right?"

"I think he means it," Juanito said.

"Nobody would volunteer to have his eyes replaced with blindsight."

"How would I know? People do all sorts of crazy things. But
if he wanted to kill you I think he'd have operated differently
when we tracked you down."

"He'll get me off Valparaiso and kill me somewhere else."

"I don't know," Juanito said. "I was just doing a job."

"How much did he pay you to do the trace?" Savagely. "How
much? I know you've got a spike in your pocket. Just leave it
there and answer me. How much?"

"Three thousand callies a week," Juanito muttered, padding
things a little.

"I'll give you five to help me get rid of him."

Juanito hesitated. Sell Farkas out? He didn't know if he could
turn himself around that fast. Was it the professional thing to do,
to take a higher bid?

"Eight," Juanito said, after a moment.

Why the hell not? He didn't owe Farkas any loyalty. This was
a sanctuary world; the compassion of El Supremo entitled Wu to

protection here. It was every citizen's duty. And eight thousand callies was a big bundle.

"Six-five," Wu said.

"Eight. Handshake right now. You have your glove?"

The woman who was Wu made a muttering sound and pulled out her flex terminal. "Account 1133," Juanito said, and they made the transfer of funds. "How do you want to do this?" Juanito asked.

"There is a passageway into the outer shell just behind this café. You will catch sight of me slipping in there and the two of you will follow me. When we are all inside and he is coming toward me, you get behind him and take him down with your spike. And we leave him buried in there." There was a frightening gleam in Wu's eyes. It was almost as if the cunning retrofit body was melting away and the real Wu beneath was emerging, moment by moment. "You understand?" Wu said. A fierce, blazing look. "I have bought you, boy. I expect you to stay bought when we are in the shell. Do you understand me? Do you? Good."

It was like a huge crawlspace entirely surrounding the globe that was El Mirador. Around the periphery of the double shell was a deep layer of lunar slag held in place by centrifugal forces, the tailings left over after the extraction of the gases and minerals that the satellite world had needed in its construction. On top of that was a low open area for the use of maintenance workers, lit by a trickle of light from a faint line of incandescent bulbs; and overhead was the inner skin of El Mirador itself, shielded by the slagpile from any surprises that might come ricocheting in from the void. Juanito was able to move almost upright within the shell, but Farkas, following along behind, had to bend double, scuttling like a crab.

"Can you see him yet?" Farkas asked.

"Somewhere up ahead, I think. It's pretty dark in here."

"Is it?"

Juanito saw Wu edging sideways, moving slowly around behind Farkas now. In the dimness Wu was barely visible, the shadow of a shadow. He had scooped up two handfuls of tailings. Evidently he was going to fling them at Farkas to attract his attention, and when Farkas turned toward Wu it would be Juanito's moment to nail him with the spike.

Juanito stepped back to a position near Farkas' left elbow. He slipped his hand into his pocket and touched the cool sleek little weapon. The intensity stud was down at the lower end, shock

level, and without taking the spike from his pocket he moved the
setting up to lethal. Wu nodded. Juanito began to draw the spike.

Suddenly Farkas roared like a wild creature. Juanito grunted in
shock, stupefied by that terrible sound. This is all going to go
wrong, he realized. A moment later Farkas whirled and seized
him around the waist and swung him as if he was a throwing-
hammer, hurling him through the air and sending him crashing
with tremendous impact into Wu's midsection. Wu crumpled,
gagging and puking, with Juanito sprawled stunned on top of him.
Then the lights went out—Farkas must have reached up and
yanked the conduit loose—and then Juanito found himself lying
with his face jammed down into the rough floor of tailings. Farkas
was holding him down with a hand clamped around the back of
his neck and a knee pressing hard against his spine. Wu lay alongside him, pinned the same way.

"Did you think I couldn't see him sneaking up on me?" Farkas
asked. "Or you, going for your spike? It's 360 degrees, the blindsight. Something that Dr. Wu must have forgotten. All these years
on the run, I guess you start to forget things."

Jesus, Juanito thought. Couldn't even get the drop on a blind
man from behind him. And now he's going to kill me. What a
stupid way to die this is.

He imagined what Kluge might say about this, if he knew. Or
Delilah. Nattathaniel. Decked by a blind man.

But he isn't blind. He isn't blind. He isn't blind at all.

Farkas said, "How much did you sell me to him for, Juanito?"

The only sound Juanito could make was a muffled moan. His
mouth was choked with sharp bits of slag.

"How much? Five thousand? Six?"

"It was eight," said Wu quietly.

"At least I didn't go cheaply," Farkas murmured. He reached
into Juanito's pocket and withdrew the spike. "Get up," he said.
"Both of you. Stay close together. If either of you makes a funny
move, I'll kill you both. Remember that I can see you very clearly.
I can also see the door through which we entered the shell. That
starfish-looking thing over there, with streamers of purple light
pulsing from it. We're going back into El Mirador now, and there
won't be any surprises, will there? Will there?"

Juanito spit out a mouthful of slag. He didn't say anything.

"Dr. Wu? The offer still stands," Farkas continued. "You
come with me, you do the job we need you for. That isn't so bad,
considering what I could do to you for what you did to me. But
all I want from you is your skills, and that's the truth. You are

going to need that refresher course, aren't you, though?''

Wu muttered something indistinct.

Farkas said, "You can practice on this boy, if you like. Try retrofitting him for blindsight first, and if it works, you can do our crew people, all right? He won't mind. He's terribly curious about the way I see things, anyway. Aren't you, Juanito? Eh? Eh?'' Farkas laughed. To Juanito he said, ''If everything works out the right way, maybe we'll let you go on the voyage with us, boy.'' Juanito felt the cold nudge of the spike in his back. "You'd like that, wouldn't you? The first trip to the stars? What do you say to that, Juanito?''

Juanito didn't answer. His tongue was still rough with slag. With Farkas prodding him from behind, he shambled slowly along next to Dr. Wu toward the door that Farkas said looked like a starfish. It didn't look at all like a fish to him, or a star, or like a fish that looked like a star. It looked like a door to him, as far as he could tell by the feeble light of the distant bulbs. That was all it looked like, a door that looked like a door. Not a star. Not a fish. But there was no use thinking about it, or anything else, not now, not with Farkas nudging him between the shoulder-blades with his own spike. He let his mind go blank and kept on walking.

Access to Space: SSX

⌐⌐

JIM RANSOM

I know how to get the U.S. permanently into space. Write me a check for a billion dollars, give me a letter of credit for a second billion I probably won't have to spend, and get out of the way. I'll take the money and vanish into the Mojave desert, China Lake for preference, Edwards Air Force Base if I must; and in about four years I'll have a Single Stage to Orbit *savable* as well as recoverable and reusable spacecraft capable of putting about ten thousand pounds into orbit at costs of about five times the cost of the fuel the flight takes. Call it Space Ship Experimental, or SSX for short.

In round terms: the ship will weigh about five hundred thousand pounds full up, of which some fifty thousand pounds will be liquid hydrogen fuel. That sells for about four dollars per pound at present, but it would be no trick at all to produce it at well under two dollars per pound; it's a matter of the costs of energy to make and transport it. Liquid Oxygen (LOX) is essentially free if you're making hydrogen in fuel quantities.

Airlines typically operate at about three times fuel costs. We'll say SSX operates at five times fuel cost; although you should understand that it takes about the same amount of fuel to fly a pound from the U.S. to Sydney, Austrialia as it does to put that pound in orbit; rocket engines, contrary to rumor, are extremely efficient.

SSX thus costs in the order of half a million dollars per flight—total operational cost—to put ten thousand pounds in orbit. Double that on general principles, and it's still one million dollars a flight for ten thousand pounds, or one hundred dollars per pound. Contrast that with NASA's tens of thousands for the shuttle.

We're not through. Once we have the ship flying, we work on the payload: we ought to be able to get that up to about fifteen thousand pounds on this size ship. Second, we work on those costs: we ought to be able to get them truly to four times fuel costs.

Even before we do that, though, understand that SSX operates both in vacuum and atmosphere: get one into orbit, and you can send another one up with fuel as payload. About twenty such flights fuels up to send SSX to the moon and back, leaving ten thousand pounds of payload on the moon, at a cost of twenty million dollars.

That's easily enough to supply a colony of five with plenty of safety factor: for example, one twenty million dollar annual flight would keep a Lunar Base going.

Is this wishful thinking? Not according to some hard eyed analysts. I've actually overstated the costs.

But what is this nonsense about giving Pournelle a billion dollars? Do I really think I could manage a project that large?

Actually, yes: it's a matter of picking the right team of bright young people and making them work twenty-six hours a day until the job is done. They can have their coronaries after SSX is flying. I know most of those we need, and I know of the rest. So, yes, I could do it. As to why China Lake, it's simple: I don't want to build an empire, and I don't want anyone who does. By putting the project in a place no one wants to live, you make the job more important than the empire.

■   ■   ■

Would this be an efficient operation, without fraud and waste? Probably not. It would merely get the job done.

Will they let me do it? Of course not. No one is going to hand a science fiction writer, even one who's a former aerospace scientist and who's been Chairman of the Citizens Advisory Council on National Space Policy for eight years, that kind of money and get out of the way. Not me, and not anyone else for that matter.

Then how can we build SSX?

One way is being done now: there's a Phase One Development contract out as I write this, and we have every reason to believe we can get funding to complete the project. The total cost, given usual government management efficiencies to prevent fraud and waste, shouldn't run much over ten billion dollars, provided the contractor gets a priority, and is allowed to run this in "skunk works" mode, thus bypassing many of the procurement regulations. The job ought to be done in six years.

Will it be done that way? Probably not. It will probably be let as a normal contract in the usual way, and let under standard regulations. Can we build the ship that way? You bet. It shouldn't cost more than about twenty billion dollars, nor take more than eight years.

That's the way it will probably go—and it will be a bargain. It's a pity we won't be allowed to just take a team out to the desert and *do* it, but that's life.

Finally, there's the private route. It's *possible* that we could have a flying SSX for about two hundred million dollars as a private venture. Possible. I didn't say I could guarantee it for that. I can guarantee it for two billion dollars, even as a government project (under my rules). On the other hand, I've seen numbers, some of them developed by the Brothers Rhutan.

I sure wish I had two hundred million.

Meanwhile, a description of SSX; the ship that could take us all into the Endless Frontier.

SSX: Spaceship Experimental
Spaceship: A vehicle designed for travel in space; not a converted
            missile
Experimental: Inexpensive and rapidly developed to gather op-
            erational data

The United States does not have access to space. The tragic
events of January 28, 1986, burned the image of a forked smoke
plume suspended in a deep blue sky into our memories. The loss
of the Space Shuttle Orbiter *Challenger*, its seven person crew,
and communications satellite payload in a fiery launch accident
was the inevitable consequence of an unforgiving design pushed
beyond its limits. Since *Challenger*, the United States has suffered
one Delta, one Atlas, and two Titan expendable launch vehicle
accidents.

Yes, we are launching Space Shuttles again, but our access to
space is neither assured nor affordable. Placing a satellite in orbit
using the Space Shuttle or an expendable launch vehicle costs
more than the satellite's weight in gold! The premium to insure
the launch of a communications satellite is currently about twenty
percent of the cost of the satellite. It does not require a degree in
math and training as an actuary to calculate the expected loss rates
from this premium.

Today, United States space transportation is about as dangerous
and unreliable as the first years of the United States Air Mail
operations in the 1920s. Air transportation became reliable through
the development of better fuels, better engines, and most important, better aircraft designs. With the arrival of the Boeing 247
and the Douglas DC-3, air transportation became reliable and
affordable. These new transport aircraft could cruise above the
worst weather near the ground, avoiding the hazards of fog and
downdrafts while keeping the passengers comfortable. The streamlined DC-3 could carry twenty-one passengers fast and economically enough to make a profit (air mail contracts subsidized the
early airlines).

Space transportation is less affordable now than air transportation was in 1920. No adult United States citizen can expect to
fly into space in their lifetime, unless they possess special scientific
or technical skills required by the government and can pass rig-
orous medical screening. A wealthy American might take advantage of an offer by the Soviets to fly a single individual into orbit
to visit the Mir space station for ten million dollars in hard cur-

rency. There are no space barnstormers and no five dollar rocket rides at the county fair.

SSX can give us assured, affordable access to space.

Spaceship Experimental (SSX)

The Spaceship Experimental (SSX) program will demonstrate a true reusable launch vehicle designed for reliability and low-cost operation. The SSX design is easy to flight test and fundamentally safe. Due to its design simplicity, modularity, and use of demonstrated technology, SSX can be developed by a streamlined "Skunk Works" program office in less than five years at a total program cost of under one billion dollars.

SSX is a Single-Stage-to-Orbit (SSTO) vehicle. Unlike the Space Shuttle and other current launch vehicles, the SSX does not drop off any booster stages or payload shrouds on its way into orbit. The SSX has only one stage to assemble, prepare, operate, and refurbish. The SSX expends only propellants.

To carry a useful size payload into orbit with only one stage, the SSX uses high-energy liquid hydrogen and liquid oxygen propellants, a lightweight structure, and a high-performance engine system. The SSX propellants are nontoxic. The SSX is a short, squat, round vehicle with the internal tanks close to spherical in shape and thus lighter in weight than those of long, slender rockets. The Space Shuttle and other rockets have a small base area; to get the necessary thrust levels, the Shuttle must use high-pressure rocket engines. The large base diameter of the SSX permits the use of a plug nozzle (or aerospike) which consists of many small, lower-pressure engines mounted in a ring around the base of the vehicle. As the SSX reaches high altitude, the engine exhaust gases push against the entire base of the vehicle and produce an engine performance equal to that of the Space Shuttle.

The SSX is Vertical Takeoff and Vertical Landing (VTOVL) like a helicopter. The SSX reenters base first just as the Apollo capsule did twenty years ago. The base area must have a thermal protection system to protect it from the hot engine gases during ascent, and the same system serves double duty keeping the SSX vehicle cool during reentry. Now almost empty of propellants, the SSX vehicle weighs only a tenth as much as it did at takeoff. Once it reaches the lower layers of the atmosphere, the SSX has a terminal velocity of only a few hundred miles an hour and is approaching the ground at exactly the same rate as the Space Shuttle does before landing. The SSX fires its engines, brakes to a stop just above the ground, hovers for several seconds to permit final adjustments in landing site, and sets down on its landing gear.

The payload sits in a large-diameter shroud atop the vehicle. The payload is away from the engines, reducing noise and vibration loads. Once the SSX reaches the desired orbit, the shroud opens, the payload is released, and the shroud closes again for reentry.

The SSX will have low flight costs because it is completely reusable and capable of rapid reflights. The low-pressure engines sustain less wear than high-pressure engines like those on the Space Shuttle. The SSX expends no hardware and has only one stage to handle.

The SSX is designed to be highly reliable in operation. One or more engines can fail *on the pad at liftoff* and the vehicle can still reach orbit. If necessary, the SSX can hover to burn off propellants and then land vertically. It does not need to achieve any minimum velocity or altitude—SSX can land safely at any point in its ascent trajectory. The SSX is a savable rocket.

The SSX is designed for low-cost, rapid development. The engine components are based on existing designs. Each engine module is small compared to those on the Space Shuttle and Titan, reducing the amount of propellant required for development and permitting the use of smaller test stands. The SSX shape is simple aerodynamically; it is very similar to the Apollo Command Module for which tons of test and operational data exist. The incremental flight test program will begin with hover flights and move progressively up in altitude to orbit, just like testing a new jet airliner. The SSX comes back every time, unlike past rockets where test flights expended most or all of the expensive hardware. Finally, the SSX is designed to have a modest but useful payload capability to keep development and facilities costs down.

The name Spaceship Experimental emphasizes the similarity to air transport development. Aerospace engineer Maxwell Hunter coined the name SSX to recall the days of experimental aircraft development at Edwards Air Force Base when hardware was built, flown, and rebuilt incorporating the flight test data in less than a year.

SSX and Current Space Operations

United States space operations can smoothly and quickly make the transition to using production SSX launch vehicles. The SSX design has inherently more reliability and lower operations costs than the current generation of space launch vehicles. Within two years after the first production SSX rolls off the line, SSX vehicles can take over the launch of at least a third of all U.S. national security, civilian, and commercial payloads.

Launch Site Support

The SSX is designed to be easy to launch from limited launch facilities. The broad base area spreads the vehicle exhaust gases over a wider area than traditional space boosters, thus reducing launch pad heating and erosion rates. SSX does not use solid rocket motors, thus it has low water deluge requirements for launch pad protection and acoustical load suppression. The short squat vehicle shape eliminates the need for large gantries and towers. For payload integration, the unfueled SSX vehicle could be rolled in and out of a modest-sized integration building, or the SSX vehicle could be serviced with a rolling payload changeout derrick plus environmental shelter. The short large-diameter payload compartment is easier to handle than the long multi-section shrouds used on the Titan IV.

New launch sites will be much easier to establish for SSX than any current space booster. The SSX liquid oxygen and liquid hydrogen propellants are nontoxic and the vehicle is modest in size, significantly reducing any environmental impacts. The intact abort capability plus highly reliable design will permit rapid FAA certification for the SSX to overfly populated areas during ascent, giving SSX an all-azimuth launch capability. For higher inclination orbits, SSX could be launched from Colorado Springs to take advantage of the higher altitude and resulting reduction in air drag losses.

Existing Payloads

Assuming an initial certified payload capability of four tons into polar low-earth orbit, the SSX can immediately launch most spacecraft now flown on the Delta, Titan II, and Scout boosters. The SSX offers a larger payload volume and lower acceleration, vibration, and acoustical loads than these boosters. Unlike the Space Shuttle, the SSX launch and landing loads are all longitudinal, and no structural modifications will be necessary to payloads designed for expendable vehicles to fly them on an SSX.

The SSX combination of low cost per launch, operational flexibility, and high-surge capability are ideally suited to the support of national security missions. The Strategic Defense Initiative space-based interceptor system and the related Brilliant Pebbles concept are both perfect candidates for launch on SSX. Lower-cost tactical support satellites (also known as CINCSats) could be flown at low cost on the SSX, with fewer size and weight constraints than the small, solid-propellant launch vehicles now proposed for the job. SSX launch vehicles can fly from dispersed launch sites into the crucial high-inclination orbits using their all-azimuth launch capability. Previous Air Force studies have shown that a complete liquid oxygen/liquid hydrogen propellant production system can be airlifted on a C-5B pallet to a site and then hooked up to electrical and natural gas supplies. Using the SSX vehicle tanks for storage, such a system could support two or more flights per week.

Future Payloads

The attributes of the SSX offer benefits for the designers of future spacecraft. The larger payload volume can eliminate the requirement for some deployment operations by permitting the launch of a spacecraft with these appendages already extended. The relatively low 3-G maximum longitudinal acceleration level during ascent plus the use of large-diameter structural interface adapters will reduce spacecraft launch loads. Spacecraft can be checked out while still attached to the SSX and returned to earth if any critical problems are detected. With the high SSX mission reliability, spacecraft program managers can have the same high confidence in the space launch portion of their launch operations as they do today in the transport of their spacecraft from the factory to the launch site in a cargo aircraft.

The SSX vehicle has a higher mass-fraction than the Centaur upper stage. After refueling in orbit from other SSX vehicles or an orbital fuel depot, an SSX could boost a payload into geosynchronous or Molniya orbit. The SSX could then deboost and return using aerobraking into low earth orbit or reenter and land, leaving no discarded upper stage or other debris.

Manned Operations

The intact abort capability of the SSX plus its inherent reliability will make SSX passenger certification a very similar process to that of commercial air transports. The certification process will include the same methodical testing of the flight and performance envelope of the SSX as currently used to certify a commercial jetliner. The vertical takeoff and vertical landing SSX design plus the low flight costs will permit an extensive test series with dozens of test flights.

The initial payload capacity of the SSX will permit the launch of a three to six person module similar to the Apollo Command Module into low-altitude earth orbits. The SSX vehicle will provide the thermal protection and propulsion systems for the attached crew module. Recent studies of similar manned modules include a Crew Emergency Rescue Vehicle (CERV) for Space Station *Freedom* performed by NASA contractors and an independent concept for a Multi-Role Capsule performed by members of the technical staff of British Aerospace. Such a module can include a working airlock assembly for crew transfer to other manned vehicles and to support extravehicular activity (EVA).

The combination of SSX and passenger module can supplement the Space Shuttle to allow more frequent crew rotation for Space Station *Freedom*. The operational flexibility, low cost, and rapid turnaround of the SSX vehicle will easily support both medical and emergency evacuation of Space Station *Freedom* crew members without incurring the development and operations costs of the proposed CERV.

Afterword to Access to Space: SSX

JERRY POURNELLE

Lest anyone get the wrong idea, I had no hand in the design of SSX. The concept has a long and honorable history, with contributions from a great number of people. It's very hard to give credit here: how do you separate those who thought up technical features, those who recognized their importance, and those who integrated them into a new design?

What I can claim credit for is chairing a meeting of the Citizens Advisory Council on National Space Policy at which the SSX was chosen as the proper ship for those who want to focus on citizen access to space. I was then part of the team that carried that concept to Vice President Quayle and helped convince him that the concept was worth an independent evaluation.

All of which is preparatory to a pitch: the L-5 Society has merged with the National Space Society (NSS), and has become yet one more part of the NASA cheering section. NSS now seems to have the typical Washington attitude that nothing of importance happens outside the Beltway, and nothing can be done without the government. As for me, as I watch The Incredible Shrinking Space Station, the redesigns of things that weren't broken, and the general bureaucratic CYA attitude, I am convinced that NASA is the problem, not the solution.

Recall Dick Rhutan patting *Voyager*'s wing after his historic flight: "See what free men can do," he said.

Well, we're going to try. Jim Ransom, Phil Chapman, and some of the other old L-5 enthusiasts have started The Lunar Society. The Society exists; it has a legal charter. It isn't precisely *looking* for members, but we'll take them. We prefer people who want to do something.

There's no big membership-services group, because the organization has no full-time employees. If you want to register, it costs one hundred dollars, and the only thing you get for that money is our personal guarantee that we won't waste the money. If you're interested, the address is: The Lunar Society, 3960 Laurel Canyon Blvd., Suite 372, North Hollywood, CA 91604. Please don't write to ask for "information." We don't have any fancy brochures. Just hard-working people trying to put a colony on the moon in our lifetimes.

Ghost Town

⌐

CHAD OLIVER

At this point in time, the future of space development is murky: the U.S.S.R. space program is losing focus because of the economic concerns of *perestroika*; the U.S. program is lost between the bureaucracy of NASA and the bottom-line mentality of U.S. mega-corps. Yet, every day we are more dependent upon satellites and space relays for communications and navigation.

The day will come when mankind will have a permanent presence in space, and I suppose whether or not those men speak Japanese, Sanskrit, Russian, or English is of lesser importance. There is real debate as to *how* mankind will live in space; I suspect the final answer will be "in any way he can."

The concept of living in bubble domes on the moon or on Mars has always been a popular idea among science fiction writers. It probably will not be so popular among spacefarers of the future. Space habitats are more efficient and reliable (no moonquakes or volcanoes) than surface domes on airless worlds—at least, for the short term.

For the long term, terraforming is probably the real best answer. Alas, even the most liberal estimates of terraforming a world, even one as hospitable as Mars, put it decades, or even centuries, away. Venus could take a thousand years to terraform, while Mercury will never be more than marginally habitable.

Yet, once these worlds have been made livable, I suspect few will remain habitat bound. Of course, there will always be habitats or space stations necessary for intersolar fuel stations and rest stops, if nothing else. Of course, a "wild card," such as my own Alderson Drive (see *The Mote in God's Eye* or *The Mercenary Prince*) which *allows* for interstellar travel in reasonable times, might instantly make them obsolete.

In such a case, they would become historic relics of the early age of space travel. And what stories they might could tell; such stories as Chad Oliver's award winning story, "Ghost Town."

CAROTH KNEW THAT they were coming.

He felt an anticipation that went beyond hate or joy or hope. The years had been long. His people were growing old.

He clasped his gnarled hands together in the firelight, seeking warmth. The pain was in him again. It throbbed from his fused neck through his powerful shoulders. He was used to pain. That did not make the hurting easier.

Caroth did not think about the pain. He thought about the hunger. It surged in him.

He knew that he had little time left, but there would be an end to waiting. The waiting was almost over.

They were coming.

Caroth was ready for them.

Rick Malina would not have admitted it to just anyone, but he had a sneaking affection for the damned things.

The ship had it on close visual now: a doughnut-shaped O'Neill like a thousand others, still rotating at the standard speed of one revolution per minute, its shielding still bright if a trifle pockmarked, the spidery appendages still swinging in a frozen dance against the stars.

Junk, of course—but valuable junk.

Space garbage—but garbage worth collecting.

Something left behind.

Rick supposed that his own ancestors—biological and professional—had felt the same way about the abandoned cliff houses in the moonlight, the rings of tipi stones that weathered in the brown grass of summer, the bits of charcoal and flakes of flint that marked an ancient campsite. You had to be a bit of a romantic to go into archeology in the first place. You concealed it later, masked it with the routine of job competence. It got covered up, just as the ruins themselves became buried in the earth.

But it was there.

And it was here. He could feel it, even on a conventional mission like this. It was a tiny stubborn flame that refused to go out.

"Hey, Doc." The commander's voice held nothing but boredom. She was not getting any younger and she was good enough for the starships. She hated shuttle flights and antediluvian spacecraft. "You going to suit up or go the Superman route?"

"Just checking," Rick said. He was not overly fond of the ship's commander, but she *was* stretching the Sacred Rules to allow him up here with the primary screen. He was basically cargo, after all. "Sometimes the optical configuration gives us a scan on the modular modification." It didn't mean a blessed thing, but it sounded impressive.

"Sure," she said with massive disinterest. "We'll be matched and ready for the dump within an hour. I assume you're still going?"

"I'm going," Rick Malina said. "Science never sleeps while the grants are awake."

He allowed himself one more look at that little artificial world floating in the cluttered space sea. He knew it up one ring of the torus and down the other. He knew it from the solar mirrors to the processing labs for nickel, iron, and titanium. He knew every dimension and atmospheric component.

He had done his homework.

This wasn't the first time his crew had worked an O'Neill.

Just the same, he enjoyed eyeballing it. It was a world. You didn't get to see them every day, even dead ones.

He executed a maneuver with the handholds that was fancier than it really had to be and drifted out of the control room.

"We'll be ready," he said.

It would be good to feel gravity again.

Caroth knew what he was. He had the kind of self-knowledge that came from endurance. Caroth was a survivor.

To survive was to continue.

He knew that his family name had once been Carothers. He knew that his people had used first names, long ago. That was before the population decline. That was when there had still been children.

Caroth was the only name he needed now. His people were few. Some of them had retained family names. Others just went by descriptive tags: One Eye, Smoke-Eater, Floater, Dreaming Woman. . . .

Perhaps, if the ape-things that had stayed behind had been a little closer genetically—

But they weren't.

Caroth was facing more than death. He was looking at extinction.

He refused to accept it.

Among other things, Caroth was a very stubborn old man.

Every O'Neill had an airlock that could be activated from outside. That was the law, a routine safety precaution. The lock could be sealed from the inside simply by dropping a metal bar into sockets, but that was an emergency procedure. An abandoned colony was never barred.

Getting inside was no problem. Transferring the supplies was no problem. Life-support tests were no problem.

It was after the shuttle had been released and the rendezvous time had been double-checked that the problems began.

"Did you see that?" asked Ann Vaughan.

"I saw it," Rick said.

Something had moved through the wild tangle of vegetation against the slight concavity of the O'Neill rim. The light was not ideal but it was sufficient. The moving form had two arms and two legs. It was about the size of a human being. It was dark and hairy.

It should not have been there.

"What the hell was that?" Pete Hurwitz stood as though he had taken root.

Rick took a deep breath. The air was not stale. Neither was it of the texture he had experienced before: heavy, full, redolent with the smells of untouched plants. This air tasted *used*. It had a greasy feel to it.

"It looked like a chimpanzee," he said carefully.

"Oh, sure," Ann said. She prided herself on her rationality. It took a lot to jolt her.

"You got a better idea?"

She hadn't.

Rick considered. Archeologists were not inclined to be fussy about such things, but he was nominally in charge. It was his job to maintain some perspective.

"It isn't the first time we've found some livestock left behind in one of these things," he said. "They can reproduce, you know. Keep going."

His explanation was on the feeble side and he knew it, Yes, they had encountered feral cattle twice before, and even those mutated chickens in the Kovar site. It made poor economic sense to remove all the animals when an O'Neill was emptied. It wasn't unprecedented for a few of them to survive.

But a chimpanzee?

Chimpanzees were valuable creatures: intelligent, trained, half-human, sometimes loved.

They were *never* left behind.

That chimp—if it had indeed been a chimp—raised some chilling possibilities.

Rick looked around in the uncertain light and tried to appear less concerned than he was. He saw nothing that he had not seen many times before. That was not surprising. He might not word it that way in his reports, but the plain fact was that one O'Neill was very much like another.

He was not reassured. He knew from experience that first impressions could not be counted upon. It took some time to ferret out the unusual or the unique. That was what salvage archeology was all about.

In the past, when archeologists had been sent into construction sites or areas destined to be flooded by building dams, it had been the same. You went in and worked your tail off, searching for new information that might otherwise vanish forever. There were times when you found nothing significant. There were times when you struck the mother lode relatively quickly. There were times when you found nothing until the last day, the last hour, the last five minutes.

It was the same with a salvage operation in an O'Neill. There was more to it than just determining what was worth saving and what wasn't.

There was history in an O'Neill. The trick was to find it.

The O'Neills that were not primarily close-in generators of solar power had been abandoned in a hurry. Few people wanted to go on living in a fossil tube, particularly when the paycredits stopped coming. Population pressure was no longer a problem on Earth, and there were more attractive worlds available than artificial colonies.

There were similarities between the O'Neills and the high mining camps that had once flourished in the Rocky Mountains of North America. Rick had seen some of those camps, restored meticulously by the Preservationists more than a century after the silver crash of 1893. Sagging cabins with the thin cold wind keening through the empty window frames, deserted log hotels inviting the guests who never arrived, cheerless corrals for long-vanished mules, tons of dirt and rock that had been torn from the mountains with rust-ruined picks and shovels. Iron stoves and schoolbooks decaying on snow-stained tables, ancient newspapers stuffed into cracks between warped and water-spotted boards—

And the graves. So many graves.

The people had been tough in those years.

Just the same, when the people moved out fast they *went*.

Only ghost towns were left.

Nobody kept records, nobody took inventory, and nobody gave much of a damn.

The idea was to leave.

Ghost towns. Waiting, perhaps. Maybe just there, like the scarred rocks and the dark trees and the cold, cold air.

The empty O'Neills were less fortunate. They remained intact and habitable, since nothing was gained by shutting down their self-contained power sources. At one time, there was even the forlorn hope that people might return to them, somehow, sometime.

Technology ruled otherwise. With the development of the stardrive, the near-space colonies of Earth lost their function. There is only one kind of stardrive that is useful, and that is one that is nearly instantaneous. If it is, then you don't need way stations.

The O'Neills were a slight navigational hazard for the starships, but that was no big deal. The critical problem was that they could not compete economically—and they all contained silent history.

The solution was neat and simple: salvage what was worth the effort and destroy the rest.

It was deeply touching.

But just for the record—

Just in case something of interest turned up—

Maybe even to ease a little collective guilt—

Check them out.

Rick Malina already felt something less than wild enthusiasm for what he had to do. He was not a stupid man. They were a team of five, and they were unarmed. They were on their own until the shuttle returned.

He had no fear of a deserted colony. It might be a bit on the eerie side, but he was used to that. He even enjoyed it, finding pleasure in the familiar details of a situation he knew well. He could run an analysis on an empty O'Neill in his sleep. When you got right down to it, all you had to do was to identify the standard features and then concentrate on what was unusual.

A chimpanzee was unusual.

Oh, yes.

This was one O'Neill that wasn't deserted.

Chimpanzees by themselves could not be taken lightly. Pound for pound, they were twice as strong as a man. In a strange environment, they could be dangerous.

The real question, though, was disturbingly simple. *What the hell else was left alive in here*?

Rick managed a smile that would not have fooled a distracted child.

"Okay," he said. "Maybe we've got us a primate colony."

Nobody laughed.

The five of them moved in.

Caroth knew exactly where they were and exactly what they would do. He understood his world.

He knew himself well but that did not mean that he had his feelings entirely under control. Conflicting emotions stormed in his gut. Pain, hunger, regret, eagerness, fear—

It would not be easy to do what he had to do.

He was sure of his power, but he could not select from a wide field. He had to take what came.

Come on, come on, he thought. *Let's get it over with.*

When you are in an O'Neill, orientation can be confusing. Horizons tend to wobble. You can go "in" by moving in a great circle around the outer rim. The sensation of gravity remains a constant determined by centrifugal force. You can go "in" by working along the shafts or spokes toward the hub of the wheel. Then things get tricky and your stomach starts to float away from you.

Rick Malina was a cautious man. He seldom acted on impulse. He knew that he would have to examine the intermediate food-producing areas and the industrial complexes clustered near the center. He didn't have to do it *now*, however.

He had seen enough to rivet his attention on the rim. When he moved toward the hub, he wanted to be very sure about what was behind him.

He felt a sense of strangeness that was alien to him. It offended his picture of the way things should be. It wasn't the curvature of the surface; that was almost undetectable. It wasn't the slime-covered spherical dwellings that sprouted like bubbles; they were standard. It wasn't the twisted shrubs and crazy trees and grotesquely overgrown gardens.

He didn't mind the phony clouds or even the see-through horizons with their shifting colors. He could even take the pale rubbery mold that squished and compressed under his boots.

It was the air—the oily air that neither smelled nor tasted *right*.

It was the shadows—fugitive shadows where shadows should not be. Chimpanzees, maybe. Still . . .

It was a power that was reaching out for him, seeking him. He could feel it in the marrow of his bones. The issue was not *if* he was going to find something outside the range of his experience. The problem was *when*.

He did not have long to wait.

He caught a whiff of it before he saw it. It took him a long minute to classify that dry pungent smell. It was one of the oldest smells of all, and should have been instantly familiar.

Familiar? Not here.

It was smoke. Plain old woodsmoke.

In an O'Neill?

He shot a look at Frances Bauerle. Fran had the best nose in the group; it was a standard joke between them. Fran smelled it too. She had come to a halt, sniffing the greasy air.

Rick's mind tensed and coiled, threatening to run away with him. The impurities could be taken out when the air was recycled, of course. If there were not too many fires. If they were located properly—

But who would build a fire? And why?

He had a wild moment when he thought of forgotten chimpanzees, chimpanzees subtly changed over the generations, chimpanzees building fires and beginning a weird new life in a world where they finally had a chance. . . .

Impossible? Not in *this* O'Neill.

He put the brakes to his imagination. He had enough problems without conjuring up phantoms.

"I see it," said Sandy Bayer. His vision had always been sharp. Fran's nose, Sandy's eyes: they covered the waterfront. "It's a fire, Rick. There are—figures—around it. I think—"

It was too late to think. Rick felt a blurring in his brain. He sensed that there were forms behind his group, cutting them off. It was as practical to keep going in the same direction as to turn back.

Why not?

They moved toward the fire.

There was really nothing else to do.

Out of the wavering light there emerged a scene not quite as old as time, but old enough. It sent a haunting chill through Rick. It fingered chords of memory he hadn't known he possessed. It had a dreamlike quality, a dream that twisted back through ancient sleeps. . . .

A crackling orange flame that hissed and danced. The sharp warm scent of blue woodsmoke. Another smell: sweet, dripping, blood-salty. Meat. Fresh wet meat sizzling in tongues of searing fire.

Yes, and figures. People? Half-naked, crouching around the licking flames. Eyes that gleamed. Sweat that glistened. Bodies that cast monstrous shadows.

Savages? (Good God, where had that word come from?)

Human?

Rick searched for the magic words and could not find them. Oh, more than a memory and more than a dream. Here they *were*. It was a situation that had not existed on Earth in his lifetime. Archeology come to life. Not stones and bones and sterile museum reconstructions. People. Or—

A man detached himself from the huddle around the fire and walked toward him. Rick had never seen such a man. He was dizzy with shock.

Human, yes. He could see that now. But the man was more than old: he *looked* old. Rick had never known a person who actually showed the signs of age. And the man was sick. He was crippled. His body was hunched forward, his spine locked into a frozen arch. In the world Rick knew, there were only healthy, perfect people.

The man had lost his hair. The skin on his skull was white and taut and blotched. Rick could see the lumps and depressions in the bone. Rick had seen plenty of skulls in his time. This one was within the range of variation for *H. sapiens*. Just one of the gang. But aged, stressed, showing the telltale signs of a body chemistry too long ignored by medical attention.

There was still power·in the man: a raw physical strength and an unyielding force that went down deep. The shoulders were uneven, but they were massive. The gnarled hands were like chunks of rock. The man's belly was creased and lined; it looked like an old leather apron. The legs were thin, all bone and gristle and sinew and knobby knees.

The man's swollen nose was too big for his face; the nostrils flared and the veins were distended. When he breathed, there was a slight bubbling noise that seemed to gurgle down and lose itself in the flaps of wrinkled skin on his chest.

His eyes were bloodshot and there was pain in them. There was more than pain. It was not hate. It was not anger. It was certainly not fear.

Resignation? Weariness? Something of that, perhaps.

But much more.

Call it pride. A hard, flinty, uncompromising pride.

Call it determination, a will that would not break.

Call it hope.

The man was now so close that he could have reached out and touched Rick Malina. Rick could smell his decaying breath.

The man stopped.

The bloodshot eyes stared at Rick.

"So," the old man said. His voice was flat. "You have come back."

In a strange kind of way, Caroth felt that it was over. He experienced a sense of letdown. All the waiting, all the planning, all the suffering—

And now this.

A child from Outside. So young, so perfect, so unmarked. There was intelligence there, of course. But the mind had never had to fight. It didn't know what endurance was. It was no match for Caroth.

He had him. It was too easy. It was like throwing a net over a young pig.

Caroth could get into Rick's head. He could twist him around and tie him in a knot. There were no barriers, no defenses. He could smother him, absorb him. He took a lot with very little effort: a name, a general life history, a swirling blur of impressions.

Caroth was not overly pleased. He had much to give. He wanted a *man* for his son, not a pliable lump of mud.

Caroth had to struggle with his disappointment. It would be easy to let go. He was hurting.

Quickly he rechecked the others. No, they were not an improvement. He had the right one. The leader.

Some leader. A child . . .

There had been one stroke of luck. Caroth took a certain satisfaction from that: he was entitled to one break. The colony had been founded by English speakers. He would not have to master a new language. The words had not changed much.

Caroth did what he had to do. He got his head jammed up against the startled face of the young man. He turned on the power, gulping at his mind.

"You are Rick," he said. "I am Caroth. I will now tell you what you are going to do."

Rick Malina felt as though he had been hit in the head with a hammer. His brain pulsed with flashes of light. The palms of his hands were dripping wet. His legs trembled.

His reaction was instinctive. He could not think.

He reached out with his two slippery hands and touched Caroth squarely on the chest. The old man's skin was rough and dry. It had iron under it.

Rick shoved Caroth back. It was not a monumental push, but it was hard enough to get the job done.

The bloodshot eyes were shocked and surprised. It had been a long, long time since any man had put a hand on Caroth.

Rick did not know what to do next. He shook his head, trying to clear it. The fuzziness would not let him go.

Still, he had a corner of his mind back. There was some grit in there, and some anger. Rick did not entirely recognize himself.

He fought without knowing what he was fighting, or why. There seemed to be three distinct personalities churning in his head. One belonged to an arrogant old man who had lived a life that was strange almost beyond belief. One still belonged to Rick Malina. *Rick Malina*. Who was he? What was he? Hang on: thirty-two years old, six feet tall, black hair, brown eyes, free from disease, archeologist, involved with several women, occasional drinker, fond of cats—

Nothing?

And a third personality. Detached, watching, taking it all in. Laughing?

Here he *was*. He was in the big fat middle of an intact society of hunters and gatherers. It was the find of the century, the opportunity of a lifetime.

And what was he doing? He was in a pushing and shoving

contest with a sick old man whose breath stank. He was struggling just to *think*.

His brain swirled. There were memories in there that did not belong to him. He remembered the ancestors of Caroth, people who had stayed behind when the exodus began. He saw a small population that had dwindled with the generations. He felt the changes. When industrial systems became pointless, the people farmed. When they were too few to maintain the crops, they hunted the feral pigs and cattle. When the bubble-houses failed, they built their own shelters. When they had nothing else, they found the security of ancient fires.

Oh, the fires were good. The fires threw the shadows back. The flames kept the chimps at a distance. The strong and patient and waiting chimps . . .

He looked extinction in the eye. It was a cold and frozen and unblinking eye. There were no more children—

Rick shuddered. He wrenched his mind free, isolating it.

He had some measure of control now.

Hang on, hang on.

Rick spoke. His voice was almost steady.

He said: "Okay. You are Caroth, and I am Rick. That's a beginning between us. I think it's kind of early for either one of us to start giving orders. Let's slow down, shall we? How about it?"

Caroth was not displeased. He could have crushed the young Outsider with little effort, but that was not the point. Caroth wanted a son.

He had not become the leader of his people by brute force alone. He had mental powers that were beyond Rick's understanding. He also had some diplomatic skills.

He used them.

"Come now, Rick," he said. His tone was as warm as he could make it. "You are welcome here. We have been waiting for you. Your people will be the guests of my people. Together, we will decide what we should do. Is that satisfactory?"

Caroth had the advantage, and he knew it. He preferred a more direct approach, but he could play with words as well as the next man. The pain bothered him. He ignored it; he had lived with pain for most of his life. He had a wedge in Rick Malina's mind. He could manipulate him to some extent.

The old man caught an errant sense impression from one of the chimpanzees, standing flat-footed and knuckle-handed outside the

range of the flickering firelight. Waiting, watching. Damn chimpanzees. He hated their guts. They kept on breeding, mocking the
people. And they were so strong. They could tear a man apart.
They had done so, more than once.

Caroth silently told the chimp exactly what he thought of him
and his mother and his mother's mother. Then he turned his attention back to Rick Malina.

"Are you hungry?" he asked. He went back to the fire and
retrieved a chunk of bloody, half-cooked meat. He held it out to
Rick. "Is this not also a good way to begin?"

The life-scarred old man was not without a sense of humor.
Rick's fight to conquer his revulsion tickled him.

Rick took the meat. He ate some of it and passed the rest to
his companions. He did not vomit.

Caroth smiled and tried to look harmless. He studied Rick with
something that was fairly close to respect.

They might get along.

That was just as well. Caroth had no intention of leaving his
world with his people. He wasn't going anywhere.

And neither was Rick Malina.

Not yet.

For Rick Malina, time began to move along two separate tracks.

In one dimension, he did the best he could to cope with what
he had found. He seemed to himself to be entirely rational. He
made the moves he had to make and he got the expected results.

Sandy managed to get the communications equipment going
again and they re-established contact with Earth. That was when
the fur began to fly.

At a time when the starships came in almost daily with tales of
wonder, it took one hell of a story to make a splash. This was
that kind of story.

Rescue was the name of the game. There had always been a
kind of lingering guilt about the abandoned O'Neills. Here was a
colony that dated from the early days of space exploration. It still
had people in it. They were caught in a lifeway that was almost
forgotten on Earth. They were sick and they had come to the end
of the line, but they were *alive*.

They had survived.

They were instantly heroic.

Rescue, yes. But rescues can get complicated. The doctors had
their certain-sure input. The media people were drooling with
anticipation. The politicians smelled votes. And the scientists—

well, this thing was too *big* to be left in the hands of a junior archeologist.

Rick did what had to be done. He had Ann and Pete measure everything from the oxygen content of the greasy air to the depth of the mold-growths that sheathed the processing machinery. Fran and Sandy took the photographs and did the interviewing.

Get it all. Get it all now.

It was a hectic time, a time without sleep.

In another dimension, Rick knew that he was reacting oddly. He was not sure what reality was—or where.

That damned old man was in his head.

Rick *absorbed* the stalking of a pig through a dripping jungle of slime-wrapped plants. He *felt* the pain that gnawed at his failing body. He *lived* with the patient chimpanzees, always gliding through the dark shadows. He *exulted* in the protection of the orange-yellow fires. He *loved* the shifting pale pastel colors of the closed-in sky.

And he remembered so much. A life time of memories: the Sorceress when she was young, the time when Stalker had tried to fly too far, the warm rain that had pelted down when there could be no rain—

Continuity. That was what it was all about. Rick had been on the fringes of it before, extracting an ancient artifact and holding it in his hand. He was not immune to wonder. He had his day-dreams. But this was genuine. So had all the countless generations been, back on Earth, back through the immense spans of time that archeologists tagged so glibly as the Neolithic and the Paleolithic. . . .

He knew that his work here would not end when the rescue ships came. His life was bound up with that of Caroth. The two of them were linked.

Caroth would stay in his world, of course.

Rick would stay with him. It was *their* world now.

Until—

Caroth had tears in his bloodshot eyes. He was ashamed of them.

The ships that came from Earth were impressive. These were no mundane shuttles on ho-hum runs. These were sleek metal fish that flashed through space with their figurative flags flying.

Caroth could not have cared less.

For a time, there were Important People in the O'Neill. There

was enough hot air from speeches to raise the temperature of the
galaxy a fraction of a degree.

Caroth did not listen to the fancy words.

The farewells were hard on him. He said little. He embraced
some and simply touched others. One Eye, Lansing, Floater, Lun-
delius, Smoke-Eater, Lastborn, Dreaming Woman . . .

His people.

He would not see them again.

Maybe the doctors could help them. Maybe not. They could
not help *him* in what was left for him to do.

He did not forget the Outsiders. He could not feel strongly about
Fran and Pete and Ann and Sandy. Still, they had been understanding. One of them might have been chosen. . . .

He knew what Rick was thinking. They were together.

When the airlock closed and the ships left, there was a terrible
silence.

Two men cannot fill an O'Neill, and there were no words.

The Important People had not been happy with Rick Malina.

Rick was not overly concerned about their opinions. He had
plenty of other things to worry about.

The law was quite specific. As long as an O'Neill was intact,
no inhabitant could be forced to leave without a vote by the local
citizens. An O'Neill was a world.

There were other laws. One of them stated that the senior archeologist on a salvage project made the final decisions about what
was to be done. Not forever, no. But for a reasonable period of
time—and it was up to the courts to figure out what "reasonable"
meant.

They could not expel Caroth until they blew the place up.

Rick could go when he was good and ready.

Just the same, Rick had not endeared himself to his superiors.
He had not behaved Professionally. He had allowed himself to
become Emotionally Involved.

He had also become, as one stern gentleman had so elegantly
put it, a pain in the butt. A glory hound.

Rick Malina didn't care.

That was all part of another world.

His world was here and now: the twisted oily-green vegetation
that seemed to grow before his eyes, the stained bubble-houses,
the spongy rot beneath his feet, the soft colors of a shifting sky.

And one irascible old man, trying to knot the final loop in his
life.

Rick's mind was almost clear. He was not entirely himself—he knew that he never would be again—but he was not a puppet dancing on an invisible wire. He had the capacity of choice, and that was a kind of freedom.

He wanted to be where he was, and what he was.

He looked at Caroth. Physically the old man was the same: the locked and tortured spine, the bald and lumpy skull, the swollen nose, the massive and uneven shoulders, the curiously fragile legs. The eyes were still bloodshot, and pain lurked behind them.

The sight of him no longer affected Rick. It was hard for him to remember his first sense of shock.

Something had grown between them.

Call it trust.

Fear was gone from Rick Malina. In its place was expectation. More than that: exhilaration, eagerness, joy.

He had never really known his father.

He hadn't known one hell of a lot of joy either.

Rick was ready. He nodded at Caroth.

"Okay, Pops," he said. "It's your move now."

Caroth had waited for a very long time.

Now that the waiting was over, an alien emotion crept through the old man: doubt.

It was Caroth who felt fear.

What if it didn't work? What if it all fell flat? What if Rick Malina could not absorb it?

What if he laughed?

The two of them were alone. Caroth would not get another chance.

He spat, disgusted with himself. He had come this far. He would not show weakness now.

"Come," he said.

Ignoring his pain, he took Rick to see the world.

Rick suspended his will and followed Caroth. It was not easy. He lost count of how many times he slept. He ate when Caroth brought him food.

The old man seemed tireless. He did not try to save himself. He used it all.

Rick was intensely alive. He found a strength he had never known before. He felt as though his whole life was converging on this place, this time, this event.

He knew that Caroth was showing him more than a world. He was showing him a life.

Rick understood, and was grateful.

He opened himself and took it all in.

There was a dark sea without waves that curved like heavy oil toward the horizon. Nameless things swam and scuttled in its shallow basin. The sea had pinpoints of light that reflected on its glassy surface.

Starlight.

The other side of the rim was translucent across that section, of course.

You could actually see Outside.

That didn't matter.

What counted was Inside.

The sea that would have been a small lake on Earth was a beginning. Caroth had been born in a nest on its shores.

Rick saw it, felt it. The nest was snug and dry and lined with flowers. Then it was sticky with blood. Caroth was a healthy and unscarred baby, but his mother died within hours. Caroth was nursed by another woman whose child had been stillborn.

Caroth survived. There were few children then, and he was indulged.

Rick followed the years of childhood. It had been a happy time: gliding through the bright corridors that were the spokes leading to the hub of the O'Neill wheel, exploring the silent and mysterious processing labs, playing the hunting game of two-on-a-side.

Caroth had not been lonely. Smoke-Eater was almost his own age; his name had been Owens then. There had been others young enough to share his life—Mac who laughed so readily, Snare who had been quick but not quick enough, Blossom who had done just that. Blossom had changed from a girl into a woman very rapidly, and she discovered sex. That had been fun for them all.

Caroth's childhood ended with the storm.

He had been looking forward to the Acknowledgment. But the storm came first.

The storm was a freak and therefore awesome beyond belief. There was not even a memory of such a thing, and the O'Neill was full of memories. Rick could feel the horror. He relived it with Caroth.

Electrical charges built up in the atmosphere. The clouds turned dark and sullen. There was *wind* in the O'Neill: a river of wind that moaned through the rim of the colony. It was strong enough to snap trees.

The rain materialized. It did not fall—it came from all directions. Huge fat drops of warm water swirled and splattered. There had been controlled rains in the early years, but nothing like this. The O'Neill would never be wholly dry again. The wind-driven globules of water smashed the world.

Lighting exploded in searing discharges. The crash of thunder was continuous. The sound could not get out. The booming echoes were so loud that people screamed to relieve the pressure in their ears.

At the end of the storm—just before the silence began—Caroth was struck by lightning.

Rick felt the stunning shock that hurled him to the wet vegetation. He smelled the acrid burning of ozone. He fought the numbness . . .

Caroth was marked. He did not know that the lightning had triggered his sickness, but he believed it. When his senses returned, it was pain that he felt. The pain chewed at him for the rest of his life. He lost his hair. His body became bent and twisted.

He worried about the Acknowledgment. What would his father think of him now?

There was a change in the way that people treated him. There was distance. Even Smoke-Eater withdrew a little, and Mac was careful with his jokes. Caroth knew their minds. He had the power. It was not uncommon among the people, a kind of compensation perhaps for shrinking numbers.

The people took it for granted that Caroth had been marked for a reason. Such things did not just happen. Caroth had been singled out.

And his father? Caroth could not read *his* mind.

They waited warily, father and son.

When the Acknowledgment came, it was strange.

The fire was like other ceremonial fires: four logs blazing on Spirit Hill. The feasting was good, but there was a sadness in the heavy air. The people were aware. Lastborn was already a child, and Dreaming Woman had seen her visions of hollow emptiness . . .

His father had always been a stern man and there was no softness in him now. He held the ancient knife with a steady hand.

His father slashed his own left arm first, wrist to elbow. Then he cut his son, deeply. He offered the knife to the flames. He grasped Caroth's arm and pressed it against his.

The red bloods mixed.

As the people chanted, his father said new words: "I will be your father, but you are not as other sons. I acknowledge you, and we are one. I charge you to continue. Remember me as I will remember you.''

Caroth responded with the old formula: ''I have heard your words.'' It was the best that he could manage.

Caroth's father seldom spoke to him again. He never explained the meaning of what he had said at the Acknowledgment. When his time came, Caroth's father climbed silently onto the traditional metal raft and poled himself out upon the waveless sea. He said no good-byes.

Rick could identify with Caroth, and more. There had been no farewell from his own father. There had not even been an Acknowledgment.

It hurt.

Emotionally spent and exhausted, Rick followed the remainder of Caroth's life. It was a world and a life that Rick knew: he had come in at the end of it. Caroth, the leader. Caroth, the unbroken. Caroth, the schemer—

An old, old man fighting the decay of his world.

Waiting, dreaming . . .

And always the dripping rot of the jungle, the pain, the mold that oozed, the fires that warmed, the dark shadows of the watching chimpanzees—

And hope, the hope that would not die.

When the journey was over, Rick and Caroth stood not far from Spirit Hill. Both men were shaking with fatigue.

''Which way do we go?'' asked Caroth. His voice was harsher than it had to be. He feared Rick's answer.

Rick still had the strength to smile. ''Do we have time?''

''There is enough.''

''The Hill first, of course. Then the other.''

Rick Malina understood.

Caroth held himself together by the sheer power of his will. He shut everything else out and concentrated on one urgent thought: *Do it right.*

It was now or never, and never was intolerable.

He took the time to kill a small pig. He gutted it with the ancient knife and got the meat ready. There had to be a feast. It was nothing without the feast.

They climbed Spirit Hill. The elevation was not great, but the ascent was a struggle. Caroth was very tired.

There was no need to gather the four logs. Caroth had put them in place long, long ago.

Rick started the fire in the old way. That gave Caroth immoderate pleasure. The boy was learning.

While the meat was sizzling in the flames, Caroth cleaned his knife.

The two men ate in silence. There were few words left. They should not be wasted.

When it was time, Caroth stood in the dancing shadows. He felt the ghost-people who once had gathered on Spirit Hill. He could hear the chanting. Ah, it was clear, so clear. . . .

Caroth gripped the ancient knife firmly. He ripped his left arm with great care, wrist to elbow. There was a lot of blood. The pain was nothing.

Rick extended his arm. Caroth slashed it. He locked their arms together with all the strength that remained to him.

The red bloods mixed.

Caroth said the words: "I will be your father, but you are not as other sons. I acknowledge you, and we are one. I charge you to continue. Remember me as I will remember you."

He offered the knife to the flames. He release was so boundless that he had almost forgotten part of the ritual. He was soaring. It was like gliding through the bright corridors of yesterday—

Caroth hardly heard Rick's response: "I have heard your words." Caroth knew that Rick would not fail him.

He was not a bad son.

Caroth could feel himself staggering. He almost fell. His will was failing him. He was ashamed.

A strong bloody arm supported him.

Rick.

There wasn't far to go.

Caroth was not used to accepting help from any man. He took it now.

He offered no thanks.

Damn son.

That was what he was *supposed* to do.

Rick Malina was so tired that he could not think. He just did what he had to do.

Caroth was too heavy to carry. He would not have permitted that in any case. The old man still had some pride.

He wanted to die with dignity.

Rick assisted him without being obtrusive about it. When Caroth stumbled, Rick caught him. When Caroth hesitated, Rick took the lead.

They made it, somehow.

The old metal raft was waiting on the shore of the waveless sea. Caroth collapsed on the raft and then struggled back to his feet. He picked up the pole.

Rick started to help him with the launch but thought better of it. He let Caroth do it for himself.

The raft drifted out and up across the surface of the dark and oily water. Caroth became small and indistinct. The last view of him that Rick had was starlight reflecting from his white bald head.

Then there was only starlight.

Nameless things swam and scuttled in the shallow basin of that sea. They were great for the ecology.

Rick staggered only a few steps before he found it. He knew that it would be there. A fresh nest, snug and dry and lined with flowers. The old devil had thought of everything.

Rick crawled into the nest. He closed his bloodshot eyes. He slept and slept and slept. . . .

When he was conscious again, Rick felt the pain in his shoulders. He examined himself. He half expected to find the body of a twisted old man.

No. There was a raw slash-wound on his left arm. Otherwise, he was the same—on the outside. He experienced a guilty surge of relief. Rick was young enough for vanity.

He picked some red berries. He knew the right ones. He swallowed them by the fistful.

Eating for two, he thought wryly.

He had his mind back. He rather liked it. It was stronger now. There was a lightness in him, a soaring.

Call it joy.

Grief? Not for Caroth. They were one. Caroth continued. He had no use for a maudlin son.

It was time for Rick to finish what he had started. There was more than one kind of salvage operation.

Rick returned to the communications equipment and sent his signal to Earth.

He built a small fire close to the airlock. He sat hunched in the shadows, waiting. There was pain in his shoulders. His arm was beginning to scar.

They were coming.

He was ready.

He had an enormous advantage now. He could see into their minds. There was much that he could do.

He could stall the destruction of the O'Neill indefinitely.

He could work with the remnant of his people.

He could bring something back to Earth more precious than artifacts. He had lived the past, and he had professional training. He was a link with all the vanished generations. He *knew* them. Not just on the O'Neill. On Earth.

He would endure. He would continue.

When the unbarred airlock was opened from the Outside, Rick Malina crossed to the shuttle with a smile on his face.

One day, he might have children of his own. Caroth had a good chance of becoming a grandfather yet.

The old man would like that.

The O'Neill waited patiently as it had waited for so many years. It was waiting for decisions. Most of those decisions would be made far away.

The air inside was fresher now. There were no more fires.

A troop of chimpanzees knuckle-walked along the trail near the airlock. There were ten of them: big old males with their massive arms, smaller females, infants with their brown gamin eyes. They barked and hooted cheerfully.

They acted as though they owned the place. They did.

There were other chimp troops, but there was plenty of food. Sweet fruits grew in the tangled vegetation. There were lots of bugs in the spongy mold. Once in a while, the chimps could catch a young pig or a calf and feast. It kept things interesting. It was fun to live in a world without humans.

They were free, and they knew it.

A female detached herself from the group. She had a child that was still so young that it rode on her shoulders, hanging on for dear life. The mother moved purposefully, without wasted effort.

She went to the airlock and examined it with her dark intelligent eyes. She muttered to herself.

She balanced on her flexible feet and the roughened knuckles of one hand. She reached up with her other hand and grasped the metal sealing bar. She was very strong. She slipped the bar from its moorings and dropped it into the sockets. It was easy.

She knew what she was doing. The airlock would not open from the Outside.

She twisted her head around. Her child leaned forward and nuzzled her.

The mother gave a low bark of pleasure.

She turned and rejoined her troop.

Poppa Was a Catcher

꒰

STEVEN GOULD

Congressman Newt Gingrich is an historian. As he is found of saying: millennium years are rare.

The United States can, in the year 2000, make an unambiguous contribution to the future of mankind. I suggest the Lunar Settlement: the first elements land in 1996; and by the year 2000, or shortly thereafter, Luna City can be completely self-sufficient, capable of keeping humanity alive no matter what, war or dinosaur-killer, might befall Earth.

By 2004, the anniversary of the Lewis and Clark Expedition, we could land the first elements of a permanent settlement on Mars.

These are not dreams. The engineers, scientists, and managers who would have to *do* the work all agree we *can* do it, and at prices we can afford—the SSX would make a nice engine for such a program. At present, the United States annually spends two hundred billion dollars more than it takes in. Any family attempting that trick would be bankrupt in no time. Even a land as rich as we are cannot forever saddle our children with the bill for our wild party.

Yet for far less than the current deficit—for perhaps twenty-five billion dollars per year, certainly no more than fifty billion dollars per year—we can insure the survival of our children, while simultaneously developing the technology and resource base that will pay off the terrible debt burden we have already placed on their shoulders.

We can do both. The key to both economic health and strategic defense is space. Whatever we do in the space medium advances both goals. We know *how* to do the job. Intelligent planning—intelligent use of the space media—will, if we'll only do it, bring in a new era of peace, prosperity, and freedom.

■ ■ ■

Poppa was a catcher on the Company team,
Slowing down the rocks as they came down the beam,
Sometimes they were low ones,
Sometimes they were high.
Sixteen tons of ore in the blink of an eye.

Momma she pushed veggies in the Company tanks,
Kept from going crazy by the Company tranks.
Bees can't stand the spinning,
Bees can't hardly stand,
Momma trucks down aisles pollinating by hand.

One day Poppa slipped up as it buzzed across the plate,
Thirty tons of ore like the black hand of fate.
Burn you mother thruster,
Thruster she won't burn.
Poppa's ship is making like a funeral urn.

Momma got called into the Supervisor's den,
Told the fate of Poppa by the Company men.
Damn your stupid husband!
Don't give us any lip.
Can't you see how much it costs to replace that ship?

Momma left the bossman in a rush of tears,
Couldn't take the sight of those Company leers.
Heaven help you Poppa,
You've gone away from me.
Batted like a homerun for the Company.

She took the elevator all the way to the rim,
Watching stars go by with a strange little grin.
Opened up the airlock,
Shook away the tears,

Her body will hit Saturn in a couple of years.
From *The Ballad of Baby Boo*
Copyright, 2053, The Delta Vees

The visitor did a number like Rockaby Baby after the bough breaks, falling freely, gracefully north of the plane of the ecliptic, three A.U. from the sun. As it fell it made pretty splashes in the sky, clouds of vaporized metal sprayed behind it to make long, brightly glowing trails. The Hadley-Apennine Observatory on Earth's moon saw them first, followed by the facility at New Eden in Lagrangian Point Five.

The clouds came in patterns broken by four-hour intervals. The first group was a single stroke of a cosmic brush. The second, oddly enough, was two dashes of luminescent cloud. The third group had three, and the fourth, to nobody's great surprise, had four.

Spectrophotometry confirmed the clouds' makeup as cesium with just a tinge of sulfur. Ballistic plotting showed the visitor's path to be a cometary hyperbolic destined to pass within the orbit of Mercury in less than three months. Informed scientific opinion showed itself to be torn in three dozen different directions by the appearance of man's first confirmed extraterrestrial visitation.

When I'd met him at the outer door, he'd said, "Percival C. Evans to see Ms. Moss, by appointment." His hair was shiny black, but his skin was waxy looking, and his eyes were bloodshot. He didn't handle ultra-low-gee well and his clothes were the latest thing from Luna, conservative, with the names of his favorite manufacturers down the seams in three-centimeter-high letters. As he shook my hand, I saw the gleam of a med-alert bracelet at his wrist.

I looked closer, saw the letters, ". . . lood substi . . ." before he dropped my hand. That was odd—he didn't seem old enough to be a fluoroglobin user. Maybe radiation leukemia. . . .

He was also worried about something.

"Yes, Mr. Evans. I'm Boo Bailey, Ms. Moss's associate." I closed the door behind him. "This way, please."

He did okay crossing to her office door, so I pretended not to see how he tended to bounce and had to steady himself against the doorway.

I let him into Grandmother's inner sanctorum without comment. "Mr. Evans?"

"Yes, Madam Commissioner."

She snorted. "I've been retired from the Commission for thirty-four years, Mr. Evans. Please don't use that form of address. Lately, it's become distasteful to me." She paused for a moment. "Please come closer, my eyes are not what they used to be." This was a lie. She'd had lens implants the year before and could see better than me.

He managed to move forward without bouncing off the ceiling. A twentieth of a gee is not much gravity and I knew he'd probably been under half a gee all the way out from Earth. I steered him toward a web chair so he'd have the illusion of normalcy and settled myself over by the bonsai. This is a nasty trick of mine since it puts the grow lights behind me and covers my face with shadow.

Grandmother's desk was circular, completely surrounding her. She pivoted her chair to face him more directly, doing something with her hand that blanked her terminal's display.

Like Mr. Evans, she had a bracelet that meant she went in every two weeks and had two liters of plasma replaced with fluoroglobin, or syntheheme, or syntheglobin—by any trademark, a fluorocarbon platelet substitute to transport oxygen and CO.

She was thin, with fine wrinkles over every visible part of her eggshell skin. She kept her scalp covered with wimple-like hoods because she was mostly bald, and covered the rest of her with loose, colorful jumpsuits that clung at the wrist and ankles, but ballooned elsewhere. She favored Soviet and Japanese corporate names and splashed them creatively across the fabric.

She was 113 years old.

"What can I do for you, Mr. Evans?"

He shifted his hands on his docs-case. "Uh, I don't wish to be rude, Ms. Moss, but what I have to say is extremely confidential." His eyes shifted briefly in my direction.

I waited to see how she would take it.

"Certainly, Mr. Evans." She stood smoothly, coming out of the chair fluidly and floating into the air. As she passed over her desk, she crossed her legs to avoid hitting any keys or switches and lowered her legs again as she floated to the floor near the only other door in the room—the one to her room. "I will leave you to your privacy." The door shut behind her.

I used the time it took him to get his mouth shut to move over to the desk. I perched on one of its bare surfaces and smiled.

He glared back at me. "What did she mean, going off like that?" He'd pulled a handkerchief from a sealflap on his vest and was blotting off his face.

I shrugged and spread my arms. "I thought she was giving you the privacy you asked for. If this still isn't private enough, perhaps I should leave the room, too. And if that isn't private enough, perhaps we *all* should leave. Boy, that sure would make this one private room." I yawned in amazement at it all.

Evans stopped glaring at me and frowned instead. "Could you get her back in here, Mr. Bailey?"

"No," I said flatly. "She rarely moves, period. Once she has, that's it for hours."

"I could go to her."

"She does not see clients in her private quarters."

"Oh." He leaned back and stared at me, clearly trying to figure out where I fit in.

Hell, I stopped trying to figure that out, *years* ago.

I could tell he was worried about my very apparent youth. He probably wasn't too thrilled with my clothes either, since they were monotone black—no company endorsements, no socio/political messages, and no statements of personal philosophy—radical.

Evans stared at me for a while longer. Then he did an intelligent thing. "What do *you* think I should do?"

"Seriously?"

"Yes."

"Tell me what this is about. At least enough to give us some idea, and I will brief her. Then she will call you at your hotel and tell you whether she will do it or not."

"And who else will you tell of this?"

I grinned. "Mr. Evans. You were sent out here by High Commissioner Rostaprovich to find something out. Didn't he tell you *anything* about Ms. Moss?"

He nodded, clearly unhappy. "He said I could trust her with anything."

I shrugged again. "Well, we won't cover up criminal activities, but she's done special projects for the various Commission Divisions ever since she retired. She does not betray confidences. Neither," I added, "does she keep people around her who talk out of hand."

He frowned again, tried glaring, but soon tired of both. Finally he pulled a magcard out of an inner pocket and handed it to me. "Please see she gets this. I think it's self-explanatory."

I took it from him and escorted him out.

Afterwards I locked up and swept for bugs.

I rarely find any, but once in a while. . . . Grandmother's been

involved in too many inter-division struggles. We've been bugged
by Belt Operations Division Security, Transport Division Security,
the Miner's Union, and several private and occasionally illegal
interests.

I even checked that thirty-six-square-centimeter magcard for a
thin-layer transmitter and battery (which is tricky, since I had to
avoid erasing the six point five megs of information on it). All
clean.

I once described these precautions to a visiting tourist and she
got the idea that we were *detectives*. Ha! Electronic security is
the first thing they teach in any of the ISRC's division schools.
On Earth they may think the ISRC is one big happy family doing
nothing but the species' work, but up here it resembles the in-
fighting of the superpowers in the 1950s. We just take ordinary,
sensible measures.

Grandmother is much closer to an outside auditor, contracted
to investigate irregularities that internal audits miss. There *was*
the time she uncovered a drug theft ring operating in Transport
Division—their cargo manifests were slightly out of balance—
but that is *not* the norm. Most of the time, she does sophisticated
computer cost/efficiency analysis and spots the problem from her
computer terminal.

She never goes out on business. Not only is she too stubborn,
but too brittle. Her bones would snap from normal use in a half-
gee field.

After I was sure (relatively) that her world was still secure, I
buzzed her on the intercom. "You can stop hiding now, the boo-
jum is gone."

She didn't answer, but after a while, she came back into the
office and took her desk. "Well, what's *his* problem?"

I said, "No problem. He came by to propose marriage, but I
told you you were far too young to be married without your
guardian's consent, and that I wasn't giving it."

She blinked and continued to look at me.

"There's a magcard by the reader with his plea. He said he'd
keep the ring until you replied."

She picked the mylar strip up and looked at it briefly, then
shoved it in the slot. After it had been loaded into main memory,
her fingers started dancing across keys.

I tried once more. "I just didn't think he was sincere enough.
He struck me as flighty—the nervous type. *I* thought he was after
your money with no consideration for the finer things in life, like
sex, or tag-team monopoly."

The keys stopped moving and Grandmother lifted her eyes from the screen. "Isn't there something else you could be doing, Boo?"

I blinked big, wide innocent eyes. "What, and abandon my ward to big, nasty fortune hunters?"

"Go outside and play."

I grinned and left.

The visitor began radio communication with all the subtlety of a battering ram. It started with a screeching warble that spanned the radio spectrum all the way from the twenty-meter wavelength to the muddy side of infrared. Radio telescopes, trained on the visitor since its initial sighting, resonated sharply. Their operators threw headphones away in startled pain. Signal-strength meters slammed over and ultra-sensitive receivers, hiked up in gain for the slightest breath of transmission, smoked.

Translation: "Is there anybody out there who speaks radio?"

Messages flashed across the Earth, jurisdiction was argued, national pride was flaunted. The UN Security Council engineered a compromise. The Lomonosov Center for Radio Astronomy with its international staff was given the task of trying to communicate with the visitor.

The Draco Project's three-hundred-meter dish antenna in lunar orbit squirted the first message at the visitor. Pulse, pause, two pulses, pause, three pulses, pause. The visitor's visual message to mankind was beamed back to it over a period of fifteen seconds at fourteen megaHertz. Forty minutes later, the visitor's unsophisticated electronic scream switched to fourteen megaHertz and began pulsing in a highly complicated systematic pattern.

The scientists at Lomonosov smiled at each other, rubbed their hands, and started to work.

I spent that afternoon doing a study in cultural biology.

Belt City is a five hundred meter diameter cylinder spinning lazily at one point nine rpm. It is seven hundred and fifty meters long and contains seventy-five percent of the human population outside the orbit of Mars.

To the best of my knowledge, it also has eighty percent of the alcohol-serving establishments in that region of space.

This equates to sixteen bars.

Which has everything to do with cultural biology.

The suspensory ligaments connected to the deep fascia of the pectoralis major support anywhere from thirty to a thousand grams of superficial fascia, glandular lobes, and lactiferous sinuses and ducts—in some cases, even more. But not in *low gee*.

Which makes an enormous difference to the attitude and positioning of a woman's breasts.

I usually start in Bogie's because it's the farthest from center, level fifty at 1.0009 gee. It also features a viewplate dance floor where you can look down and see the stars spinning by, just as if it were glass.

In a one-gee field breasts, even small ones, sag. And I find that perversely interesting.

Which usually means I have to take the elevator up to Ariel's at the hub to see what no gravity does. Ariel's, though, is a tourist trap, with high prices to cover the extra cost of zero-gee bar equipment.

In a zero-gee field breasts, even large ones, don't sag. They achieve elastic balance not unlike malleable soap bubbles.

And I still don't know which is more interesting . . . but I keep researching the matter.

I wish I could give you a glib answer as to my fascination with this particular part of female anatomy, but I can't. Supposedly I was breast fed a normal length of time as an infant. Maybe it's because I lost my mother at an early age, but I doubt it. The closest I can come to explaining it is that women have them and I don't, and this seems reason enough.

Martha Goodwin, owner/operator of Archie's, flagged me down as I was leaving her place. I jumped over a table to join her. (Archie's is on level twelve, point two two gee.)

She grabbed my legs before I came down and spun me in a quick circle, upside down. "Lout," she said.

"Twit."

"Nerd."

"Ohhh!" I said. "You have wounded me to the quick. You have brought blood welling to the surface. You have clasped death's hand on my soul and. . . ."

"Shut up, Boo," she said, and flipped me right-side up again.

"How come you never call me, Martha? Here I am, bearing your child, and you won't even call me once a month."

"I couldn't call you Martha—your name is Boo." She lifted me by the belt until my stomach was in front of her face. "Hmmm, you do seem to be putting on weight."

"Ouch!" I broke her hold with a wrist twist and floated to the floor. "I resemble that remark."

She shook her head. "Two guys were asking after you this morning. They looked like rock miners, but they had money."

"Maybe they hit it big. A half percent finder's commission on a kiloton of praseodymium would pay a lot of bills."

"Ha! You think a find that big wouldn't be all over the belt by now? No, I've never seen these guys before but they looked like the type you find on the wrong end of a lock accident."

"So what did they want with me?"

"They didn't say. Your number's in the city directory, right?"

"Yeah." I didn't get it. What's more, I didn't want to.

"So they probably wanted to find you without *you* knowing about it in advance."

I shook my head. "You have a nasty, suspicious mind. Maybe they're just smart and don't trust the phones. But if they expected *this* to be a safe place, they sure goofed up. Everyone knows *your* tables are bugged."

She made a half-hearted swing at my head with the back of her hand. As I ducked, I couldn't help noting her characteristics *vis à vis* cultural biology, which led to another conversation entirely.

Anyway, it was approaching 1930 when I got home. I'd hit twelve of the bars and gave up happily due to fatigue.

I wasn't droned. The closest I'd come to pharmaceuticals was a glass of chocolate liqueur that Henri Montard of the *Belle* had wanted me to taste. Every place else serves me my usual, tonic and lime, without asking.

Grandmother was torturing plants again.

"Have you talked to your suitor lately?" I asked, doing a two-finger handstand on the edge of her desk.

From over by the plants, she said, "I talked to Mr. Evans thirty minutes ago."

"Oh? When's the wedding? I warn you, I *won't* be maid of honor. I look terrible in pink."

She resumed threading a wire around the branch of a pygmy pine to start it warping in downward curve. She also plucked a handful of particularly healthy looking needles, to cut down sugar production in that area of the plant. "Mr. Evans brought some very interesting data from Misha."

"Misha?"

She nodded absently. "The High Commissioner. Michael Rostaprovich. Around fifty years ago, I had an affair with him. But the man's inconsistent—never could take a set routine. Would never have worked."

"Sure," I said. "I'll bet Evans is exactly the same way. Inconsistent." But my heart wasn't in it. I've seen pictures. She was a heartbreaker, even at sixty.

She began misting, putting a fine sheen of moisture on her pride and joy, the stunted bamboo she'd trained into a double helix over the last fifteen years. "I want you to look at a graph I've produced," she said. She turned toward the computer and called out, "Harken, graphics file G,R,A,P,H,3,3,5." She spelled out the file name for the computer.

I stopped dancing on the ceiling and flipped down into her chair. The flat screen produced a three-color line graph. The horizontal units were in years stretching from 2019 to the present, 2078. The vertical units were in International Monetary Units corrected to 2070 inflationary values. "Pretty," I said. "I may not know art, but I know what I like."

She finished pruning the bamboo and danced lightly over. "The green graph is the cost of equipment outlay for the development of ISRC divisions over the last fifty-nine years. The red one is the predicted percentage of equipment destroyed, damaged, or lost. The orange line is the actual equipment loss."

I nodded. The green line started out at a nice forty-five degree slope, increased almost to a vertical line, then leveled off to a seven-degree increase over the last twenty years or so. The red line crept along the bottom of the chart, pretty much matching the dips and climbs of the green but at half a percent of its vertical component. The orange line was lower than the red line and became lower still until around 2048, when it started climbing erratically until it crossed the red line, and kept rising until it represented about four percent of the green. Then, to further confuse things, a fourth line of dashed red broke off from the main red line around 2056 and climbed above the orange line, then matched its path, but keeping about three percent above it.

"Okay," I said. "At first, the expected disasters weren't as bad as predicted, and, as time went on and experience increased, they got even less so. That makes sense even to me, but what's this back in '48? I see by equipment outlay that there was a big push along then, but that doesn't explain losses even worse than the opening days of space development."

Grandmother nodded, pleased. "That's right. It doesn't." She crossed her legs in lotus and floated gently to the desk top. "But, there's more." She pointed at the broken red line. "Sometime in '56, the annual report started using this figure for overall expected equipment loss. And nobody knows where it came from! They didn't even question it; just checked to make sure that actual loss was below it and thought they were doing good!"

I stared at the screen. "Okay. Someone is trying to make the increase in equipment loss seem normal. Why?"

She crossed her arms. "My working hypothesis is that they're trying to cover up sabotage. Perhaps interdivisional. I don't have the figures yet as to which divisions suffered the greatest losses. Mr. Evans is going to see that I have access to the Commission network."

I leaned back. "I thought there had to be a reason *you* were called in. You're going to start checking the data base for tampering?"

"Right. If there's nothing tricky, we know it was personnel with access at the time—a small group. If it gets tricky, that might tell me something, too."

"Derekin will have a fit." Roberto Derekin was head of Belt Operations Division Security. He thinks there ought to be a commission reg against Grandmother. He's none too fond of me, either.

Grandmother smiled, something she does less than once a month, and nodded her head. "I know."

Director Derekin called the next morning while I was doing body maintenance in the exercise room. Since Grandmother knew I was home, she didn't answer it. I quit stretching and activated the phone.

He's uglier full size, but at half size his features still made me grin. "An honor, Director. To what do we owe the pleasure?"

"Connect me with Anita, Bailey."

"I'm doing well, thank you, and how are you and Mrs. Derekin?"

"Connect me."

I nodded. "Glad to hear it. You know, you really don't call often enough. It's a shame we don't see more of you."

"Bailey!" His face turned red.

"I must say that your skin is looking much better than the last time you called—have you seen a dermatologist?" This was a cheap shot. Everytime he got upset, his face broke out.

He took a deep breath. Paused. Took another.

"Could you hold the line a minute, Director? I have to check on some laundry."

I flipped him to hold and buzzed Grandmother. "Hell hath no fury like a man ignored. One of your other suitors is on the phone—Roberto."

On the screen, she frowned slightly. "Very well, Boo. I'll speak with him. Perhaps you should stay off-camera. You know how you excite him.''

"That's 'incite.' I'll patch him through."

I flipped a few buttons and the screen split—Grandmother on one side and Derekin on the other.

Grandmother nodded. "Good morning, Roberto."

That's another thing that burns Derekin about Grandmother. She treats him like a child and he's fifty-two years old. Still, that's sixty-one years younger than she is. Besides . . . she treats everybody like a child.

"We have a request from a Percival Evans to open your terminal lines to the Commission Network with full access." He stopped and looked at her.

She just sat there, waiting.

"Well?" he said.

"Well, what, Roberto? Did you ask a question?"

"What justification do you have for needing this access?"

"I would think that is Mr. Evans' business. Did you ask him?" Derekin frowned harder, if that's possible.

Grandmother shook her head slowly. "Either Mr. Evans has the authority to grant the access or he doesn't. If he didn't, you wouldn't be trying to find out what I'm going to do with it. And if he didn't tell you *why*, then I'm certainly not going to." She clucked her tongue at him. "When will the access be changed?"

He started to say something, but choked it off. Then he said, "I was told you would be on line by 1330. You will have full read-access to any section, but will be completely write-protected."

Grandmother nodded.

Derekin broke the connection without another word.

The United Nations' Agreement on the Moon and other Celestial Bodies created the International Spacial Resources Commission over sixty years before the visitor dropped into man's solar system. For over half a century, the ISRC, or "Company," as it was known, held a virtual monopoly on the exploitation of space. When the visitor began discussing trade between the peoples of Earth and its creators, the Company screamed.

From debate on the floor of the United Nations in General Assembly:

The Australian Representative:

    Sacred Trust! They scream to us of Sacred Trust? For sixty years the ISRC has exploited outer space only to pump their profits back into further exploitation, building vaster empires for the Commission's Chairmen. We keep hearing that our foothold must be secure in the heavens before these "angels" we've created can descend to help the Earth. Bah! I say we should disband the Commission and turn its parts over to private enterprise—to companies that will keep the customers satisfied, rather than keep up the same sort of tyranny OPEC practiced when oil mattered. Under no circumstances should the relations with our first interstellar visitor be handled by this parasite of the human race.

The American Representative:

Colleagues and Friends, much as it grieves me to do so, I must in part agree with the Representative from Australia. The body that so ably undertook the opening of space to commercial exploitation has grown to be an overlarge and unwieldy instrument for the furthering of man's place in the universe. Surely, it can be said that the joining of two sentient races is much too delicate an affair to be handled by the ISRC?

In Assembly of the United Nations of Earth, February 17, 2045, it was overwhelmingly decided that all relations with extraterrestrial races would be handled by the peoples of the planet Earth by their chosen representatives on Earth. The International Spatial Resources Commission was granted no authority in this area. In fact, pending were debates as to whether the ISRC should have any authority whatsoever.

Meanwhile, at Lomonosov Crater on the Earth's Moon, a team of thirty scientists, backed up by thousands on Earth, were trying to pin the visitor down to a definition of terms.

I spent the next three days reading, writing, and programming—minor consulting jobs for minor clients. I also kept an eye on the news, since the debates about ISRC's involvement with the visitor probe were being beamed in from Earth.

One evening, while Grandmother was maiming plants, I asked her opinion of the matter.

She said, "A dollar short and a day late. The chances of the ISRC being allowed to handle it are negligible. For too many years an ISR Commission seat has been a reward for political favors on Earth. Once a Commissioner is appointed, he milks it for all it's worth."

"You," I said, "were different, of course."

She ignored me and went back to the bonsai.

Friday, four full days after Evans showed up for his appointment, he came again, at Grandmother's request. He was handling low gee even worse, so I surmised he'd been spending all his time on the lower floors of the Hyatt.

"Good afternoon, Mr. Evans," she said when he'd been seated.

"Good afternoon."

"I asked you here to brief you on our progress to date and get some instructions."

He nodded.

"First of all, your surmise that the predicted equipment-loss figures had been tampered with is absolutely correct. Not only have they been changed, the files have been completely replaced."

"How can you tell?"

She frowned, remembered that he was the client, and said, "I wrote the original specs on the current network over forty years ago. You may remember that my commission seat was over Information Services Division."

He nodded again.

"In the particular operating system currently being used, there are thirty-four different ways to create a file. What method is used is dependent on such considerations as file size, number of users, how often it is to be accessed, what sort of access, and what form of information is to be stored in it. This lets the system use the most efficient method in accessing them. Suffice it to say that the files reflect this information in their header blocks, and by examining them, I can tell which method was used.

"The files in question are normally created using a catastrophe analysis program called RISKAN, and use one particular method of file creation. The header blocks did not reflect this. In fact, the method of file creation used is common to any of several file examination and repair programs."

Evans spoke. "But if the headers have been changed, why was the master budget program able to access the information?"

She leaned forward. "Because it doesn't matter to the operating system. If the expected method doesn't open the file, the OS just runs down the various file types until the file opens. It won't report an error until it has tried every one of the thirty-four ways. This is obviously less efficient, but is more forgiving when different computer systems have to interface."

"Now, more to the point, I have also been able to determine which terminal group generated the file in question. So, I pulled the personnel files for that area and time to see who would have access and the knowledge to create and insert the new file."

"And?"

She leaned back. "None of them could have done it. The terminals in question are palmprint locked to a group of file clerks, all of them barely competent at their own jobs, much less sophisticated computer crime."

Evans frowned, leaned forward. "Maybe one of them accessed the system and let someone else use it."

"I considered that," Grandmother said, "but decided to check something else . . . I examined the header blocks on the personnel file—it too had been replaced. For that reason, I think that the person who made the changes *was* in that file, but wiped his own record to avoid tracing."

"We could question the clerks directly. They could probably pinpoint a fellow clerk who doesn't show up on the personnel roster."

"Good luck, Mr. Evans. That change was made in '56, twenty-two years ago. According to records, those clerks no longer work for the commission. You may be able to track them down, but even then, who's going to remember?"

Evans licked his lips. "What do you suggest?"

"I programmed a search of commission personnel files, system wide. I looked for the same sort of altered files at any date later than 2070." She held up a sheet of hardcopy. "These seven departments are the result. Four of them are in Belt Operations, one is in Transport, and two are in Systems Administration, on Luna."

Evans blinked his eyes rapidly. "I never dreamed anybody but personnel could change those records."

Grandmother shook her head. "A system programmer or analyst of sufficient rank could. Also security."

"What is the next step?"

"That's for you to decide. I would recommend that you turn this information over to someone with the authority to question the employees in these departments. Some trace of the perpetrator should turn up."

"No," Evans said flatly.

Grandmother nodded. "I thought that would be your attitude. You are unwilling to release this information until you know who is behind it and why."

"It could be *anybody*. Can you continue the research?"

"Only if you can authorize me and my agents to question any Commission personnel necessary. Also, you can expect interference from local Security. They will want to know what is being investigated.''

"Director Derekin has already been pressing me for info." He mulled it over. "Okay, I'll have to telex the High Commissioner, but I'm sure you'll have authorization by tomorrow."

"Very well," she answered. "We'll prepare a course of investigation."

After I saw him out, she leaned back in her chair and sighed.

I nodded in sympathy. "That was tactless of him, sticking to business when you were dying to throw yourself into his arms."

She grimaced, then hit a key on her console. "What's my next step?"

I laughed. "*You're* asking *me*?"

"Call it an exercise in education. What would you do next?"

"Part of it's obvious. If the personnel files in Trend Analysis were tampered with to hide whoever had been tampering with the stat files, then what are they trying to conceal in these other seven departments? What files have been switched or modified? What sort of information changed?"

"Surely. I've started that search."

"Well, then, how about examining the incidents of equipment loss over the last twenty years for patterns?"

She nodded. "That one has also been initiated."

"Oh." I gnawed on it a little more. "Then why don't you send me out to buy some software?"

"That does not follow logically."

"Sure it does. We're talking about an individual or individuals who are more than just competent at system interaction. I've got a line that should work without heavy authorization, and better yet, without alerting our target. I'll give you three-to-one odds on my finding something before the authorization comes through."

Grandmother pursed her lips. "It would get you out of my hair." She nodded. "I'll download the personnel files to your console. Prepare yourself."

I grinned and jumped.

"Well, what on Earth does the bloody thing say?"

The analyst pushed his chair back and flipped his pen into the air. It floated up in a leisurely arc until it just brushed the ceiling, then descended as slowly. Without looking, the analyst reached out and captured it again.

"That's hard to say," he told the reporter. *"You've read the document, haven't you?"*

"Sure I have, but I've also read The Canterbury Tales *in the original. I needed help with those, too.*"

The analyst chuckled. "All right, you want the Reader's Digest *condensed version with all the lumps removed.*" He picked up a sheet of printout from the console before him. "*In essence, the treaty is a general agreement between the Peoples of Earth and the Builders of the Visitor to maintain a steady social and economic intercourse at the first opportunity. The document guarantees them the right to sample all the world's markets, to taste the complete diversity of our world's cultures.*" He paused and looked out the window to the distant crater walls. "*They don't have faster-than-light travel, so it isn't worth their trouble to send a manned trading expedition to a suspicious closed world.*"

The reporter scowled. "*But I thought the visitor said trade could begin as quickly as seven years from now, and there isn't a star within seven lights-year of us in the direction it came from.*"

The analyst sighed. "*I warned them against playing that up. We've gone over that point with the probe several times, using several different time definitions—the orbits of planets, the speed light travels from the sun to Earth—and we get the same answer. We've decided that there is already an expedition heading in this direction. Whether it decides to stop in our solar system or not depends on the visitor's success in obtaining this treaty.*"

"*What about the language of the thing? All these terms like 'Creatures of Planet 500 light-seconds Out of System Primary' and 'Makers of Probes.'*"

"*Well, what do you expect? We have barely begun to learn how to communicate with the visitor. The experiences we share are extremely limited. In fact, it's highly improbable that the probe even thinks, but is instead an extremely sophisticated computer with some capacity for self-programming. If we could bring the visitor down to Earth and show it what we're discussing, share with it more background experience, then we could make great leaps and bounds in progress.*"

The reporter tilted his head and spread his arms. "*Well, why don't we? Send a ship after it and bring it here?*"

The analyst snorted. "*Didn't they teach you anything about physics before your agency sent you here, or are you sleeping with the publisher's wife?*"

The reporter thumbed his nose. "*My business. Answer the question.*"

"*We can't even get close to the probe. It's in an orbit completely perpendicular to the plane of the ecliptic.*" He held up his hands *at right angles to each other. "Even if we had a ship close, it would still be in the plane of the ecliptic. There isn't any sense in an orbit at any angle to the solar system's plane unless you're going to Pluto. That is, there wasn't any sense until now." He crossed his arms. "The most we could manage is a flyby when the visitor rounds the sun inside the orbit of Mercury. Even then, the relative velocity would be almost sixty thousand kilometers per hour. Sort of like trying to read a sign on a train when it's going the opposite direction of the train you're on. Here it comes, flash, and it's gone."*

Preston T. Pau was department supervisor of Equipment Inventory Control for Belt Operations. He was from Malaysia and his English had a British flavor.

I entered his office and said, "It was kind of you to see me on such short notice."

He waved me to a chair. His offices were in the high-gee section of the Commission's end of Belt City, and the seat was welcome. "Think nothing of it, Mr. Bailey. We're always glad to clear problems up. What can I do for you?"

"Well, let me tell you a story. Sometime in August of 2072, our client, Horstman Software, received a demo copy of a software package that was unique, well written, but not particularly useful—at that time. They returned the package with a polite note rejecting the software, but asking to see any future work that person did. They never heard from them again and the file with the name and address was subsequently wiped." I paused and shifted in my seat. "In the meanwhile, a certain type of software came into wide use—one that dovetailed very neatly with the software package Horstman received that August. Now they want that particular package and badly. They feel it would make a fortune for them and the author, but they no longer know who the author was!"

Pau frowned. "I see their problem, but fail to see where we could help."

I nodded. "Horstman has recalled one thing aided by hypnoanalysis—the address on that package was your department."

Pau blinked, then leaned back in his chair. "August of '72? Hmmmmm. I was transferred into this department in '74, so I have no personal knowledge of the period." He touched a button on his desk and a voice answered.

"Stayson."

"This is Preston, Joseph. Do you have a minute?"

"I could find one."

"I'm going to send a Mr. Bailey to talk to you. He'll be right up."

"Send him on."

Pau stood. "Joe Stayson has been with his department since '69. If anyone can help you, he can." He walked me out his door and down the hall to a lift. "He's on level eight. Take a right out of the lift, and it's the first office on the right."

I smiled and thanked him profusely. He shook it off like a shower and went back to his office happy to have delegated another chore. A good executive.

I got off the lift *much*, lighter than when I got on and followed Pau's directions.

Joseph Stayson was a young, rumpled man with a receding hairline. I found him standing loosely behind a chest-high desk piled with computer hardcopy and empty coffee mugs. Stayson stuck out an arm and loosely shook my hand. His greeting was artificial, clearly memorized for social occasions. I didn't waste a lot of charm on him, but simply repeated my story.

He blinked twice, and said, "Jean Rowan."

"I beg your pardon?"

"Jean Rowan. If your client is right about the address and the time, the author was Jean Rowan."

"How certain are you?"

"Positive. I'm a good programmer, but she was better. She came in July of that year to do an audit of computer procedures and left in September. I recall it vividly. She was a better analyst than I was and she wouldn't have a thing to do with me." He blinked again. "I remember. I was in love with her."

I tilted my head to one side. "Do you know where she is now?"

"No . . . and I've tried to find out."

"City guide? Commission directory?"

He shook his head. "Negative. I tried personnel, but they don't give out anything. The only clue I ever had was a picture of her in what she said was her apartment. She gave it to me the last day she was here—pyrrhic victory."

I straightened up. "May I see it? I won't hurt it, but it could be very important for her."

He frowned, and his mouth looked like he'd just bitten into something rotten. Then he pulled open a drawer and shifted papers around until his hand came out with a twelve-by-sixteen centimeter photograph. He took it by the corner and flipped it through the air at me. "Take it," he said. "I never want to see it again."

■ ■ ■

Robin Wilson, of Belt Operations Accident Control, looked at the picture and said, "Roberta Ash, but she was blond when I knew her," and "No, I've no idea where to find her."

Sally Mander, of Belt City Sewage Control, eyed the photograph and said, "Linda Maples looked better as a redhead," and "I thought she went back to Earth."

F. X. Herzig, of Seismic Surveying, handed the picture back to me and said, "Darlene Birch, with darker hair than usual," and "Whatever became of her?"

I said, "I don't know . . . but I'm going to find out."

Grandmother used a digitizer on the photo and put it on the wall screen one meter square. I bounced slowly between the ceiling and the floor while I looked at it.

Jean Rowan a.k.a. Roberta Ash a.k.a. Linda Maples a.k.a. Darlene Birch—in other words, the person in the picture, was a woman anywhere from twenty to forty years old. She had fair skin and a nose slightly too large for her face. Her eyes were green and she seemed slightly underweight, but this was hard to tell because she wore a flowing caftan that concealed everything but her head and hands.

She was seated in a circular lounge chair, the kind made for an intimate two at the most. Behind her on the wall was a graphic print of an early Soyuz launch in a chrome frame. The wall itself was light blue. Beside her on a small table was a tall clear glass with a straw and a dark liquid in it. In a small vase behind that was a flower.

"What's the flower?" I asked Grandmother, since I have limited experience with these things.

She frowned. "It's an orchid. Stupid plants—they're epiphytes . . . parasitic." She leaned closer to the wall. "I've tried to make an I.D. on the face, but any record has apparently been wiped. She's not in the records anymore."

"Too bad. What about the apartment? Think we can locate it?"

She stopped frowning and stepped back from the picture again. "Perhaps. Tell me, Boo. What level is it on?"

I looked at her out of the corner of my eye. She wasn't looking at the picture, so I knew she'd spotted something. I looked at the blowup again and tried to see it myself.

If I'd ever seen Jean Rowan in the flesh, I might be able to tell something from facial sag, or lack thereof. Because of that voluminous caftan, I couldn't tell whether her breasts were sagging or just small. The orchid could have been old and just curled up from lack of hydrostatic pressure, or fresh and bowed down by a full gee of gravity—or plastic, even. I didn't know beans about orchids.

"I don't know."

"Look at the drink."

"Damn. The straw. The fluid's pretty high, isn't it?"

She nodded, satisfied. "Yes. That apartment, if it's in Belt City, is somewhere between levels ten and four."

I moved back to her console and was calling up the city map when the phone beeped.

Grandmother turned the wall screen off. I turned on her desk phone and found myself looking at Mr. Percival Evans.

"Good afternoon, Mr. Evans."

"Mr. Bailey—I have a favor to ask of Ms. Moss. I have been invited to dine with Commissioner Hall and some of his staff this evening and was asked if Ms. Moss would join us, as well." He paused. "It's probably an attempt to find out what I'm investigating, but they *might* reveal something themselves. What are the chances of Ms. Moss joining us?"

I looked over the screen at Grandmother. She was thinking it over. I asked, "Where is this dinner to be held, Mr. Evans?"

"Roark's, on the twelfth of level of the Hyatt. According to the Commissioner, that's the only restaurant Ms. Moss frequents."

Grandmother moved around until she was in the camera's range. "I would be delighted to accept, Percy, if the invitation is extended to Boo."

He nodded sharply. "Done. Apparently the Commissioner knows you quite well. He said, 'and she'll probably want to bring Boo Bailey if she decides to come.' I'll see you at nineteen, then?"

"Certainly, Percy."

He clicked off.

I raised an eyebrow at Grandmother. "Percy, is it? My, my. His suit is going better than I thought. I guess you synthetic blood types have an affinity for each other."

She looked at me. "Mr. Evans uses a blood substitute?"

I shrugged. "He wears the bracelet."

"Interesting. There aren't that many of us." She walked over to the bonsai. "See if you can run down the probable location of that apartment in the next half hour before you have to get ready for dinner. Mustn't keep Uncle Hal waiting."

Outbound, the visitor received the news from Earth.
In General Assembly of the United Nations of Earth, the human

race ratified an agreement of general intent—that the beings in-
habiting the third planet from the sun would welcome and en-
courage trade with the builders of the extraterrestrial probe known
as the "visitor."

There was a pause as the message traveled the ever-increasing
distance to the probe. Then the message was repeated back to
Earth rephrased, but unaltered in content, with an affirmative
behind it followed by a specific inquiry symbol. "This is what you
are saying—yes?"

Earth confirmed with a triplet of affirmation symbols and held
its breath.

Fifty minutes later the visitor replied with the symbol for Earth-
lings and the symbol for its builders, joined with the strongest
conjunction of their makeshift language.

Then it vanished.

Roark's was a leisurely thirty-meter stroll out of the apartment
and around the curve to the Hyatt proper, then up a "stairway"
to level twelve. Grandmother will *not* get on a lift. Who knows
when some minor malfunction will take it *down* instead of up,
and she'll find herself in a hostile acceleration gradient?

The restaurant had a balcony overlooking Central Park, a cylinder within a cylinder. You can look down (or up) to see grassy
slopes, trees, and swimming pools. The grass was at level 40—
three-quarters gee.

We were shown to the private room in the back. Gathered there
was Commissioner Halloran Hall, head of ISRC Belt Operations;
Roberto Derekin, his security chief; Anne Bogucki, Belt Operations Personnel chief; Laura LeHew, Legal Section; and Percy.
They were standing around a bar at one end of the room drinking
and talking.

When we entered they shuffled around, smiles and good cheer.
Uncle Hal came forward, pecked Grandmother on the cheek, and
shook my hand firmly. "How's it going, Boo?"

I just smiled.

Let me explain something now. "Uncle" Hal is not my uncle
any more than Anita Moss is my grandmother, but they are family
just the same. Both my parents died when I was two and several
executives in the ISRC adopted me. There was no family to send
me to back on Earth, and they felt responsible. Like real family,
I'm also stuck with them. *I* didn't choose them any more than one
chooses real relatives, but I'm happy that some of them ended up
"related" to me.

Uncle Hal is one of them I'm mostly happy about.

I won't say how I feel about Grandmother—she might read this and I'd rather bug her.

Offers of drinks were made and I took tonic and lime. Grandmother took a glass of mineral water. The conversation resumed where it had stopped when we came in: when, not if, the UN would dissolve the ISRC.

It was interesting the way they polarized. The older they were—Percy, Uncle Hal, and Grandmother—the more inclined they were to see it as a natural step, while the newer appointees—LeHew, Derekin, and Bogucki—were resentful. I kept quiet and listened, looking for the odd probe into Percy's investigation.

While the waiters loaded the buffet, Derekin looked at Grandmother and asked, "How's your investigation going, Anita?"

I shook my head. Subtle stuff.

Grandmother just smiled.

LeHew and Bogucki were arguing a point of space law with Uncle Hal by the buffet. LeHew snared a few samples off the passing trays. Bogucki leaned over the lobster almondine and inhaled the fragrance. "Good stuff," she said. Uncle Hal tested a piece of ham and said, "Better come and eat before we throw it out."

Derekin stepped aside for Grandmother, but she just waved him on. As I moved up to the buffet I saw her snare Percy with her eyes. He hung back and listened to her for a moment. I saw him shake his head in response, then they joined us.

During supper, we talked about the visitor.

"What are its makers like, I wonder?" said Laura LeHew.

Uncle Hal told her, "They are the most hideous form of life in the galaxy—capitalists."

"Just so they aren't bureaucrats," I said.

This got a bigger laugh than it deserved, but it was the first thing I'd volunteered all evening.

Laura started a complicated lecture comparing the language of the original UN ISRC charter and the statement of intent negotiated with the visitor. I tuned her out and watched the group.

Grandmother was doing her usual imitation of a bird, sampling this and that, but not eating heavily. She did, however, send me back for more of the lobster. Uncle Hal was doing justice to everything, while Anne was a close second. Percy ate a lot of the lobster, but stuck to salad and bread after that. Derekin was too busy trying to watch everyone to eat much. And Laura was talking too much to eat a lot.

Grandmother had put down her fork and was starting to dismantle the whole of Laura's argument with a few well-chosen questions when Percy keeled over.

In a twentieth of a gee, one doesn't fall very fast. I had an arm under him before he was halfway to the floor. My other hand checked his pulse.

He didn't have one.

Uncle Hal is the division commissioner. Grandmother knows everybody, from several heads of state to the High Commissioner. Laura LeHew and Anne Bogucki are bigwig department heads. So who do they pick on?

"Again—why'd you put the poison in his food?"

There weren't any bright lights. They weren't towering over me and screaming in my ears. But it wasn't pleasant.

Derekin would have loved to take me back to his office and have a go at me with all the wires hooked up and the reticular formation of my brain awash with phenobarbital. Instead, he had to sit back in the corner of the room and let Captain Vaslov of the U.N. Civil Police conduct the interview.

"What poison?" I asked for the sixth time.

What upset Vaslov was my lack of fear. He was used to fear— he expected it even in the innocent. This was the Russian attitude and the result he got even with non-Sovs.

I was so tired of sitting there in police headquarters at a full gee that I decided to try logic.

"Okay—try this for size. If you've questioned the others, you know I sat at the end of the table away from Mr. Evans. He went through the buffet line *after* I had already sat down, and there was *no way* I could have sprinkled poison on his plate."

Vaslov grimaced. "We know that—the poison was put in the lobster almondine on the buffet."

I looked at Vaslov. "Damn selective poison—what was it? An allergen that Evans was sensitive to?"

Derekin growled. "We're asking the questions, Bailey."

"Hey, guys. I've got a right to know. If I didn't put it on the stuff, then someone did it before I served myself. What did I eat?"

Vaslov exchanged glances with Derekin.

"It was a diamine amino acid analog," said Vaslov. He watched my face carefully as he said it.

I shrugged. "Is that supposed to tell me something? I didn't think amino acids were poisonous."

"This one isn't. Not to me or you, but then we don't have two or three liters of fluorocarbons floating around our bloodstreams, do we?"

I stood up so quickly that Derekin's hand dove toward his pocket.

"*What are you talking about! Where's my grandmother? How is she?*"

Vaslov held out a restraining hand. "Hold on. Hold on. Your grandmother's fine. I was told that she left the clinic a half hour ago and is resting at home."

"What did the stuff do to her?"

"Nothing," Vaslov said.

The intercom buzzed. Vaslov said, "*Slushaiyoo.*"

"We've received the samples from Robertson Clinic, Captain. It is as I thought."

"Very well, Kareega. We'll be right there." He then turned to me. "Come down the hall with us. I want you to see something."

I'd never been in a morgue before.

Kareega was from Zaire. He was a forensic chemist. When we entered the room he was pouring a translucent fluid out of a bottle into an open beaker. When we were closer he began lecturing.

"This is a mixture of blood plasma and fluorocarbon blood replacement removed from Anita Moss an hour ago. We've already determined that it contains a proportion of the diamine analog distributed evenly through the solution." He held up the bottle and peered through it.

"What does that do to oxygen transport?" I asked.

Kareega blinked, thought about it. "Nothing, I should think. It should also still carry CO_2 four times better than oxygen."

I was still a little shaky. I interrupted him, "Then what killed Evans?"

Vaslov said, "Excuse him, he's young."

"Right," I said. "And that's my Grandmother's life fluids in that jar."

Kareega ignored us and went on as if nothing had happened. "Evans was killed when the fluoroglobin in his circulatory system polymerized."

"Huh?"

"The fluorine groups of the fluoroglobin underwent nucleophilic attack by the amine groups of the analog with acid catalyst, forming long-stranded polyelastomers."

I looked at him blankly.

"Look." Kareega took a medicine dropper out of another bottle and held it over the beaker. "This is carbonic acid." Three drops fell. Almost instantly, the fluid changed color, became darker. He took a stainless steel spatula, dipped it into the mixture, and brought it up. Draped over it were irregular strips of translucent material. Kareega looked from the solids on the end of the spatula to me.

He spoke slowly, as if speaking to an idiot, "His blood turned to rubber."

I looked at Vaslov. "Are you *sure* Ms. Moss is all right?"

He nodded.

"Why wasn't my grandmother affected?"

"She's not a diabetic," said Kareega.

When I didn't say anything, he went on.

"The reaction is twofold. After the diamine analog attaches to the perfluorocarbons, an increase in acidity is sufficient to catalyze the resulting polymerization. Mr. Evans is an advanced diabetic. His blood tends to acidosis normally."

Derekin spoke. "Which is fortunate for your grandmother. Her blood pH was normal, as you know."

I stared at him. Impatience got the better of me and I said, "You really are an asshole, Derekin."

"You and your grandmother engineered it, didn't you?"

I turned back to Kareega. "You're saying that my grandmother's normal blood pH kept the same thing from happening to her?"

Kareega's eyebrows went up. "There *is* hope for you. Diabetics have a tendency toward blood acidosis because they accumulate organic compounds like Beta-hydroxybutyric acid, etcetera. Still, even if he hadn't, the balance would have been tipped when he slept—that would have accumulated enough CO. Ditto for your grandmother."

"How did they treat her?"

"Total blood replacement plus administration of some compound with a high affinity for the diamine analog. Probably something with a long arm of carbohydrate moieties so the liver would get rid of it."

I nodded and stared over his shoulder. My mind was racing and getting nowhere at all.

Vaslov took me back to his office. Derekin came, too.

Pity.

"I'm willing to adopt a working hypothesis, Bailey. For the time being, I will assume you didn't have any direct connection with Mr. Evans' murder."

"Whoopee."

Derekin said, "Watch it, Bailey."

Vaslov continued. "But this still leaves the matter of *what* you and Ms. Moss were investigating for Mr. Evans and High Commissioner Rostaprovich. I have no choice but to assume that this inquiry was the reason behind his murder." He sat down behind his desk and folded his hands together. "We have asked you before—what was the goal of your investigation?"

I blinked. It was two in the morning. I was tired. "As I said, you'll have to get that information from Ms. Moss. I am not at liberty to say."

"You realize that whoever was trying to get Evans was trying to get Ms. Moss, as well?"

I shook my head. "Possible—but not definite. It could have been coincidence."

Vaslov leaned back and suddenly looked tireder than I felt. He said, "*Obrataet*," and his intercom buzzed again.

"Yes, Captain?" a voice asked.

"Alert lock control of an egress prohibition for Anita Moss and Boo Bailey. Forward their retinal patterns from records for their scanner."

"Anita Moss and Boo Bailey. Yes, Captain, at once."

He turned back to me. "That leaves you the run of the city. On pulling your record, I see you haven't been out in two months, anyway."

I didn't say anything.

"I will be calling on your grandmother tomorrow at ten. Please inform her."

Grandmother was waiting for me when I got home.

"You should be resting," I said tiredly.

She snorted. "Do you think I stayed awake through the blood replacement? I was asleep for hours."

"Oh."

"Tell me about it briefly—you can give me more in the morning."

"Vaslov is coming tomorrow at ten. He wants to know what we were investigating. I didn't tell him. He's restricted us to the city and told lock control to make it stick." Then I told her about the poison.

She nodded. "Dr. Rao told me that. It would have been interesting to see it polymerize, though." She raised her index finger to her nose. "I've sent a coded telex to High Commissioner Rostaprovich asking him for direction. Hopefully, I'll get a response before Vaslov arrives."

"Okay. Anything else?"

"Set your alarm for eight."

Five hours sleep isn't at all bad in a twentieth of a gee. Not the six hours I usually get, but enough. I found Grandmother at her desk.

Before I'd opened my mouth, she asked briskly, "What progress did you make in tracking down the apartment of that Rowan woman?"

Well, good morning to you, too, I thought back. "It was either in the Hyatt, the Hilton, or in the block of condos closest to the North Lock. I know our neighbors in this area, and every other residential area is in heavier gee."

"Okay—get out of here and track it down before Derekin or Vaslov shows up. You can eat breakfast someplace else. If you find anything, call on the scrambler and see if it's safe to come back."

"Oh, yeah?" Awareness dawned. "*You* got a response from the High Commissioner."

"Yes." Her voice shook. I was shocked when I realized it was barely contained rage. "The Commission denies any involvement or responsibility for Percival Evans' actions. They say to the best of their knowledge, Evans was on vacation. That's the official line."

"Nuts! Does that mean there's an unofficial line?"

"Misha sent me a coded response. Although he approved of Evans' investigation and privately supported it, the majority of the commissioners felt that this wasn't the time to rake up dirt—with the debates on the ISRC Charter Renewal coming up. He says he can't be implicated." She folded her arms. "Derekin also cut my access to the network."

I nodded. "Figures."

She made shooing motions. "Get out of here. I'll handle Vaslov, but I don't want to hand him everything until I know what's going on."

I ate breakfast at Archie's.

"Those two guys were here again, two nights ago."

I looked up from my eggs and roe. "Sit down, Martha. I want to play footsies."

"Ha! That was never a part of anatomy that interested *you*." She sat opposite me.

"Were these persons asking after me again?"

She nodded. "They were indeed. Do you still not care?"

I scooped the last bit of roe onto toast and chewed. "I guess I've gotten to the caring stage. Can you tell me what they looked like?"

"Better. I can show you."

"Oh? You tape them?"

"Yeah. Got them on the cashier's camera."

I dropped my napkin on the table and followed her back to her office.

"I thought you said they looked like rock miners?"

She looked up from the screen. "Well, that's how they looked the first time I saw them. I hardly recognized them when they showed up like this."

"This" was in formal evening wear, tight pants, and padded jackets. The big one, slightly balding, went in for typical corporate ads—a Stolichnaya Vodka logo on his jacket and ad copy down the seams. The other guy, about my size, went in for abstract juxtapositions of male/female anatomy. Across his shoulders was the statement, "Treats Women with Respect."

I didn't recognize either of them, but the population of Belt City is over 60,000, plus a large transient pool.

"Never seen them before, kid, but I'll keep an eye out."

In return for certain economic incentives, the bell captain in the Hyatt said, "Not in this hotel. I guarantee it."

I knew the bell captain of the Hilton, so the incentive was a promise of dinner and dancing, before she told me, "No. We don't have anything that looks like that. The furniture is all wrong."

That left Cramer House, the exclusive set of condominiums near North Lock.

I stopped at Lily's Fashions to make one purchase. Then I started the approach I'd decided on.

It worked the fourth time I tried it.

She was a waitress at the small cafe owned and operated by Cramer House. I sat down at one of their undersized tables and when she came up with the menu, I said, "Just coffee, please, but perhaps you could help me in another matter."

"Sir?"

I lifted the purse I'd bought at Lily's. "I found this purse down the hall. When I looked inside, all I found was this picture and an awful lot of money. I'm betting this woman owns the purse, or would at least know who does. Do you recognize her?"

She picked up the picture. "Sure. That's Ms. Oakley. She lives in twenty-six."

Bingo.

"Well, thank you. Here, forget the coffee, but take this." I laid a ten-IMU note on the table. "I'm sure Ms. Oakley would want you to have it. Does she eat here often?"

"No, sir. She used to, but I haven't seen her in months."

I left.

The condo was on level four, slightly under a twelfth of a gee. Number twenty-six was fifteen meters down a corridor from a public lift. I had a *Below the Belt News* terminal print me a copy of the latest edition, and settled down on a bench with a clear view of her door.

Evans' death had made it past ISRC censors. Vaslov hadn't issued a press release, but Derekin had, claiming that progress was being made in the investigation, and that certain suspects would be arrested within forty-eight hours. There wasn't the slightest mention of what the motivation might be. Evans was described as a senior ISRC official vacationing in the Belt.

I hoped Vaslov was pissed at Derekin.

In other news, a large molybdenum strike stimulated trading on the world steel markets. The appropriate bodies had been accelerated and would arrive in the vicinity of the Belt City smelter in two weeks.

In a freak accident, a scow carrying two hundred cubic meters of raw sewage from Ceres station lost two valves and half its cargo sixteen thousand kilometers from Belt City. There was some concern at first, but calculations showed that mirrors in the vicinity of Belt City were in no danger of fouling. Certain scatological puns were made.

Bellomy's was having a sale on recreational drugs, and K. P. Mitchell's was advertising second-skin suits at twenty percent off.

Rowan/Oakley left her domicile on my third time through the paper, three hours after I began my vigil.

At first, I didn't know it was her. All I saw was a woman dressed in red coveralls with Bell Aerodyne logos come out of the door marked twenty-six. She was carrying a large bag, the kind typically used to carry personal pressure equipment, and she turned right, going away from my station.

I was on her quick, jogging down the same corridor and passing her, like a man in a hurry. She glanced at me as I went by.

It was her all right.

I took the next right and slowed down. The first phone booth I came to was occupied, but the second wasn't. I ducked into it and pulled off my jacket, all the while looking back toward the other corridor. She went straight. I slung my jacket over my shoulder and followed.

She ended up where I was afraid she would—North Lock.

I lingered with a mixed crowd of executives, tourists, and private pilots while she processed through Lock Control. The crowd was upper crust. At South Lock, the industrial port, the crowd would've been miners, techs, catchers, and pitchers.

I scrambled up a side passage, floating more than walking, to the observation lounge. There was no way I could follow her through Security. Even if I did get past them, there was no way traffic control would allow me clearance for the *Johnny-Go-Lightly,* Grandmother's rock buggy. Not with Vaslov's down-check.

Through the glass I saw Rowan/Oakley skip over to the women's lockers. Fifteen minutes passed before she came out. She had on her skin suit, plus an insulative coverall, zipped open to her waist. Her helmet hung from her shoulder, on a strap. She carried a small hard case for her vacuum sensitives.

I groaned. If she'd just gone to the terminal side of the lock inside of the private pilots' port, I'd have had some idea where she was headed. I pulled myself down the rail until I was looking out into the huge circular hangar bay, and open space.

For a charge, you could listen in to the lock radio traffic. I slipped some IMU fractions into the slot and put on the headphones.

She came through the lock ten minutes later, taking plenty of time to test for suit problems. I switched the channel selection to traffic control. She kicked across to one of the thirty staging platforms where the lock crew had already stationed a medium-range, two-ton ship. She must have phoned ahead, arranging for fueling and staging before she left the condo. I jotted the registration number and name down on the back of my right hand as she entered and pressurized.

"Traffic control, this is November Zebra one eight three, requesting clearance for egress."

"Roger, Ms. Oakley. *Black Orchid* is cleared for egress on pre-filed flight plan at eleven five six. Repeat—one one five six."

Damn. No mention of destination.

The *Black Orchid* was resting on three extended pads, very slight centripetal force keeping it in place. She waited the five minutes until 1156, then kicked off the pad with a burst from side thrusters and moved out of the hangar against a backdrop of slowly revolving stars. As I watched, the ship seemed to start turning, but I knew she was killing the two-RPM rotation she was carrying from the city.

Once clear of the lock she kicked in her main engine and drifted out of sight. I reached in my pocket for more fractions and moved down to where the radar repeater tanks were.

The first one didn't work when I dropped the money in. I walloped it over the fraction reader, but it didn't do anything. Swearing under my breath, I moved to the next one and put my last half-IMU piece in.

It lit up.

Black Orchid, identified in the tank by a small blip with the designation NZ183 below it, was accelerating with respect to the orbit of Belt City, staying in the plane of the ecliptic, and incidentally the plane of Belt City's rotation. I took down the vectors and watched for a change in acceleration that would indicate she'd stopped thrusting. It came five minutes later. I noted the velocity attained, forty meters per second. That jibed with the average acceleration for a ship that size, about fourteen micro-gees.

An idea, unbidden, unwanted, and dangerous flashed into my brain. I grabbed the rail for a moment, while reaction washed through me, twisted my guts, and left me gasping. I wanted to throw up, but controlled the urge. When the feeling passed, I was grinning.

It might work.

"No, I forbid it."

"Don't be silly," I said. "I haven't asked your permission."

I was in a public phone booth, on level thirty, having just made certain arrangements with a retailer of vacuum gear. When Grandmother answered the phone and found scrambler garbage on the screen, she'd keyed our code and synched in.

"I can tell Vaslov about the girl and have him send a vessel after her."

I could tell by the way she said it that it was the last thing in the world she wanted to do.

"How *was* your interview with Vaslov?" I asked.

Her voice started shaking again. "That *man!* I . . . are you determined to do this?"

I nodded. "For many reasons."

She looked at me for a full ten seconds. "Very well. I'll give your gear to Ms. Goodwin, when she comes by. Have her be careful. Vaslov was *not* pleased when you weren't here earlier. I'm sure he left someone outside."

"Right. See you later."

"I hope so."

She switched off, and suddenly I found myself looking at my reflection in the darkened screen—a very young, very uncertain reflection.

I thumbed my nose at it and left.

The man was wearing a faded Rolling Stone vest ensemble with patches. Quite a change from the Stolichnaya suit I'd seen him in on Martha's tape.

His accent was Australian and he had a knife.

"They can do wonders with dacron, boy. You survive the blood loss and they'll build you a new trachea."

I stood very still while the cutting edge rested against my throat.

I had been heading for Archie's when an arm had come out of a side hall and grabbed my jacket collar. The next thing I knew, I was standing in a maintenance closet next to vacuum cleaners and mops.

The door opened again and his co-star appeared, the short one who'd worn the erotica on the tape. He closed the door behind him. "It's clear to the lift. Light traffic."

The big one tightened his grip on my collar. The knife moved slightly on my neck. "Listen very carefully, Mr. Bailey. We're going to walk casually to the lift, get on it, and go down to level fifty. I'm going to walk behind you. My friend here is going to walk beside you. He also. . . ." The short one's arm moved and something went *snick*. Something long and shiny appeared in front of my eyes. ". . . has a knife," continued the big one.

"Why?" I croaked.

"He gets lonely without a knife." The grip relaxed marginally. "It was asking questions that got you into trouble in the first place. Let's not reinforce any bad habits."

The door opened outward and the short one moved out into the hall, holding his knife blade down, by his leg. The knife came away from my throat and the big guy gave me a gentle shove.

As I cleared the door, I slammed it on him.

"What . . . !" said the short one, before I rebounded off the door into him. I tried to make the contact all knees and elbows. He didn't have time to lift the knife until after he hit the far wall. The big one grunted something and managed to get around the door, but I was four meters down the hallway and accelerating.

They recovered quickly. I was hoping they wouldn't be able to handle themselves very well at a fifth of a gee, but they ran right along behind me, sort of skating instead of thrusting hard enough to bounce off the ceiling. That meant they were local, or maybe from Luna. I gained some room when I banked around a corner by running on the wall. That was a trick they didn't seem to know.

Still, I thought the little one was gaining on me.

There wasn't anybody around. It was early afternoon and I'd run the only direction I could, toward the Hyatt. Unfortunately, that was through a residential section. Everyone in that area was either at work or occupied within.

I entered the Hyatt proper and weaved past a room service attendant pushing somebody's late lunch. There was a crash behind me. I looked over my shoulder. The little one was down, waiter and food scattered. The big one sailed over the whole mess and kept coming.

I reached the railed walkway that ran along the side of the Hyatt opening on Central Park. At that point it was one hundred and seventy meters to the parkland below. I ducked left, checked that I was hidden from my chaser's sight, and dove over the edge.

I dropped sideways, tangential to the walkway, at a little under ten meters per second, the rotational velocity of level ten. Above and to the side of me, I heard footsteps go pounding past, apparently missing my impromptu exit. I fell, moving down in what would look like a looping spiral around the central axis if viewed from the park below.

Earth tourists are particularly nervous when they see someone go over the edge, but they don't realize that in a spinning structure like Belt City, gravity is only *apparent*. Once I left the walkway, the only force working to increase my velocity was wind as I dropped into areas of faster-moving air.

It took me fifteen seconds to reach the slides, and my velocity had only increased by seven meters per second by the time I got there.

The slides are stainless steel concave slopes, polished, running from thirty meters up the base of the walls to forty meters out from the wall. They are primarily a recreational device and secondarily a safety feature.

I tucked my bare forearms and feet out of the way and made contact with my back and the seat of my pants. My vertical speed was not that much of a problem, but I seemed to be skimming over the surface of the slide over twenty meters per second *side-*

ways. In actuality, it was the slide slipping past at a rotational velocity thirty meters per sec faster than the level I'd left. I had a lot of velocity to make up.

I fetched up at the bottom of the slide with my pants and back warm from the friction. When park diving is done recreationally, one wears a helmet and a neck-to-toe padded coverall. You tend to lose less skin that way.

I headed for the nearest exit.

I phoned Martha from a public phone and said, "Don't say it, but you know what sort of plants my grandmother grows?"

She started to open her mouth, stopped, and nodded. "Sure."

"Key on that word."

I switched over to scrambler and punched in BONSAI. The screen showed garbage for the next thirty seconds. I was about to switch back, sure she'd misunderstood me, when it synchronized and cleared.

"Sorry, I had to look up the spelling," Martha explained. "I thought you were coming by?"

"I did, I was, I didn't. Those two guys you told me about tried to take me for a walk, maybe out a maintenance lock on the rim, but I didn't let it get that far. I'd just as soon not go near your place right now, because that's where they picked me up the first time."

She stared at me, with her mouth slightly open. Finally, she closed it and said, "Oh."

"Could you go get a package for me from Grandmother? She knows you're coming."

She looked pained. "Is it important? I mean, my second-shift manager took a day of anxiety leave and I'm short-handed."

I sighed. "Okay. I understand. You're scared of the man Vaslov has stationed outside Grandmother's and also of these two jokers with the knives. I can find someone else." I pretended to reach for the cutoff switch.

She brought her hand up. "You son of a bitch! Where do I meet you?"

I grinned. "At a maintenance lock, on the rim." I told her which one and her eyes widened. "And, Martha," I said, dropping the smile, "I owe you."

"You sure the hell do," she growled and switched off.

The retailer of vacuum gear I'd talked to earlier was true to his word. I picked up a bag of equipment from him, stopped by a florist, and then went to the public library to borrow a computer.

The calculations came out the same using three different algorithms. I was satisfied. I compiled a list of windows and left in a hurry.

"Where have you been?" Martha said, as I panted up to her in the full gravity of level fifty. "I've been here ten minutes." She looked around her and shuddered slightly. "My feet hurt and it's spooky here."

I nodded and grinned. "That's what people say. It'll keep us from being interrupted." The cover plate to the lock control circuit came off with the aid of an allen wrench. I jumped two wires and pulled another one off its terminal post.

"What are you doing?"

I pushed a button. The inner door opened. "Normally, to open one of these locks, maintenance control pushes a button at the same time. I bypassed that, plus the line that tells them this lock is open." I took my jumpers out and closed the panel again, leaving the one wire disconnected.

"You look like you've done it before."

I smiled. "Once a year, Martha, since I was sixteen. Just early this time, I guess."

She helped me move the equipment into the lock. "You know that tape of those two characters?" I asked her while I stripped to underwear and started putting on my skin suit.

She helped me get the suit straight. "Yeah, what about it?"

"Get it to Grandmother and tell her that they tried to get me."

"Okay."

When she tried to hand me my aluminum oxygen tanks I held up my hand.

"Sorry, Grandmother didn't need to send those. I made other arrangements." I opened the bag I'd gotten from the retailer and took out another set of tanks—bigger and more oblong. "Spun fiberglass—radar transparent."

I connected them and pulled on my insulative coverall. The skin suit, with its open-weave mesh, would handle any cooling problems, but this far from the sun, the problem was usually keeping warm. Next, I connected a fiberglass hydrogen peroxide tank with catalytic nozzle and controls to my belt by a short line. All in all, there was less than two kilos of metal in my equipment, including electronics.

"Hand me that box, would you?"

Martha handed me a cardboard container. I opened it clumsily with suit gloves and took from it a white rose. I handed the box back to her and tucked the rose stem beneath a velcro seal flap on my coverall.

"For mother," I said.

She nodded, stepped forward, kissed me gently on the mouth, and helped me seal my helmet. Then she gathered up the bags, box, and tanks and pulled them outside the lock. I pushed a button and the inner door closed.

Pumps whined and it became easier to inhale than exhale. The amber light came on and I opened the outer lock.

I still had to walk down a flight of stairs in vacuum to reach one of the exterior monorail stations. Repairs on the exterior of Belt City are difficult, since it takes a major catastrophe to get the City Council to order spin stopped. So rails run along the outside skin for monorail cranes and work stations, enabling work crews to reach anywhere on the exterior despite the greater-than-one-gee acceleration.

I found myself standing on a balcony of steel grating, able to look down through the holes at the stars spinning by. Looking "south," I could see the mirrors floating kilometers away, by the smelter. Off to one side, a thin silver pencil hung in space—the Slingshot Mass Driver, three kilometers long.

A tiny disk of sun set and rose twice a minute.

Guardrails surrounded the platform except where the monorail passed it. There, chain was stretched across a gap. There was no crane or work station at this lock. They were kept near the center, and this lock was near the North End. "Overhead" was the city, curving out of sight to my right and to my left, and stretching seven hundred meters ahead of me and fifty behind.

First things first. I walked to the railing, unvelcroed the rose, and dropped it. It sailed away on a curving path, a bright white speck soon lost in the black.

After a few minutes I looked at the chronometer in my helmet. I had four minutes to my first window.

One hundred meters of rope came out of a coverall pocket. I snapped it to the railing and tossed it over the side. It sailed out in a curve, but soon straightened, hanging straight "down." I threaded the top end through brake cars clipped to my belt and climbed over, struggling with the hydrogen peroxide tank. It took me thirty seconds to reach the end of the rope, infinitesimally slowing Belt City's rotation in the process. The chronometer said I had one minute and forty seconds left.

The hundred seconds seemed to last forever. I was hanging by my belt with an apparent gravity of one and a half gee. My back was arched uncomfortably and my blood seemed to be pooling in my head and feet—throb, throb. I took a small pair of wire cutters from a pocket and set them against the rope.

The chronometer reached zero—*snip*—and I was falling.

My velocity relative to Belt City was on the order of sixty-nine meters per second, or about two hundred and fifty kilometers per hour. I had sufficient oxygen and CO_2 scrubber for fifteen hours. If Rowan/Oakley kept on her current course with her last known velocity, I would catch her in one hour and forty-seven minutes. And since there weren't any registered bodies or installations in this direction for over six hundred kilometers, I was pretty sure I'd catch up with her before she got where she was going.

I fiddled with the radio, switching to transponder frequency and cutting in the directional antenna. I set my helmet sextant at a simple one-eighty and wiggled around until Belt City was squarely in the bullseye on the mirror. Faintly, I got the electronic warble I was looking for. The LCD display above my forehead showed me the letters "NZ183." The *Black Orchid* was still on course.

For a while, I listened in on Traffic Control, checking to see if anyone had noticed my exit. My coverall was matte black, with as low an albedo as possible, and I seriously doubted that normal radar would pick me up. I was right. Nobody noticed. Nobody cared whether I'd died or moved to El Paso . . . or something like that.

I went to sleep.

Beep, beep, beep.

I was dry-mouthed and groggy. The alarm was going off. I told it to shut up and tried to roll over on my stomach.

Beep, beep, beep.

The alarm didn't shut off, and rolling over supposes that one direction is *down*. I came to complete wakefulness and checked the time. I'd been asleep for one hour and fifteen minutes. I shut off the alarm and took a swig of water from the nipple to get rid of the cotton mouth.

Per calculations, Rowan/Oakley should be fifty-seven kilometers ahead of me. Belt City was a bright speck three hundred and fifteen kilometers behind. I did a transponder check to see if *Black Orchid* was still in the right direction. She wasn't. I started checking in a circle around her estimated position and got her transponder fifteen degrees off. I started scanning visually and spent five minutes trying to decide which of the three stars ahead of me was her.

She was the one on the right.

I started deceleration thirty minutes later, grabbing the handle of the hydrogen peroxide tank and lining it up with Belt City, plus a fifteen-degree offset to pull me back to *Black Orchid*'s course. Steam, turning almost immediately to ice crystals, blasted out of the two nozzles by the grip at a forty-five degree angle to my suddenly strained arm. I kept this up for twelve seconds before I released the trigger.

When I turned around again, I decided she was within range of my suit's laser ranging system. *Black Orchid* was now three thousand and twenty-two meters in front of me with a relative velocity of −0.32 meters per sec. Her main viewport was still pointed away from me, but Rowan/Oakley could have a check port or a camera pointed my way.

I wasn't worried. At three kilometers I was just another black piece of space.

We passed within five kilometers of several 500- to 1,000-meter-diameter rocks. Ordinary asteroids probably, since they were this close to Belt City and unprocessed. I was getting hungry—I hadn't eaten since breakfast, seven hours earlier.

She turned the ship three incredibly long hours later. Belt City was almost a thousand kilometers behind us. A few minutes later, she began decelerating.

Things got tricky for a while. She was slowing over a prolonged period of time. If I just sat there, I would soon zip past or run into her. I wanted to keep the comfortable gap I had, but my motor didn't push me at fourteen micro-gees—it was more like two hundred and fifty micro-gees. So, I would give a one-second burst every time our relative velocity exceeded two and a half meters per second, correcting lateral errors as best I could. Graphed, my path would be a wavy line wandering over the straight line of her course.

We seemed to be matching velocities with an installation of some kind. When *Black Orchid* began decelerating, I'd noticed a large kilometer-plus-diameter asteroid almost dead ahead. It was equipped with a transponder broadcasting the registration code "SS453." With that "SS," I didn't need a *Registry* to tell me it was a scientific station.

I gave myself an added vector—ninety degrees to my course—enough to pass the asteroid on the side opposite *Black Orchid*. I killed the rest of my relative velocity a few minutes later and nudged myself into the rock.

SS453 looked like carbonaceous chondrite—dark brown, low

albedo, high in nickel iron ore—but I was ready to swear that it wasn't. No gravity. None I could detect, and I've been on a lot of rocks. For it to have the pull it was exhibiting, it would have to be incredibly light ore, strewn with pockets.

I scrambled around the horizon, kicking off in tangential leaps and using the HO thruster to bring me back into the surface. I came within sight of the installation on the dark side and hid behind an outcropping.

I was wrong—SS453 was chondrite. It was also hollow.

In the dim light of stars and the ship's own exterior lights, *Black Orchid* was being warped into a hole fifty meters across by two space-suited figures. To one side of the hole, a parabolic antenna, over twenty meters in diameter, pointed into space. Beside it was a heavy-duty communications laser, as large as any I'd seen. It was pointed a different direction. Cables from both ran across the rock and down into the hole.

I flipped through the suit channels, searching for some communication, but couldn't get anything. They were either maintaining radio silence or using a nonstandard channel.

The ship and figures dropped from sight. I stayed where I was for ten more minutes, then followed.

It was dark inside.

The hole faced away from the sun and SS453 didn't rotate—otherwise they would have floated their antenna and used some sort of relay. I found a rigged line and pulled myself four meters down into the asteroid, where I stopped.

As my eyes adjusted, I glanced at the communications laser where it was outlined by stars, then at the stars themselves. Ursa Minor and Polaris—what was that laser doing pointing above the plane of the ecliptic? Maybe it wasn't being used and that was a convenient direction—or maybe the rock did rotate and that used to be the right attitude. I pulled myself on into the asteroid.

In the early days, when the crushers couldn't handle the rocks they do today, they'd mine the large rocks inside out. It made sense—when you blasted you wanted the rubble to hang around, not go flying through space and incidental humans. Later, they just picked the right size rocks and crushed them whole. SS453 was obviously a holdover from those days.

I took some random rangings with the suit laser. There was enough volume within SS453 to hold Belt City. I spotted a lighted lock door set in the side of the hole, then a larger lighted port, and froze against the rock. Spacesuit lights came around a corner where the hole intersected the interior surface and moved up the

far side of the hole to the lock. There were three of them—Rowan/
Oakley and the two who'd docked her. They cycled through the
lock while I thought dark, cold, ancient thoughts, suitable to a
slab of chondrite.

It worked; they didn't see me.

I moved into the interior, around the corner, and turned on my
lights.

Grandmother was going to be pleased.

"Ahoy, SS453."

I floated on the "day" side of the asteroid, away from their
laser, but still in line of sight for one of their ordinary radio
antennae. I wondered what they were doing inside? Probably
checking their radar screens and looking for a transponder transmission.

"Ahoy, SS453."

They could always send some men out, but they'd have to figure
I was nearby and I'd turned my gain way down.

"This is Scientific Station SS453," said a cautious male voice.
"Who's calling?"

I grinned. Their proper response should have been to chew me
out for improper radio procedure. More proof.

"Boo Bailey, here. Please connect me with Ms. Oakley, also
known as Darlene Birch, also known as Linda Maples, also known
as Roberta Ash, also known as Jean Rowan."

There was a moment's silence on the other end.

"Excuse me, but you're not making a lot of sense. None of
those persons are aboard this station."

"Strange. Registered space vessel NZ183, carrying Ms. Oakley, was moved into your asteroid's interior twenty-three minutes
ago."

There was no hesitation; the person on the other end was good.
"Oh, really? If that's the case, it's not something I'm aware of."

"Maybe you should talk to your boss. Maybe somebody's not
telling you something."

"My name is Dr. William Reese. I *am* in charge of this installation."

I hesitated for a moment. Could he be completely unaware of
what was going on? I decided not. "My mistake, Doctor. I'll just
turn the matter over to ISRC Security and the U.N. Civil Police.
Sorry to bother you."

"Why should the police be interested?" he got that question in
quick, before I could even pretend to sign off.

"Well, I could talk about missing equipment, raw materials, even computer tampering, but the cutest one is several thousand cubic meters of sewage. Dr. Reese, you have enough equipment and materials in that asteroid to build an O'Neil colony. I'm amazed. You must have been acquiring supplies for the last decade."

I recognized Rowan/Oakley's voice from her exchange with traffic control when she'd left Belt City.

"Stop. Please don't transmit anything else. We're on open frequencies."

I nodded at that. It was unlikely that anyone had picked up my weakened transmission, but to tell them that would tell them where I was. "I can scramble," I said. "Key in the place you worked as Jean Rowan, okay?"

"Initials or full name?"

"Initials."

I keyed in EIC for Equipment Inventory Control, and waited until I heard her say, "Can you read me?"

"Yes."

Over the radio came a deep, tired sigh. "Okay . . . what do you want?"

"I want you to talk to my grandmother."

"Your grandmother is . . . ?" I couldn't decide whether she was faking or not.

"Anita Moss."

"You don't mean the systems expert?" She sounded excited at the prospect. "The person who wrote FASKAN Relational Filing?"

"Yes—that was one of hers."

Her voice became wary again. "Why does she want to talk to me?"

I grinned. "Wrong. The question is why do you want to talk to her? The answer is, you'd rather talk to her than Captain Vaslov of the uncivil police. In one of their boats, he could be there in ten minutes."

"I must confer with my colleagues."

"Confer away. I'm not going anywhere."

I would've loved to have had a bug in that room. She was back in five minutes. "Okay, I'll call her. Do you have a scrambler reference?"

"Wrong again. You'll go see her in person—now—at highest possible acceleration. This business will *not* be transacted by phone."

"But my work . . . !" She paused, then said tiredly, "As you said, I don't have much choice. I'll leave in ten minutes."

"A real pleasure talking with you. Bye."

Came a rapping, came a tapping. . . .

She'd been accelerating for five minutes when I matched velocities and dropped onto her main port. I must've scared her to death.

"Who the hell are you?" she said over standard hailing frequencies.

"Boo Bailey, again. Look, could you let me in? I've been in this suit for seven hours and I need a *bathroom*." I didn't mention that I didn't have the reaction mass to get back to Belt City before my life support was depleted.

I made her run her tanks dry on the way back. With constant acceleration, the trip took an hour and thirty-three minutes. I didn't say much to her except to ask what name she preferred.

"Mary," she told me. "Mary Oakley."

The rest of the time I spent making sure she didn't kill me.

Not that she tried, but she and her "colleagues" were the best suspects I had for Evans' murder. I watched her carefully.

Lock control was funny.

I went through the line close behind her, answering the standard questions. "No, I have not been in contact with nonquarantined humans. No, I am not carrying any pharmaceuticals, prescription or otherwise." Then I stuck my face up to the retina scanner to see if I was a registered criminal.

Confusion. "Uh, there's an egress prohibition linked with your record."

I nodded. "Right."

"You're not allowed to leave the city."

"Right."

"According to our records, you haven't been outside the city in two months."

"Look—what's the problem? I'm not leaving. I'm entering. Do I have an entrance prohibition on my record?"

"Uh, no."

"Why worry about it?"

"Uh, right." He waved me on, but I saw him turn to the phone as we left.

Grandmother was relieved to see me.

It wasn't obvious—not to anyone who didn't know her, but

when she saw me enter the office, she actually *smiled*.

"Mary Oakley, this is Anita Moss." I escorted her to the web chair, the same one Evans sat in for the last time thirty-six hours before. She sat carefully, apparently composed, but I noticed her fingers were white where she clamped onto the edge of the chair.

"How do you do?" asked Grandmother.

"Uh, fine."

Grandmother sat back and looked from Oakley to me. I was tired, grumpy, and still keyed up from watching Oakley.

I said, "About a third of your missing equipment and supplies are sitting inside a hollow asteroid masquerading as scientific station SS453. It's one thousand kilometers up orbit."

Oakley snapped, "It's a legitimate scientific station! We do work on closed-system ecologies and zero-gravity calcium loss."

"Do you also work with the Search for Extra-Terrestrial Intelligence?" I asked.

She looked wary. "No, we have nothing to do with SETI."

Grandmother narrowed her eyes. "Why do you ask, Boo?"

"They have a heavy-duty communications laser pointed toward Polaris and a twenty-meter parabolic antenna pointed somewhere else. I don't see what that sort of communications equipment has to do with closed-system ecologies or zero-gravity calcium leaching, especially when they can route stuff through the facilities here at Belt City."

Grandmother turned back to Oakley. "Well, Ms. Oakley?"

"What has that got to do with anything? What do you want? Why did you have this juvenile megalomaniac blackmail me into coming here?"

I raised my eyebrows. Grandmother blinked and looked at me.

"Well, I *did* suggest that we would rather talk to you than Vaslov or Derekin. Is that not the case?" I asked, turning back to Oakley.

She leaned back in her chair and looked defeated. "I suppose so."

Grandmother leaned forward. "Does that mean you're willing to answer my questions?"

Oakley crossed her arms. "To what end? What are you trying to find out? Are you working for yourself or are you representing the ISRC?"

Grandmother frowned, but answered her. "I am representing myself. I *was* investigating the theft or sabotage of ISRC equipment over the past thirty years, but that commission, if it ever existed, has been repudiated by the ISRC. I am currently investigating the murder of Percival Evans.''

I'd been waiting for this moment. It's one reason I didn't mention the murder on the radio—I wanted to *see* her reaction.

She frowned. "Who?"

"Percival Evans—special assistant to the High Commissioner. He was poisoned approximately twenty-four hours ago.''

Oakley cocked her head to one side and closed one eye. "Look, you have me at a disadvantage. You know about items in our possession that we have no legal claim to—though I can make a case for a moral claim. Regardless, you could have me punished and imprisoned for theft, fraud, and, I suppose, embezzlement. But you've got to believe me—I don't know anything about murder!''

"Where were you last night at 2130?"

Oakley thought for a moment. "I was eating supper with Dr. Rory Herzig, at the Hilton.''

"Dr. Herzig, the physicist? From the Deep Space Institute?" Grandmother asked.

"Yes. He corresponds with Dr. Reese on various projects.''

"Did you eat in the public dining room?"

"Yes.''

Grandmother pursed her lips. "How many people know of the existence of your stockpile of materials and equipment?''

Oakley uncrossed her arms and clamped her mouth shut.

"Come now, Ms. Oakley. I haven't asked you to name names. I just want to know how many people might have killed Mr. Evans.''

"Why would we have killed him?"

"If Mr. Evans' investigation was successful—and you see that it was—he would have uncovered your illegal stockpile. Killing him, and perhaps me as well, would've hindered such an investigation.''

"So? If you started digging, do you know how many such activities you'd uncover?''

Grandmother nodded. "I've considered that. Before my access to the Commission Network was cut, I'd noticed some tampering that didn't have your fingerprints.'' She steepled her fingers. "You said something earlier, about having a moral claim to that equipment. I'm curious as to what that might be.''

Oakley sat still for thirty seconds, staring at Grandmother, brow wrinkled. Finally she said, "One of the reasons I agreed to talk to you was your reputation. Dr. Reese claims that you resigned your Commission seat because you were fed up with the corruption—the graft.''

Grandmother frowned. "I'm not that lily-white, but that was part of it.''

Oakley nodded. "But you still have that reputation for integrity.''

"Get on with it," Grandmother said irritably.

"We're stockpiling that equipment to create an independent colony. We want to keep it from being wasted and stolen by greedy bastards—twits who don't give a damn about keeping us out here.''

Grandmother waved a hand. "So it's altruistic, eh?''

"Hell, no!'' said Oakley. "We want to make money, too, but we also want to stay out here. This is our home.''

I felt something curious when she said that—a tingling around my stomach and in the cheeks. I asked her, "How long do you think you'll last—even with your equipment—once ISRC finds out? They'll keep your ore from reaching Earth and the things you'll need from Earth from reaching you. You have to go through them.''

Oakley started to say something, then stopped. Instead she said, "We'll manage. After all, the charter comes up for renewal in twelve years. It won't pass.''

"Twelve years is a long time to wait," Grandmother said. "Especially if you don't have the equipment and are in prison.''

Oakley looked at the floor. "I guess I didn't sell you.''

"You are ambitious and idealistic. I have no qualms about your *stated* objective—I just don't know how much is acting and how much is conviction. I will make a deal with you," said Grandmother, leaning forward. "*If* you and yours turn out to have nothing to do with the death of Percival Evans, I will keep to myself any knowledge of your unorthodox acquisitions. In return, you'll acquaint me with as many of the *other* parties engaged in embezzlement and theft of ISRC materials as you've run across in your own activities.''

Oakley looked up again, eyes alive again. "Agreed.''

I scratched my head and looked at Grandmother. "I hope you know what you're doing.''

Vaslov showed up fifteen minutes later. I checked him on the door monitor and told Grandmother, "Vaslov—alone.''

Oakley had been answering a steady stream of questions while I'd showered and changed. Now she almost lost it. "Is he here for me?'' Her eyes were wide, staring at Grandmother.

I shook my head and looked at the ceiling.

"No, Ms. Oakley. He is here to harass Boo and me. I imagine he heard about Boo's entry into the city and now wants to know where he's been—among other things.''

The doorbell rang again.

"If you would wait in the kit . . . exercise room while we take care of this, you can avoid him entirely.''

I showed her the room on my way to the door and waited until that door was closed before I let Vaslov in.

"Captain Vaslov," I said, nodding.

His eyes narrowed and he walked past me without a word. I shrugged, shut the door, and followed. Before I entered the office again, I locked the door to the kitchen. Grandmother may have been working on the hypothesis that Oakley wasn't the murderer, but I noticed she was avoiding an opportunity to be poisoned again.

Vaslov was getting excited in the office.

"You are in the jurisdiction of the U.N. You can be deported!"

Grandmother smiled. "Perhaps you could get me deported—I am a citizen of the United States of America. But Boo's a citizen of the U.N. He was born here. You couldn't deport him.''

"I can *imprison* him," said Vaslov.

Grandmother shook her head. "For what? This is not the Soviet Union, Captain.''

Vaslov whirled around when I entered the room. "Where have you been for the last eight hours?"

I said, "Walking, talking, sleeping, and weeping. Where have *you* been?"

"You see?" he said to Grandmother. "Obstruction of justice!"

"You see?" I asked Grandmother. "Invasion of privacy."

The doorbell rang again.

It was Derekin. I let him in, to get under Vaslov's skin.

"Vaslov," nodded Derekin, as he entered the room.

Vaslov put his arms behind his back, parade rest style, and faced Derekin. I could see his arms shaking from where I stood. "Director Derekin, I wish you'd consulted with me before issuing your press release."

Derekin said, "I've no time for that nonsense, Vaslov. I'm ready to name the murderers—are you interested?"

Vaslov's eyebrows rose. "You are sure of your information?"

"Yes."

"Then I am interested."

"Boo Bailey and Anita Moss, as I thought all along!"

"Damn," I said. "And I thought we were going to get away with it."

Vaslov looked at the ceiling. "I don't suppose you bothered to acquire proof?"

"Damn right, I acquired proof." He pulled a bottle from his pocket. "Your own forensic chemist has identified this as the diamine amino acid analog that killed Evans." He paused for effect. "It was found in *The Johnny-Go-Lightly*, Ms. Moss's personal rock buggy, usually piloted by Boo Bailey."

Grandmother spoiled it by laughing.

Vaslov held out his hand. "Did you look for fingerprints?"

"Of course—it had been wiped." Derekin handed the bottle to Vaslov. "Do you think I'm stupid?"

Vaslov refrained from answering. Instead, he turned to me. "So this is what you were doing outside the city."

"That's right," I said. "In addition, I slipped back to Earth, overthrew three small African nations, and killed Commissioner Rostaprovich." I held out my arms, wrists together. "Take me away, I'm a dangerous man."

Vaslov almost smiled. "Try to be serious. Do you have any constructive comments?"

I looked closer at the bottle. "Glass bottle, plastic lid, right?" He nodded.

"Why do I store it in the buggy when I can go to the rim, jimmy a lock open, and just let go? It's radar transparent—who'd see it? Gone forever and ever. Or, for that matter, why not just flush it down a toilet? It's a plant. The only question is, did Derekin do it to preserve his cute little theory, or is it a real clue?"

Derekin turned red and I could almost see the pimples forming. "I do not plant evidence!"

Vaslov looked skeptical.

I grinned. "When did you get the message telling you to search the buggy?"

Derekin's mouth dropped open. "How . . ."

"What good is a plant if nobody finds it?"

Grandmother cleared her throat. "Then there's the matter of method. Has it been determined that the poison was put on the lobster after it arrived in the room?"

Vaslov looked at Derekin before saying, "Yes. There were no traces of it in the preparation pans and the dish was filled in the dining room under the supervision of the maitre d'. Both he and the waiter support each other's story and I've questioned them under Clifton multigraph as well."

"I see."

She reached into a drawer. "There are two men shown on this tape. There is reason to believe they are involved in some way with the murder of Percival Evans."

Derekin reached for the tape, but Vaslov beat him to it. "What makes you think this?"

"Because they tried to kidnap me this morning," I said. "And the only thing I got out of them was that 'it was asking questions that got me into this mess in the first place.' They also carry concealed knives. I believe that is a violation of the municipal statues."

Derekin interrupted. "What bullshit is this? Aren't you going to arrest them, Vaslov?"

Vaslov turned to Derekin. "I suggest you remain quiet as long as you continue to have nothing constructive to say."

I liked his phrasing.

"Please give me the details of this kidnapping."

I gave it to him—short, but complete. He looked at the ceiling for a moment. "Why didn't you report this then?"

"I offer it now in a new spirit of rapprochement."

Vaslov's eyes narrowed.

Grandmother asked, "Have you investigated the availability of the poison?"

Vaslov was talking easier now. "It can be synthesized in a well-equipped laboratory—but it does require some expertise. There are no supplies of the finished product in the belt."

"Have you checked the educational background of all the persons at the dinner to see if one of them had the expertise?"

"*Da*. None of them per their personnel files. We are checking from the other end—looking for people with the expertise and then trying to link them with the suspects. This is a slow process."

"Assuming Director Derekin did indeed find the poison aboard my ship, check your records to see if one of them went out of North Lock today."

Vaslov nodded. "I had considered that already." Derekin was scowling at the corner of the room. "You still haven't pressed them about what they were investigating."

"That is true. Are you ready to tell me anything?"

"Only what I've said before. We were investigating an unusual trend in equipment loss. Apparently, someone learned of our investigation and was worried about what we would discover."

Vaslov asked, "When do you think they found out about Evans' investigation?"

Grandmother shrugged, then saw me frowning.

"What is it, Boo?"

"Those two men—the ones who tried to grab me? According to a friend of mine, they started looking for me the day before Evans first came to us."

"Well, then," said Grandmother. "If they are involved, then that puts the leak beyond us. Perhaps even on Luna."

Derekin said, "I've got a telex on my desk that says Evans wasn't investigating anything! I say you're creating a smokescreen to hide behind."

Vaslov considered that. "Do you have a response to that?"

"Authorized or not, Evans asked us to begin an investigation. That's all I have to say on the subject."

Vaslov grunted. "I think I will start checking on these things we've discussed," he said, hefting the tape. "I will talk with you later." He started to leave. "By the way, I've left a man outside your door. Please clear any excursions with him." He walked to the office door.

Derekin stood where he was for a second.

Grandmother said, "Goodbye, Captain Vaslov. Goodbye, Director Derekin."

"I'm still not satisfied, Anita," said Derekin, obnoxious to the end.

Grandmother cut in sharply. "It is not required that you be satisfied. This dwelling is not ISRC property. You are invited to leave."

Derekin scowled for a moment, then stormed out, passing Vaslov as if he wasn't there.

After they'd both left I came back and said, "You know, Grandmother, I don't care what we find out. If Derekin didn't kill Evans, we should give serious consideration to framing him."

"Look at this."

I held it out on my palm at arm's length, a small black dot about two millimeters across, with a hair-thin wire antenna.

"My word," said Grandmother.

I took it into the bathroom and flushed it down the toilet.

Grandmother had wanted to bring Mary Oakley back into the room, but I'd insisted on sweeping for bugs first.

When I came back in she was frowning. "Which one left it?"

"It must have been Vaslov. It was on the wrong side of the room to be Derekin or Oakley. Anybody else been here?"

"No."

I prepared supper for Grandmother, Mary Oakley, and myself. We ate in the kitchen while Oakley continued to answer Grandmother's questions.

"Most of the theft is all on paper. Over half of the equipment loss is materials that were never delivered. Various officials "destroy" them on paper and pay the vendors who "supplied" them in the first place. Then, large portions of that payment end up in the officials' New Eden bank accounts."

"When did you start your acquisitions?"

"In '73. I'd been working for ISRC for three years and was starting to see what was going on. My parents worked for the ISRC and I was mostly raised out here. There were others who felt as I did. We started small and slowly recruited high-quality personnel. Very few of them actually know about the equipment—that was accomplished by a dedicated few acting over a decade."

I swallowed a bite and said, "Then you weren't responsible for changing the original expected-loss figure back in '56."

"How old do you think I am? That was somebody else—it was something I was taking advantage of, though."

"How much of the rest is physical theft?" Grandmother asked.

"We're not sure. At least some of it is. We suspect that a few commissioners are setting up to go private sector with ISRC equipment after the charter is defunct."

"They're taking the long view," I said. "Twelve years is a long time to wait."

Grandmother shook her head. "Twelve years is the blink of an eye." She turned back to Oakley. "So you don't really know actual individuals?"

"Not really."

Grandmother pushed her plate away and wrinkled her brow. I started cleaning up.

Finally Grandmother said, "Thank you, Ms. Oakley. You've been most helpful. I'll keep my promise. Please let Boo know where you can be reached." Then she went back to her office.

When I went to bed three hours later she was at her desk staring at nothing, her fingers steepled and tapping gently against each other.

I wondered what she'd thought of.

Next morning my alarm went off at eight. I didn't remember setting it. I hadn't. There was a note taped to it—a printout of instructions from Grandmother.

I made a call.

Inspector Vaslov said he would be glad to be there at 1330 and would ensure the arrival of another guest. I asked him if he'd had any luck with my kidnappers.

"Yes and no. We have identified the two men in the tape—they arrived from Luna two days before Evans. They are a Mr. William McKeel and a Norren Warwood. What's more, they passed through North Lock control yesterday at 1500 and back in again at 1532."

"Ah."

"On the other hand, they have not been back to their hotel rooms since they checked in three days ago. A search has found no luggage or personal belongings there."

"I see. Which one was which?"

"McKeel was the larger of the two," Vaslov said.

"Excuse me, Captain, but isn't it against U.N. policy to be so cooperative?"

Vaslov didn't blink an eye. "I offer it now in a new spirit of rapprochement." He signed off.

As I fixed breakfast, I couldn't help but think that a cooperative Captain Vaslov was too much to handle.

Grandmother received the telex at 1245, beep, beep, at her computer terminal. She had it print out and read the message to herself. "Good enough," I heard her say. Then she retired to get ready for company. Oakley had left the night before, but was due back later that afternoon.

Vaslov arrived at 1320, early. As I was letting him in, up came Derekin.

"I didn't even talk to him about it," said Vaslov. "I knew he'd be here. One day I will get rid of his spy in my office, but then I will have to phone him myself when I want him somewhere."

Derekin ignored him and walked on into the office. Vaslov followed. I looked out in the hall for Vaslov's man, but he'd apparently been dismissed.

Ann Bogucki arrived three minutes late. I met her at the door. She was breathing fast, balancing a briefcase and a pile of file folders in her arms. "Sorry I'm late. Just came from the Union Contract negotiations." She looked around, saw the small table next to the front door, and set the whole mess there. "That should keep. Well, what's going on? Why did Captain Vaslov ask me to come here?"

"Beats me," I said honestly. "I'm only the hired help." I

showed her into the office and seated her in the web chair. Then I went over and stood by the bonsai.

Grandmother came in seconds later.

"Good afternoon, Ms. Bogucki, Director Derekin, Captain Vaslov."

Assorted returned greetings. Derekin fidgeted in the background, Vaslov stayed still, but watchful, and Bogucki toyed with a small shiny object hanging from her jacket on a clip. It looked like cosmetic air brush.

"How can I help you, Ms. Moss?" asked Anne Bogucki. "I thought that Captain Vaslov had asked all the possible questions."

Grandmother nodded slightly. "That's undoubtedly true. However, he may not have asked them of the right people. I'd like to go over what happened two nights ago, the evening Mr. Evans was killed."

Derekin shook his head angrily. "We're been over that enough already. Is this why we're here?"

Vaslov smiled—sort of. It was a smile that made me glad I wasn't a Soviet citizen. Derekin saw it and shut up.

"As I remember it," Grandmother continued, "Commissioner Hall, Laura LeHew, and you were talking over by the buffet as it was loaded."

Bogucki nodded.

"Laura was snatching things off the trays as they came by, then you sampled the lobster and Commissioner Hall tried the ham. Is that essentially it?"

"We have been over this quite a few times, Ms. Moss," Bogucki said. "What's the point? Any of us could have put the poison in the lobster."

"True. But only one of you had the expertise to make it. What do you know of biochemistry, Ms. Bogucki?"

"What most people know, I suppose."

"Nothing special? No particular *expertise*?"

"No," Bogucki said flatly. She looked calm enough, but she was gripping the object on the clip tight enough to whiten her knuckles.

Grandmother shrugged. "Captain Vaslov, I suggest you arrest Anne Bogucki for the murder of Percival Evans."

Derekin raised his arm in the air. "This is too much! Trying to pin it on Anne isn't going to get you off the hook."

Grandmother lifted the piece of paper off her desk and held it up until Derekin ran down.

"I have here a telex I received one hour ago in answer to one

I sent last night. At my request, the Panzer Detective Agency in Manhattan did a quick investigation into Ms. Bogucki's background. Before acquiring her doctorate in business administration, she received a bachelors in biochemistry and worked two years as a research technician for Carroll Pharmaceuticals. For those who don't know, Carroll Pharmaceuticals is the manufacturer of fluoroglobin, the most widely used blood substitute on the market.''

Vaslov frowned, swore, "*Chyort vosmoi*, but what about her personnel file? None of that is in her record.''

Grandmother smiled. "That's right—but tell me, Captain Vaslov, what is Ms. Bogucki's job?''

Vaslov nodded grimly. "Director of Personnel. It was a small matter to change her own file, wasn't it?''

"Just as important," added Grandmother, "she had access to my old file and Evans' current file. She knew we were fluoroglobin users.''

I was watching Bogucki. She was sitting very still, looking straight ahead at Grandmother. Suddenly she sighed.

"Just one thing—how close were you to implicating me in the equipment hoarding?''

Grandmother shrugged. "Not very close. We discovered that the activity was going on, but what you apparently don't realize is that several different groups are engaged in the activity.'' She paused. "If you hadn't killed Evans, chances are we never would have found you out.''

Derekin looked at Bogucki, eyes large, shocked.

Bogucki looked sad, then pulled the cosmetic air brush off the jacket clip with a sharp little jerk.

The front of the apartment blew up.

Her briefcase.

Smoke and dust, following the shockwave, billowed into the room. My ears rang. I blinked dust from my eyes, picked up the nearest plant, and threw it as hard as I could at the door to the office.

Grandmother screamed, "*Not the bamboo!*''

Norren Warwood came through the door and took it, pot first, in the face. His burp gun, set on automatic, carved chunks of plastic out of the ceiling as he went back over.

I kicked off the plant bench hard, knowing how difficult it would be to get any traction in a twentieth of a gee. Halfway to the door I flipped over, feet first.

William McKeel saw me through the doorway and brought his

burp gun up. I thought I was dead, but he had to jump over Warwood to avoid tripping and, accustomed to lunar gravity, he jumped too hard. His head bounced off the ceiling and the gun fired off to my left. My right foot connected with his face and I felt his collar bone snap under my left heel.

Rebound took me slightly back into the office, but McKeel had done a wonderful job of absorbing most of my momentum. He bounced off the hall wall. I scrambled for their burp guns and backed off quickly, but they weren't moving.

I became aware of someone screaming.

It was Derekin—he'd taken a stray bullet in the thigh. Grandmother was trying to lay him down so she could put a compress on the wound. Vaslov was standing over Bogucki's chair, a strange expression on his face. I wondered why she just sat there, looked closer, and vomited.

A large percentage of her head was missing.

Mary Oakley rang the bell to the hotel suite early that evening. We were in the president's suite of the Hilton, at even lower gee than the apartment. Still sweating from moving the last of the bonsai, I opened the door and showed her where Grandmother was still fiddling with the grow lights, trying to get them just so.

"Growing bonsai in this gravity is a tricky situation, Mary. In low gravity, plants have a tendency to explode into growth, not having to allocate much of their production to support structures. Bonsai are mostly support structure, gnarled twisted trunks and branches—thick where the low gee tendency is to be thin." She paused and decided they were finally getting enough light. "An analogy could be made for human expansion in space. The ISRC is like me, making twisted, thick organizational structures when we could be growing like thin vines through the belt."

Oakley nodded to be polite. Grandmother moved over to a chair and sat. I sat myself, by the door to the room, still nervous. Grandmother was still mad at me.

"Oh, well. Thanks to you and your colleagues, the days of the ISRC are numbered."

Mary Oakley blinked. "Us? Why give us the credit?"

"Because you built the visitor. When did you launch it? No, wait—it was summer of '66, wasn't it?"

Oakley looked flustered. "What are you talking about?"

"What does it matter, Mary? If you want to claim otherwise, that's your right, but '66 would have been right for an orbital assist from Jupiter. Your vehicle did a gravity well maneuver to throw it up above the plane of the ecliptic, then fell back in toward the sun for the next ten years. Nice touch."

Mary frowned, looked around the room.

My mouth dropped open. "So that's what you were doing with that laser. You were listening in on the broadcasts from Earth to the probe and then telling the probe what to respond with a tight laser beam so nobody could hear. It was nothing but a fancy relay station!"

Oakley stopped frowning and smiled slightly. "Don't be ridiculous."

Grandmother went on as if she hadn't heard. "It doesn't matter now. You've got your agreement with Earth. They may be a little upset when they find you're human, but I'll bet they honor it. They're looking for any way to get around the ISRC Charter. You'll be a handy means."

Oakley smiled even more when she said, "If we were behind the probe, what you say would undoubtedly be true, but naturally, the Republic of Kepler would never engage in such a fraud."

Grandmother looked at her for a moment, smiled, and said, "Of course."

I looked from Grandmother to Oakley and back again. "Nuts," I muttered.

Grandmother then said, "It would be nice to know when the Republic of Kepler gets around to accepting applications for citizenship."

"Somehow," Oakley said, "I think you'll be the first to know."

"So why did it have to be the bamboo, Boo?"

It had finally come out. She wasn't going to sulk anymore, but confront me with it.

"Why do you think? It was because I knew it was your pride and joy—your favorite plant. Why pick something else when I can save your life and break your heart at the same time?"

She opened her mouth, closed it, opened it again. "You could have given me heart failure!"

"How long did it take you to train that plant?"

Her eyes narrowed, went steely on me. "Fifteen years."

I grinned. "Then I knew you had at least fifteen more to live. That's how long it will take you to do it again and *you* won't die until you do." I tilted my head. "Honestly, Grandmother, did you think I did it on purpose? I just grabbed the first one I could and threw it. If they'd made it into the room they would have killed all of us, wounded Bogucki to give her an alibi, and run.

We'd be dead, Bogucki would be alive, and Vaslov wouldn't be on his way back to Luna with sixteen arrest warrants.''

She leaned back, closed her eyes, and rubbed at her temples with parchment-covered fingers. ''Oh, I suppose you're right. But fifteen *years* . . . !''

I sighed. ''Are you done with me?''

''I suppose. What are you going to do now?''

I smiled and strode to the door. ''I've an appointment with Martha Goodwin . . . something about cultural biology.''

The ship was approaching high Earth orbit when it made its first transmission. This consisted of the query symbol followed by a tentative recognition symbol. When excited operators acknowledged the transmission, the ship returned with a verbatim repeat of the Agreement of Intent negotiated by the probe. The next transmission from Earth invited more effort toward refining their shared language. The ship's reply was in English.

''Don't bother. It's an interesting language, but we can probably get along better in this one. We are open for video transmission.''

Screens were switched on and voices raised in outrage. ''What sort of hoax are you trying to perpetrate? You aren't aliens!''

A human stared back from the screen. ''I could dispute that, but it's not important. What is important is that we're the builders of the visitor.''

''Impossible. The visitor entered our system from the direction of the head of Draco. Mankind hasn't strayed from the plane of the ecliptic.''

''Let me show you something,'' said the human.

He flicked a switch and his image vanished off the screen to be replaced by a recorded film. The image in the screen now was the slingshot. A voice was talking. ''In September of 2066 the remote probe known as the visitor was launched from the ISRC belt operations mass driver out of the system, specifically at a rendezvous with Jupiter.'' The screen changed to an animated plot of the solar system, showing the visitor's path outbound from the asteroid belt. ''Upon reaching the close proximity of Jupiter, the probe was directed into a gravity well maneuver.'' The dotted line dipped abruptly below Jupiter and came up at over ninety degrees off its original course. The dotted line started climbing high above the plane of the ecliptic. ''As you can see, the visitor was in orbit for over twelve years before it made itself visible to the observatories of the system.'' A bright line appeared between a spot in the asteroid belt and the probe. "The visitor was controlled by laser link from the capital of the Republic of Kepler, Independence." The screen switched to the exterior of Independence, once known as Scientific Station SS453. "Once the trade agreement was negotiated, the probe was given the command to self-destruct. This was by means of a small chemical explosion too small for visual identification. The resultant debris should re-enter the inner system in another seventeen years."

The man's image appeared back on the screen. "I have on board this ship twenty metric tons of praseodymium, which I am willing to trade to the highest bidder. I don't have to tell all the uses for this rare earth. We will await offers on this frequency."

"But wait a minute, even if you did build the probe, you aren't extraterrestrial. You're from Earth! The agreement is void!"

"The agreement says nothing about planet of origin, and even if it did, I wasn't born on Earth and I have never, I repeat never, been on Earth in my life. If that isn't extraterrestrial, then I don't know what is." He switched off.

"Do you think it will work?" he asked his wife.

The woman smiled. "Of course it will. Even if we didn't fit the exact wording of the agreement, they'd find some excuse. They've had to bear the ISRC for too long. I'm just wondering how they'll word it in the papers."

The man stretched back and locked his fingers behind his neck. "Oh, that's simple. Another 'first contract' story."

In Appreciation
ROBERT A. HEINLEIN
7/7/1907–5/8/1988

JERRY POURNELLE

On a high hill in Samoa there is a grave. Inscribed on the marker are these words:

> *"Under the wide and starry sky*
> *Dig my grave and let me lie.*
> *Glad did I live and gladly die*
> *And I lay me down with a will!*

> *"This be the verse which you grave for me:*
> *Here he lies where he longed to be,*
> *Home is the sailor, home from the sea,*
> *And the hunter home from the hill."*

These lines appear another place—scrawled on a shipping tag from a compressed-air container, and pinned to the ground with a knife.

That shipping tag is not yet on the Moon. It will be.

Some years ago when the United States flew space craft instead of endlessly re-designing them, I had the extraordinary fortune to be sitting with Robert A. Heinlein in the cafeteria at Cal Tech's Jet Propulsion Laboratory during the landing of the Viking probe to Mars. We were in the cafeteria because, while I had both press and VIP credentials, Mr. Heinlein did not. I had brought him to

JPL because I thought he belonged there; but there hadn't been time to get him credentials, so the NASA authorities ordered him out of the Von Karman Center.

I was outraged, and wanted to make a scene, but Robert would have none of that. He trudged up the hill to the cafeteria.

There is sometimes justice in this world. At the moment our first spacecraft landed on Mars, most of the network news cameras were in the cafeteria trained on Mr. Heinlein, rather than down in the center recording what NASA's officialdom thought they should be watching.

On Sunday, May 8, Robert A. Heinlein died peacefully during a nap. Like one of his beloved cats, when it was time he left us without fuss. He was cremated and his ashes scattered at sea from a warship. If we want to take his ashes to the Moon, we will have to take a pint of seawater. I think he'd find that acceptable.

Mr. Heinlein began writing science fiction before World War II, at a time when most strategists thought that battleships would dominate naval warfare and the battleships' analog fire control system was the most advanced computer technology in the world; when the Norden bombsight was top secret technology. After the war, while Dr. Vannevar Bush was telling Congress that the US would never be threatened by intercontinental missiles, Robert Heinlein gave us *Space Cadet* and *Universe*.

He wrote the outline of his "future history" in 1940–41. He was ridiculed for predicting in that history that the first rocket to the Moon would fly as early as 1976—and that it would usher in a "false dawn" followed by a long hiatus in space travel during the "crazy years" of mass psychosis toward the end of the twentieth century. Alas, some of that is chillingly accurate.

Robert Heinlein had as much to do with creating our future as any man of this century. It was not remarkable that the science reporters for the networks chose to follow him to exile in the cafeteria. They, like most of JPL's scientists and engineers, would never have been there if his stories had not called them to study and learn so that they could make his dreams a reality. His stories have caused more young people to choose careers in science and engineering than all the formal recruitment pitches ever tried.

He created our future in other ways. His stories made us ready, convinced us that it could be done. Robert Heinlein was truly *The Man Who Sold the Moon*.

Twenty years ago, Robert Heinlein took the time to review the first novel of a young space scientist turned professor turned novelist. My novel. Five years later, he read the first draft of *The*

Mote in God's Eye and sent us a 70 page single-spaced critique that has more about how to be a successful writer than all the creative writing courses ever taught.

I owe a great part of whatever success I've had as a writer to help and encouragement Robert Heinlein gave me over the past thirty years. I once asked him how I could pay him back. His answer was simple: "You can't. You pay it forward."

He changed our lives in many ways. His dreams prepared the way for space flight. We are all in his debt.

No debt was ever easier to pay. Indeed, it costs nothing, because we get back tenfold everything we invest.

We can pay Robert Heinlein forward by keeping the dream alive: A dream of an endless frontier where free people know no limits and knowledge has no bounds.

Ad Astra and Goodbye.

The Long Watch

ROBERT A. HEINLEIN

"Nine ships blasted off from Moon Base. Once in space, eight of them formed a globe around the smallest. They held this formation all the way to Earth.

"The small ship displayed the insignia of an admiral—yet there was no living thing of any sort in her. She was not even a passenger ship, but a drone, a robot ship intended for radioactive cargo. This trip she carried nothing but a lead coffin—and a Geiger counter that was never quiet."

—from the editorial *After Ten Years*, film 38, 17 June 2009, Archives of the *N.Y. Times*

I

JOHNNY DAHLQUIST BLEW smoke at the Geiger counter. He grinned wryly and tried it again. His whole body was radioactive by now. Even his breath, the smoke from his cigarette, could make the Geiger counter scream.

How long had he been here? Time doesn't mean much on the Moon. Two days? Three? A week? He let his mind run back: the last clearly marked time in his mind was when the Executive Officer had sent for him, right after breakfast—

"Lieutenant Dahlquist, reporting to the Executive Officer."

Colonel Towers looked up. "Ah, John Ezra. Sit down, Johnny. Cigarette?"

Johnny sat down, mystified but flattered. He admired Colonel Towers, for his brilliance, his ability to dominate, and for his battle record. Johnny had no battle record; he had been commis-

247

sioned on completing his doctor's degree in nuclear physics and was now junior bomb officer of Moon Base.

The Colonel wanted to talk politics; Johnny was puzzled. Finally Towers had come to the point; it was not safe (so he said) to leave control of the world in political hands; power must be held by a scientifically selected group. In short—the Patrol.

Johnny was startled rather than shocked. As an abstract idea, Towers' notion sounded plausible. The League of Nations had folded up; what would keep the United Nations from breaking up, too, and thus lead to another World War. "And you know how bad such a war would be, Johnny."

Johnny agreed. Towers said he was glad that Johnny got the point. The senior bomb officer could handle the work, but it was better to have both specialists.

Johnny sat up with a jerk. "You are going to *do* something about it?" He had thought the Exec was just talking.

Towers smiled. "We're not politicians; we don't just talk. We act."

Johnny whistled. "When does this start?"

Towers flipped a switch. Johnny was startled to hear his own voice, then identified the recorded conversation as having taken place in the junior officers' messroom. A political argument he remembered, which he had walked out on . . . a good thing, too! But being spied on annoyed him.

Towers switched it off. "We *have* acted," he said. "We know who is safe and who isn't. Take Kelly—" He waved at the loud-speaker. "Kelly is politically unreliable. You noticed he wasn't at breakfast?"

"Huh? I thought he was on watch."

"Kelly's watch-standing days are over. Oh, relax; he isn't hurt."

Johnny thought this over. "Which list am I on?" he asked. "Safe or unsafe?"

"Your name has a question mark after it. But I have said all along that you could be depended on." He grinned engagingly. "You won't make a liar of me, Johnny?"

Dahlquist didn't answer; Towers said sharply, "Come now— what do you think of it? Speak up."

"Well, if you ask me, you've bitten off more than you can chew. While it's true that Moon Base controls the Earth, Moon Base itself is a sitting duck for a ship. One bomb—*blooie!*"

Towers picked up a message form and handed it over; it read: I HAVE YOUR CLEAN LAUNDRY—ZACK. "That means every bomb in the *Trygve Lie* has been put out of commission. I have reports from every ship we need worry about." He stood up. "Think it over and see me after lunch. Major Morgan needs your help right away to change control frequencies on the bombs."

"The control frequencies?"

"Naturally. We don't want the bombs jammed before they reach their targets."

"What? You said the idea was to *prevent* war."

Towers brushed it aside. "There won't be a war—just a psychological demonstration, an unimportant town or two. A little bloodletting to save an all-out war. Simple arithmetic."

He put a hand on Johnny's shoulder. "You aren't squeamish, or you wouldn't be a bomb officer. Think of it as a surgical operation. And think of your family."

Johnny Dahlquist had been thinking of his family. "Please, sir, I want to see the Commanding Officer."

Towers frowned. "The Commodore is not available. As you know, I speak for him. See me again—after lunch."

The Commodore was decidedly not available; the Commodore was dead. But Johnny did not know that.

Dahlquist walked back to the messroom, bought cigarettes, sat down and had a smoke. He got up, crushed out the butt, and headed for the Base's west airlock. There he got into his space suit and went to the lockmaster. "Open her up, Smitty."

The marine looked surprised. "Can't let anyone out on the surface without word from Colonel Towers, sir. Hadn't you heard?"

"Oh, yes! Give me your order book." Dahlquist took it, wrote a pass for himself, and signed it "by direction of Colonel Towers." He added, "Better call the Executive Officer and check it."

The lockmaster read it and stuck the book in his pocket. "Oh, no, Lieutenant. Your word's good."

"Hate to disturb the Executive Officer, eh? Don't blame you." He stepped in, closed the inner door, and waited for the air to be sucked out.

Out on the Moon's surface he blinked at the light and hurried to the track-rocket terminus; a car was waiting. He squeezed in, pulled down the hood, and punched the starting button. The rocket car flung itself at the hills, dived through and came out on a plain studded with projectile rockets, like candles on a cake. Quickly it dived into a second tunnel through more hills. There was a

stomach-wrenching deceleration and the car stopped at the underground atom-bomb armory.

As Dahlquist climbed out he switched on his walkie-talkie. The
space-suited guard at the entrance came to port-arms. Dahlquist
said, "Morning, Lopez," and walked by him to the airlock. He
pulled it open.

The guard motioned him back. "Hey! Nobody goes in without
the Executive Officer's say-so." He shifted his gun, fumbled in
his pouch and got out a paper. "Read it, Lieutenant."

Dahlquist waved it away. "I drafted that order myself. *You* read
it; you've misinterpreted it."

"I don't see how, Lieutenant."

Dahlquist snatched the paper, glanced at it, then pointed to a
line. "See? '—except persons specifically designated by the Executive Officer.' That's the bomb officers, Major Morgan and
me."

The guard looked worried. Dahlquist said, "Damn it, look up
'specifically designated'—it's under *'Bomb Room, Security, Procedure for,'* in your standing orders. Don't tell me you left them
in the barracks!"

"Oh, no, sir! I've got 'em." The guard reached into his pouch.
Dahlquist gave him back the sheet; the guard took it, hesitated,
then leaned his weapon against his hip, shifted the paper to his
left hand, and dug into his pouch with his right.

Dahlquist grabbed the gun, shoved it between the guard's legs,
and jerked. He threw the weapon away and ducked into the airlock.
As he slammed the door he saw the guard struggling to his feet
and reaching for his side arm. He dogged the outer door shut and
felt a tingle in his fingers as a slug struck the door.

He flung himself at the inner door, jerked the spill lever, rushed
back to the outer door and hung his weight on the handle. At once
he could feel it stir. The guard was lifting up; the lieutenant was
pulling down, with only his low Moon weight to anchor him.
Slowly the handle raised before his eyes.

Air from the bomb room rushed into the lock through the spill
valve. Dahlquist felt his space suit settle on his body as the pressure
in the lock began to equal the pressure in the suit. He quit straining
and let the guard raise the handle. It did not matter; thirteen tons
of air pressure now held the door closed.

He latched open the inner door to the bomb room, so that it
could not swing shut. As long as it was open, the airlock could
not operate; no one could enter.

Before him in the room, one for each projectile rocket, were the atom bombs, spaced in rows far enough apart to defeat any faint possibility of spontaneous chain reaction. They were the deadliest things in the known universe, but they were his babies. He had placed himself between them and anyone who would misuse them.

But, now that he was here, he had no plan to use his temporary advantage.

The speaker on the wall sputtered into life. "Hey! Lieutenant! What goes on here? You gone crazy?" Dahlquist did not answer. Let Lopez stay confused—it would take him that much longer to make up his mind what to do. And Johnny Dahlquist needed as many minutes as he could squeeze. Lopez went on protesting. Finally he shut up.

Johnny had followed a blind urge not to let the bombs—*his* bombs!—be used for "demonstrations on unimportant towns." But what to do next? Well, Towers couldn't get through the lock. Johnny would sit tight until hell froze over.

Don't kid yourself, John Ezra! Towers could get in. Some high explosive against the outer door—then the air would whoosh out, our boy Johnny would drown in blood from his burst lungs—and the bombs would be sitting there, unhurt. They were built to stand the jump from Moon to Earth; vacuum would not hurt them at all.

He decided to stay in his space suit; explosive decompression didn't appeal to him. Come to think about it, death from old age was his choice.

Or they could drill a hole, let out the air, and open the door without wrecking the lock. Or Towers might even have a new airlock built outside the old. Not likely, Johnny thought; a *coup d'état* depended on speed. Towers was almost sure to take the quickest way—blasting. And Lopez was probably calling the Base right now. Fifteen minutes for Towers to suit up and get here, maybe a short dicker—then *whoosh!* the party is over.

Fifteen minutes—

In fifteen minutes the bombs might fall back into the hands of the conspirators; in fifteen minutes he must make the bombs unusable.

An atom bomb is just two or more pieces of fissionable metal, such as plutonium. Separated, they are no more explosive than a pound of butter; slapped together, they explode. The complications lie in the gadgets and circuits and gun used to slap them together in the exact way and at the exact time and place required.

These circuits, the bomb's "brain," are easily destroyed—but the bomb itself is hard to destroy because of its very simplicity. Johnny decided to smash the "brains"—and quickly!

The only tools at hand were simple ones used in handling the bombs. Aside from a Geiger counter, the speaker on the walkie-talkie circuit, a television rig to the base, and the bombs themselves, the room was bare. A bomb to be worked on was taken elsewhere—not through fear of explosion, but to reduce radiation exposure for personnel. The radioactive material in a bomb is buried in a "tamper"—in these bombs, gold. Gold stops alpha, beta, and much of the deadly gamma radiation—but not neutrons.

The slippery, poisonous neutrons which plutonium gives off had to escape, or a chain reaction—explosion!—would result. The room was bathed in an invisible, almost undetectable rain of neutrons. The place was unhealthy; regulations called for staying in it as short a time as possible.

The Geiger counter clicked off the "background" radiation, cosmic rays, the trace of radioactivity in the Moon's crust, and secondary radioactivity set up all through the room by neutrons. Free neutrons have the nasty trait of infecting what they strike, making it radioactive, whether it be concrete wall or human body. In time the room would have to be abandoned.

Dahlquist twisted a knob on the Geiger counter; the instrument stopped clicking. He had used a suppressor circuit to cut out noise of "background" radiation at the level then present. It reminded him uncomfortably of the danger of staying here. He took out the radiation exposure film all radiation personnel carry; it was a direct-response type and had been fresh when he arrived. The most sensitive end was faintly darkened already. Halfway down the film a red line crossed it. Theoretically, if the wearer was exposed to enough radioactivity in a week to darken the film to that line, he was, as Johnny reminded himself, a "dead duck."

Off came the cumbersome space suit; what he needed was speed. Do the job and surrender—better to be a prisoner than to linger in a place as "hot" as this.

He grabbed a ball hammer from the tool rack and got busy, pausing only to switch off the television pick-up. The first bomb bothered him. He started to smash the cover plate of the "brain," then stopped, filled with reluctance. All his life he had prized fine apparatus.

He nerved himself and swung; glass tinkled, metal creaked. His mood changed; he began to feel a shameful pleasure in destruction. He pushed on with enthusiasm, swinging, smashing, destroying!

So intent was he that he did not at first hear his name called. "Dahlquist! Answer me! Are you there?"

He wiped sweat and looked at the TV screen. Towers' perturbed features stared out.

Johnny was shocked to find that he had wrecked only six bombs. Was he going to be caught before he could finish? Oh, no! He *had* to finish. Stall, son, stall! "Yes, Colonel? You called me?"

"I certainly did! What's the meaning of this?"

"I'm sorry, Colonel."

Towers' expression relaxed a little. "Turn on your pick-up, Johnny, I can't see you. What was that noise?"

"The pick-up is on," Johnny lied. "It must be out of order. That noise—uh, to tell the truth, Colonel, I was fixing things so that nobody could get in here."

Towers hesitated, then said firmly, "I'm going to assume that you are sick and send you to the Medical Officer. But I want you to come out of there, right away. That's an order, Johnny."

Johnny answered slowly. "I can't just yet, Colonel. I came here to make up my mind and I haven't quite made it up. You said to see you after lunch."

"I meant you to stay in your quarters."

"Yes, sir. But I thought I ought to stand watch on the bombs, in case I decided you were wrong."

"It's not for you to decide, Johnny. I'm your superior officer. You are sworn to obey me."

"Yes, sir." This was wasting time; the old fox might have a squad on the way now. "But I swore to keep the peace, too. Could you come out here and talk it over with me? I don't want to do the wrong thing."

Towers smiled. "A good idea, Johnny. You wait there. I'm sure you'll see the light." He switched off.

"There," said Johnny. "I hope you're convinced that I'm a half-wit—you slimy mistake!" He picked up the hammer, ready to use the minutes gained.

He stopped almost at once; it dawned on him that wrecking the "brains" was not enough. There were no spare "brains," but there was a well-stocked electronics shop. Morgan could jury-rig control circuits for bombs. Why, he could himself—not a neat job, but one that would work. Damnation! He would have to wreck the bombs themselves—and in the next ten minutes.

But a bomb was solid chunks of metal, encased in a heavy tamper, all tied in with a big steel gun. It couldn't be done—not in ten minutes.

Damn!

Of course, there was one way. He knew the control circuits; he also knew how to beat them. Take this bomb: if he took out the safety bar, unhooked the proximity circuit, shorted the delay circuit, and cut in the arming circuit by hand—then unscrewed *that* and reached in *there*, he could, with just a long stiff wire, set the bomb off.

Blowing the other bombs and the valley itself to Kingdom come.

Also Johnny Dahlquist. That was the rub.

All this time he was doing what he had thought out, up to the step of actually setting off the bomb. Ready to go, the bomb seemed to threaten, as if crouching to spring. He stood up, sweating.

He wondered if he had the courage. He did not want to funk—and hoped that he would. He dug into his jacket and took out a picture of Edith and the baby. "Honeychile," he said, "if I get out of this, I'll never even try to beat a red light." He kissed the picture and put it back. There was nothing to do but wait.

What was keeping Towers? Johnny wanted to make sure that Towers was in blast range. What a joke on the jerk! Me—sitting here, ready to throw the switch on him. The idea tickled him; it led to a better: why blow himself up—alive?

There was another way to rig it—a "dead man" control. Jigger up some way so that the last step, the one that set off the bomb, would not happen as long as he kept his hand on a switch or a lever or something. Then, if they blew open the door, or shot him, or anything—up goes the balloon!

Better still, if he could hold them off with the threat of it, sooner or later help would come—Johnny was sure that most of the Patrol was not in this stinking conspiracy—and then: Johnny comes marching home! What a reunion! He'd resign and get a teaching job; he'd stood his watch.

All the while, he was working. Electrical? No, too little time. Make it a simple mechanical linkage. He had it doped out but had hardly begun to build it when the loudspeaker called him. "Johnny?"

"That you, Colonel?" His hands kept busy.

"Let me in."

"Well, now, Colonel, that wasn't in the agreement." Where in blue blazes was something to use as a long lever?

"I'll come in alone, Johnny, I give you my word. We'll talk face to face."

His word! "We can talk over the speaker, Colonel." Hey, that was it—a yardstick, hanging on the tool rack.

"Johnny, I'm warning you. Let me in, or I'll blow the door off."

A wire—he needed a wire, fairly long and stiff. He tore the antenna from his suit. "You wouldn't do that, Colonel. It would ruin the bombs."

"Vacuum won't hurt the bombs. Quit stalling."

"Better check with Major Morgan. Vacuum won't hurt them; explosive decompression would wreck every circuit." The Colonel was not a bomb specialist; he shut up for several minutes. Johnny went on working.

"Dahlquist," Towers resumed, "that was a clumsy lie. I checked with Morgan. You have sixty seconds to get into your suit, if you aren't already. I'm going to blast the door."

"No, you won't," said Johnny. "Ever hear of a 'dead man' switch?" Now for a counterweight—and a sling.

"Eh? What do you mean?"

"I've rigged number seventeen to set off by hand. But I put in a gimmick. It won't blow while I hang on to a strap I've got in my hand. But if anything happens to me—*up she goes!* You are about fifty feet from the blast center. Think it over."

There was a short silence. "I don't believe you."

"No? Ask Morgan. He'll believe me. He can inspect it, over the TV pick-up." Johnny lashed the belt of his space suit to the end of the yardstick.

"You said the pick-up was out of order."

"So I lied. This time I'll prove it. Have Morgan call me."

Presently Major Morgan's face appeared. "Lieutenant Dahlquist?"

"Hi, Stinky. Wait a sec." With great care Dahlquist made one last connection while holding down the end of the yardstick. Still careful, he shifted his grip to the belt, sat down on the floor, stretched an arm and switched on the TV pick-up. "Can you see me, Stinky?"

"I can see you," Morgan answered stiffly. "What is this nonsense?"

"A little surprise I whipped up." He explained it—what circuits he had cut out, what ones had been shorted, just how the jury-rigged mechanical sequence fitted in.

Morgan nodded. "But you're bluffing, Dahlquist. I feel sure that you haven't disconnected the 'K' circuit. You don't have the guts to blow yourself up."

Johnny chuckled. "I sure haven't. But that's the beauty of it. It can't go off, *so long as I am alive*. If your greasy boss, ex-Colonel Towers, blasts the door, then I'm dead and the bomb goes off. It won't matter to me, but it will to him. Better tell him." He switched off.

Towers came on over the speaker shortly. "Dahlquist?"

"I hear you."

"There's no need to throw away your life. Come out and you will be retired on full pay. You can go home to your family. That's a promise."

Johnny got mad. "You keep my family out of this!"

"Think of them, man."

"Shut up. Get back to your hole. I feel a need to scratch and this whole shebang might just explode in your lap."

II

Johnny sat up with a start. He had dozed, his hand hadn't let go the sling, but he had the shakes when he thought about it.

Maybe he should disarm the bomb and depend on their not daring to dig him out? But Towers' neck was already in hock for treason; Towers might risk it. If he did and the bomb were disarmed, Johnny would be dead and Towers would have the bombs. No, he had gone this far, he wouldn't let his baby girl grow up in a dictatorship just to catch some sleep.

He heard the Geiger counter clicking and remembered having used the suppressor circuit. The radioactivity in the room must be increasing, perhaps from scattering the "brain" circuits—the circuits were sure to be infected; they had lived too long too close to plutonium. He dug out his film.

The dark area was spreading toward the red line.

He put it back and said, "Pal, better break this deadlock or you are going to shine like a watch dial." It was a figure of speech; infected animal tissue does not glow—it simply dies, slowly.

The TV screen lit up; Towers' face appeared. "Dahlquist? I want to talk to you."

"Go fly a kite."

"Let's admit you have us inconvenienced."

"Inconvenienced, hell—I've got you stopped."

"For the moment. I'm arranging to get more bombs—"

"Liar."

"—but you are slowing us up. I have a proposition."

"Not interested."

"Wait. When this is over I will be chief of the world government. If you cooperate, even now, I will make you my administrative head.''

Johnny told him what to do with it. Towers said, ''Don't be stupid. What do you gain by dying?''

Johnny grunted. ''Towers, what a prime stinker you are. You spoke of my family. I'd rather see them dead than living under a two-bit Napoleon like you. Now go away—I've got some thinking to do.''

Towers switched off.

Johnny got out his film again. It seemed no darker but it reminded him forcibly that time was running out. He was hungry and thirsty—and he could not stay awake forever. It took four days to get a ship up from Earth; he could not expect rescue any sooner. And he wouldn't last four days—once the darkening spread past the red line he was a goner.

His only chance was to wreck the bombs beyond repair, and get out—before that film got much darker.

He thought about ways, then got busy. He hung a weight on the sling, tied a line to it. If Towers blasted the door, he hoped to jerk the rig loose before he died.

There was a simple, though arduous, way to wreck the bombs beyond any capacity of Moon Base to repair them. The heart of each was two hemispheres of plutonium, their flat surface polished smooth to permit perfect contact when slapped together. Anything less would prevent the chain reaction on which atomic explosion depended.

Johnny started taking apart one of the bombs.

He had to bash off four lugs, then break the glass envelope around the inner assembly. Aside from that the bomb came apart easily. At last he had in front of him two gleaming, mirror-perfect half globes.

A blow with the hammer—and one was no longer perfect. Another blow and the second cracked like glass; he had trapped its crystalline structure just right.

Hours later, dead tired, he went back to the armed bomb. Forcing himself to steady down, with extreme care he disarmed it. Shortly its silvery hemispheres too were useless. There was no longer a usable bomb in the room—but huge fortunes in the most valuable, most poisonous, and most deadly metal in the known world were spread around the floor.

Johnny looked at the deadly stuff. ''Into your suit and out of here, son,'' he said aloud. ''I wonder what Towers will say?''

He walked toward the rack, intending to hang up the hammer.

As he passed, the Geiger counter chattered wildly.

Plutonium hardly affects a Geiger counter; secondary infection from plutonium does. Johnny looked at the hammer, then held it closer to the Geiger counter. The counter screamed.

Johnny tossed it hastily away and started back toward his suit.

As he passed the counter it chattered again. He stopped short.

He pushed one hand close to the counter. Its clicking picked up to a steady roar. Without moving he reached into his pocket and took out his exposure film.

It was dead black from end to end.

III

Plutonium taken into the body moves quickly to bone marrow. Nothing can be done; the victim is finished. Neutrons from it smash through the body ionizing tissue, transmuting atoms into radioactive isotopes, destroying and killing. The fatal dose is unbelievably small; a mass a tenth the size of a grain of table salt is more than enough—a dose small enough to enter through the tiniest scratch. During the historic "Manhattan Project" immediate high amputation was considered the only possible first-aid measure.

Johnny knew all this but it no longer disturbed him. He sat on the floor, smoking a hoarded cigarette, and thinking. The events of his long watch were running through his mind.

He blew a puff of smoke at the Geiger counter and smiled without humor to hear it chatter more loudly. By now even his breath was "hot"—carbon–14, he supposed, exhaled from his blood stream as carbon dioxide. It did not matter.

There was no longer any point in surrendering, nor would he give Towers the satisfaction—he would finish out this watch right here. Besides, by keeping up the bluff that one bomb was ready to blow, he could stop them from capturing the raw material from which bombs were made. That might be important in the long run.

He accepted, without surprise, the fact that he was not unhappy. There was a sweetness about having no further worries of any sort. He did not hurt, he was not uncomfortable, he was no longer even hungry. Physically he still felt fine and his mind was at peace. He was dead—he knew that he was dead; yet for a time he was able to walk and breathe and see and feel.

He was not even lonesome. He was not alone, there were comrades with him—the boy with his finger in the dike, Colonel Bowie, too ill to move but insisting that he be carried across the line, the dying Captain of the *Chesapeake* still with deathless challenge on his lips, Rodger Young peering into the gloom. They gathered about him in the dusky bomb room.

And of course there was Edith. She was the only one he was aware of. Johnny wished that he could see her face more clearly. Was she angry? Or proud and happy?

Proud though unhappy—he could see her better now and even feel her hand. He held very still.

Presently his cigarette burned down to his fingers. He took a final puff, blew it at the Geiger counter, and put it out. It was his last. He gathered several butts and fashioned a roll-your-own with a bit of paper found in a pocket. He lit it carefully and settled back to wait for Edith to show up again. He was very happy.

He was still propped against the bomb case, the last of his salvaged cigarettes cold at his side, when the speaker called out again, "Johnny? Hey, Johnny. Can you hear me? This is Kelly. It's all over. The *Lafayette* landed and Towers blew his brains out. Johnny? *Answer me.*"

When they opened the outer door, the first man in carried a Geiger counter in front of him on the end of a long pole. He stopped at the threshold and backed out hastily. "Hey, chief!" he called. "Better get some handling equipment—uh, and a lead coffin, too."

"Four days it took the little ship and her escort to reach Earth. Four days while all of Earth's people awaited her arrival. For ninety-eight hours all commercial programs were off television; instead there was an endless dirge—the Dead March *from* Saul, *the* Valhalla *theme,* Going Home, *the* Patrols' *own* Landing Orbit.

"The nine ships landed at Chicago Port. A drone tractor removed the casket from the small ship; the ship was then refueled and blasted off in an escape trajectory, thrown away into outer space, never again to be used for a lesser purpose.

"The tractor progressed to the Illinois town where Lieutenant Dahlquist had been born, while the dirge continued. There it placed the casket on a pedestal, inside a barrier marking the distance of safe approach. Space marines, arms reversed and heads bowed, stood guard around it; the crowds stayed outside this circle. And still the dirge continued.

"When enough time had passed, long, long after the heaped flowers had withered, the lead casket was enclosed in marble, just as you see it today."